Praise for Sharyn McCrumb and IF EVER I RETURN, PRETTY PEGGY-O

"McCrumb writes with quiet fire and maybe a little mountain magic. . . . Like every true storyteller, she has the Sight."

—*The New York Times Book Review*

"McCrumb draws you close, makes you care, leaves you with the sense, sought for in most fiction, that what has gone on has been not invention but experience recaptured."

—*Los Angeles Times*

"A masterful tale of suspense . . . This fine novel is the product of a gifted and accomplished writer."

—Steven Womack
Nashville Banner

"Filled with believable, complex characters, dead-on social observations and evocative settings, this novel is too good to miss."

—*Atlanta Journal & Constitution*

Please turn the page for more rave reviews . . .

"SHARYN McCRUMB IS A BORN STORYTELLER."
—MARY HIGGINS CLARK

"Sharyn McCrumb, like every fine writer, has an abiding sense of place, a deep understanding of her world and the forces, human and otherwise, that shape it."
—*San Diego Union-Tribune*

"This suspenseful novel gets four stars for insight into the human heart above and beyond the call of the usual thriller, as well as a jarring climax."
—*West Coast Review of Books*

"[A] masterpiece of a suspense tale . . . Powerful."
—*Booklist*

"SUSPENSEFUL AND ABSORBING."
—The Orlando Sentinel

"Sharyn McCrumb makes small town Tennessee come to life with the same love/hate William Faulkner found in describing rural Mississippi. This is one terrific book by an extremely talented writer."

—STUART M. KAMINSKY

"A post-Vietnam Ruth Rendell, set in the Tennessee mountains."

—Roanoke Time & World News

"In its finely crafted portrayal of Appalachia . . . IF EVER I RETURN, PRETTY PEGGY-O shows the maturing of a bright new talent."

—MARGARET MARON

By Sharyn McCrumb:

The Elizabeth MacPherson novels
(in chronological order)

SICK OF SHADOWS*
LOVELY IN HER BONES*
HIGHLAND LADDIE GONE*
PAYING THE PIPER*
THE WINDSOR KNOT*
MISSING SUSAN*
MacPHERSON'S LAMENT*
IF I'D KILLED HIM WHEN I MET HIM . . .*

The Ballad Novels
IF EVER I RETURN, PRETTY PEGGY-O*
THE HANGMAN'S BEAUTIFUL DAUGHTER
SHE WALKS THESE HILLS

BIMBOS OF THE DEATH SUN*
ZOMBIES OF THE GENE POOL*

**Published by The Ballantine Publishing Group*

IF EVER I RETURN, PRETTY PEGGY-O

Sharyn McCrumb

BALLANTINE BOOKS • NEW YORK

 Published in the United States by Ballantine Books, a division of Random House, Inc., New York, and simultaneously in Canada by Random House of Canada Limited, Toronto.

The epigraph on page 57 is taken from "Strange Days," written and composed by Ray Manzarek, John Densmore, Robby Krieger, and Jim Morrison, and is reprinted with the permission of the Doors Music Company.

http://www.randomhouse.com

Library of Congress Catalog Card Number: 89-24337

ISBN 0-345-36906-8

This edition published by arrangement with Charles Scribner's Sons, an Imprint of Macmillan Publishing Co.

Manufactured in the United States of America

First Ballantine Books Edition: September 1991

OPM 29 28 27 26 25 24 23 22 21

To Jim Wayne Miller

With Thanks from a Bricoleur

AUTHOR'S NOTE

I WONDER WHO *lives in that house,* I thought for the hundredth time.

One source of inspiration for my Ballad novels is an attempt to make sense of the inexplicable by making up my own "legend" to satisfy my curiosity, most notably in *If Ever I Return, Pretty Peggy-O,* which began as an attempt to answer the question: I wonder who lives in that house.

That house is a white-columned mansion set amid stately oaks on Highway 264 on the outskirts of Wilson, North Carolina, an hour east of the state capital, Raleigh. My parents lived farther east still, in Greenville. The only direct way to reach Greenville from points west was to take Highway 264, which meant that I had been driving past that white mansion for nearly twenty years: home for weekends from UNC–Chapel Hill, back from my job as a newspaper reporter in Winston-Salem, and later back from the Virginia Blue Ridge, where my husband and I were attending graduate school at Virginia Tech.

In the spring of 1985 I was driving home by myself when I passed the big white house on Highway 264, and I said for at least the hundredth time: "I wonder who lives in that house." I still don't know who really lives there: it isn't the sort of place that invites drop-in visits from inquisitive strangers. As I drove past on that spring day, I decided to answer the question with my imagination. *A woman lives in the house,* I thought, beginning the invented legend. *She bought the house with her own money. She didn't marry to get the house, and she didn't inherit it. Who is she?*

A folksinger.

I pictured a sixties singer, who would have made a substantial amount of money during the sixties so that she was able to buy the house, but in order for her to be able to take up residence in a small Southern town, her singing career would have to be over.

A character began to take shape. This folksinger had attended UNC–Chapel Hill in the sixties, as I had, I decided. She was still young-looking, a trim blonde woman in her early forties who had once been a minor celebrity in folk music, but her popularity waned with the change in musical trends, so now she has bought the mansion in the small Southern town, looking for a place to write new songs so that she can stage a musical comeback, probably in Nashville. *She doesn't know anybody here,* I thought.

I had loved folk music when I was in college, and I had grown up listening to my father's mixture of Jimmy Rodgers songs and the ballads collected by Francis Childe. As I continued the drive, I began to consider what songs this folksinger character might have recorded in her heyday. Since I was alone in the car, I could sing my selections as I drove along. After a couple of Peter, Paul, and Mary tunes, I happened to recall an old mountain ballad called "Little Margaret." I was reminded of it because I had heard Kentucky poet laureate Jim Wayne Miller sing it in a speech at Virginia Tech only a few weeks earlier. The song is an American variant of a Childe Ballad. It is four centuries old, and it is a ghost story.

Little Margaret sees her lover William ride by with his new bride, and she vows to go to his house to say farewell, and then never to see him again. When Margaret appears like a vision in the newlyweds' bed chamber that night, William realizes that he still loves her, and he goes to her father's house, asking to see her: "Is Little Margaret in the house, or is she in the hall?" He receives a chilling reply: "Little Margaret's lying in her coal-black coffin, with her face turned to the wall."

I sang that verse a few times because some instinct told me that the heart of my story was right there. Suddenly the pieces fell into place.

The owner of the house is a folksinger. She has moved to a small town, where she doesn't know anybody, and one day she receives a postcard in the mail, with one line printed on the back: *Is Little Margaret in the house, or is she in the hall?* The folksinger's name is Margaret! The line would terrify her with its implied threat, and she would take the message personally, because her own name was in the line. Having sung the song many times in her career, she knows the next line: *Little Margaret's lying in her coal-black coffin, with her face turned to the wall.*

I pictured her calling the local sheriff in a panic and saying that someone is threatening her life, but the sheriff sees no threat in the line on the postcard. He tells her that the message is simply a prank. I thought: Suppose something or someone close to her is violently destroyed that night. Then she will know that the threat was serious. Then all she can do is wait for the next postcard to come, as she and the sheriff try to find out who is stalking her.

As I drove toward my parents' house, I followed the thread of the plot so that by the time I reached Greenville, I knew who lived in that house (which I had mentally relocated to east Tennessee), and I had the seeds of the first Ballad novel. That hour of inspiration was followed by several years of hard work, researching the high school reunions of sixties' graduates, talking to Vietnam veterans, and interviewing law enforcement people, but the idea itself came from an old mountain song.

The theme of *If Ever I Return, Pretty Peggy-O* came from a more modern melody: the Doors' tune "Strange Days." I thought: Suppose "strange days" tracked everybody down one summer in an east Tennessee village. For the baby boomers it is their twentieth high school reunion, forcing them to come to terms with their shortcomings; for the sheriff and his deputy, it is the memory of Vietnam, which haunts them both for different reasons; and for Peggy Muryan, the once-famous folksinger, strange days track her down in the form of a stalker who still remembers her days of celebrity. For Appalachia itself, the strange days refer to the time when the traditional folkways began to be lost in the onslaught of the media culture. Childe Ballads gave way to radio's Top 40; quilts featured cartoon character designs; and the distinctiveness of the region began to erode as it was bombarded by outside influences. In each case "strange days" meant the sixties.

Music is a continuous wellspring of creativity for me. When I was writing the subsequent Appalachian Ballad novels, I would make a soundtrack for each book before I began the actual process of writing. The cassette tape, dubbed by me from tracks of albums in my extensive collection, would contain songs that I felt were germane to the themes of the book, and sometimes a song that I thought one of the characters might listen to, or a "theme song" for each of the main characters. Generally, the songs I use to focus my thinking do not appear in the novel itself; they are solely for my benefit, although I have thought of providing a "play list" in the epilogue to each book.

When the cassette tape is finished, I make one copy of it for my car, and another one for my office. Then, during the months that I am researching, before I write a word of the book itself, I play the car tape whenever I am driving so that I can absorb and internalize the sound and the themes of the novel-to-come. I suppose the music serves as both the means of directing my thoughts along the lines of motivation, characterization, and theme during the planning phase of the novel and later for the creation of mood when I am in my study actually working on the book.

The songs I listen to also provide the titles for the Ballad novels. *If Ever I Return, Pretty Peggy-O* is a line from the Joan Baez recording of "Fennario," a minor key variation of a Scots folk song alternately called "The Bonnie Streets of Fyvie-O."

I do more than listen to music in order to portray the culture of the Southern mountains in my Ballad novels. I read. I study. I interview people who are experts in the subject of the current work. I have hiked the Appalachian Trail with a naturalist, and explored country music with Skeeter Davis. I researched woodworking with a master dulcimer-maker, and I have sat in Tennessee's electric chair. I try to write interesting, compelling stories because I think it is the duty of a fiction writer to entertain, *but*: beyond the reader's concern for the characters, I want there to be an overlay of significance about the issues and the ambiguities that we face in Appalachia today. In my novels I want there to be truth, and an enrichment of the reader's understanding of the mountains and their people. I have been known to warn folks not to read my books with their brains in neutral. Dickens: "Never be induced to suppose that I write merely to amuse or without an object." I have a mission.

Appalachia is still trying to live down the stereotypical "backwoods" view of the region presented in the media. I think one of the best ways to combat this negative portrayal is to educate the general reader about the real character of the region, and particularly about the history and origins of Appalachia and its people, both culturally and environmentally. Like Charles Dickens, I think that in order to win hearts and minds, one must reach the greatest possible number of people, and so I am pleased when my novels make the *New York Times* bestseller list, because that means that millions of people have been exposed to my point of view. Millions of people watched *The Dukes of Hazzard*: surely the opposite opinion deserves equal time. I am passing along the songs, the stories, and the love of the land to people who did not have a chance to acquire such things from heritage or residence.

Perhaps my own theme song ought to be the song recorded by Joan Baez on an early album called *One Day at a Time*: "Carry It On."

Carry It On.

Sharyn McCrumb
November 5, 1997
Shawsville, Virginia

IF EVER I RETURN, PRETTY PEGGY-O

CHAPTER 1

Days of loathing and nights of fear
To the hour of the charge through the
streaming swamp,
Following the flag,
Till I fell with a scream, shot through the guts.
Now there's a flag over me in Spoon River!
A flag! A flag!

EDGAR LEE MASTERS

SPENCER ARROWOOD DROVE the patrol car into the cemetery and took a sharp right turn into the past. It was seven o'clock in the morning, too early for any other visitors to come, even on Memorial Day. Spencer wanted to be out of there before anyone spotted his sheriff's car and rushed over to offer him sympathy. It had been a long time, and he scarcely felt anything anymore except a sense of obligation to come here, but he wanted to be gone before the little American flags began appearing on the flat bronze markers.

He parked on the asphalt loop near Cal's grave, picked up the paper bag from the passenger seat, and threaded his way through the wet grass and the plastic flowers toward the family plot. The Arrowood graves had once been surrounded by a wrought-iron fence, but it had given way to a curbing of stone. Easier for the mowers. The last vestige of Victorian pomp was the marble angel over his Confederate great-grandfather. Albert Arrowood had been a teenaged corporal, whose only war wound was frostbite, but he had made money in later life, and his widow had been a fanciful woman with a taste for the baroque.

The empty-eyed angel presided over inscribed blocks of granite that diminished in size by generation, ending in the stark simplicity of the most recent memorials: flat bronze markers that didn't try to upstage the azaleas and the dogwoods. Most of the cemetery's recent graves were flat markers, but people hadn't come to terms yet with this modern austerity; they insisted on adding a pot of plastic flowers for decoration. In a cemetery bright with pink-flowered crown vetch and sweetbay magnolia, Spencer wondered why they bothered. Because of winter, he supposed, and perhaps out of the guilt of neglect. Graves that went unvisited from one year to the next could avoid the look of desolation, thanks to perpetual upkeep and plastic flowers: imitation remembrance.

No flowers for Cal.

He held the paper bag between circled thumb and forefinger, reading the grave markers as he walked past them. He smiled as he passed the grave of Odell Watson, who had shoveled shit in Louisiana during World War II and died of a heart attack in '74: little American flag number one.

No flowers for Cal. His mother would bring them later and chide him for not having visited the cemetery. "And on Memorial Day, too!" she would say. If he didn't manage to head her off, that remark would degenerate into a whole conversation about how wonderful Cal had been, and how he was up there with Jesus waiting for the family to join him, and how Spencer didn't love him. "Even tore up the last letter your brother ever wrote without letting the rest of us read it:" *The ones who really loved him,* she meant. Spencer had heard it all before, at least twice a year since 1966; he avoided his mother on her Cal-days. Martha knew by now not to put her calls through.

Just past the boxwood hedge was Bobby Beaupre. Spencer remembered him as "one of the big boys," older than Cal, even, whose attitude toward the younger kids alternated between bullying and condescension. Spencer never passed his grave without remembering their first encounter in the cemetery.

It was Halloween, and Spencer was six years old. He had pleaded to be allowed to go trick-or-treating with Cal, but Cal didn't want any babies tagging along after him and his gang. Spencer had been sent off in his pirate costume with two little girls, and they were warned to stay together and to look out for bad boys who might take away their bags of candy. Spencer had been on his way home with half a sackful of Tootsie Rolls, jelly beans, and Double-Bubble. He said he was cutting through Oakdale because it was a shortcut, but it was really to prove his bravery to the sniffling fairy princess and the plastic-masked witch, who refused to enter the dark cemetery. The shortcut also served to get rid of them.

He had been just about to this point by the boxwood hedge when he saw a white-sheeted figure coming at him. In the moonlight, Spencer could see white socks and high-topped sneakers beneath the sheet. He tucked his candy under his arm and sprinted for the low stone wall, heedless of the shouts behind him. Later at home, Spencer squirmed in embarrassment as Cal made everyone laugh with a whole routine about how Spencer thought he saw a ghost and hightailed it out of the graveyard, when it was just Bobby Beaupre in a bedsheet. Spencer tried to explain that he knew it was a live person in disguise; he had thought it was a candy thief, but no one paid any attention to him. Cal's version made a cuter story.

Bobby Beaupre was soon to be flag number two when the civic committee came around to decorate the graves of the glorious war dead. Bobby had made it back from Korea with sergeant's stripes and a few shrapnel scars, and then wrapped his Plymouth around a tree on 611 after a Saturday night at the tavern.

A clump of pink azaleas triggered a later memory: the itch of an old Army blanket and a breath of White Shoulders cologne.

Oakdale Cemetery was really two places in Spencer's mind, both occupying the same space geographically: like Persia and Iran, different connotations for the same piece of ground. The Oakdale Cemetery of Spencer's childhood was a place reserved for "dead people" in the ghost story sense of the term. Nobody they really knew was there, except perhaps an aged and scarcely familiar grandparent. That cemetery had been a place to give an extra charge to hide-and-seek; it served as a fitting backdrop for a night spent telling horror stories with the guys. ("Give me back my gol-den arm!") In his teens he'd snuck a few beers in Oakdale, or used it for make-out sessions with Janice Waller or Sue Karyl Simmons. It had been a stage set in those days, with the horrors no more authentic than the Jaycees' Fright House on Halloween.

Lately, though, and he saw it as a sign of aging, the cemetery had turned into a subdivision of Hamelin, with more and more of his acquaintances moving out there. First went old people he knew at church, then his grade-school teachers, and lately it had been his parents' friends. A familiar name appeared in each new obituary column. He could remember when he hadn't bothered to read it at all. Sprinkled through the lists of each current generation-to-die had been friends his own age, of leukemia or drowning, and Vietnam had claimed another handful. Soon, he supposed, people his age would be dying of cancer or heart disease, and then the terrors of Oakdale would be past anything the Jaycees could conjure up. Just now, he was still a stranger, a semi-interested party, visiting people with whom he had little in common.

The Arrowood plot was well tended and devoid of plastic flowers. His mother brought real ones often enough. Spencer stood with his back to the granite angel and stared down at his brother's grave. The letters on the marker were Brasso bright, like an Army belt buckle: JOHN CALVERT ARROWOOD OCTOBER 25, 1946—MAY 26, 1966 PRO PATRIA. He had often wondered what Cal would make of that inscription, after getting straight D's in high school Latin. He set the paper bag down beside the grave and knelt to brush off the bronze lettering bits of dried grass from the last mowing; the marker felt cold to his touch. The sunny field was bright but unnaturally silent. Not even a birdsong to cover the sound of his own breathing, which seemed unnecessarily loud, as if he were flaunting life before those who no longer possessed it.

He glanced back at the patrol car, parked alone on the gravel circle. He still had the place to himself; the old ladies who were the regulars wouldn't come until the mist lifted and the sun burned away the dew.

"Hello, Cal," he said to the staring metal slab. "I wish to God you'd grow up." Spencer Arrowood, at thirty-eight, had a streak of gray at the temples and a tendency to squint at fine print; but Cal, lying down there in Marine dress blues, stayed nineteen years old. He wouldn't age in Spencer's mind, and he wouldn't take on that spectral dignity assumed by the dead, those solemn white-robed figures who replaced people one had actually known. Cal was no granite angel. He existed in a series of mental filmclips: in his Scout uniform, in shoulder pads and smudged eyes, in a crew cut and wrinkled fatigues. When Spencer visited the grave, for ten minutes' awkwardness on the dates specified, the memory of Cal might assume any of these guises, but always he would be sneering at his sissy kid brother: "Ya-aah, candy-ass! You brought me flowers!"

The fact that he outranked Cal by twenty years did nothing for Spencer's sense of inferiority. He was still the younger brother, the one who had to prove himself. He had spent a childhood taking dares and getting stitches to earn his right to tag along. And then suddenly on the night of the senior prom, as he was dressing in that room full of trophies, there was a scream from downstairs. And then sobbing. He went down and heard the solemn uniformed messengers say again that Cal was dead. Ever a slave to middle-class civility, his mother had offered them coffee, but the soldiers declined politely and left, so that she could have hysterics without offending the sensibilities of strangers. Spencer stood around awkwardly for a while, feeling like an eavesdropper to his parents' grief, and then he went back upstairs to a room that had just become a shrine, without even calling Jenny to say he wasn't coming.

Suddenly Cal had become a saint. At the funeral his parents seemed to be burying somebody else: someone who was kind and wise and solemn. But Spencer couldn't ever find that somebody in his mind. When he came to the cemetery, he always met the sneering Cal, unhallowed by death and spoiling for a fight. "Ya-aah, candy-ass! You brought me flowers!"

Cal was a jeering witness to the incident at his own funeral. Spencer wished he could visit the grave just once without thinking of it. He was standing with his parents under the green canopy provided by the funeral home, shaded from the bright June day around them. The sky was cloudless blue, and the new-mown grass mixed its sweet smell with the scents of funeral flowers and his mother's perfume.

Spencer remembered the square cardboard fans with the wooden tongue-depressor handles that the funeral home provided. He had stared at the picture of a red-robed Jesus surrounded by sheep. "Onward Christian Soldiers." He had counted the sheep to block out the sounds of grief around him.

Reverend Noll had just finished reading the service, and the mourners had begun to wander away. Cal's gun-metal gray coffin squatted in a blaze of wreaths, waiting for the family to leave so that it could sink into the earth. Spencer had stood there in his hated double-breasted blue suit, wondering whether the shame was in crying or not having to. His mother wept silently; his father had his look of smug stoicism, like a man who has withstood the dentist's worst tortures and remained unbroken.

"Do you want a flower to remember him by?" he had asked Spencer.

Not wanting to seem irreverent, Spencer nodded. He reached out to the nearest wreath and pulled off a red carnation.

Then the old bastard had turned to his wife. "Do you want one, Jane?" She'd said no. "Neither do I," he announced. "I don't believe in these sentimental gestures at funerals."

Spencer hung his head, knowing that he had failed an unannounced test, and that only he would remember it. Only he and, of course, the dear merciless departed. "Ya-aah, candy-ass! You brought me *flowers*!"

He lifted the paper bag and unscrewed the metal bottle cap. "Not this time, buddy," said Spencer, pouring the quart of beer on his brother's grave. Pabst Blue Ribbon—in high school Cal had called it PBR, and he'd chugged it in tasteless gulps as a rite of manhood. "Not this time."

His respects paid to the dead, Spencer carried the empty beer bottle back to the patrol car. He did not look back.

The quickest way to downtown from the cemetery was to take Ashe Lane, a street that Spencer had not thought of as "Cal's paper route" for years. Now, with the memories freshly stirred, he remembered each yard by dog or shrubbery. (Here was the German shepherd who used to collect his own paper and the two from next door, and lay them in a soggy heap on the welcome mat.) Spencer sometimes went with Cal to deliver papers, in bad weather when he took the car. Cal would drive along slowly while Spencer pitched the rolled-up paper at each porch, pretending to be lobbing passes at a wide receiver. The Dandridge place, a big white house with a circular driveway, had been a tough one. Too many trees in the yard. It had changed hands just recently, he recalled. Martha had been full of speculation on the new owner, a folksinger named Peggy Muryan. From what he could gather, most of the women in town were dying to meet her, but so far she had kept to herself.

He slowed down to look at the Cape Cod on the corner of Ashe and Belmont. It was surrounded by scaffolding: the wood was being replaced with aluminum siding, he decided. What color had it been in the paper route days? Green? Brown? The houses had changed some since those days; in fact, Spencer could no longer remember exactly how they had looked back then, because he passed them so often. The changes in the town were gradual things scarcely noticed, like the lines on his own face. He had lived there all his life; you could plot his entire biography on a survey map of Hamelin, except for college and the service. Most of it was right there, though, from the white frame house he had been born in to the sheriff's office that occupied most of his waking hours.

A few flags hung limply at intervals along Main Street; the rest would be out before noon. As he approached the park benches in front of the courthouse square, he slowed the patrol car to a crawl, looking for Vernon Woolwine, whoever he was today. Spencer hoped it wasn't the Nazi storm trooper. Not on Memorial Day.

He had heard that every Southern town had one resident oddball, a picturesque nonconformist who, in the local parlance, was a few bricks short of the load. The uncontested eccentric of Hamelin was Vernon Woolwine. Physically he was somewhere in middle age, although in some of his incarnations it was hard to tell, and he had a boot-faced plainness that argued against a flair for drama, but there it was: Vernon Woolwine was a welfare-funded exercise in street theater.

On all but the coldest, wettest days, Vernon Woolwine was an attraction in downtown Hamelin. Nobody seemed to know where he had come from. When Spencer came home after being stationed in Germany, Vernon was already installed as a fixture in Wake County, a curiosity that was both exotic and familiar, like the covered bridge, or Carver Jessup's tree-climbing coondog. Spencer had always meant to find out more about Vernon Woolwine, but he never got around to it. After all, Vernon was harmless, and the sheriff wasn't even sure that flamboyant vagrancy constituted a crime.

Vernon Woolwine just wasn't himself. Ever.

Every day at mid-morning, he would appear in the vicinity of the courthouse in an elaborate costume, and he would spend the rest of the day strolling up and down the streets of Hamelin, or lounging on the park bench, acknowledging the stares from strangers with a courtly nod. Sometimes he would be Elvis: a white jumpsuit and a shaggy blue-black wig, or he would impersonate Rooster Cogburn/John Wayne with cowboy duds and a black eyepatch. There was no set schedule to his impersonations, and nobody seemed to know where he got the costumes. Knoxville, most likely. He probably saved up handouts and small sums from his government checks so that he could purchase new identities from time to time. He didn't attract much attention anymore. People just kind of noticed who Vernon was today, and let it go at that. Once some high school boys had tried to beat him up, but some of the old-timers from the VFW had run them off. Spencer wondered why adolescents felt so threatened by anything out of the ordinary.

A flash of red at the door of Denton's Café caught the sheriff's attention, and he slowed down for a closer look. There was Superman, complete with red cape and black boots, emerging from the café, balancing a fried pie on the top of his coffee cup. Spencer gave him a wave that was half salute, and the pudgy Superman bowed in return.

At the courthouse intersection, Spencer turned left; the sheriff's office was around back. He noticed that the wreath hadn't appeared on the statue of the Confederate soldier yet. Sooner or later there would be trouble over that, he reckoned; but not this year. The liberals didn't outnumber the old guard yet; he kept track by reading the editorial page of the *Knoxville Journal*. Hamelin, Tennessee, was still bound by traditions, even when their meanings had been obscured by time. People who took integration pretty much for granted still stood up when they played "Dixie" at the high school football games.

This loyalty to the familiar might go a long way toward explaining why Spencer Arrowood got elected sheriff. He was a hometown boy, kid brother of Hamelin's football star and war hero Cal Arrowood. Sometimes Spencer wondered if he had got the job as a posthumous tribute to the golden boy, but most of the time he didn't let it worry him. He was a good sheriff, competent enough, and he knew a lot of people, which made it easy to get the job done without a lot of unnecessary theatrics. It helped him to know which kids were more scared of their parents than of jail cells, and which drunks to go looking for at nine-thirty, before they got tanked enough to cause trouble.

Spencer didn't think he was the equal of his predecessor, Nelse Miller, but given the way the world had changed since those days, maybe nobody could be. Sheriff Miller, a silver-haired gentleman given to wearing a white Stetson, had known everybody in Wake County, and most folks had considered him a friend of the family, but the county was smaller then. Nowadays strangers lived in the old frame houses, kept to themselves, and commuted forty miles to work. They didn't go to church, and they didn't frequent the night spots. As a peace officer he would encounter them only during license checks, or when somebody burgled their cozy little homes, which was seldom. Spencer didn't think anyone could know *everybody* in Hamelin anymore.

There wasn't much call to use a gun around Hamelin, but Spencer could if he had to; he'd spent a lot of his childhood roaming the woods with one weapon or another. When he had decided to go into law enforcement, he thought that was a pretty good background to have, but four years' experience had convinced him otherwise. Now he thought that a few courses in typing and public speaking might have served him better.

Today's big job was a speech at the high school on drunk driving, and he dreaded it. High school students hated to be told the consequences of drunk driving; they resented the implication that they were mortal. Today the students would be even less receptive to the message, because they were in school making up a snow day while the rest of the world took the holiday off. Getting the message across wouldn't be easy. That speech needed a big, scary-looking hulk to freeze the message into the kids—exactly the right job for Deputy Godwin, and probably the only thing he was good at, but Godwin was on night duty for the week. The other deputy, Joe LeDonne, was a wiry five feet eight, too small to impress the beer-guzzling jocks and too quiet to accept the assignment. That assembly full of foot-stomping show-offs wouldn't see into LeDonne's silence to know that he'd be the one who could pull them out of a wreck piece by piece without losing his cool or his supper. Of course, LeDonne was a Vietnam vet. Spencer wondered if Cal would have been like that if he had come home: a thin crust of snow over a pit of ice water.

The outer door to the office was open, and Spencer could hear the sound of Martha's typewriter over the drone of the fan. She was always early; she liked to finish her first cup of coffee before eight. Besides, Martha was between husbands, so there wasn't much to stay home for. As he eased his way around the screen door, trying not to let in any more flies, he could see her head bent over the typewriter, a mare's nest of Orphan Annie curls that made him long to duck her head in a bucket of water. She might land husband number three in spite of it, though; the scrawny look she'd had in high school had stood her in good stead, now that most women her age were running to fat. In a small town, a gaunt, tanned woman of thirty-eight passed as a desirable date, if not as a beauty.

Martha Ayers heard him come in and switched off her

typewriter. "Where were you last night?" she asked in a stern voice.

She didn't mean it the way it sounded. They'd got that straight between them years ago.

"Good morning, Martha," he said, sighing. "Where was I supposed to be?"

"Spencer, I don't know where your mind is these days! At the high school."

He flipped the page of his desk calendar. "I have it down for today. One o'clock."

"That's your speech to the kids. I'm talking about the meeting of the planning committee." He still looked blank. "For the high school reunion," she finished patiently. "This is the twentieth year, you know."

Spencer sighed. "Is there more of that coffee?"

She nodded toward the pot on the filing cabinet. "Now I got elected reunion chairman, so I have to contact everybody, because I have access to a typewriter and all. The reunion starts on August eighth—that's a Friday, and there'll be events all weekend."

"I might look in on it," said Spencer politely.

"You'll do more than that!" Martha shot back. "There aren't many members of the class of '66 still in town, so everybody's going to have to pitch in."

Spencer eyed her warily. "Pitch in?"

"Don't worry, Spence. Nobody's going to ask you to hang streamers in the gym. But you *are* the sheriff of Wake County, and that makes you a pretty important person in our class. I'd like you to do some of the asking about arrangements."

"Like what?"

"For starters, you could see about getting the high school gym for a dance on August ninth. When you're out there making your speech today, ask the principal about it. I need to get places reserved before I can get the announcements printed up."

"Why don't you give him a call?" asked Spencer. He didn't want to be associated with a high school reunion. He wasn't even sure he wanted to attend.

Martha ignored him. ". . . and we decided we want you to present our alumni gift to the school at the banquet."

"Why me? Chuck Winters is a lawyer in Knoxville. He's used to making speeches."

"No, everybody said it ought to be you. We're giving the school a plaque inscribed with the names of all the boys from school that got killed in Vietnam. Since Cal was the first one, and him so popular and all, we thought it was only right for you to give the speech."

"I don't know," he muttered, over the ringing of the telephone.

"And don't forget today is Memorial Day. Every drunk in Tennessee will be on his way to the beach!" She snatched up the phone before he could reply.

As Spencer walked back to his office, Martha cupped her hand over the receiver, calling out again, "Memorial Day, Spencer!"

"I won't forget," he promised.

"Memorial Day," grunted Joe LeDonne. "When the country honors its war dead by pulling a three-day drunk. You bet."

He had come in about ten past eight, acknowledged Martha's existence with a nod, and strode past her into Spencer's office. He sat perched on the arm of a chair, still wearing his aviator shades, his rolled-up sleeves offsetting his tie. "Do you want me on a speed trap?" he asked.

Spencer shook his head. "The highway patrol ought to have that covered. I just wanted you to be aware of possible problems. You'll be on patrol today—I have to make a speech."

"The drunk-driving routine?"

"Yeah. Any ideas on what I should say?"

Martha appeared in the doorway carrying the mail. "Why don't you read them 'Please, God, I'm Only Seventeen' out of Ann Landers? I always cry over that one."

Spencer and LeDonne looked at each other. "I don't think I could do it justice," he said cautiously. "I guess I'll just stick to statistics and quote the penalties."

"Well, I hope they stay awake for it," she sniffed. "Oh, by the way, Spencer, there is something else you could do for me about the reunion. I have to write to the out-of-towners, and I'll need Jenny's address."

"I don't have it," he said quietly.

"Don't you really? I know where both my ex's are." Having taken this small revenge on behalf of Ann Landers, Martha swept out.

"Reunion?" asked LeDonne, when the door closed behind her.

"High school. Twentieth."

LeDonne considered it. "I guess mine is about two years off. I hope to God they can't find me."

"You wouldn't go?"

"Oh, hell, what for? For the women to ask me war stories as a turn-on, and the men to give me a lot of crap about why they didn't go? I don't need it."

"Don't tell them you're a vet."

"Doesn't it show? I always know one." A grim smile. "Wheelchairs are a tip-off."

"No, really, how can you tell?"

"Things I can't explain. Okay, I'll give you one example. You ever notice the way I walk?"

Spencer wasn't sure what he was getting at. "You don't limp," he said.

"No, but I don't walk like most guys; most Americans, anyway. See? I put all my weight on one foot, and then shift all my weight onto the other foot. It comes from walking patrol in the jungle. You walk that way, you live longer."

"Interesting."

"Yeah, I'm a regular episode of *Wild Kingdom*: the almost extinct species of jungle grunt. Anything else I can do for you before I hit the road?"

Spencer grinned. "Can you think of a way to get Martha off my back about this reunion crap?"

"Yes," said LeDonne, easing off the chair. "But if you do it in this country, people get upset about it. See you later, Spence."

Spencer managed to get through half of the monthly crime statistics and two more cups of coffee before Martha interrupted him again. "Mrs. Traynham is here, Sheriff," she said in a carefully neutral voice.

Spencer tossed his pencil at the "in" basket. That would shoot the morning. "Send her in." He sighed.

Jessie Traynham had lived in Hamelin since 1945, almost long enough to be considered a local. Before that she had been married to one of the top scientists at Oak Ridge, on the other side of Knoxville. The Traynhams had been stationed there during World War II, while he worked on a secret governmental project that the scientists did not discuss with their wives. Two weeks after Hiroshima, when the news of the bombing of Japan made headlines around the world, the Oak Ridge workers danced in the streets: their project had been a success. Finally the wives found out what all the secrecy had been about. One week after that, Jessie Traynham had arrived in Hamelin, carrying a suitcase and inquiring into Tennessee divorce laws. She'd been there ever since. In 1958, when Dr. W. Albert Traynham died of cancer, he had left his money to his former wife (people still argued about what that meant), and she had bought the big gray Edwardian house on Ashe Lane.

"Good morning, Spencer Arrowood," she said crisply, in a voice still bearing traces of an Alabama accent.

"Morning, Miz Traynham," Spencer replied cautiously.

When he was a kid, ladies her age wore crinkly-permed hair and georgette shirtwaist dresses. Jessie Traynham's blond-rinsed hair was cut in a Princess Diana bob, and she wore a white jogging suit. "Your mother tells me that you have been too busy to start that garden patch for her yet," she said. "I wonder what you are about. It is well-nigh June!"

"Yes, ma'am, I've been meaning to get over there, but something always comes up."

"If you don't get on with it, you will lose your tomatoes to frost!"

"Well, I thought I might start with bedding plants instead of seeds, and—"

"I did not come here to discuss gardening with you, Sheriff!" she said briskly, as if he were wasting her time. "I want to know what you intend on doing about this!" She put a white-gloved hand into a paper bag and drew out something wrapped in a paper towel. Before Spencer could protest, she dumped a still-moist turd in the center of the monthly crime stats.

"Did you bring me some fertilizer, Miz Jessie?" asked Spencer patiently.

"No, sir, I brought you a crime!" she said, nodding at the evidence seeping into the pages of the report.

Spencer frowned. "Was it a burglary?" He had heard of cases in which burglars left their biological calling cards to taunt the police. It was supposed to show how much time they had to spare.

"It was in my flower bed," snapped Mrs. Traynham. "Put there by that damned dog who belongs to the folksinger."

"Peggy Muryan's dog!" He understood now. When the minor folksinger bought the big white house in Hamelin a few weeks back, the story made a paragraph in "People" columns throughout the country, even though few people had thought of her since the early seventies. No out-of-town reporters had shown up to pursue the matter, though, much to the disappointment of the John Sevier Motel and Grill. "Did you tell her about this?"

Jessie Traynham hesitated. "I didn't think it would do any good, with her being a celebrity and all. I haven't even spoken to her."

"Real neighborly of you," Spencer commented, but he understood how she felt. If Peggy Muryan had been an average nobody, half the old ladies in town would have been to call on her, ogling her wallpaper and inviting her to join every club in town. As it was, they were shy, afraid she'd mistake them for celebrity hunters.

"Well, she hasn't called on me either!" she retorted, determined to bluff it through. Spencer knew he had her, though.

"All right, Miz Jessie, I'll tell you what I'll do. I'll drop by this afternoon and ask her to keep her dog out of your yard if you'll promise to pay a call on her this evening. Take her some of your preserves, or something. Or ask her to give you something for the rummage sale next week. Is it a deal?"

She sighed. "I suppose so, Spencer. She can't do much more than slam the door in my face."

The sheriff smiled. "I don't think you need to worry

about that. As I recall, she used to sing an awful lot of songs about peace and love."

Jessie Traynham's lips twitched. "Well, if she wants to know 'Where Have All the Flowers Gone,' tell her to ask that dog of hers!" She nodded toward the evidence seeping into his monthly report form. "Get that thing off your desk, Spence!"

She was gone before he could think up a suitable reply.

CHAPTER 2

I'm going to see my brother, who's serving in
the army,
I don't know where he's stationed, in Cork or
in Killarney;
Together we'll go roaming o'er the mountains
of Kilkenny,
And I swear he'll treat me better than my
darling sporting
Jenny . . .

"WHISKEY IN THE JAR"

AS COMPENSATION FOR the lack of an AM-FM radio in his patrol car, Spencer had developed an automatic Muzak in his mind. Without his conscious thought, his mind would provide a continuous background hum of popular songs to entertain him while he drove. Sometimes, he'd noticed, he could tell how he felt about something by analyzing the songs going through his head: "Good Day, Sunshine" meant a good mood; "I'm Looking Through You" told him that he was pissed off. The songs were seldom of a later vintage than 1970; maybe an occasional Eagles or Elton John, but that was it. He supposed that all his moods were set to music while he was young, and neither songs nor emotions had troubled him much since then.

Today as he drove up the steep, tree-lined street to the

high school, his mind presented him with a medley of Peggy Muryan songs, probably inspired by his conversation with Jessie Traynham. She hadn't had many hits, but because she'd got her start at the University of North Carolina, she'd had a regional following even before she made it on the national charts. Spencer could remember "Mason County Love Song" complete with his own personalized video: scenes from his senior year in high school, times when the song was playing in the background, like the homecoming dance when he was slow dancing with Jenny.

Jenny.

The FM station in his subconscious got its cue from his mood change, shifting from Peggy Muryan tunes to the Peter, Paul, and Mary version of "Whiskey in the Jar," his Jenny song. The aptness of the words didn't even register anymore, but he could feel his heart beat faster and his muscles tense as the tune clanged around inside his head.

He had not seen Jenny for at least ten years; even so, it was odd that he should still picture her as a girl of seventeen. She had been a mousy girl with light brown hair and dreaming eyes, seeing more wonders in Hamelin than ever were. Cal, for instance.

Spencer remembered her shyly proffering her yearbook in algebra class. Could he possibly get his big brother, Cal, to sign it for her? They were sophomores then, still in awe of the mighty seniors. Spencer had returned it to her the next day with a neatly printed inscription: "Farewell to you and the youth I have spent with you. It seems but yesterday we met in a dream. You have sung to me in my aloneness, and I of your longings have built a tower in the sky. John Calvert Arrowood—Class of '64." She had recognized it as a quotation from *The Prophet*, that poetic touchstone for romantic souls in

'64. Spencer had squirmed uncomfortably as she reread the inscription, her eyes misting. He had written it himself; Cal couldn't be bothered.

The Jenny he had started dating the summer after Cal died, the Jenny he'd been married to for two-and-a-half years, the Jenny he saw in a car one Christmas when she was home on a visit—that was somebody else.

"She sighed and swore she loved me, and she never would deceive me," his mind sang, "but the devil take the women for they always lie so easy. . . ."

He swung into the high school parking lot and pulled up in a visitor space. The song stopped when he switched off the ignition. Spencer was grateful that he wouldn't have to hear the last verse.

The auditorium was hot, its un-air–conditioned temperature heightened considerably by the presence of 150 squirming hostages who didn't give a rat's ass about the penalties, legal or medical, for drunk driving. Spencer stood at the podium flanked by the red velvet curtains and stared at the blank faces that might have been his own classmates.

If elected student body vice-president, I promise to . . . Although we didn't win the championship, those of us on the team would like to . . . As we graduating seniors leave these familiar scenes behind to go out into the world . . .

He reckoned he didn't look all that different. He could still wear some of his jackets from high school, and silver strands don't show up much in blond hair. His short hairstyle was pretty much the one he'd worn back then. His wouldn't have stood for the Flower Child look, even if he'd wanted it. He didn't feel all that different, either, some of the time. Not with people his own age. Maybe that was because he was still single, so there were fewer milestones around him to measure his aging. He could still imagine pulling an all-nighter over beer and pizza with the old gang. He wasn't *that* old.

He was in *this* crowd, though. It was as if he were still eighteen, and they were all eighteen, but they were from another planet. His eighteen was frozen in a time of Beatles and LBJ and *That Was the Week That Was*. These aliens of the Reagan era, with their heavy metal noise and their California plastic personalities, made him feel not so much old as lost.

He felt like an impostor, trying to be grown-up and stern in the same auditorium where he'd shouted at pep rallies and giggled through Chapel. He straightened his khaki tie and glanced down at his badge. The round faces were staring up at him in utter boredom masked as polite attention. When the assistant principal introduced him in a squeaky voice, Spencer heard muffled laughter; once he would have been part of it. Now he solemnly thanked the little bureaucrat and stepped up to the microphone to be The Establishment.

"As most of you know, I am the sheriff of Wake County," he began. The microphone gave a little screech, and two boys ran to the controls. "I'm here to talk about one of the greatest killers of young people . . ." Other than war, he finished silently.

As a matter of form, Spencer gave them statistics about reaction times, cited the consequences of a drunk-driving conviction, and even tried to play on their emotions by describing the sorrow of parents he had to confront with the news, and the nightmare of a twisted car whose occupants weren't . . . quite . . . dead. They didn't show any signs of having been affected by his speech, but he hoped it had sunk in for some of them. Lacking any other comparable experience, Spencer thought of wars as long successions of battered cars bloodied by mangled occupants; if he saw action at many more wrecks, maybe it would add up to a year of combat.

"... like to thank the High Sheriff for taking the time to be with us today ..." the principal was saying. He had scooted up to the microphone as Spencer fielded the last question from the audience. All four inquiries had involved drinking and getting away with it. The last questioner, a thin-faced blonde in gypsy earrings, had asked: "What if you make him drink coffee and take a cold shower?"

Spencer smiled. "You get a wide-awake, freezing drunk, ma'am."

He had shifted awkwardly during the brief speech of thanks. The assembly had already been dismissed before he remembered that he was supposed to ask the principal for the use of the gym-auditorium. As he threaded his way through a tangle of bodies toward the retreating plaid sports jacket, someone touched his arm. "Could I talk to you, sir?"

Spencer decided that it was a boy. The tiny elfin face surrounded by fine, gold-flecked hair could have belonged to a young girl. It was a face of cat's eyes and flower lips that hinted at pointed ears beneath the flowing hair. But it wore an Army camouflage jacket, boys' sneakers, and no makeup; male, then.

"What can I do for you?" asked Spencer, in his genial sheriff-voice.

"I liked your speech a whole lot, but I wanted to ask about something else if you've got a minute." It was a soft voice, managing without the squeakiness of adolescence to commit itself to neither gender.

Spencer motioned him to one of the folding chairs set up on the gym floor. "I'm Pix-Kyle Weaver, sir," the boy was saying. "My dad's Wilsie Weaver, that has a farm in Dark Hollow. I'll be a senior next year."

Some things didn't change, Spencer thought to himself. Adolescents still have to identify themselves by explaining who their parents are. No paycheck, no identity. He tried not to look surprised at the fact that the boy was an upperclassman. He had figured the kid for fourteen at the most. "What was it you wanted?"

"Well sir, for history next year, I've signed up with Mr. Withrow to do an independent study for one semester. I know I'm starting early on it, but I'm real interested, and I thought I could spend the summer boning up on things."

"What things?"

"Vietnam."

Spencer looked away. "Can't help you there."

"Oh, I know you didn't go, but your brother did, and I wondered if you had any stories of his that you recall?"

"No. I never talked to him after he went."

"Well, what about your deputy? Ain't he a vet?"

"LeDonne?" Spencer's lips twitched. He could picture this elf-faced kid trying to interview Joe LeDonne. "Yeah, but don't count on him telling you anything. He doesn't talk about it."

Pix-Kyle Weaver gave the sheriff a salesman's "You haven't heard the last of me" smile, and shook his hand. "Guess I'll go back to reading books, then."

There was no sign of the principal. He had probably gone to his office to work on his end-of-the-day announcements. Spencer wanted to leave without talking to him, but he figured he'd get no peace from Martha until the thing was settled, so he went along to the office to get it over with. On his way down the hall, he recognized a kid he'd gone to high school with; then he realized that the kid would now be thirty-eight years old; maybe it was a son or a nephew, or maybe there was one jug-eared kid in everybody's high school class, standard issue.

The sports jacket bounced up as soon as the sheriff entered the office, and Ray Beasley produced a stricken smile while he wondered what those little hellions had done now. Stolen the hubcaps off the patrol car, perhaps? When Spencer explained his errand, the smile brightened to a state of lesser anxiety. Mr. Beasley didn't know, he was sure. It was a matter to be taken up with the school board . . . if the sheriff would care to be put on the agenda? Spencer backed away, saying that he would convey the information to the reunion committee. They exchanged wary good-byes, and Spencer hurried out to his car. He didn't stop to look at the trophy case in the hall, where a familiar face would leer at him from the team picture of the 1964 District Football Champs. Even on Memorial Day, once was enough. "Got to see a girl about a dog," he told himself and any ghost who might be lingering in that familiar hall.

His Muzak played "We Can Work It Out" all the way there.

Peggy Muryan's house was known locally as the old Dandridge place after its original owner, one of the town's founders, even though the last Dandridge to live in it had died in 1930. The folksinger had bought it from the grown children of the attorney who had owned it since 1945. Spencer could see why she'd wanted it—it looked like a movie set, and she'd bought it in the spring, when the azaleas were blooming and the oaks formed a canopy of leaves above the rolling lawn. He wondered if she'd last out a winter in it. Now, though, it was a white-columned splendor, sporting fresh paint and bright green shutters. He supposed that she would eventually get tired of the house and the small town, and then the place would become a lawyer's office or a funeral home.

That's what happened to most small-town mansions. A damned shame. He was glad of its temporary reprieve.

He didn't see any sign of a dog.

After a few minutes' wait on the woven doormat, Spencer had come to the conclusion that the bell was broken. He rapped on the glass panel in the door, calling out: "Anybody home?"

His efforts were rewarded by the sound of bare feet running, and the accompanying click of dog's nails. A moment later, the door was flung open, and Peggy Muryan changed her smile to a wide-eyed stare.

Spencer was used to making people nervous. It went with the uniform. He gave her his most reassuring smile as he studied Hamelin's only celebrity. She'd been making records when he was in high school, so she must be over forty, he supposed, but she had the well-cared-for look of one who can afford to fight off time. Her blond hair was the color of moonlight, and her slender figure in jeans and a Carolina sweatshirt suggested someone who exercised more than she ate. He looked down at her hand, clutching the collar of a white German shepherd.

"Blondell! Down!" she ordered, still eyeing him nervously.

He could tell that it wasn't a trained guard dog. It would bark out of instinct and scare off prowlers, but its attitude was that of a friendly dog that had needed more training and attention than it got.

"Good afternoon," said Spencer politely. He introduced himself as the sheriff of Wake County and said he hoped that she was settled in all right.

"Everything's okay," she said, obviously wondering what he wanted. "I guess you know who I am."

"In a town this size it'd be hard not to," he agreed, stooping to pet the dog. "She doesn't bite, does she?"

"No! She's just a big baby. See what I mean? Blondie,

get down! Don't lick the sheriff's face! You'll get me arrested. Unless I am already."

Spencer knew that the wrinkles appearing around her eyes probably meant that she had a couple of joints in a box on her nightstand. With the locals it would have been a fruit jar of home brew under the sink. A few years in law enforcement had taught him that clear consciences were in short supply. It made him sad sometimes to think about it; and sometimes it made him feel like a hypocrite. He had a few fruit jars of his own.

He tried a reassuring smile. "Just a small problem. Nothing talking won't solve."

"You'd better come in, then." With a glance around her to check the housekeeping, she pulled the door open wide enough to let him in. "I'm sorry about the way it looks. . . ."

People often said that when they let him in, as if he were a health inspector instead of a sheriff. He had once gone to arrest a murderer who had let him in with just those words. The only remorse she'd shown, in fact.

Spencer followed the woman and her dog across a white-carpeted hall to the parlor, a rather bare-looking room that seemed in the process of redecoration. Baskets of green plants and a weeping fig tree brightened a room otherwise in need of paint and new curtains. Some of the furniture looked like antique shop finds in need of refinishing, while others were modern reproductions from an upscale catalogue's version of "country," with duck decoys on the end tables and heart-stenciled lampshades. It bore little resemblance to the furnishings of real country people. The presence of a grand piano with a Martin guitar leaning against its leg was the only indication that the house belonged to a musical celebrity. He had expected autographed pictures of Joan Baez and Pete Seeger. There was nothing to suggest the hippie origins of the woman's career, except perhaps the clutter. Several days' worth of newspapers littered the floor, and the remains of a sandwich sat on a tray on the coffee table.

"The house needs work," Peggy Muryan remarked, curling up in a leather chair near the fireplace. "But these big places are hell to keep up. Maybe I ought to hire some help."

Spencer lifted a damp towel from the sofa and sat down. "Maybe."

She ruffled her hair and frowned. "The thing is, I'm supposed to be working. I'm not a *housewife*, for God's sake. Are handymen cheap around here?"

"There's people who need the money," he said carefully.

"Oh God! I can't believe I asked that!" she said, picking up on the tone of his answer. "New Left Folksinger Seeks to Exploit the Working Class. Inquire Within. I can't *believe* I said that. But we're not as rich as people think we are, and this house is a monster to clean. It's not that I'm lazy. It's just that I have to work."

Spencer raised his eyebrows. "Isn't that working?"

"Not for me," she said. "For me, working is sitting at that piano staring at a blank wall. I'm supposed to be writing songs for a new album."

"I thought you sang folk songs."

She frowned. "Even then you have to arrange them. Some of those old ditties are absolute stinkers in their natural state. The taste of the people is not all it's cracked up to be. But, anyhow, it's not 1968 anymore."

"I am relieved to hear it."

"Yeah, me, too, in a way. I could be young in 1968, but I don't think I could be old in it. Folk music doesn't sell anymore, unless you want to be a nostalgia act, singing all your golden oldies for drunks on the club circuit, which is like impersonating yourself. Hey, do you think Elvis is alive and working as an Elvis impersonator?"

Spencer shook his head. "Elvis is bound to be dead. Look at all the vultures in his vicinity." She laughed, and that made him feel clever, so he decided she might be all right.

"I want a real career, not a rerun of the old one. My agent wants me to try nightclub tunes, the sort of stuff Maudie is doing now. I mean Sylvia Tyson. You know."

Spencer shook his head. He'd never heard of Sylvia Tyson.

"She used to be half of Ian and Sylvia in the old days. God, what harmony! But they got divorced, and that broke up the act. They had made it big, too. God, he'd have to have been an ax-murderer for me to have cut him loose. They were so *good* together. Well, times change. Anyhow, she's a big star on Canadian TV these days, doing slick easy-listening music."

"What about Ian?"

"Owns a ranch in Alberta, I think. Still records. But it's not the same, friend. Half magic is no magic at all."

She stopped remembering and seemed to register who he was. He wondered if this was the patter she gave reporters. "This isn't what you came for, is it? You don't have a guitar in the trunk of the squad car, or anything? God, not *Officer* Johnny Cash . . ."

"I guess you get that a lot," said Spencer politely. He did play the guitar, in fact, and had thought of passing along a few of the old songs. "Well, the fact is I did come about something in particular," Spencer admitted, leading up to it as gently as he could.

"I'm not into drugs," said Peggy quickly. "Those things on my patio are tomato plants."

Spencer smiled. "You're not the problem, Miss Muryan.

Your dog is." In the most diplomatic of language, he told her Jessie Traynham's complaint about the flower bed.

"Oh God," said Peggy, raking her hair with her fingers. (Short nails, he noticed. No polish. Guitar player's hands.) "She's got me in trouble with the neighbors before I've even met them."

"Nothing major," Spencer assured her. "Just stay with your dog when you let her out and see that she doesn't go over into the other yard. Miz Traynham isn't mad at you; she's just shy about you being so famous and all."

Peggy groaned. "I'm not exactly a household word. Hell, if I had a thousand dollars for every time they spelled my name *right*, I'd still be poor. Maybe they still remember me around here, though. Should I make some kind of celebrity gesture to get on her good side? An album? An autographed picture?"

Without meaning to, Spencer grinned, imagining Jessie Traynham being offered an autographed photo of her next-door neighbor.

Peggy covered her face with her hands. "I'm sorry," she said in a small voice. "It's going to take me a while to move in to a small town—mentally I mean. I can't *believe*—well. What do you suggest?"

Spencer thought it over. "Did you see the article in the *Hamelin Record* about the Women's Club holding a rummage sale?"

"No. I don't take the paper. I saw one issue and didn't know a soul mentioned. There was no real news—just kids' birthday parties and recipes. A rummage sale. Do you think they'd like me to donate something?"

"I'm surprised you haven't caught 'em going through your garbage," Spencer drawled. "I think they'd be delighted."

"Well, I guess I could come up with something. There's stuff I need to get rid of. I brought a carload of junk down from my father's house when I moved here. I haven't even opened the boxes. They're just taking up space in the attic. Maybe I'll go through them sometime."

"If you're sure you want to give them something, you'd better do it now. The rummage sale is tomorrow. I doubt if they'd even accept a donation from anybody but you."

"Rummage sale. Would they want something like old clothes, or like celebrity things?"

"Whatever you've got."

"Whatever I can find." She waved her hand at the clutter about them. "You can imagine what the attic is like. If I start going through those boxes, I'll be up there for days, and I'd probably want to keep everything. They have to have it today? Okay, I'll just go up and pick one and give it away before I can change my mind. Wait right here!"

Before Spencer could tell her to wait and give the stuff to Jessie Traynham, she had hurried out of the room. Blondell made a move as if to follow her, thought better of it, and stayed to get better acquainted with this interesting stranger. Spencer didn't know whether to be amused or insulted that the local celebrity thought the sheriff was an errand boy. Taking her looks into account, he decided to be amused.

Spencer tried to remember the Peggy Muryan he had expected to see: someone looking more like forty, he supposed, with a hardness to her features, wearing some sort of slinky Rodeo Drive outfit. He walked around the room with Blondell at his heels, hinting to be petted. He stacked the newspapers beside the couch and turned to examine her record collection, which didn't seem to be in any particular order. He found a lot of jazz and soul music, which surprised him. He'd expected autographed albums from her contemporaries. The Kingston

Trio, maybe, or Joe and Eddie. Nancy Ames. He hadn't thought about Nancy Ames in twenty years. She'd probably show up in his Muzak now, with "South Coast" or "Cotton Mill Girls." As he flipped through the record collection and read the titles of her albums, his mind supplied a soundtrack, a Childe Ballad from her first album. "True Thomas, he pulled off his cap, and bowed low down to his knee; 'All hail the mighty queen of heaven. . . .' " He patted Blondell absently.

Strange that somebody famous would want to live in Hamelin. If he got to know her well enough, he'd ask her. He wondered if she had ever been married; Martha would know. He checked the mantelpiece for photographs, but there were none. No clues there. Still, there didn't seem to be a husband in evidence. If he asked her out to dinner—would The Laurels be classy enough, or would he have to take her to Knoxville? He wondered what LeDonne would think of her. Had she sung against the war? He couldn't remember.

He plunked a tentative finger on a piano key. " 'Oh no, oh no, True Thomas,' she said, 'That name does not belong to me. I am the queen of fair Elfland, and hither come—' " He had forgotten the rest. The sheet music of an unfinished song lay propped on the rack. Spencer squinted at the words: "I am the redwood woman. Cut me down; count my rings." Different from her old stuff. Maybe she was going to take a shot at Nashville.

SONG FOR TRAVIS was penciled across the top of the sheet, then crossed out. He glanced over the words.

"You interested in music?" asked Peggy from the doorway.

He winced at the ice in her voice. "And me with no search warrant," he said with a wan smile.

"It's okay. They're not very good. I'm embarrassed to

let anyone see them." She set a cardboard box on the coffee table. "Here's the box. It's mostly letters and trinkets from fans, I think. I put a couple of albums in there, too. Watch out; it's dusty. It ought to appeal to somebody as sixties memorabilia."

"Or tinder," said Spencer solemnly.

She sighed. "I used to sign people's *hands*, you know?"

"It's not 1968 anymore."

"I'll be back, folks. Want me to sign your hand now, avoid the rush?"

"This doesn't seem like your style," said Spencer, indicating the sheet music.

She brushed a smudge of dirt from her cheek and wiped her hands on the seat of her jeans. "Maybe it will be."

"Who's Travis?" he asked, nodding at the title.

She gave him a crooked smile. "Do you also run the local newspaper?"

He grinned. "Nope. I'm just naturally inquisitive."

She flopped down on the couch with a sigh of exasperation. "Travis was my singing partner back in college. Peggy and Travis. We played the YMCA coffeehouses doing a two-thirds rendition of Peter, Paul, and Mary, and some mountain songs Travis learned from his kinfolks. God, we were young then! He was the first guy I ever slept with. We went to a free flick on campus—*On the Beach,* you know that film? The world has been destroyed by nuclear war, and all these people are in Australia just waiting for the radioactive clouds to come and get them. I cried for an hour after the movie, and suddenly sex didn't seem like such a big deal anymore. I mean, we were all going to die anyway."

"And now we're not?"

She shrugged. "Yeah, but now we have less to lose. I mean, I was *nineteen* then. Do you remember how you felt back then? Wasn't it like standing on the edge of a cliff holding hands?"

"Sometimes." He couldn't remember. "So what ever happened to the guy?"

"We split up when I went national."

"Maybe you could team up again," he said, thinking of what she'd said about that Sylvia person in Canada.

"I don't think so." She looked up at him. "Now, what about you? Aren't you a little young to be a Southern sheriff? I thought y'all had beer bellies and faces like bulldogs."

He smiled. "And I thought you'd wear love beads and iron your hair."

"Maybe I did once. 'But that was in another country, and besides the wench is dead.' Shakespeare," she added.

He smiled. "It's Marlowe. My deputy, Joe LeDonne, says that a lot, but he means something else altogether." The mention of LeDonne reminded him that he had places to go. He tucked the box under his arm. "I guess I'd better get back to work. Today's Memorial Day."

"Memorial Day. Were you in the war?"

"Memorial Day is a real pain in law enforcement. Traffic. Parties. Sometimes fireworks. Not much of a holiday."

"You didn't answer my question. Were you in the war?"

"Nope. I enlisted in '71 and chased paper clips around Germany. Lost a brother in 'Nam, though."

"It seems like a long time ago, doesn't it?" she said sadly.

"Half my life, I guess. How about you?"

She shook her head. "I guess my hindsight isn't very good. The more I look back, the more confusing it all becomes. It seemed rather clear back then, though, didn't it? Let us run the world, and we'll fix it. Only now we do, and we haven't." She sighed. "We ended a war, deposed two presidents, desegregated the South, established rights for women. It *seems* like a lot. But it feels like so little."

"Yeah. Did you sing against the war back then?"

"I sang against war in general," she said thoughtfully. "All of us did. But I sort of lost somebody there, too." She shivered and drew closer. "Is there something people do on Memorial Day—if there's no grave to visit?"

Spencer shrugged. "My deputy is a vet. He says we honor our dead by pulling a three-day drunk. I'm not recommending it."

"No." She turned away. "Maybe I'll get back to work now."

Spencer hesitated in the open door. "Since you're new in town, maybe you'd like to go out to dinner sometime?"

She grinned. "Sheriff *and* Welcome Wagon? You're not married, are you?"

"Not anymore."

"At our age, that's the best answer. I guess I could go—if we agree not to turn it into a wake for the Year That Was."

"It won't be a problem after today," said Spencer. "Memorial Day. I keep thinking it's overcast, but it isn't."

"Thinking about your brother?"

"Among other things."

Peggy walked him to the door. "Memorial Day . . . I wonder if I ought to be somewhere." She caught a glance of herself in the hall mirror and shivered. "The Ghost of Decade Past. God, what a pall you've cast over my day. And I've agreed to see you again. I guess it's just the occasion, though. Where was I then? I can't even remember. I *will* snap out of this!"

He gave her a reassuring smile. "Sure. When today is over, we'll be right as rain."

They both glanced up at the sky, but it was still a cloudless blue. You couldn't blame the weather.

As he drove back to the courthouse, his mind played an old Doors tune from '67, the one that said: "Strange Days Have Tracked Us Down." It was a prophecy of the approaching summer.

Animal blood can be used to gel gasoline for use as a flame fuel that will adhere to target surfaces.

Homemade napalm.

He ran his finger down the list of instructions and smiled.

The ragged paperback was his favorite book. About the size of his hand, it had a rough black cover with no writing on it at all. No title, no publisher, nothing. He had found it in an Army surplus store, a stapled-together manual full of black-and-white diagrams, and simple instructions. Real simple instructions, like for morons. They told you that gasoline could be found at a service station, and that animal blood came from slaughter-houses or "natural habitat." Yeah, like the neighbor's pet. He supposed that it was some sort of an Army field manual for commandos. He had never seen anything like it.

He wanted to give it a name, so he had written in pencil on the inside cover Hell's Cookbook. He liked to read it by candlelight, savoring the recipes for destruction and thinking of how he might use them.

Hand grenades can be made from a piece of iron pipe. . . . Build a timer to detonate explosives from dried seeds in a glass jar, or set off a booby trap with a light bulb. . . . Rig a grenade with nails and a blasting cap. . . .

A very informative little book. The possibilities were endless. Just the sort of homemade stuff the VC rigged up in Vietnam, and here were all the instructions sent to him in a neat little book, so that he could continue the war.

Right here in the mountains of Tennessee.

CHAPTER 3

We have done with Hope and Honor, we are
lost to Love and Truth,
We are dropping down the ladder rung by
rung;
And the measure of our torment is the measure
of our youth.
God help us, for we knew the worst too
young!

KIPLING

MARTHA AYERS WAS staring at a name partway down the reunion list. Cathy Brown. Big doll-like eyes and rich black hair that always stayed put. Had she been a cheerleader? A Homecoming candidate? Martha couldn't remember anymore. All four years of Cathy Brown's high school existence had impacted into one frozen moment. They were in a car, coming back from some field trip with the journalism class. Martha was crammed into the back seat between Cathy and Jimmy Templeton, the staff photographer (a skinny nobody; probably a lawyer now). Suddenly Jimmy had decided to take a picture of Cathy. "Move out of the way, Martha!" he told her, as if there were any place she could go. But Cathy Brown wouldn't hear of it. "Oh, no-ooo," she cooed. "You have to take my picture and Martha's too!" She had flung her arm around Martha and aimed her dazzling smile at Jimmy's lens. Nothing had ever come of that photograph, but the scene stayed clear in Martha's mind, tinted with her own humiliation, backlit with rage that didn't fade. She slipped the reunion form letter into the envelope addressed to Cathy's parents. She didn't care what had become of Cathy Brown. No success would compound the injury; no tragedy would even the score. High school was a life unto itself.

The reunion was nine weeks away, more or less. Too early to ask Joe to go with her. She thought of paving the way by bringing him homemade bread or cookies, something that she could pass off casually "because I was making some for the church group, anyway." She discarded the idea as being too obvious. LeDonne saw too much as it was. If he knew the hot, clutching feeling she got in her stomach when she looked at him, he would be amused. Oh, he might find it convenient, even pleasant, to go to bed with her; it was the fact that it mattered to her that would amuse him. Sometimes Martha felt that Joe had been dead for a long time; she wondered if that was the core of it.

Like that Egyptian story she'd read once when she ran out of fairy tales, and before she discovered historical romances. The king of the gods, Osiris, had a fight with somebody—the details of it escaped her. Whoever it was had killed Osiris and cut his body into a million pieces so he couldn't come back; but Isis, his wife, had hunted for the fragments of the god until she found his penis, and she'd used it (how?) to get herself pregnant. That had been the birth of Horus, the hawk-faced one. Did it bring Osiris back to life? Martha couldn't remember.

LeDonne came in a little after eight; Spencer was off today. The deputy was wearing his aviator shades, and his tie was loosened in anticipation of the coming scorcher.

"Want some coffee?" she asked, keeping her voice even.

He held up a can of Pepsi. "Breakfast. It's too hot for coffee."

She tried to think of some other pleasantry to prolong the conversation before they got down to the business of the day. LeDonne had begun to examine the notes on the desk as if he had forgotten she was there.

"I have to tell you one thing that isn't written down there, Joe."

"What?"

"You have to do something about Roger Gabriel."

Suddenly LeDonne looked tired. "Tell me about it," he said. There was no trace of interest in his voice, but she saw that his hands were shaking. He put down the notes.

"Well, we had a complaint about him."

"Why? He just lives out there in his cabin and keeps to himself. He don't even hunt, far as I can tell. Only time I see him around is the first of the month when his disability check is due at the post office."

Martha shrugged. "The complaint came from Denton's. He went in there to get a hamburger, had a couple of beers, and ended up tearing up the place."

LeDonne glanced toward the door that led to the holding cells. "He in there?"

"No. He went off home after it happened, and Spencer thought it'd be best if we left it for you. On account of him being a vet and all."

LeDonne tilted his head back and looked at her. "And just why is that?"

"We think it might have been a flashback."

"Maybe it was. So what? I didn't know him out there. He wasn't in my outfit. Hell, he might have been a spook down south, for all I know. I bet we weren't even there the same year. If you think he's nuts, why didn't you call the VA?"

"Spencer wanted you to talk with him first. If that doesn't work, we'll see. . . . "

He gave her a hollow smile. "There must'a been another article in the paper on post-Vietnam syndrome, I guess."

"Go talk to him, Joe. Maybe he needs help." She raised her voice a little, as if the faraway effect of talking to LeDonne had something to do with distance.

"Okay, lady, y'all pay for my time," he answered, strolling toward the door.

"Joe!"

He stopped and looked in her direction.

She flushed. "You doing anything for lunch?"

"Going to Denton's Café. Twelve o'clock or so."

"Mind if I tag along?" She tried for casual and succeeded only in sounding strained.

"It won't spoil my appetite." He turned to go, canceling her presence as thoroughly as if he had hung up an invisible telephone.

Martha went back to her list, pausing at the name of Robert Laurie, who had killed himself their senior year. She still shuddered when she got to that page in the yearbook, no matter how many times she said the word "coincidence" to herself.

The yearbook staff had been looking for a way to do group shots without resorting to the inevitable semicircle of bland faces posing in front of the camera. For the school newspaper reporters, somebody had come up with the idea of making it look as if they were covering a story. Four girls and a guy; that's why they singled him out—it was an obvious move. The black-and-white photo midway through the yearbook showed them on the roof of the school. Robert was teetering on the edge of the building as if he were going to jump, while his fellow reporters (Martha on the far right) stood a few paces back with notepads and ghoulish grins. Cute picture, with the caption "One jump away from a lead story." When Robert Laurie shot himself the next year, the cuteness of the photo began to fade. Martha hadn't known him very well, wasn't sure why he'd done it; but she still felt an irrational resentment toward him for spoiling her yearbook with the taint of his memory. It had been a good picture of her, too.

The dirt road wound through a thicket of trees and underbrush before it reached Roger Gabriel's shack. In early June, the drive was too green and too quiet for Joe LeDonne; his hands were cold with sweat. I am not driving a jeep, he told himself. He wondered if it ever bothered Roger Gabriel. The rain probably did. Pellets of loud rain on big leaves probably made his muscles tighten and his heart beat faster. Even the feel of moist rain-laden air in his nostrils would bring it on: the memory of having lived through a time when it rained for weeks and you couldn't get out of it, when your socks rotted in your boots. LeDonne wondered what it was about Denton's Café that had triggered the memories.

Roger Gabriel's shack had never seen better days. It was hard to imagine it new, or to picture some builder proud of his work. The place was a small lopsided square with a sagging front porch and the remnants of a coat of cheap white paint. No sign of a garbage dump; he probably hauled his trash to one of the county's metal Dumpsters near the highway. Anyway, people who ate dinner out of a tin can didn't generate much garbage. LeDonne looked around for the dog, wondering if it would be a shepherd or a collie. They all kept dogs.

They'd had them over there. It was something you could touch without having your skin crawl.

LeDonne's dog had been a mostly black German shepherd named Boots. While Joe was out on a day patrol, the dog jumped over the chain-link fence, hanging himself by his lead chain. Joe burned the body with gasoline from the motor pool. They eat dog out there. He had a white husky now, a silent, remote animal who tolerated his caresses. It didn't love him as Bootsie had. They were even.

As LeDonne approached the house, a dusty Labrador crawled out from under the porch. He wagged his tail warily, standing his ground while awaiting further developments. LeDonne stopped ten feet from the porch. He knew he had been seen, but for form's sake, he cupped his hands and called out: "Anybody home?"

The three minutes of silence that followed did not surprise or disturb him. He stood motionless, smiling at the dog. Roger would be watching him from one of the windows, or perhaps from the cracked glass panel in the door. The dog broke the stillness, being the most alive. It edged toward LeDonne in a sidestepping dance, its head low, but curious, interested. Joe, who had stood with his arms at his sides, slowly stretched his hand toward the dog, palm up.

"You here by yourself?" he asked the dog as it nuzzled against him. "Guess you don't get too much company out this way."

He squatted in the grass and began to scratch the Lab's ears. Over its head he could see a dark line between the sill and the front door. "Good boy!" he murmured, still watching the door.

He spent a few more minutes chatting with the dog, making the kind of small talk that most people make to other people, all the time edging closer to the front porch.

"And I had this dog named Bootsie that I bet you would'a liked," he told the Lab, as he eased himself down on the top step. He could feel the presence of someone behind him, watching, and he knew how easy it would be for that person to waste him where he was. It was not a new feeling to LeDonne, only a meaningless one. He was past caring. "How'd you get so dusty, boy? Leading the buried life, are ya?"

He heard the door open and felt the vibration of Roger Gabriel's footsteps on the wooden porch. LeDonne continued stroking the dog, talking softly. "Nice dog," he remarked when the presence felt near enough. "He got a name?"

"Chao," said Roger.

Good-bye in Vietnamese. LeDonne's hand stiffened on the dog's neck, but he saw it prick up its ears and realized that it had been an answer to his question. "Good dog," he murmured, this time in Vietnamese.

Roger sat down beside him on the top step. "Want a beer?"

LeDonne shook his head. "I'm going to lunch pretty soon—at Denton's Café."

"Better have two, then," said Roger, still in an expressionless voice.

Chao lay down on the step below their feet, within easy reach of whatever hand chose to pet him. Head on his forepaws, he waited.

"What was it?" asked LeDonne after a long companionable silence.

Roger could have said, "What do you mean?" and LeDonne could have explained how the previous night's disturbance had been reported to him, and that the sheriff had sent him out to check on things. But those cut-and-fill conversations take place mainly for form's sake, because people seem to feel that the structure is necessary for social order. Roger understood the question and saw no reason to prolong the discussion. Nothing was at stake for either of them.

He sighed. "The ice machine."

"Yeah?" LeDonne was interested. He'd expected to hear about ceiling fans.

"They got an automatic icemaker on the fridge, and when that thing kicked on, it sounded like an AK-47."

It had to have been something like that. What could LeDonne tell the guy? Don't do it anymore? Have your nightmares in private? "There's a support group in Knoxville. Have you tried it?"

Roger smiled. "There's a support group in hell. Until I get invited to join that one, I'll stick to beer."

Martha dabbed at her mouth with a lipstick-smeared napkin. The cheeseburger had been rubbery and the potatoes slick with cooking oil—hardly the ideal food for a lunch conversation—but she had tried. It was like lobbing mudpies off a glass wall: you can only see your own efforts, not any response from the target.

"What's he like?" she asked, having given up more promising topics, like the weather and the upcoming rummage sale.

"Gabriel? He's okay."

He certainly wasn't that, Martha thought, but you had to consider the source. Anyone more messed up than Joe LeDonne she could not imagine. "What does he look like?" If she could keep him talking, she might learn something—the way in, perhaps.

Joe pushed a mouthful of cheeseburger into his cheek. "Beer gut. Hair like pinestraw. Some scarring on the face, I think. That must be what the beard is for. Loves his dog. Drinks too much. Can't sleep worth a damn. Can't hold a job. Alternates between depression and nirvana—I'd say he's your type, Martha."

She shrugged. "I don't mind trouble, if there's something worth saving." She wasn't sure about Joe. Sometimes she thought that there wasn't anything at all behind those aviator shades except a soul that she'd built herself. But she wasn't going to give up without a better shot at finding out.

LeDonne rattled the ice in his paper cup. "How come you didn't think your husband was worth it?"

Martha almost smiled. "Which one?"

He shrugged. "Take 'em in order. It'll take me that long to finish my pie."

"Maybe there was something to save about Leon," she said slowly. She hadn't thought of it before—objectively, the way Ann Landers might look at the case. It was fifteen years ago by now, so she might as well be Ann Landers; she certainly wasn't the girl who'd married Leon Jarvis. "I was twenty then, and I remember all my girl friends were getting married, and I kept thinking, Martha, what's wrong with you? When are you going to find Mr. Right?"

Joe nodded. "Wouldn't it be nice if we knew what year things were going to happen to us, so we wouldn't try to force them?"

"Lord, it would kill me to know! Imagine some fairy godmother telling me when I was twenty that here I'd be thirty-eight and still not have found the right one! I'd have jumped off a bridge."

"Or married Leon Jarvis."

"Same thing. Uh-huh. It was a beautiful wedding, but I knew all along that I hadn't ought to do it. I remember the night before the ceremony, my maid of honor and I went out to the county park and sat there on one of those picnic tables in the dark smoking a whole pack of Benson

& Hedges and talking till after midnight. You know, I can't remember one word of what we said, but I remember thinking, *If she'll just say, 'Martha, don't do it!' why, I won't.* But she didn't say it, so I thought maybe I was doing the right thing and just didn't know it."

She traced the rim of the coffee cup with her finger. It felt greasy, too. "I wanted to be the wife Mama had been to Daddy, but you couldn't do that with Leon. Why, he couldn't even hold a job or balance the checkbook, much less take care of me! So I got a job, and then I made more money than Leon, and . . . well, he's married to a beautician now, in Knoxville, and they have two little girls. I guess it's all for the best."

"Possibly so."

"And . . ." She sighed. "I was almost thirty by the time I married Howard. Around here, if a man is thirty and not married, there's a reason."

"Had a reason, did Howard?" Joe asked lightly.

"Yes, and it was nothing that was going to change on account of me." Martha dropped her rolled-up napkin into the pool of ketchup on her plate. "I got to get back to the office, Joe. Time to shut up the time capsule. You coming?"

"Back to the present? Oh, yes, ma'am. But not back to the office. I'm riding the roads. Want me to fix you up a date with old Roger?"

Martha shook her head. "I can find my own Lost Causes."

If he knew what she meant by that, he gave no sign of it. But he paid for her hamburger. She thought that might be a good sign.

The Hamelin Women's Club rummage sale, held each year in the basement of the Methodist Church, had been a bigger event in the days before yard sales were fashionable. Even now it had a good many contributors: those of the old school who thought that a yard sale was an admission of poverty, and young moderns who had neither the time nor the patience to hold one and would rather donate their junk for the tax deduction. Jane Arrowood was one of the former; her son Spencer, the latter.

Each year they assembled a collection of *National Geographics* (always popular among those with school-age children), unmatched dishes, unfortunate Christmas gifts, and things they were just plain tired of, and Spencer carted them down to the sale committee for sorting and pricing. This purging never gained them much in the way of additional space, however, because Women's Club supporters were also expected to attend the rummage sale, and almost no one escaped without buying at least one white elephant from someone else. One memorable year Jane Arrowood really *had* purchased a white elephant: the ceramic planter trailing vines of philodendron still stood on the wrought-iron table on her sun porch.

"I am not going to buy anything this year," she told Spencer. "This time I mean it."

He nodded. She always said that, but he had worn a gray sweatshirt and jeans in anticipation of hauling her dusty bargains home in his pickup truck. "Just make sure I can lift it by myself," he told her as she wandered off toward the stall of books.

He was glad that it was his day off and he wouldn't have to wear his uniform. His mother's bridge-playing friends were only too glad to see a peace officer if they had a noise complaint or a stolen lawn mower, but that was seldom. The rest of the time they seemed to view his occupation as something akin to being a circus fire-eater: someone who risked his life unnecessarily for a modest salary. His mother still told her friends that this was a phase, and that he would reapply to law school at the end of his next term. At thirty-eight, though, that possibility was seeming more remote to both of them. Perhaps his mother still found it trying to listen to tales of Chuck the lawyer, or Johnny the dentist, with their upscale homes and their Sharper Image toys. Spencer didn't listen much anymore. At least she didn't say that Cal would have done better. Cal would have cashed in on his days of pigskin glory by selling insurance.

Spencer was *around*, though. He thought he deserved credit for that. Most of the whiz kids went home the way they went to church: one holiday a year. The fact that he lived in town, and saw to the yard and the furnace and the storm windows, meant that his mother could keep the house. There wasn't much she could do after his dad died. She'd been like an old cocker spaniel dumped by the side of the road, and she could no more look after herself in the world than it could.

Spencer looked at the linen-suited ladies fingering lace tablecloths and porcelain whatnots with their soft wrinkled hands. Well-spoken, carefully dressed creatures, keeping comfortable homes—and every one of them just *one man* away from Welfare. He wondered if they had made good wives, these suburban geishas, who had gone from Rainbow Girls to Junior League. Maybe . . . if intelligent conversation was not on your list of priorities. Most of his generation would never be able to afford to find out.

He wondered what Peggy Muryan would be like at their age. Maybe it depended on the success of her comeback.

"Are you just going to stand there staring into space, Spencer Arrowood, or are you going to buy something? We have no stolen goods, I assure you." It was Jessie Traynham calling to him from her stall of postcards and magazines.

He ambled over and began to sift through the postcards. Some of them had penny stamps on the back and short messages in copperplate script: "Arrived in Bristol safely. Have seen Carl. Home by Friday. Jack." Why had Jack gone to Bristol to see Carl? A family illness? Trouble with the law? Postcard senders never seemed to write with any consideration for future voyeurs.

"Things going all right for you, Miz Jessie?" he asked, still studying the cards. He set aside some from World War II, a picture of a destroyer, and an artillery shot labeled "Camp Davis, North Carolina."

"Tolerably so. That woman's dog has stayed out of my flowers."

"Did you go and see her?"

"I did. But she came out and talked to me on the porch. Seemed nervous."

Spencer looked up at Jessie Traynham. Her hair was lacquer-perfect, and her green crepe dress was set off by real pearls. "Did you drop by unannounced?" he asked her. "Wearing gloves?"

"Well, naturally . . ."

He grinned. "Uh-huh. I wouldn't have let you in, either, Miz Jessie. You are a combination health inspector and town crier in that getup, and anybody'd be afraid to find you on their stoop. Give her some notice so she can run a dust rag across the furniture, and I reckon she'll be more pleased to meet you."

Jessie Traynham sniffed, her opinion of his generation's manners and housekeeping. "She did say that she had given you a box of memorabilia, as she put it, for the rummage sale. What might that have been?"

"I just glanced at it. Seemed to be papers. Letters, maybe. I was mindful of the deadline, so I brought it straight here. Maybe I'll have a look through it now, though. Maybe there'll be an autograph from Janis Joplin."

"Well, buy those postcards before you wander off, because I don't want to have to put them back in order."

Spencer handed her a couple of quarters. "Any idea which stall would have her things?"

Jessie Traynham shrugged. "Try Miscellaneous Collectors. That's where we put the baseball cards and the Jim Beam Christmas decanters."

He checked that stall and most of the others before his mother asked him to load a magazine rack and a floor lamp into the truck, but he never found Peggy Muryan's donation.

TEAPATCH SERVICE CLUB
SHU LIN KOU AIR STATION

9TH, TUES MORN, 1 A.M.

DEAR PEG,

JUST BECAUSE I'M OUT OF SIGHT DOESN'T MEAN I'M OUT OF MY MIND. . . . (AM I OUT OF YOURS?) . . . I MEAN, IT'S NOT LIKE I'M IN EXILE. I'LL ASSUME THAT YOU MEANT TO WRITE, INDEED YOU MAY ALREADY HAVE, BUT YOU'VE BEEN SO BUSY. I'VE ASKED THE BASE RADIO STATION TO PLAY YOUR ALBUM. I SUPPOSE I'LL HAVE TO BUY IT AND GIVE IT TO THEM TO GET THEM TO DO IT. HAVE YOU MADE THE CHARTS YET?

I SUPPOSE I WISH I WERE GETTING THE CHANCE YOU HAVE TO MAKE IT BIG, INSTEAD OF GETTING A SHOT (NO PUN INTENDED) AT BEING AMERICA'S NEXT WAR NOVELIST, OR WHATEVER. ANYWAY, I JUST WISH YOU'D WRITE. LET ME KNOW YOU'RE OKAY.

WHAT'S BEEN HAPPENING TO ME LATELY? OH, I THOUGHT YOU WEREN'T GOING TO ASK.

I HAVE ARRIVED IN THE FAR EAST, AS MISS WALKER USED TO CALL IT IN FIFTH GRADE. I HAVE ARRIVED. THAT'S ALL I HAVE TO SAY ABOUT LIVING IN THE "LAND OF THE DWARFS." . . . ACTUALLY, THIS ISN'T A BAD PLACE AT ALL IF YOU LIKE MILITARY DICTATORSHIPS. SHANGHAI JACK (OR WHATEVER HE CALLS HIMSELF)—THE GENERALISSIMO, YEAH, THAT'S IT. HE RUNS THE SHOW OVER HERE. REAL OLD MAN. YOU CAN CATCH HIM EVERY NITE AS TV GOES OFF THE AIR (YES. THEY HAVE TV) ON THE PATRIOTIC TRAILER THAT RUNS AT THE END OF EVERY BROADCAST DAY. HEARTWARMING SHOTS OF THE GEEMO HISS SELF, BIGGER'N SHIT, A KINDLY OLD MAN, AMIABLE YET FIRM, RESOLUTE, UNSWERVING, FATHER TO THE MASSES.

HIS WORD IS LAW. YESSIR. DON'T NEVER FORGET THAT—AT LEAST NOT WHEN YOU'RE OUT HOBNOBBING WITH THE LOCAL PEASANTS HERE. ONE NEVER KNOWS WHO MIGHT BE HOVERING . . . WATCHING.

I LIVE IN THE BARRACKS. SECOND FLOOR; TWO ROOMMATES. SORT OF. ONE OF THEM IS GOING HOME. SEEMS HE HAS SUGAR DIABETES BAD ENOUGH FOR A DISCHARGE. WELL, AT LEAST HE'S GOING HOME. MY OTHER ROOMMATE, WHAT'S-HIS-NAME, KEEPS A PLACE DOWNTOWN SOMEWHERE, SO WHEN OUR BREAKS BETWEEN SHIFTS ROLL AROUND, HE DISAPPEARS. I HARDLY EVER SEE HIM. WHICH IS JUST AS WELL. I VALUE MY PRIVACY.

I CAN SEE RIGHT NOW WHERE IT'S GOING TO BE A LONG 10 MONTHS WITHOUT A STEREO SETUP. I THINK I SHALL PURCHASE ONE. AM

VERY BORED. TAIPEI IS BORING, WORKING IS BORING, NCO CLUB IS SAME, IBID FOR TEA-PATCH SERVICE CLUB, SNACK BAR, ETC.

BUT CONSIDERING THE ALTERNATIVE, IT'S A LITTLE MORE BEARABLE.

DO WRITE AND TELL ME HOW THINGS ARE. NEWS FROM THE HOME FRONT AND ALL THAT. TELL ME ABOUT YOUR CAREER. HAVE YOU MET DYLAN YET? . . . SPARE ME NOTHING. I'M NOT ANGRY WITH YOU, PET. REALLY I'M NOT. AND I'M NOT CARRYING A TORCH, AS MY OLD MAN WOULD SAY. JUST WRITE ME, WILLYA?

YOUR MAN IN TAIWAN,

T.P.

CHAPTER 4

Strange days have tracked us down.

THE DOORS

THE FACE LOOKING up at Martha from page 37 of *The Papyrus* was eighteen years old, but it was still intimidating. Martha didn't see it as a young face, because she was seeing it through young eyes: in 1966 that face had meant power, achievement, and status. Tyndall Johnson. Martha wondered what the hell she was doing back in Hamelin.

Tyndall Johnson's straight blond hair in a shoulder-length flip made Martha think of Dippity Doo, for the first time in twenty years. In the era of ramrod-straight hair, that pink gelatinous goo had plastered many a wavy mane into rigid conformity with fashion. Martha ruffled her short brown curls, remembering the cotton candy feel of straightened hair. She wondered if Tyndall Johnson's hair had been naturally straight. Probably so. Some people are born to fit the times.

Tyndall's golden flip, her Pepsodent smile, and her collection of pastel-colored Fair Isle cardigans appeared on about half the pages of *The Papyrus*, Hamelin's yearbook. There was Tyndall with a rose "Best All Around," Tyndall in the homecoming honor court, Tyndall in the student council, and Tyndall in all the candid shots of the "class"—actually about the same six people—shooting pool, having a snowball fight, riding golf carts. . . . Everybody at the reunion would want to know what happened to Tyndall.

The caption under her senior portrait said "Katherine Tyndall Johnson." It had to be her. Martha looked again at the social item in the local paper: Mrs. Katherine Tyndall Garner was visiting her mother, Mrs. Evelyn Johnson, in Willow Creek. The article didn't say why or for how long. The next paragraph was all about the Adamses' shopping trip to Knoxville. Not much happened in Willow Creek.

It was Tyndall Johnson, back in town. Martha was sure of it. And because she was sure of it, she made herself a cup of tea and waited another ten minutes before she looked up the Johnsons' number in Willow Creek. Finally she dialed it.

Someone answered with a weary hello, and Martha said: "My name is Martha Ayers. Could I speak to Tyndall Johns—" She glanced again at the paper. "To Mrs. Garner?"

"Speaking," said the voice. "Martha Ayers . . . are you a friend of my mother's?"

"No," said Martha. She didn't consider saying, I'm a friend of yours. That had never been true. "We were in school together," she said at last. "And I'm planning the class reunion. Since you're in town, I thought you might like to be on the planning committee."

There was a pause long enough for Martha to wonder if she had hung up, but then the voice said, "Are you free for lunch?"

"I guess so," said Martha. It was her day off. (Do I have to get my hair done for this? she wondered.)

"One o'clock. Denton's. Will that be all right?"

"Sure. Fine. I eat there a lot."

As far as Martha was concerned, the conversation wasn't over, but Tyndall Johnson said, "I'll see you there," and quietly hung up.

"Still bossy after all these years." Martha shrugged. But what the hell. A reunion committee could use a little bossiness. And she could use the help.

Martha spent ten minutes longer than usual deciding what to wear. Denton's did not encourage upscale dressing, but she didn't want to feel at a disadvantage: *nothing* polyester. One of the put-downs in Tyndall's crowd had been: "He buys his shoes at the Shoe Show," a discount place in the shopping center. *They* all had Bass Weejuns, purchased from the correct department store downtown. This was years before the *Preppie Handbook* came out. Martha used to wonder if they had secret meetings to decide what clothes were "in." How did they all choose Villager shirts, London Fog raincoats, and madras skirts at the same time? Some wardrobe hotline? Martha thought it was no coincidence that the secret headquarters in *The Man from U.N.C.L.E.* was at the back of a tailor shop.

In the end she decided to go with a scoop-necked navy silk tee and a challis skirt. Small gold earrings and a simple gold chain. She still had a gold circle pin in her jewelry box, but she hadn't worn it in twenty years. She couldn't even remember the symbolism anymore. If you wore a circle pin on your left breast, did that mean you were a virgin or going steady? Such rituals had seemed so important back then.

At least she was thin. Thank God for that. She picked up the yearbook and the manila folder of reunion notes, and headed out to the car. She thought about seeing if Spencer Arrowood wanted to join them for lunch, but she decided that he'd be more trouble than he was worth.

Tyndall would probably feel obliged to be charming to him, and Martha would end up feeling like a third wheel, and they wouldn't get a damned thing done. Spencer was no help with the reunion, anyway. Best just to give him a task and tell him to get on with it, after someone else had seen to the planning.

Denton's had been a hangout in high school. Maybe it still was for Hamelin's youth. She was never there at three-thirty to find out. But a Hamelin banner adorned one wall, along with photos of a few championship football teams. The wooden booths and the paintings of mountain scenery stayed the same from one decade to the next. Just now the place was reasonably packed with the second-hour lunch crowd, but there were no fortyish women alone. Martha smiled: not a Fair Isle in the house. She grabbed a booth just as its occupants were leaving, and sat on the side facing the door. The yearbook was open to "J."

The Papyrus. Martha wondered how the yearbook got saddled with that name. It had always been that, even in her mother's day. Nothing changed but the year. Even the faces seemed pretty standard: beefy, florid boys and little field-mouse boys; cameo-featured rich girls, and frumpy girls, and tawdry girls with raccoon eye makeup. They had all turned into somebody else by now, one way or another. *The Papyrus* indeed, thought Martha. They ought to call it *The Book of the Dead.*

Tyndall Johnson was about ten minutes late. Martha recognized the oval face and the cover-girl nose, but Tyndall Johnson, with short-cropped hair and a scrubbed, thin face, was wearing a jean skirt and a baggy T-shirt. She didn't look as if she were dressed for a luncheon engagement. Martha smiled carefully and waved her over. Tyndall Johnson, she thought, looked every minute of her age.

"Hi," she said, handing over a menu. "I'm glad you could come."

Tyndall reached for the yearbook. "I'm sorry," she said. "It was so long ago." She turned to the A's.

"I think we were in Chorus together," murmured Martha.

"I never could sing, but it was that or—what was it, Shop?"

"Yes. Most of the guys took Shop."

"We should have. I've refinished a lot of furniture since those days, and God, the times I've wished I'd had some real instruction in using tools!"

Martha giggled. "I can see you out there using the jigsaw with a bunch of greasy-haired guys with cigarette packs rolled up in their shirtsleeves."

"Yeah. Remember Billy Hillyard? He even had his own adjective: *grungy*. I wonder where he is now."

"I don't know. Maybe through this reunion committee we can find out."

Tyndall sighed. "A reunion, huh? When is it?"

"August. I think we should send out some kind of announcement. To the ones we can find, anyway. Of course, some people have left town. You're just visiting, aren't you?"

"Yeah. You could call it that. How about you?"

"Oh, I still live in town. I'm the dispatcher for the sheriff's office. You know who the sheriff is?"

Tyndall shook her head. "Not one of the jocks, I hope?"

"No. Cal Arrowood's little brother. Spencer."

"Really? He hasn't got shades and a beer gut, has he?"

"No. He's okay. He *looks* okay, anyway. And what about you? You went to Meredith College, didn't you?"

"Three years. I quit when Steve graduated from N.C. State. Worked for a while as a secretary, until he became solvent. And we have three kids: Steve Jr., Nell, and Elissa. God, I miss them!"

Martha hesitated. "You're . . . separated?"

Tyndall Johnson Garner smiled. "Only by distance." Her thin fingers rumpled her hair. "My mother has Alzheimer's disease, so I come down here when I can to look after her. She's in one of her bad spells right now. She doesn't even know me half the time."

Martha sat back, her mouth still open. "I'm sorry," she said at last.

"So am I. We don't know what to do. If I stay home with my husband and my kids, I feel guilty for leaving her with paid help, but when I come down here I feel guilty about neglecting my own children. Life seems to be a choice between two wrong answers."

"The Statler Brothers were right," said Martha.

"Excuse me?"

"The Statler Brothers. They had a song called 'Class of '57' that said something about life getting complicated once you pass the age of eighteen. I guess it does. Maybe the reunion will be sort of sad."

"I want to work on the committee, Martha. Lord knows, I never thought I'd find myself back in Hamelin, but here I am. For a couple of weeks, anyway. And I can do typing and address envelopes at home with Mother, so please let me help. I need something to take my mind off house arrest."

Martha opened the yearbook. "Maybe we should see if we know where some of these people are. . . . "

Tyndall nodded. "We can draw up a form for them to fill out. Maybe put together a booklet of addresses and updates. Debbie Shaw. Remember her? Valedictorian. That girl was a whiz in class—either that or she worked all night studying. I wonder what happened to her."

"She didn't go to college," said Martha. "She works as

a bookkeeper at the mill. Lives with her kids in a trailer in Dark Hollow. You think we ought to order lunch before we get started on this?"

"I'm not hungry," said Tyndall.

Something in the conversation with Homer Ramsay had made Spencer think about Peggy Muryan, but he couldn't figure out just what it was. He had found a phone message on his desk that morning to call her, but there had been no answer when he called, and then it had slipped his mind until just now. He figured he'd try again when they got this Ramsay business straightened out. He glanced at the grizzled old man in the chair beside the booking desk. He was studying the ducks and hunting dogs on the office wall calendar with a look of grave concentration.

"We can't book this guy," the sheriff had said to LeDonne, in an undertone, as they filled out the paperwork.

"Why the hell not?" said LeDonne. "I got him dead to rights."

"Because the prosecutor will wet himself laughing, that's why!"

Joe LeDonne had leveled his aviator shades at the sheriff, cocked one stiff finger, and said, "Rabies!" Then he turned around and walked out.

He had a point. Homer Ramsay was breaking the law, and the potential for harm was present in the crime. Spencer pulled up a chair. Maybe they could talk it out. "Mr. Ramsay, I understand your position as a sportsman, but we can't have you committing illegal acts."

"Bullcrap. State of Ohio oughtta gimme a medal." Homer Ramsay still wore his gray felt hat, indoors or not. He wasn't dressed like a hunter—not in that suit jacket and black dress shoes—but then he hadn't been out hunting today. He had been driving. LeDonne had pulled him over for speeding and had found the back of his pickup filled with caged raccoons. They were in the department parking lot, still in the back of his truck under a shade tree. It was ninety degrees today: too hot for some exhibits to be brought into the office. Spencer went out into the parking lot, took a good look at the fourteen smelly, ill-tempered raccoons, and let it go at that.

"Why should Ohio give you a medal?"

"For transporting coons. You think they want them things in the city? Bullcrap. They's a nuisance. You can't tell a city coon nothing. Man, they've seen it *all*. You take a Tennessee coon. Now, if you surprise him a-stealing out your garbage, why, he'll turn tail and run away. But an Ohio coon, he'll just sit back on his haunches and look you dead in the eye. He ain't afraid, nossir. Seen it all."

"Mr. Ramsay, what are you doing with a truck full of city-bred raccoons?"

The old man rubbed his chin. "Restocking. The local population has been considerably depleted by hunters. Hardly any sport for the hounds atall anymore. You can walk around for hours and never even catch scent of one. I say we need the coons, and downtown Ohio sure as hell don't."

Spencer heaved a weary sigh. Maybe the game warden could handle this. He looked up at Homer Ramsay. "I am going to have to look up this bit about transporting animals across a state line, but I'm pretty sure it's against the law. State or federal. One or the other. Suppose one of those animals has rabies?"

"Bullcrap," said Homer Ramsay. "I know a sick coon when I see one. Nothing wrong with these coons but high cho-les-ter-ol. Steady diet of Kentucky Fried Chicken and half-eaten Big Macs. Do 'em good to get to Tennessee woods. Make 'em fit."

Yeah. Until somebody shoots their asses to kingdom come. By the time he said, "Mr. Ramsay, you cannot run a boot camp for raccoons," they were both laughing fit to kill. Finally he sent Mr. Ramsay and his truckload of ring-tailed city slickers to the game warden in the county office building. Then he called Peggy Muryan. The funny story would break the ice, and then he would see what she wanted, and maybe he could tell how things stood with them. If things seemed okay, he would ask her out. He figured he could catch up with LeDonne later and tell him that he hadn't exactly dismissed the case.

Taking a date to the Mockingbird Inn on the highway for spaghetti night, that was no big deal. You could pass that off as just not wanting to eat alone. He even went there with Martha sometimes, and no one thought a thing about it. But the Parson's Table in Jonesborough was an altogether different proposition.

It was an old steepled brick church, garlanded with ivy vines, and still looking like an old-fashioned house of worship. It was just across the railroad tracks, perched up on the hill above tiny, historic Jonesborough, but the church's interior had been remodeled into an elegant restaurant, with pastel table linens and little vases of fresh flowers on each table. They had home-baked bread and entrees that Spencer wouldn't have tried to pronounce. Ratatouille. Boeuf Bourguignon. . . .

You went to the Parson's Table, you were serious. Spencer had taken Jenny to Regas in Knoxville the night they got engaged. It was the place of choice to impress your date. But that was kids, he told himself. Knoxville was too far to drive on a weeknight, and the Parson's Table was just as fancy. He figured Peggy Muryan was used to nice places.

He watched as she sipped her Potage Saint-Germain with a worried frown. He hadn't used the wrong spoon, had he? The Mockingbird Inn would have been safer from that standpoint, but Peggy Muryan was *somebody*. She was probably used to places with menus in French in New York . . . L.A. He hadn't brought her here to impress her, but just to accommodate the lifestyle he assumed she had. He hadn't counted on its making him nervous to be here with someone so much at ease. She was wearing a simple dress of flowered silk, but it looked expensive. Even her short hair was different somehow; he could tell because the tiny diamond studs sparkled in her earlobes. Best keep talking, he thought, so as to have less time to fret about table manners.

"How's your work going?" he asked.

Peggy shrugged. "Okay, I guess. It's hard to judge your own work. Anyway, I do a lot of revising, so nothing is really finished yet. Still, it beats having a real job."

Spencer smiled a little. "How would you know?"

She set down her spoon. "How would I *know*? What do you think I've been doing all these years? Sleeping in a glass case in Woodstock?"

"I hadn't thought about it." He didn't think there was anything to think about. Peggy Muryan had made records that actually showed up on the national charts. He figured she'd made a few million—well, *a* million, anyway—and then had gone off to California to enjoy herself by the swimming pool. Isn't that what they did?

"You thought I was rich," she said with an accusing smile. "Homes in Paris and L.A.? A couple of Rolls-Royces? Millions in a Swiss bank? Is that what you thought? I hope you aren't interested in me because of my money."

"Well, no, I—"

"Because there's damn little of it."

"But you're famous."

"So is Tiny Tim. Remember *him*? 'Tiptoe Through the

Tulips.' Got married on the Johnny Carson show with half the country watching. He works in a *circus* these days, and they don't pay him much, let me tell you." She waved a breadstick. "Being famous is not all it's cracked up to be, Sherlock. Remember that the record companies get most of the money from an album, and you get maybe ten percent, if you're lucky. So, from a six-dollar album, that's around sixty cents. And not many people sold a million albums. Elvis. The Beatles. Not Peggy Muryan. I was lucky to sell fifty thousand. So what's that: about thirty thousand dollars, out of which you pay a manager, maybe a publicist, and your musicians, and you have to buy costumes, and go to the right parties. No matter how much you make, it doesn't sit in the bank."

He looked at her face, glowing in the candlelight. It was still a young face: the lines didn't show much, the way his did when he looked in a mirror. She had not had a hard life, whatever she'd done. "So where have you been all these years?"

She inclined her head. "Around. I got married in the early seventies. Record company production executive. *That* didn't last long. I still get a Christmas card. And for a while I toured. The money is better."

"Ticket sales, huh?"

"Not so much that. See, you produce your own album. Just pay a small studio to actually make it, and then you sell it after the concert, and *you* keep ninety percent of the take. And you can do Cause concerts. Some group uses you for a fund-raiser, and you split the gate receipts fifty-fifty with them. I've sung for peace, for whales, and for El Salvador. I've even sung for striking garbagemen. But the road is no place to grow old. Bad food, bad hours, bad times. So I went to work, like everybody else. Did you know that one of the Highwaymen is some big shot in the federal government now?"

Spencer shook his head. "You don't think of people getting to be famous more than once."

"Yes, I know exactly what you mean. There are so many people who are still alive, but . . . not as far as the public is concerned, you know? It's like being reincarnated without having to die. Tom Lehrer. *That Was the Week That Was,* remember? He played the piano and wrote those great satirical songs, like 'The Vatican Rag.' He's a college professor in California now. And one of the Black Panthers just did a cookbook. It's as if they got another life, one that isn't connected at all to the one we all know about."

"Had a secret life, did you?"

She frowned. "No. Just an ordinary one. I was Visiting Artist in the Northern California public schools, teaching kids about folk music and giving a performance with a lot of sing-along involved. I'd do small concerts every now and then, or play cafés on weekends. The money was enough to get by on, and it was peaceful."

"So why are you here?"

"Because my grandmother died."

"Okay."

"No, really. She died at the age of eighty-six, and I was the only grandchild. My granddad had been an executive in textiles, and there was a modest estate. Anyway, enough for a down payment on the house here and to live for a couple of years, if I'm careful. Compared with California, houses here are dirt cheap. I figured if nothing else, it would be a good investment. If I succeed at my comeback, then I sell the house at a profit; and if not, I go back to working with schoolchildren and doing local gigs, and I'll keep the place."

"Did your grandmother live around here?" It was still a long way from California. It didn't quite make sense.

"No, why? Oh—you mean, how did I decide to move

to Hamelin? I came through here once, a long time ago, and liked the look of the town. It looked like a nice place to live. An Ozzie and Harriet sort of place, I guess. When I was on the road, I used to dream of having a house of my own. And I remembered the big white house, and I thought, Someday when I'm successful, I'm going to live there. Of course, if I had really been successful, that's the last place I could have lived. An apartment in New York would be more like it. But now that I am comfortably unsuccessful, here I am."

Spencer raised his wineglass. "To your homecoming."

She frowned. "I need to show you something first."

In the time it took her to rummage through her purse, Spencer prepared himself for the "I don't think we should see each other again" speech, only it was Jenny's voice he was hearing in his mind. By the time he concentrated on what she actually wanted—the advice of a sheriff, and not a dinner date—he was somewhere between relieved and wounded.

She handed him a color postcard and pushed the candle closer to his plate. "This came in the mail yesterday."

It was a photograph of a log cabin, Davy Crockett's birthplace in Limestone, Tennessee. It wasn't too far from Hamelin—not that many people made the pilgrimage, but the postcards were for sale in most of the drugstores and restaurants in the area.

So she's getting hate mail, thought Spencer, examining the card carefully. There was probably no question of fingerprints by now, though. He guessed it was inevitable that people would be jealous of a celebrity in their midst sooner or later. Everybody thought she was worth a bundle, and there were always people who resented that. He turned the card over. It was addressed to "Peggy Muryan, Hamelin, Tennessee," with the right zip code. The postmark was Knoxville, but that didn't prove anything. Knoxville was the sorting station for most of the mail from the surrounding small towns.

The message, though, was not what he expected. Printed in all capital letters in grease pencil on the message side were the words:

IS LITTLE MARGARET IN THE HOUSE,
OR IS SHE IN THE HALL?

Spencer shook his head. "I don't get it. Do you know who it's from?"

"No. But it's meant to frighten me."

He read the lines again. "I was expecting a poison-pen letter. Some variation of the old Hanoi Jane business, but this doesn't make any sense to me at all. If it's meant as a joke, it's gone clear over my head."

He could see that it wasn't funny, though. The folksinger's eyes were wide, and she was nearly as pale as the candle. She reached for the Davy Crockett postcard.

"I'm pretty sure it's a threat. You see, my name is Margaret." His still-blank look made her sigh in exasperation. "Some fan you are! Don't you remember the song?"

"It's not on *Carolina Blue*."

"No. It's earlier. These lines are from an old English folk song. They still sing it in these mountains. 'Little Margaret.' We used to do it in our act."

We? thought Spencer. Peggy Muryan had always sung alone. "So . . . somebody is wanting to know if you are at home?"

Peggy managed a tense smile. "You do not seem equipped to handle this matter. Perhaps you should deputize Bascom Lunsford."

"Someone who knows folk songs, you mean." Bascom

Lunsford was synonymous with ballads down around Asheville, but he had passed away quite a few years back.

"You said you sang this song, so I'm asking you. What's it about?"

"It's about a revenant. That's a folklore term. Little Margaret's lover marries someone else, and she shows up on his wedding night, but when he goes to her house to find her—that's when this line comes in. He says: 'Is Little Margaret in the house, or is she in the hall?' And her people answer him: 'Little Margaret's lying in her coal-black coffin, with her face turned to the wall.' "

Spencer considered it. "A revenant is someone who dies and comes back?"

"Yes. I think the point of the message is that Little Margaret is *dead.* And I don't like it. Can you find out who sent it?"

"I doubt it. Even if we got prints, they may not match any that we have on file. Maybe it's just a prank. I don't even think it's illegal."

"It's a death threat!"

" 'Is Little Margaret in the house, or is she in the hall?' Where's the threat? They'd laugh you out of court. Maybe it was meant to scare you, but you'd have a hard time proving it."

"You don't think I need police protection?"

"Not in Hamelin. The crimes I see are about as straightforward as a knife between the shoulder blades. This reminds me more of the old ladies who call us talking about burglars in the garage, and it turns out to be a raccoon in the garbage can. I think you're looking awful hard for trouble."

Peggy's lips tightened for a moment, but then she wrinkled her nose and grinned at him. "I was about to get mad at you for telling me that I'm safe. I guess I ought to be grateful. After all, you're the expert."

"This isn't the big city. Folks around here are pretty friendly, and even if they take a dislike to you, they'll show it a deal plainer than that postcard. So I'd say it's just a piece of foolishness."

He resolved not to talk about the postcard anymore that evening. It was a subject for disagreement, and they both sensed that their acquaintance was too new to bear the weight of an argument. To keep things light and sociable, Spencer took some trouble to be amusing about legends of East Tennessee. He told her about the impersonations by Vernon Woolwine, about Indian Graves Gap, and about his great-grandparents' farm back in one of the hollows near the North Carolina line.

"I wish you could have met them," he said. "You're so interested in the old ways. They *were* the old ways. They lived to be nearly a hundred. My great-grandfather, the Reverend John, was a circuit preacher back up in these hills. You know what that is?"

She nodded. "Little country churches can't afford a pastor, so they take turns having a preacher. The circuit rider visits each church, in turn, and preaches the Gospel."

"He married Great-Grandmother Mary in 1892 and took her on horseback over the mountains to his farm. She was eighteen years old. A tiny thing with long black hair and cat-green eyes. They say she was Irish. My dad used to tell Cal and me how she rode sidesaddle on her mare, following behind her husband, and she had cut a mulberry switch to use as a riding crop. When they got to the farm, she got off her horse and stuck that old stick into the wet ground, and didn't think no more about it."

Peggy hid her smile behind the rim of her coffee cup. *Think no more about it.* He was repeating the story as he'd heard it, a litany from the family history.

"But that riding crop took root there in the yard and

grew into a great, spreading mulberry tree. Dad used to play in it when he was a little boy. Some trees will do that, you know. Sprout from a cutting. Sometimes even fenceposts will take root."

"Maybe you ought to be writing ballads," said Peggy.

Spencer blushed. "No. I never was inclined to music. Not much, anyway. I wish you could have met my dad. When I was a freshman in college, I took up playing the guitar."

"Didn't we all? Three chords, right? C, F, and G7?"

"G, C, and D7. I never could get my fingers to do that F chord." He looked down at his fingers, approximating their position on the frets. "They just don't bend that way. Well, anyhow, I learned a couple of songs off a Joan Baez record, and when I came home for Thanksgiving, I was practicing my chords. There I was, singing 'A Fair Young Maid, All in the Garden' when my dad walks into the room, and he joined in."

" 'John Riley.' " Peggy nodded, recognizing the line.

"Right. From the very latest Joan Baez album. Now, I knew that my dad was not into the counterculture, and he didn't know Joan Baez from Betty Crocker, so how come he knows my new song?"

"New song." Peggy smiled. "Four hundred years old."

"Yeah. He said he'd heard it from his grandmother. Mary of the riding crop. His tune was all wrong—sounded like Ernest Tubb—but he was letter perfect on the words."

"Did you get any other songs from him?"

Spencer shook his head. "I spent the whole weekend trying. But he didn't know Grand Ol' Opry from Childe Ballad. They were all mixed up in his head as songs from childhood. You might have had better luck, but you're ten years too late to try."

Peggy shrugged. "It's ten years too late to matter. Folk is out."

Spencer hesitated, trying to make the question casual. "How does 'Little Margaret' go?"

She shrugged. "I can sing it if you like."

Spencer glanced around the restaurant, and Peggy laughed. "I'm not gonna stand up on the table and yodel, Spencer. I'll lean toward you and sing softly, so people will think we're talking private."

Nobody was within ten feet of them, anyway, and he thought it might be important to hear what the song was about, in case its sentiments were echoed by the sender.

Peggy closed her eyes for a moment, summoning the words from her memory, and then she bent close to him and began the old, mournful ballad in a voice just beyond a whisper.

Little Margaret's sitting in her high hall door,
Combing back her long yellow hair,
She saw sweet William and his new-made bride
A-going down the road so near

She threw down her ivory comb,
She threw back her long yellow hair.
Says: "I'll go down and bid him farewell,
And never more go there."

It was all lately in the night,
When they were fast asleep,
Little Margaret appeared all dressed in white,
A-standing at their bedfeet.

It's: "How do you like your snow-white pillow,
And how do you like your sheets?

And how do you like the fair young maid
Who lies in your arms asleep?"

"It's fine I like my snow-white pillow,
And it's fine I like my sheets,
Much better do I like the fair young maid
A-standing at my bedfeet."

He called to his serving man to go
And saddle up the dapple roan.
He rode to her father's house that night,
And he knocked on the door, alone.

Peggy paused for breath, and Spencer felt a spasm of cold as he anticipated the next verse. He had forgotten about the Parson's Table and the other diners.

"Is Little Margaret in the house,
Or is she in the hall?"
"Little Margaret's lying in her coal-black coffin,
With her face turned to the wall."

"Fold back, fold back those snow-white robes,
Be they ever so fine,
Let me kiss those cold clay lips,
For I know they'll never kiss mine."

Once he kissed her lily-white hand,
And twice he kissed her cheek,
Three times he kissed her cold, corpy lips,
And he fell in her arms asleep.

Spencer waited a moment for the spell of the old tragedy to evaporate in the noise of the restaurant-that-used-to-be-a-church. Peggy toyed with her wineglass, looking into the candle as if she'd forgotten he was there.

"There is no violence implied in the song," he said at last. "She seems to have died of a broken heart, and maybe he dies of grief. 'He fell in her arms asleep.' Does that mean he died?"

Peggy shrugged. "Depends on your sense of drama, I guess."

"Anyway, he feels guilty about what he's done. He jilted Margaret and married someone else, and she dies of sorrow." He frowned. "Does any of that apply?"

"Not even the 'long yellow hair,' anymore," she said, touching her short-cropped hair. "No. I just think the implication of the coffin is rather ominous."

"Maybe not," said Spencer. "Maybe someone meant it more kindly than you took it."

When he heard her voice on the phone the next morning, he would know that he had been wrong.

Later when they were driving back to Hamelin, she settled back in the passenger seat and sang "The House Carpenter." Her clear, strong voice echoed around him in the closed car, blending with the night outside. It made him shiver. "What hills, what hills are those, my love, that look so dark below?" He looked out at the black shapes of the mountains framed by pine shadows, and he thought that, but for the ribbon of asphalt, it could be any year at all. The small silver moon slipping in and out of tangled branches was like a dime in a street grate, or a sixpence in a troubadour's hat. It was everybody's moon, since time began.

"Those are the hills of Hell, my love, where you and I must go." He felt the coldness settle into the pit of his stomach.

Peggy's song had ended, and she let the quiet seep in

for a mile or two, before she said, "You talk a lot, Spencer, but I'm not learning much. You told me about your great-grandparents, and your folks, and the scenic wonders of Wake County, Tennessee, but I still don't know much about you."

"That *is* me."

"Part of you, maybe. It's background. But what about your life? You were in the Army, and now you're a sheriff, and you used to have a wife. What became of her?"

"She left. We were high school sweethearts, I guess. It's been a long time."

Not long enough. He could feel Peggy Muryan watching him in the darkness, but he kept his eyes on the two pools of headlights in front of him. Jenny, like the Limestone postcard, was too much weight for a fragile friendship to bear. Maybe he could talk about her later, but it would take more than one evening to break the long habit of silence.

"Do you know 'Whiskey in the Jar'?" he asked her.

"Sure."

"Why don't you sing that one?"

She settled back in the darkness again and took up the tale of the robbing of Colonel Farrell on Gilgarra Mountain, and the robber's betrayal by Darling Sportin' Jenny. She tells the police what he'd done, and she renders his weapons useless, but he manages to escape during the trial. When Peggy got to the verse about the robber going to find his brother, who's serving in the Army, Spencer reached for her hand and held it as if to keep himself from falling.

DARKNESS AND SILENCE, but if you strained toward it, it turned out not to be darkness or silence at all. In the blackness were stars, pinpoints of light, aimed at your eyes, and the sky had a luminous haze from man-made lights somewhere far off, so that no matter how much you wanted to slip into darkness, the light wouldn't let you go. The light was broken glass and your eyes were bleeding. . . . But you have to keep them open. . . . Listen! . . . Beneath the surface of the silence were pinpoints of noise. The drone of mosquitoes . . . the bending of leaves . . . and the rustle of grass. His own footsteps. His heart. But he could turn off the night sounds with the noise in his head. Put your M-16 on rock and roll, and tune your head to the DJ of Oldies . . . moldies . . . ghoulies . . . ghosties . . . Is it dead or is it Memorex?

The song drowns out the thudding, the buzz, the rustle. That was Otis Redding for you, soldier, "Sitting on the Dock of the Bay."—SIR! Would that be Cam Ranh Bay, SIR?—Soldier, you know that it would. If Otis sings in your head, but the radio's dead, does it make the leaves move? The cover is not too thick, here, though. Single canopy.

It's time to kill something.'Cause that's what they do in a war.

Edging forward slowly. Staring at the dark until the

shapes burn through. Let's get this zippo mission on the road.

Jamming in your helmet . . . jamming in your head. . . . But no jamming in the rifle, man. No firearms tonight, though. Tonight is for quiet death. . . . Tiger, tiger, burning bright in the forests of the night. . . . Hey, man, did you know that you can sing that to the tune of "Twinkle, Twinkle, Little Star"?

Nothing to be scared of. We have met the enemy, and they are us. And yea, though I walk through the valley of the shadow of death, I will fear no evil, 'cause I'm the meanest son of a bitch in the whole damned place.

And I am stoned.

The Objective is a few hundred yards in the distance. Breathing loud in the quiet. Unseeing, Move quiet, Point Man. Let the mosquitoes drown you out. Let the wind in the grass be louder than the rasp of steel easing from leather. Let the songs in your head be louder than the little voice that says "Kill."

Cut a chogie now. We're in dead space. . . . Move it!

Closer. Faster. Quieter. NOW! Get her now, before she knows what you are. Before she has a chance to fight . . . Chao, Mamasan . . . Struggle. Choke on the cry in your throat. Die. That's an order.

Blood at night is darker than the summer sky. The newly dead are quieter than the teeming night. . . . Darkness and Silence come later.

DEAR PEG,

AND WE'RE BACK. HELLO.

I'VE BEEN TRYING TO THINK OF SOMETHING TO RUN OPEN ABOUT, BUT NOTHING SEEMS TO GEL, ALTHOUGH THERE ARE SOME THINGS THERE. EITHER THAT OR I DON'T ESPECIALLY CARE TO GO INTO THEM. OR US. YOU AND ME. AN AUTOPSY OF A DYNAMIC DUO. LOVE, OH LOVE, OH CARELESS LOVE.

THAT'LL BE ENOUGH OF THAT, T.P. IT'S NOT NICE TO BORE FAMOUS PEOPLE. SHE PROBABLY HAS COUNTRY JOE AND THE FISH ON HOLD WHILE SHE READS YOUR LETTER.

WHEN BOB HOPE CALLS, TELL HIM YOU ALREADY GAVE TO THE BOYS OVERSEAS. TELL HIM YOU GET THESE HYSTERICAL LETTERS FROM AN OLD FLAME, AND YOU ACTUALLY TAKE TIME OUT OF YOUR SPARKLING LITTLE OL' LIFE TO READ THEM.

JUST HAD A ONE-STAR GENITAL STOP BY WITH A SMALL GAGGLE OF OTHER OFFICERS . . . GUESS THEY'RE MAKING THE ROUNDS TO SEE HOW WE ENLISTED SWINE ARE HACKIN' IT. . . .

RIGHT NOW I'M FILLING MY HEAD UP ON

SOUNDS, GRACE SLICK AND THE JEFFERSON AIRPLANE. NO WONDER I'M SO FUCKED UP. I MEAN, I GET ALL MY NEWS FROM EITHER THE PACIFIC STARS AND STRIPES OR NATIONAL LAMPOON.

IF NOTHING ELSE GOES ON, 'MAGINE I'LL BOOK ON UP TO THE NCO CLUB AND MAINLINE A FEW VODKA TONICS. LISTEN TO THE BAND AND WATCH THE ORIENTAL DANCING MAIDENS GO THROUGH THEIR BUMPS AND GRINDS ON THE RUNWAY.

THE CLINIC HERE MADE UP A TWO-PAGE QUESTIONNAIRE FILLED WITH SHRINK-TYPE QUESTIONS. THIS EFFORT ON THEIR PART WAS DIRECTED AT THE 6908TH BECAUSE THEY HOPE TO SCREEN OUT SOME OF THE LOONIES WE HAVE RUNNING LOOSE. ROTSARUCK. THE AIR FORCE SECURITY SERVICE HAS THE HIGHEST INCIDENCE OF ALCOHOLISM, THE HIGHEST INCIDENCE OF DIVORCE, THE HIGHEST RATE OF ATTRITION IN A.F. TECH SCHOOLS, THE HIGHEST RATE OF DRUG ABUSE AND HOMOSEXUALITY OF ANY OTHER COMMAND IN THE AIR FISH. THIS IS BY NO MEANS A COMPLETE LISTING, YOU UNDERSTAND, BUT IF YOU WANT IT, CHANCES ARE THAT WE HAVE IT. NO REQUEST TOO RANDOM. NO TASTE TOO BIZARRE. COME ONE, COME ALL.

THIS IS BECAUSE THE AIR FARCE PLANNED IT THIS WAY. NO, NOT INTENTIONALLY. BUT BY SKIMMING THE BEST, MOST HIGHLY QUALIFIED, BETTER EDUCATED, ETC., THE SECURITY SERVICE VIRTUALLY GUARANTEED THAT THEY WOULD GET ALL THE RUMMIES,

ALL THE EX-HIPPIE DOPERS, ALL THE FAGS, THE MALCONTENTS, THE SENSITIVE.... NO WONDER THEY HAVE A PROBLEM. TOUGH SHIT.

AND TO THINK THAT I SPECIFICALLY REQUESTED THE SECURITY SERVICE. AM I INSANE? WELL, I HAVE DELUSIONS. I THINK MY EX-GIRLFRIEND IS NOW A MAJOR RECORDING STAR. IT DON'T GET MUCH CRAZIER THAN THAT. THE CRAZY PART IS THAT WORD "EX." OH, I BELONG HERE. I DO. FORGET ABOUT KANSAS; I AM WEIRD ENOUGH FOR OZ.

TIME TO WRITE THE FOLKS NOW. AN EXERCISE IN THE PRETENSE OF NORMALITY. "THE FOOD IS FINE, MA." LIKE OUR ESTEEMED GOVERNMENT, I BELIEVE THAT TRUTH SHOULD BE RATIONED.

AND YOU HAVE MINE.

YOUR FAITHFUL PENPAL,

tepee

CHAPTER 5

Time will run back and fetch the Age of Gold.

MILTON

HELLO, CLASS OF '66!

How are you?—What have you been doing for twenty years?—Everybody wants to know. . . . We know, you've been *really* busy—too busy to keep in touch. Well, now is your chance to catch up!

Do you wonder what some of your old friends have been doing? Do the cheerleaders still look good? Are the class sweethearts still together? Did the runty little guy with glasses become a millionaire computer tycoon? Do you think that *nobody* could have been married more times than you? Do you ever wonder what *he* looks like now? And is Joe Kool really the night-shift drive-in window cashier at Burger King?

When you come to a class reunion, you always get surprises. And you'll always be remembered by more people than you would have thought possible. Why don't you come HOME TO HAMELIN for your TWENTY-YEAR REUNION?—Someone is bound to miss you if you don't! Here's the plan:

Friday night—August 8—8 p.m. until . . .
The American Legion Hut, Hamelin

Lounge will be reserved for Class of '66 and Guests only.

Saturday night—August 9—8 to 12 P.M., High School Gym: Buffet line with a variety of entrees, including chicken and barbecue. Cash Bar and D.J. to play all the oldies. Dance, Romance, or Pass around the Baby Pictures!

$13.00 per person—$26.00 per couple

And even if you can't make it, fill out the enclosed form and tell us all!

Tyndall Johnson Garner and Martha Ayers,
REUNION COMMITTEE

Martha had a stack of mimeographed reunion announcements on one side of her desk and a stack of stamped envelopes on the other. The list of addresses was in a loose-leaf notebook between them. About a third of the class had been easy to find. Tyndall was doing the phoning and postcard writing to track down what she could of the rest. Spencer wouldn't mind Martha's addressing envelopes on county dead-time, but she couldn't tie up the phone. She addressed Spencer's invitation and glanced at his office door. Ajar. And the telephone light for his extension was not on, so he wasn't busy. She hand-carried the reunion announcement to the inner sanctum.

Spencer had a small office, with sand-colored walls, an old wooden desk with a green blotter and a beer stein full of pencils, and one pine bookcase filled with reports and books on police work. On its top shelf was a scraggly brown-tipped philodendron, whose life depended on Martha, and a picture of Cal Arrowood in his Hamelin football uniform. Martha glanced at the familiar boyish face, with its squinty grin, and then at Spencer, who was staring at a report on his desk. The resemblance seemed to fade from one year to the next, Martha thought. Cal had an air of foolhardy confidence passing for invulnerability that Spencer never did have. The years had given Spencer a little weight, a little dignity, and an ordinary conservative haircut, blurring an already tenuous family resemblance. From her high school days Martha remembered that Cal was handsome; the photograph did not tell her so.

"Special delivery," she said, laying the invitation on his desk.

He read the headline and made a face. "Might go fishing that weekend," he grunted.

Martha folded her arms. "I'd like to know what *you* have to run from? An ex? I've got two! A life in the slow lane? Hell, you're *my* boss, so what does that make me? And don't tell me it's your looks, Spence, because I'll laugh in your face."

He shrugged. "I survived high school. I don't feel called to wallow in the experience, though. I guess I just haven't lost anything in the class of '66."

"Then don't expect to find anything. Just take it as a three-hour party at the American Legion Hut and forget the heavy implications. Bring your new friend."

"Peggy?" The idea had not occurred to him.

"Lord, yes, wouldn't that be a thrill? Just like when Lizbeth Barnes invited Joan Baez to our graduation exercises. Only she got back a note from a secretary saying that Joan would be in Chicago and couldn't make it. Only this time, the celebrity would actually show up. Maybe we could get her to sing."

"Now, wait a minute . . ."

"Think it over, Spencer. It would be a great addition to

the reunion. And she might enjoy it. She doesn't get too many chances to play celebrity these days, does she?"

Spencer folded the announcement and stuck it in his hip pocket. "I'll let you know."

"Don't leave it too long. She'll want the publicity if she comes. Channel Five and all." The phone on her desk was ringing. Martha hurried to answer it, glad of the distraction. Spencer might talk himself out of the whole idea if they discussed it anymore. She shouldn't have said that bit about the TV station. "Wake County Sheriff's Office," she said, snatching up the phone. She thought she recognized the voice, but after years as a dispatcher, she knew when someone was in no mood to chat. She wondered if it could be as bad as she sounded. "Yes, ma'am, he's in," she said. "I'll put you through."

She heard Spencer pick up the phone and say, "Slow down! Just tell me what happened!" Then she went back to addressing reunion envelopes.

Two minutes later, Spencer hurried past her desk. "Get LeDonne! Tell him to meet me at the Dandridge place!"

"What's going on?" asked Martha.

"Just get him!" And Spencer was gone.

He kept replaying last night's conversation in his mind. Remembering the postcard.

IS LITTLE MARGARET IN THE HOUSE,
OR IS SHE IN THE HALL?

Maybe he should have believed her instincts instead of the face value of the evidence. It just seemed so . . . effete. Literary quotations on a postcard did not square with the kind of spontaneous, anger-driven violence that he was accustomed to. Mostly, he thought, if some of those old boys could verbalize, they wouldn't use their fists so much.

Last night had been quiet. Spencer had checked the night reports when he came on duty in the morning, and there were no new ripples in the town's activity. No suspicious foreigners lurking in anybody's neighborhood . . . no screams in the night . . . no theft of weapons from store or residence. There had been one drunk arrested, a near-brawl at the Mockingbird Inn out on the highway, and two traffic tickets, just as usual. If a nocturnal butcher had been prowling the streets of Hamelin, he had been unobserved and unreported.

Near the courthouse, Vernon Woolwine had taken up his post for the day, conspicuous in a black cape and costume, with a metallic black mask over his face. Darth Vader. Erect and menacing, he faced the stream of traffic with brooding solemnity. People knew not to wave at him when he was Darth Vader or Freddy Krueger. Nods were not acknowledged. Spencer drove on.

The town seemed just as usual. It was another bright, hot day. People in shorts were out mowing their lawns or washing cars. Spencer waved to a couple of familiar faces, and they waved back. The normality seemed reassuring, as if the community were trying to convince him that he *did* know his town. He let himself see the pleasant houses, the bright flower beds, and the laughing children without looking for a darker side to any of it. Sure, there were undercurrents in Hamelin. Wife-beaters, petty thieves, addicts. After a couple of years in law enforcement, nothing surprised him anymore. But this had taken him off guard.

He had wanted Peggy to find the peaceful little town she had been looking for. There was more arrogance in that wish than concern, he knew. How many times had he boasted: We're not New York. We don't have crazies here. We don't lock our doors here. We can get a wrong number and still talk. Her phone call had shaken his claims.

He made a mental note to tell his mother to start locking her door.

The Dandridge house was white and shining among its wreath of trees. He was relieved to see no broken windows or sprayed paint on the walls. He eased the car up the circular driveway toward LeDonne's car, parked by the front porch. There was no sign of Peggy. The trouble, then, was out back. She might be there. He remembered the fear in her voice and the way she kept saying over and over, "But I told you." She might be waiting for them out at the edge of the woods—at the scene of the crime. But he didn't think so.

From a distance it looked like a piece of muddy white cloth dangling from the tree limb—like one of those stuffed-sheet ghosts people put in their yards on Halloween above the cardboard tombstones. The blood had dried to the color of rust on the white fur. The wire was hanging from a thick branch of the oak—one that was close enough to the ground to be caught and swung down for tying purposes. You wouldn't have to be very tall to reach that branch, Spencer decided. It wouldn't take much in the way of strength, either.

He looked at the body suspended from the wire, its head lolling. Blondell. Peggy's German shepherd. Its eyes were still staring widely at nothing, and its feet almost touched the scarlet-matted grass beneath—but that wouldn't have mattered. Spencer wondered where its entrails had been dumped.

He glanced back at LeDonne, who was looking up at the carcass with impassive interest. He had made no move to lift the camera.

Spencer touched his sleeve. "You wanna get some shots of this so we can take it down? I don't want Peggy having to look at this. Make sure you save the knot when you take down the wire. Put the whole thing in an evidence bag, in case we get a suspect."

"I hope I find out who did this," said LeDonne.

"I expect we will."

"Not *we*. I. They wanted to take the woman out, they should've left the dog out of it." He edged toward the body, adjusting the f-stop on the camera.

Spencer glanced toward the hedge that separated Jessie Traynham's house from Peggy's. He'd have to question her, of course, since she'd complained about the dog a while back, but he knew better than to think she had anything to do with it. Now if the dog had been poisoned, sure. He'd have suspected anybody in that case. Poison was clean and easy, and you didn't have to watch it happen. But strangling a dog with wire and then cutting its guts out with—what?—had been a long and messy job. He didn't think he could have done it.

"This is weird shit," he told LeDonne. "All I can figure is bikers. Some kind of initiation ritual, maybe."

"Nope, not bike gangs. Not unless they're vets, anyway. Don't you recognize—" He broke off, frowning. "Well, no, you wouldn't. Take a look at this." He pointed to a triangular patch of blood on the animal's neck.

"Some kind of tattoo?"

"Pretty much. I'd say it had to have been done with a razor. A diamond with a shape in it. It's an emblem. I can find out for what, but I think we know pretty much as it is. This is a commando-style killing, Spence, straight out of you-know-where. And that means we're looking for a grunt."

Spencer stepped back as if he expected more signs of the war to come at him from the woods. "You sure?"

LeDonne raised his camera. "It's not the first one I've seen. Why don't you go look to the lady, and let me finish up here?"

Spencer hesitated. He would have to calm her down enough to get some answers. He kept thinking about the postcard. Some disgruntled vet who hadn't liked the message in her songs, maybe? It seemed a little far-fetched. Too many years. Unless it was a question of recent opportunity meeting an old grudge. A vet. His mind clicked. "Roger Gabriel?" he said aloud.

LeDonne kept shooting. A close-up of the patch, this time. "I'll ride out there," he said calmly. "Offhand, I'd say it isn't him, though."

"He's had flashbacks, you said."

"Yeah . . . but . . . It isn't him. Now if it was your woman hanging there with her insides ripped out, I'd say maybe, but, Spencer, this was a *dog*."

In the end, he left the crime scene to LeDonne and went up the hill to the house. Scraggly camellia bushes flanked the back steps. They looked undisturbed. No footprints marred the damp earth around them. Nobody had been looking in the windows, then. He tapped on the screen door and heard Peggy call out, "It's open."

He stepped into the kitchen, latching the door shut behind him. There was a pile of breakfast dishes on the countertop, but the white tile floor was clean, and the sun shone through net curtains onto an aloe plant on the windowsill. A yellow dog dish stood on a mat beside the refrigerator. The bowl was full. This morning she must have put a handful of kibble into the bowl and then gone in search of the white shepherd. He listened for sounds of sobbing, but the house was silent.

Peggy was on the sun porch, glassed in on three sides with big rectangular windows. The slope of the hill was too steep for her to have watched them investigate the crime scene. From the back windows, he could see only the top of the tree, not the weighted branch with its grisly burden. He doubted if she had tried to observe them, in any case. She sat curled up on a wicker love seat, surrounded by a jungle of tall plants. Her face was pale, and she had the bloodless look of a woman over thirty without lipstick. There was no makeup for the tears to ruin.

When she looked up at him, her eyes were wet and angry. "What kind of redneck enclave are you running here?" she demanded.

He sat down on the rush mat in front of her. "I'm sorry about the dog."

"You said that postcard was nothing to worry about. You said it was just a prank!"

"I know. I'm just glad it wasn't you. I need to ask you for some details about this, so that we can get whoever did it."

She rubbed her eyes. "I didn't see or hear anything unusual. You brought me home last night, and I let Blondell out, and then I went to bed. I meant to wait up to let her back in, but I was too tired. Then this morning, I called her and she didn't come, so I went out to look for her. . . . " Her voice trailed away into silence.

"You didn't hear her bark?"

"No. She wasn't much of a watchdog, you know. Do you think she suffered?"

Spencer hesitated. "I don't know," he said. He was pretty sure she had suffered like hell, but there didn't seem to be any point in saying so. "I'd like to take that postcard with me. We'll see what we can find out. We think we're looking for a male suspect—"

Peggy snorted. "You *think*? Do you suppose that old tabby next door would butcher a dog?"

"No. But I'll have a talk with her anyway, in case she

heard something. What I need from you is something more to go on."

She was rubbing her thin fingers together as if they hurt. "I don't know what to tell you."

"Whoever sent you that postcard knows your material. He knew that you would recognize 'Little Margaret.' And, whether he knows you personally or not, he sure as hell has a grudge against you. Do you have any idea what that could be about?"

She shook her head. "I don't know anybody here."

He thought for a moment. "Have you had any other complaints about the dog? Has it killed someone's cat . . . anything like that?"

"No."

Spencer stood up. "Okay, I'll do what I can. If anything suspicious happens, you call me at once. LeDonne will take care of the dog's remains."

"Fine," she said absently.

He had expected her to cry, and he had been going over the possibility in his mind, wondering what he ought to say and whether he could hold her without seeming to be coming on to her, but the occasion did not arise. She seemed calmer than he felt. Shock, maybe. He'd look in on her in a day or so. Finally he left her there on the sun porch. When he said good-bye, she waved him away without looking up, as if her thoughts were somewhere else.

Joe LeDonne sat on the edge of Martha's desk, sipping his usual Pepsi and staring contentedly at the kitten poster above her typewriter.

"I can't believe somebody would kill a dog," said Martha.

LeDonne considered all the road kills he drove past each day, and the tethered dogs he had seen for sale in the marketplaces in Southeast Asia, and the animal shelter he had just visited, which had agreed to add the white shepherd's body to the pile of destroyed animals to be burned later today. It didn't seem to be worth mentioning. He took another sip of Pepsi.

"Spencer said he was going to talk to Mrs. Traynham, in case she might have seen something."

"She didn't," said LeDonne, thinking of the mark on the body of the dog. "I drove out to Roger Gabriel's place to ask him some questions, but he wasn't around. I'll try again later."

"Do you think he did it?"

LeDonne told her about the marks on the animal and the way that it was killed. "I'd say he rates an official visit, anyhow," he said. "Especially after his dustup in Denton's. The Vietnam connection is there."

"Well, I just don't understand it," said Martha. She was putting her pencils back in their ginger jar, careful not to look at the deputy. "I mean, I'm sure you're right about the connection, but I don't see why y'all can't let go. You only spent—what?—a year in Vietnam? Two, at the most. And you're thirty-five years old. That's a pretty small percentage of your existence. I just don't see what the hang-up is."

LeDonne picked up a book of speeding tickets on her desk, ruffled its pages with his fingers, and smiled. "Look, Martha. Say you're eighteen years old. The age when kids today are playing video games, *pretending* to shoot down planes. Only you get to play for real. You walk through the jungle with two of your friends, and between the three of you, you are carrying enough firepower to have won the Alamo all by yourselves. You could have taken Shiloh in half an hour . . . you can make people *die*. And you have to be on full alert, all the time.

Here, if you're half asleep, half stoned, or just bored shitless, you can still function. Hell, nobody even notices. But there you were at full throttle." He took a long swallow of Pepsi. "I figure I lived more in that year in Vietnam than in ten watered-down years back home."

Martha sniffed. "That's your fault."

"No. See, we were eighteen. We were *young*, and they gave us this incredible power. This experience where every day was literally life or death. One whole young year in overdrive." He tossed the crumpled can into Martha's wastebasket. "And then they ship us home. And we have to feed parking meters. And return library books on time. And get to work at exactly eight o'clock. This whole goddamn world is so *trivial*, Martha!"

"I'm sure last year's Miss America feels the same way!" snapped Martha. "And anyway, I don't see why it happened to you."

"Ask my draft board."

She sighed impatiently. "Not the war. The hang-up about it. Ray Elgin went to Vietnam, and he's perfectly fine. He's got a nice dental practice, a beautiful family. No mental problems at all!"

"I don't know, Martha. Maybe he wasn't in combat. Maybe old Ray is a tougher dude than the rest of us. Or maybe he was so shallow that no one else's pain meant a thing to him. Or maybe he suffers in silence. I don't know the man. Ask *him*."

"I'm just saying that it seems strange that some of you are so affected by it, and some of you aren't. And when I inquire about it, you give me a speech about the Alamo versus parking meters!"

He shrugged. "You asked. When Spencer gets back, tell him I'm on patrol. I'll meet him back here at five."

As he ambled toward the door, Martha wondered how

many more years it would take Joe LeDonne to get the hang of triviality.

It was past nine o'clock before the light finally faded from the sky, but Peggy Muryan had locked her doors long before twilight. She had made herself a sandwich around seven, eating at the kitchen countertop, the carving knife close at hand. Gradually this fear of solitude and silence had ebbed, and she had tried to get on with her work. For once she wished she owned a television set. The noise and bright lights would have made a welcome distraction.

Peggy Muryan paced her cluttered living room, not so much straightening as shifting piles from one place to another. She would pick up a few magazines and then lay them down again before she had really decided what to do with them. Her thoughts were elsewhere. She sat down at the piano, idly tapping a few notes, then shrugged and walked away.

"Well, kid," she said aloud."Just how tough *are* you?"

She wanted a cigarette. Great. Just what she needed at the start of a new singing career. A nicotine habit to tear up her throat. What did people do with their hands when they didn't smoke? She could vacuum the room. The white dog hairs in the carpet made her shudder. She didn't want to think about the tree in the backyard . . . and Blondell, hanging. . . . *Just how tough are you?*

She looked at the telephone. There wasn't anybody to call, though. Spencer Arrowood would just remind her of all of it, and if she phoned anyone else, she'd have to be cheerful or relive the whole terrible day again by explaining what was wrong.

What *is* wrong, Peggy?

Well, somebody sent me a song about a revenant, and I'm afraid a real revenant has come back looking for me. . . .

Yeah, sure. Tell it to Shirley MacLaine.

But there's a little matter of a dead dog in my tree. Blood everywhere. Guts ripped out. That message comes through loud and clear. It could have been you, it says.

She answered her own fears with a shrug. If you go into show business, you make yourself a target for crazy people. People who have never met you fall in love with you. Lonely people build you a soul, and then get angry if it doesn't fit you. People hear messages in your songs that you didn't put there. *Helter Skelter.* And sometimes they make you the image of whatever they're angry at. Their parents . . . their girlfriend . . . their job. . . . Celebrity is having ten thousand friends and five really sick enemies, all of whom you have never met. *Will* never meet, if you're lucky. Either you accept that and resolve to live with it, or you get out of the spotlight and hope to God you left in time. Because if anybody still remembers you from one flash of fame twenty years ago, then anonymity is not an option.

She wondered who had killed the dog. Somebody with a long memory, or somebody in this small town who resented her arrival? Or do you believe in ghosts? she asked herself.

"Little Margaret." Tight mountain harmony, holding the notes in counterpoint. She had not sung that song in a very long time. She had never sung it alone.

It wasn't much of a room. The walls were grimy from the wood stove last winter, and the paint on the ceiling was beginning to peel away. The black vinyl-covered couch leaked stuffing, and the food stains on the coffee table covered up most of the cigarette burns. No curtains at the windows. Just shades.

But the stereo was state of the art.

One whole wall was devoted to the music system:

sleek black machines with glowing green and amber lights, touches of chrome, and simulated wood paneling. Large, black-webbed speakers sat on either side of it, like high-tech sculptures. One flick of a knob, and those speakers could make the walls throb and make your eardrums rattle against the skull. The lights would wink, and flicker—red, green, gold. The machines could scoop into a groove of recorded sound and make you hear the musicians breathing as they played.

It was a futuristic masterpiece of plastic and steel. It was a time machine. But it only went to the past.

Roger Gabriel sprawled on his shabby couch and stared at the little lights across the room. Under the coffee table Chao slept, with one ear up, eyelids flickering. Roger's sleep, when he got any, was much the same.

The sounds weren't so loud just now. The bass was set so that each drumbeat rippled across the floor, but the tune was a quiet one, a soothing trickle of notes in a minor key. Roger wasn't exactly listening. He only listened to the Doors' tunes, and, of course, to the Grateful Dead. Yeah, the Dead. They talked about *him* in their music. They knew what went down, all right. You could tell, if you listened real carefully, you could tell that they were talking about 'Nam.

His record collection looked out of place in the polished, simulated wood cabinet. The album jackets were torn and dirty, with bits of cellophane peeling off the covers. He always meant to take that off. Cellophane is no good for records. Never got around to it. The records themselves were in pretty good shape, considering that they were well played and twenty years old. Nothing newer than '72. Nothing on wax had said anything to him since then.

The records were the sound track of his own private movie. His own version of *Apocalypse Now*. His own *Deer*

Hunter. Starring himself. Only it hadn't started out being a movie. It had all really happened—the jungle fighting . . . the pain . . . the incredible noise of a firefight . . . the itch of socks rotting inside your boots. The cinematic quality came later, when he had relived it so many times that he was only *remembering* remembering.

Remembering. He took a slug of Coors as he savored the word. An interesting term for an act of memory. It sounded as if it should mean reattaching a limb. Sometimes it felt that way: as if a part of you went missing a long time ago, somewhere else, and the force of recall could make you whole again. Most of the time it was okay when he remembered Vietnam. It was worse when Vietnam remembered him. Sometimes he would be lying in a sweaty sleep, tangled up in blankets, and suddenly a sound in his head would slap him to the floor and send him rolling under the bed for cover. Dodging a rocket that had exploded in cinders twenty years before. Seeing a face that was rendered to bone in the decade before last. Feeling the same tightening of muscles and chilling of flesh that he'd lived through at eighteen. Sometimes, when he wasn't thinking about the war at all, it would reach out and drag him back into its Now time, and he would be trapped for however many seconds or minutes it took him to find his way back to his own Now.

The stereo time machine was one way of controlling it. He could turn it on, pop in the right set of sounds, and crank up the cerebral movie. Sometimes it worked so well that he was free for the rest of the night, even for a couple of days. But it never lasted long.

Remembering was not a permanent grafting. The body always rejected the foreign tissue.

DEAR PEGGY-O,

INSTEAD OF SENDING CHRISTMAS CARDS THIS YEAR, I THOUGHT I'D GO CAROLING. IT MAY BE A LITTLE HARD FOR YOU TO HEAR ME FROM THE OTHER SIDE OF THE WORLD, SO I'LL WRITE DOWN THE WORDS FOR YOU. DON'T JOIN IN, THOUGH. THIS IS A SONG FOR MALE VOICES. HERE GOES:

Dashing through the mud, in a jeep that should be junk,
O'er the hills we go, half of us are drunk,
Wheels on dirt roads bounce, making asses sore,
Christ, I'd rather go to hell than finish out this tour.

(chorus)
Jingle bells, mortar shells, VC in the grass,
No more Merry Christmas shit until this year has passed.
Jingle bells, mortar shells, VC in the grass,
Take your Merry Christmas cheer and shove it up your ass.

* * *

AND A MERRY CHRISTMAS TO YOU, PET.

BY THE WAY, I SMOKE NOW. I JUST BOUGHT MY SECOND CARTON TODAY. (PAYDAY—$50.) (IMPRESSIVE, ISN'T IT?) I SMOKE . . . FOR NO REALLY GOOD REASON. BUT I MUST ADMIT, IT SEEMS TO GRATIFY SOME SORT OF OBSCURE PSYCHOLOGICAL FACTOR. (DON'T TELL ME. I DON'T CARE TO HEAR IT.)

YES, I'M HAPPY ABOUT MY DECISION—NO NOT SMOKING. I'VE CHANGED THE SUBJECT. DIDN'T YOU NOTICE THE PARAGRAPH CHANGE? I MEAN MY "LOT IN LIFE." THE AIR FIERCE. WHAT I HAVE ENDED UP IN IS ONE OF THE AIR FORCE'S MOST HIGHLY SPECIALIZED SKILLS. MAYBE I TOLD YOU ALL THIS AT FIRST—BUT MAYBE YOU FORGOT. THE VIETNAMESE COURSE (HANOI DIALECT) WAS 48 WEEKS LONG, WITH 2 TWO-WEEK LEAVES, MAKING 52 WEEKS. THEN I WENT TO GOODFELLOW AIR FORCE BASE IN TEX-ASS FOR RADIO INTERPRET ANALYSIS.

NOW . . . PICTURE MY JOB . . .

I'M IN A DESOLATE LITTLE JUNGLE OUTPOST SOMEWHERE IN THE HIGHLANDS OF, SAY, LAOS, OPERATING MY RADIO GEAR & LISTENING TO WHAT THE NORTH VIETNAMESE ARE UP TO. WHEN ALL OF A SUDDEN, IN BURST AT LEAST 7 MILLION GUERRILLAS, PRECEDED BY DISTANT GUNFIRE AND SCREAMS OF PAIN AND DEATH (ISN'T THIS EXCITING?).

TIE MY HANDS BEHIND ME.

DRAG ME OUTSIDE.

MUZZLE TO HEAD.

FADE-OUT.

OH YES, I THINK ABOUT THESE THINGS. I

MAY HAVE DRAMATIZED A BIT, BUT MY JOB IS EXACTLY THE SAME SORT OF JOB THAT THE PUEBLO (WE REMEMBER THE PUEBLO, DON'T WE?) WAS ON WHEN IT WAS CAPTURED. DITTO THAT NAVY EC121 THE NORTH KOREANS ALSO SCORED ON.

THE FACT THAT ANY OF MY LETTERS COULD BE THE LAST YOU GET SHOULD COMPENSATE IN SUSPENSE FOR WHAT I LACK IN PROSE STYLE. STAY TUNED. SEE IF YOU NEED TO INVEST IN A "HAPPY 23RD BIRTHDAY" CARD FOR TEPEE. SEND ME A FRUITCAKE. SWEETS TO THE SWEET.

FADED LOVE,
TRAV.

CHAPTER 6

Farther along we'll know all about it,
Farther along we'll understand why,
Cheer up, my brother, live in the sunshine,
We'll understand it all by and by.

"FARTHER ALONG"

FOR MAYBE THE thousandth time in her life, Tyndall Johnson Garner was sitting at the kitchen table in her parents' house, talking to Sally Howell. When they were in grade school it had been hot chocolate and Fig Newtons. Then in junior high, when Sally used to ride her bike over and stay the night, they had snacked on Cokes and homemade cheeseburgers with mayonnaise, as they practiced the steps to the Continental on the red-and-white squares of the kitchen linoleum. As oh-so-sophisticated seniors they had contemplated college, the Peace Corps, and *going all the way* over beer and Benson & Hedges menthols.

Tyndall poured Sally another cup of tea. "Do you remember when we used to sing all the Everly Brothers hits in harmony? 'Cathy's Clown,' 'When Will I Be Loved?' "

Sally nodded. "I was Phil." Sally didn't look the way she had in high school, but she didn't look much older—just different. Her thick brown hair was feathered in short wisps about her round face, and her large brown eyes and child's pouting mouth suggested a winsome innocent. Except for Sally's steely expression, which never quite faded from her features. She was a history professor now at the University of Tennessee-Knoxville, teaching freshmen for whom JFK and Vietnam *were* history.

In the hall, the grandfather clock chimed eight times. Tyndall tensed and started to get up. "I'm always afraid the clock will wake Mother," she explained. "Sometimes she gets up at night and wanders around by herself. Listen, do you think you could just stay here while I run out for some groceries? The Magic Market said they would deliver things, but it's getting late."

Sally Howell went to the wall telephone. "Who took your order? Wade? Good." She punched in the number, which was penciled on the calendar beside the phone. "Hello, is that you, Wade Turley? This is Dr. Sally Howell, calling from the Johnsons' residence in Dark Hollow. We phoned in a grocery order a good while back, and I want it here in twenty minutes. Wade, I don't *care* about your personal problems. You know the situation here. *Twenty minutes,* Wade!" As she slammed down the phone, her fierce expression softened and she and Tyndall began to giggle.

"God, I love impersonating a grown-up!" she snickered.

"Is he coming, *Dr.* Howell?"

"You have nineteen minutes to turn on the porch light. A Ph.D. is a useful tool for intimidation." She took another sip of her tea.

Tyndall nodded. "People think you're a tough bitch."

"They may be right." Sally sighed. "It worries me. You know, I used to think that with no great effort on our part we would grow up to be Jane Wyatt."

"Father Knows Best," murmured Tyndall. "Loving husband, three charming kids, you mean?"

"Not specifically that," said Sally, frowning. "Middle-class child that I was, I guess I thought that being grown up automatically meant that one would live in a nice house, well-decorated and clean. That one would eat attractively arranged, balanced meals off china plates in the dining room. And that life's problems would be on a par with whether or not you could make a speech at the Garden Club Luncheon."

"Like Jane Wyatt on the TV show."

"Exactly. Only I grew up to be Robert Young. My mistake. No wife."

Tyndall poured herself another cup of tea. "I'd better go turn on the porch light now." As she hurried from the room, she called back, "I can't picture you as a housewife, Sal."

Sally thought about it until Tyndall came back. "Neither can I," she admitted, reaching for a packet of saccharin. "I didn't think it through back then. I guess I thought that I would go out and have my meaningful career, and then go home to the perfect house and whip up a gourmet meal." She sneered. "My dining room table is buried under several layers of *Newsweek*, towels I've been meaning to put away, and seventy-four freshman term papers."

Tyndall smiled. "Nobody wanted to *be* Jane Wyatt, but everybody would like to live with her."

"No, in a way I wanted to be her. She was always calm and kind and loyal and self-assured. She never yelled. She *haunts* me, Tyndall. I swear, sometimes when I'm threatening to sue an auto mechanic who has mistaken me for an imbecile, or when I turn down some failing student trying to cop a D, or when I stand up in the faculty senate and tell the administration that we won't take any more crap from them—a little voice in my head says, 'Jane Wyatt wouldn't do this.' "

"Jane Wyatt probably would, Sally. She was a working actress; maybe she had it as tough as you did. Her *character* wouldn't have done those things, but then she didn't have a life, did she? None of our mothers did. They just stayed home and heard reports of the outside world from their husbands and their children. Suburban shut-ins."

"Sometimes their lives sound like a prison to me, and sometimes I think of them as pampered house cats. Did any of us grow up to be one?"

Tyndall shrugged. "I guess I did."

"No, it's different, somehow. You were on the school board, weren't you? And you and Steve go hang gliding, for God's sake! My mom played bridge. Period."

"It'll be interesting to see what *did* happen to the girls in our class. Do you think that most of them have careers?"

"They will have," muttered Sally. "Maybe not at this reunion, but by the next one, there'll be a lot of just-dumped divorcees studying data processing at the community college."

"I hope you're not going to share that thought with the class of '66."

"If they provoke me I might. If too many good old boys get on my case about being *Dr.* Sally, or if people want to know how come I'm not happily married." She shuddered. "I don't even know why I'm going to this thing."

"Vulgar curiosity, I expect." Tyndall laughed. "As long as you are going, Martha was hoping you'd do the reunion booklet. You're the only one we know with a computer."

"The only *woman*, you mean," growled Sally. "Martha Ayers? Good Lord, I hadn't thought about her in ages. What's she doing?"

"She's the dispatcher for the sheriff's department. I guess you get home from Knoxville often enough to know that Spencer Arrowood is the sheriff."

"Yes. It's odd, isn't it? He wasn't the political type or the macho type. It's hardly the job I'd have expected him to have. Now *Cal* Arrowood was another matter." She looked thoughtful. "I wonder if Jenny is coming to the reunion."

Outside in the darkness a horn blew. Tyndall jumped up. "That will be Wade with the groceries. Before I go . . . about Jenny. Martha says Spencer doesn't know where she is. And she told me something else about Spencer. Do you remember Peggy Muryan?"

"Of course. *Carolina Blue.* I read the article about her arrival in Hamelin. Why?"

"Martha says that Spencer is dating her. And she's been receiving hate mail. And somebody just killed her dog in a really gruesome and deliberate way."

They looked at each other significantly for a moment, and then the horn blew again, and Tyndall hurried away.

It was going to be one of those nights that were too hot for sleep, and besides, the sky was all wrong. LeDonne closed the door of his old Volkswagen as gently as he could and leaned against it, looking up at the stars. He wondered why the stars were so faded in the summertime. They shone feebly through a grayish haze, as if the breathless night had stifled even them. LeDonne missed the crisp blackness of December, when the heavens were like black velvet, sequined with stars. He always slept better in the winter.

It was past eleven now, but LeDonne decided that it was better being out doing something than lying wide-eyed in bed staring up at the ceiling—or working up a hangover to ruin the next morning. He didn't think it was too late in the evening for visiting. He'd give good odds that Roger Gabriel wasn't sleeping either.

He thought about blowing his car horn when he first drove up, but that might seem belligerent. Roger Gabriel wouldn't respond well to a confrontational approach. LeDonne could see a small patch of light in the living room window—probably a reading lamp. The black Labrador was not outside. Probably inside for the evening, then, keeping his master company. LeDonne glanced down at the brown envelope he was holding. Time to see what Old Roger thought of these.

For a few moments, on his way to the front porch, LeDonne was aware of his vulnerability: an easy, unprotected target, well within range of almost any weapon. He forced himself to consider the possibility of ambush, and his response was, So what? It had always made Death lose interest in him before.

By the time he was close enough to knock, he could hear the strains of music from within. The Grateful Dead. LeDonne wondered if that meant anything or not. He rapped twice on the door, just loud enough to be heard over the bass notes.

A moment later he could feel someone peering out at him from the closest window. LeDonne stood very still. Inside, the music faded to a murmur. "You mind if I come in and talk to you?" he called out in carefully neutral tones.

The door slid inward a few inches, emitting a crack of yellow light and the funky smell of cheap grass. Then Roger Gabriel's expressionless face filled the opening. He waited. LeDonne said nothing. Finally Roger said, "Welcome home," and motioned him inside.

Welcome home, the password among vets. LeDonne nodded and followed him in.

"I came for a consultation," he said, holding up the

envelope. "It's not a summons. You got any beer, or is that your only vice?" He nodded toward the joint in an old clam shell on the table.

Roger Gabriel motioned for him to come in. Chao was standing just past the door, waiting to take his emotional cue from his owner. When he saw the deputy, his tail wagged once, as if to acknowledge their prior acquaintance.

LeDonne looked at the shabby couch, the threadbare rug, and the state-of-the-art music system. He nodded and motioned for Roger to sit down, but his still-expressionless host walked away. "A beer, you said."

"If you can spare it." LeDonne rubbed Chao's dusty head, wondering as always what dogs meant by that earnest, alert expression they have—as if waiting for you to tell them something really important. He waited in silence while Roger hauled the cans out of the refrigerator.

He returned with the beers, turned the stereo up a notch, and sank down into the couch cushions. He slid one wet can along the coffee table toward LeDonne.

"Is 'consultation' a cop word for drug bust?" he asked, reaching for the joint.

LeDonne shrugged. "Looks like a Marlboro to me. Thanks for the brew." He took a long swallow and reached for the envelope. "Something's come up on the job, and I'd like a second opinion. It might spoil the taste of the beer," he warned.

The corners of Roger Gabriel's mouth twitched. "I believe I'll manage. What's this about, anyway?"

LeDonne didn't look up. "Have you ever heard of Peggy Muryan?"

"Sure. And James Taylor, and Marianne Faithfull, and Buffy St. Marie. My taste ran more to Joplin and Gracie Slick, though. Why?" He nodded toward the stereo. "Are you going to ask me to play requests?"

"What did you think of her music?"

"A little subdued for me. A jolt of electricity does wonders for a guitar."

"I meant politically. Was she one of those antiwar folkies?"

"How should I know?" Roger Gabriel shrugged. "She didn't sing any duets with Marvin Gaye, that's all I know."

"She's in town. Did you know that?"

He smirked. "And you need a date for the concert, pal? Is that it?"

LeDonne scowled. "I mean she lives here now. And she's the victim of harassment."

"Go on."

"Threats. And this." LeDonne opened the envelope and placed a stack of color pictures face up on the coffee table.

After a moment's silence, Roger Gabriel picked them up. Impassively, he examined LeDonne's shots of the crime scene, placing each picture slowly and carefully at the bottom of the stack after he had examined it. LeDonne waited. When he got to the close-up of the carving on the dog's body, his eyes widened, but he said nothing. Finally he set the pictures facedown and looked at LeDonne.

"Interesting," he said.

"I thought so."

"It does take you back, doesn't it?"

LeDonne tapped the topmost picture. "You ever do anything like that over there?"

"Or over here? I'm not your man. I can see why you'd ask, though." He didn't sound offended.

"So you agree with me about the suspect's . . . service record, shall we say?"

"I'd say he graduated with honors from the University of Vietnam, yeah. You going to grill everybody at the VFW?"

LeDonne shook his head. He sifted through the stack

of photographs until he found the close-up of the razored patch. "I don't know if you can make this out. It's a diamond-shaped patch with some shape sliced inside it. It's hard to see."

Roger Gabriel nodded, making no move toward the picture. "I saw that. Ten to one it's a lightning bolt."

"The Electric Strawberry. A line company. Not yours, though, was it?"

Roger Gabriel shook his head. "I was a Screaming Chicken. You knew that."

"The One-oh-Worst." LeDonne smiled. The 101st Airborne Division had not cared for that name. They preferred Screaming Chicken because of the eagle insignia on the division's shoulder patch.

Gabriel didn't want to swap war stories. "Was this her dog? The folksinger's?"

"It was."

"Well, I think I'd ask her if she had any enemies in the Twenty-fifth Infantry."

"You know of any Strawberries around here?"

Roger Gabriel reached down and absently stroked the neck of his dog. Chao heaved a sigh and collapsed at his feet to continue his nap. "Not offhand," he told LeDonne. "The Twenty-fifth seems an odd outfit for this kind of job, though, doesn't it?"

"I thought of that," said LeDonne. "Anything else occur to you?"

"Well . . . something I'd have expected to see, maybe. But it isn't there in any of your pictures."

"The ace of spades?"

"So it *was* there?"

"No," said LeDonne. "It wasn't."

Sometimes Spencer Arrowood wished that he hadn't quit the softball team, but he told himself that he didn't have time for the practices, and the nature of his job would prevent him from making some of the games. It wasn't that he was getting too old to play. It was a reminder, though, that those days were not far off. Still, he missed the exercise.

He leaned against the wall in front of the bleachers, watching younger guys chasing a ground ball toward the white picket fence in the distance. He knew most of them. The umpire, Fred Hovis, had been a friend of Cal's. Now, with a spare tire around his middle and a pudgy red face, he seemed to have lost his identity, to have become "some old guy." The way, when they were kids, they characterized people in middle age, as in: "Some old guy told us not to play around the dump," or "We were doing bike tricks in the road, but some old guy blew his horn at us and made us move." Umpire Fred was looking very self-important, as if he didn't know that he had been demoted from *person* to *annoyance*.

The first baseman and the left fielder were people that Spencer remembered from high school. They had been a few classes behind him. And the skinny long-haired kid up at bat looked familiar. Where did he know him from? It took him a few minutes to remember his speech at the high school and to place the eager youth who had asked Vietnam questions. Something Weaver. Pix-Kyle, that was it. He wasn't wearing his camos tonight. He was relieved that the kid had given up war stories in favor of baseball. He didn't look like he'd be much good at it, though.

"Evening, Sheriff," said someone coming up behind him.

Spencer turned, trying to make the smile look genuine. "Hello, Jeff," he said carefully. "What's new with you? *Nothing* is new with me."

Jeff McCullough just looked at him through horn-rimmed glasses, an expression that didn't indicate disbelief or satisfaction. Just a silent "Well?" suggesting that he knew what you were keeping back, and didn't you want to tell *your* side of it to the Press (himself)? That prodded most people into saying more. It was McCullough's chief journalistic gift, but it was generally wasted on the *Hamelin Record*, where people were all too eager to give you their news: a daughter's wedding, a toddler's birthday party. But McCullough, who was still shy of thirty, had a degree from the U.T. j-school and ambitions beyond a small-town weekly. He wrote occasional stories for bigger markets, and in the rare event of an item of interest in Wake County, he covered it for the Associated Press. The extra money came in handy, but if he stopped being a single mobile home dweller, he would have to get a second job. Thirteen thousand a year wasn't far from food stamps. You covered county politics and high school sports, and the rest of the paper was filled with community columns written by local old ladies, heavily edited wedding and award news (which came in misspelled and handwritten), and public service press releases that came by the handful each week, like the USDA gypsy moth article, which got a three-column headline on page four. It took up space. But Jeff McCullough was learning his way around his newly adopted town, and he was beginning to pick up the undercurrents. He didn't print them in the *Record*, but he found it useful to know of their existence.

Just now, the reporter/editor of the one-man operation was in search of bigger game than *Hamelin Record* social news. He looked at the sheriff and waited.

Spencer developed a sudden interest in the outfielders. Finally he said, "Did you hear about Homer Ramsay smuggling raccoons from Ohio?"

McCullough smiled. "Yes, indeed. I have interviewed Homer, the game warden, a few local hunters, and the district attorney. The *Record* slant will be sympathetic: concern for the supply of game. I think I can do a wire service piece, though, that will be a hoot. 'The Case of the Kidnapped Coons' or 'How You Gonna Keep 'Em Down on the Farm, After They've Seen Cleveland?' One of those goofy features that gets printed everywhere, like the one from Michigan, where a guy took a church congregation hostage, and they took up a collection and *bought* his gun."

"Doesn't sound like he has much of a future as a terrorist. Is that a true story?"

"Yep. From a town not much bigger than this one. Sometimes reporters get lucky."

Spencer nodded. "Good luck with the raccoon story."

"Well, that wasn't the one I wanted to discuss with you," said McCullough. "There's talk going around that somebody murdered Peggy Muryan's dog. Now that story might make *People* magazine."

Spencer let out his breath in a long sigh. It wasn't really unexpected. Once they had started questioning people about the incident, the news was bound to spread. Jeff McCullough found out a lot of things just because people stopped him in the street and asked about them, thinking that the local newspaperman would know more about it than they did. "I wish you wouldn't do this story just yet, Jeff," he said. "There isn't a lot to tell right now. And you know that we don't have to let you see the police reports until we make an arrest, so all you've got is hearsay."

"Is it true that her dog was killed in some kind of commando-style execution?"

"That's one theory," said Spencer carefully. Even

Jessie Traynham knew that much. "But we have no suspects, no motive. I don't even think you can assume that the individuals knew that it was Peggy Muryan's dog."

McCullough looked wistful. "It's a hell of a story, though. Disgruntled vets punish peacenik folksinger. A Jane Fonda angle. Maybe call Jane Fonda for a quote."

"Not yet, Jeff. You got no follow-up. And you might keep us from solving it, which would really shoot your story in the head. I tell you what: if you agree not to print anything about it until I say so, I'll give you the whole story—first—when we break the case."

McCullough looked more dubious than he felt. The sheriff was right. It wasn't much of a story yet. But it had a hell of a lot of potential. With convincing reluctance, he said, "Okay, Sheriff. You know the *Record* always cooperates with law enforcement. You give me an exclusive later, and I'll write nothing now. But I'm going to start doing some background checks on Peggy Muryan, just in case I get a blank check on word limit. If anything interesting turns up, I'll let you know."

"Deal." Spencer turned back to the game. That ought to keep the media off Peggy's doorstep for a while, anyway. He didn't want any publicity until they had an arrest, not so much for Peggy's sake, but as a precaution. Some kooks thrive on publicity. It prompts them to do more outrageous acts. He didn't want any more incidents. The sheriff felt a tap on his shoulder. It was McCullough again.

"Can I have a quote for the raccoon story?"

It was past midnight, and Hamelin was dark. The streetlights offered a faint shine, but the stores had been black for hours. Crime was only a remote possibility, but costly electric bills were certain. The Gulf station was closed, but its Pepsi machine blazed in the darkness. In the sheriff's office, the radio was tuned to an all-night country station in New Orleans. There had been no calls since nine-thirty.

Those who were awake were elsewhere: in the hospital in the neighboring county; in brick houses up the mountain, catching the last of Carson; or waiting for a car door to slam, and listening for the footsteps of an adolescent, home at last. Those who wanted to sleep, but couldn't, sat up with a bottle or a paperback, always alone.

In the pasture off the highway, up Price's Run, deer wandered down from the hills to drink at the pond, and an owl swooped at the sound of a field mouse rustling in the long grass. The two human nonsleepers saw nothing in the darkness around them and felt only the dampness of the cooling earth. It was as late as it gets. They crouched together in the field, looking up at the stars. One of them yawned.

"It's late. Isn't it late?" The reply was a shrug. "Maybe we should go back."

"You scared?"

"Well . . . not tonight. But maybe you shouldn't do this."

"Do what?"

A brief silence. The argument had been abandoned. "What are we going to do?"

"We're going on patrol in the jungle. When we get there. First we have to make sure this field isn't mined. You know how to do that? Get down on your hands and knees, and—"

"Let's . . . risk it."

"No. I'm ordering you to do it. Get down on your hands and knees."

"Okay. Okay."

"Say 'Okay, Sergeant.' I'm your sergeant."

"Okay."

"Say it!"

"Okay . . . Sergeant."

"Turn the boom box on. I wanna hear 'Break on Through to the Other Side.' No earphones tonight. I want you to hear it, too."

"Suppose somebody else hears you?"

"Then I'll blow them away."

NO,

I HAVEN'T FORGOTTEN ABOUT YOU, MARGARET ANNE MURYAN. SEE, I EVEN REMEMBER YOUR NAME. (I MAY FORGET A FACE, BUT I NEVER REMEMBER A NAME.) (?) LET'S SEE, IF I REMEMBER CORRECTLY, YOU SHOULD HAVE YOUR NEW ALBUM OUT BY NOW. IT WAS THIS MONTH THAT IT WAS BEING RELEASED, WASN'T IT? I HOPE YOU'RE HAPPY. I THINK YOU'VE EARNED IT, PERSONALLY. BUT THEN, WHAT DO I KNOW?

WELL, I JUST CAME BACK FROM A MISSION OVER NORTH VIETNAM THIS MORNING. AGAIN.

ALL LETTERS OF THANKS AND CONGRATULATIONS SHOULD BE ADDRESSED TO ME, YOUR AMERICAN FIGHTING MAN IN BLUE. MONEY ALSO ACCEPTED.

A LITTLE WHILE AGO I GOT THROUGH WRITING MOTHER DEAR FOR THE SECOND TIME SINCE I'VE BEEN HERE. AND I'VE BEEN HERE SIX MONTHS. SO WHAT IS LIFE AT THE TOP REALLY LIKE? IS BUFFY ST. MARIE REALLY AN AMERICAN INDIAN? WITH ALL THAT LONG, STRAIGHT BLACK HAIR AND

THOSE ALMOND EYES—IS SHE SHORT?—MY ASSOCIATES HERE CONTEND THAT SHE LOOKS LIKE A DINK (A MILITARY TERM, MEANING PERSON OF ORIENTAL PERSUASION. OR ONE WHO WEARS BLACK PAJAMAS IN THE DAYTIME). YES, THANK YOU, I KNOW ALL ABOUT THE INDIANS WALKING ACROSS THE BERING STRAITS DURING THE ICE AGE, THUS BEING ORIENTAL IN ORIGIN. I DID LEARN THAT IN SIXTH GRADE. MISS WALKER WAS NOT LAX. MY COMRADES IN ARMS HERE ARE NOT IMPRESSED BY THAT LITTLE NUGGET OF ANTHROPOLOGY. IN FACT, I BELIEVE I CAN STILL GET 8 TO 1 ODDS HERE THAT BUFFY DINK MARIE WEARS "CHARLIE" PERFUME. (CHARLIE IS THE VC'S FIRST NAME.) THE ONES ON OUR SIDE (NOMINALLY, I ADMIT) ARE CALLED ARVN. ARMY OF THE REPUBLIC OF VIETNAM, AND THEY MAKE TWELVE HUNDRED PIASTERS A MONTH. THAT'S TEN BUCKS—WATCH THE SIX O'CLOCK NEWS, PEGGY, SO I WON'T HAVE TO EXPLAIN THESE THINGS. IT EATS INTO MY LIMITED SUPPLY OF PAPER, WHICH WOULD FORCE ME TO PURCHASE MORE, THUS DEPLETING MY FUND FOR BEER ACQUISITION.

JUST GOT BACK FROM A SECRET SECURITY BRIEFING. (I.D. CARDS REQUIRED FOR ADMITTANCE.) (I REALLY SHOULDN'T BE TELLING YOU THIS, BUT IT'S NOTHING THE KGB DOESN'T CONSIDER COMMON KNOWLEDGE.) ACTUALLY, I MAY NEVER SEE VIETNAM EXCEPT FROM 40,000 FEET . . . IF I'M LUCKY. I MEAN, CONSIDER THE ALTERNATIVE. WE GO AIRBORNE IN EC-135'S (MILITARY VERSION

OF THE 707—YOU DO KNOW WHAT A 707 LOOKS LIKE?), AND WE FLY TO VIETNAM FROM OUR BASE IN (. . .) (WELL, WHAT DO YOU CARE, PET? ASK BOB HOPE), THEN WE REFUEL AND FLY AROUND FOR TWELVE HOURS OR SO, MONITORING TRANSMISSIONS & WHATNOT, AND THEN WE RETURN.

THAT GIVES ME FLIGHT PAY AND COMBAT PAY, ON TOP OF MY BASE PAY. NOT BAD AT ALL. R&R IN AUSTRALIA OR HAWAII. I CAN LIVE WITH THAT.

AT LEAST I HOPE I CAN.

NOT THAT I WOULDN'T RATHER BE WEARING MY FELT HAT AND JEANS, PLAYING MY GUITAR, OUT THERE ON STAGE WITH YOU. HOT LIGHTS IN MY FACE. SONGS TAPED TO THE NECK OF THE GUITAR. AND THERE YOU ARE IN THAT LONG GREEN VELVET DRESS . . . THE ONE WITH THE SQUARE BODICE . . . BLOND HAIR STRAIGHT AND SHINING . . . TAMBOURINE TUCKED BEHIND THE FOLD OF THE DRESS . . . AND WHEN WE SING, IT'S LIKE LETTING GO OF THE TRAPEZE AND SUDDENLY CATCHING HANDS SIXTY FEET ABOVE THE GROUND, BECAUSE WITHOUT YOU I'D FALL . . . I'VE MADE LOVE AND I'VE SUNG COUNTERPOINT. COUNTERPOINT IS CLOSER. DO YOU EVER FEEL LIKE YOU'RE FALLING, OUT THERE WITH NO ONE TO CATCH THE NOTES?

SHU, SHU, SHU, LA ROO . . . REMEMBER THAT ONE?—OH MY BABY, OH MY LOVE, GONE THE RAINBOW, GONE THE DOVE, LA DA DEE DEE (FORGOT THE VERSE), JOHNNY'S GONE FOR A SOLDIER. AND SO HAS,

TRAVIS

CHAPTER 7

I am a poor wayfaring stranger
Wandering through this world of woe;
There is no sorrow, no toil or danger
In that bright land to which I go.

"POOR WAYFARING STRANGER"

LEDONNE HANDED MARTHA the key to the reunion post office box and a stack of letters. "All your little pigeons are coming home to roost," he said.

Martha frowned. "Well, it took them long enough. The reunion is two weeks away. I don't know how they expect me to get a booklet prepared to hand out at the party on two seconds' notice!" She began to flip through the envelopes. Company stationery, a few stickers with a rose or a flag beside the return address, some handwritten addresses.

"Ronny Jessup," she grunted, tearing at the flap of one long envelope. "Remember him, Spencer? Short, pudgy guy who hung out with the greasers?"

The sheriff looked up from his coffee cup and nodded. "He went to our church."

"Listen to this! 'I am getting my master's in business administration from Western Carolina University. My wife, Paula, teaches kindergarten. She is blond, 5'1", and she weighs 105 pounds.' " Martha made a face and tossed the letter in a typing paper box. "Still a toad."

"What's the box?" asked LeDonne.

Martha shrugged. "Also rans. They won't get much space in the reunion book. And no accompanying picture from the old yearbook."

"Yeah," said LeDonne, nodding sagely. "High school and equality are forever incompatible. Where do the letters of the Chosen go?"

Martha held up a blue letter-sized envelope. "I still need a picture of you, Spencer."

Spencer set his mug down next to the coffeepot and headed for his office. "Put me in the cardboard box!" He called, "LeDonne!"

The deputy picked up the rest of the mail and followed.

Martha opened another envelope. "Mary Mason," she said aloud. The letter was postmarked San Diego, but the stationery said "Mts Pegasus, Epirotiki Lines." Mary had been in the Navy Reserves for a dozen years: Japan, Korea, Thailand. She still loved to travel—Ireland, Greece—but she couldn't make it back for the reunion. Martha finished reading the letter and wrote down, "Mary lives in San Diego with her dog, Rosebud, a Samoyed-boxer mix. . . . " She put the letter into the blue envelope of success: Mary had made it to California and she had seen the world. Martha hadn't been out of Tennessee more than twice.

She picked up a square brown envelope with British stamps. Another traveler? Folded into the letter was a picture of two women in riding clothes standing next to a horse. Martha sighed. Eugenia Carr. Everybody thought she'd grow up, but they had been plainly mistaken.

Eugenia Carr had been an outsider in Hamelin. Her parents came from up north somewhere, and she was a quiet girl who made satisfactory grades without being too interested in academics. For as long as anybody could remember, Eugenia Carr had been a loner, and she had been saying that she was going to ride horses . . . train horses . . . live horses, and to hell with "becoming a grown-up." From her first barrel-shaped pony to the half-thoroughbred hunter she'd had in high school, Eugenia had been adamant about an equestrian career. Her classmates had suggested that she would outgrow this phase, as most teenage girls did. Martha had expected her to be married to a nice insurance agent, living in Knoxville. But there she was, still long-haired and longer-legged, holding the reins of her mount and smiling at her fellow horse fanatic. Still taking riding lessons and mucking out stables. Martha tossed the picture and the unread letter into the cardboard box.

Didn't anybody in this damned class get married or stay married, she thought, other than Ronny the Toad?

Apparently not. Martha thought you could divide the women of the class into Mary Tyler Moore and Mrs. Peel. They had lived on the cusp of an era, when *Beaver* Cleaver went out and *Eldridge* Cleaver came in, and nobody quite knew what to do about it. Martha thought about her two laughable attempts at the Great American Way. She got married, and nobody wrote "The End" across the sky. Decades stretched out in front of her—it had seemed like a long time then—and it had seemed so pointless, all the cleaning and working for dirt wages to pay paltry bills. She wondered why her mother's generation didn't mind it. Maybe they didn't know that they could.

She closed her eyes and drew another envelope from the pile. Please be normal, she thought, and wondered what she meant by that.

The sheriff opened a manila folder on his desk. "So what have we got?"

Joe LeDonne leaned back in the visitor's chair and

closed his eyes. "We got a dead dog. That's about it, Spencer."

"Maybe not." He handed a typed report across the desk. "Have you seen this complaint that was phoned in this morning?"

Le Donne opened his eyes and took the paper. A few lines into it, he sat up straight. "A dead sheep?"

"Last night. Wayne Wyler—has a farm over past Willow Creek. Says he found the sheep with its throat cut this morning. *He* says it's coyotes."

"Could be, I guess. Nobody else has been hit, though." LeDonne looked up from the report. "And what do we think?"

Spencer shrugged. "A dead dog. A dead sheep. Maybe it's a pattern. Maybe it's vandalism. I thought I'd send you over there now to check it out. See if there is anything carved on this one."

LeDonne nodded. "No further developments with Peggy Muryan? No more postcards?"

"Not that I know of. I thought I'd stop by and make sure, though. And Jeff McCullough over at the newspaper is looking into Peggy Muryan's background to see if there's anything in her past that might tie in. Some group she offended with a song, maybe."

"You're going to see her this morning?"

"Yeah, I thought I'd stop by. Why?"

"Remember that tattoo on the dog's neck? Ask the lady if she ever knew any Strawberry ground-pounders."

"Any what?"

"Servicemen in the Twenty-fifth Infantry Division," said LeDonne with mocking precision.

"I'll ask her."

LeDonne walked over to the county map mounted in Plexiglas on the wall above the copy machine. Wyler's farm was up a gravel road that connected to the main highway near Willow Creek. There weren't a lot of people out in that part of the county, and most of the nearby landowners had been Wyler's neighbors for forty years. There hadn't been trouble out there before. Or coyotes. "Hope Wyler had the sense not to burn the carcass," he said.

LeDonne strolled into the outer office and retrieved his hat and sunglasses from his desk. "I'm going out to Willow Creek to check on a dead sheep," he told Martha. "Anything else new with you?"

Martha shook her head. She was making notes on the reunion mail. LeDonne picked up the photograph that had been lying faceup in the cardboard box: two women beside a horse. "Now that's a familiar face," drawled LeDonne.

Martha looked up. "Eugenia Carr? How do you know—"

"Eugenia Carr? Classmate of yours? Why is she standing next to Princess Anne?"

Martha snatched the photo and peered at it intently. As LeDonne took the keys to the patrol car and ambled toward the screen door, Martha retrieved the letter with the British stamps and put it with the picture into the blue envelope reserved for those who had made it.

Not much went on in a town of nine hundred people on a weekday. A lot of people had driven to work, at one of the factories in the next county, as likely as not. The kids were at the pool in the county park, or getting up a sandlot ball game. On Main Street, Vernon Woolwine was lounging on the covered stoop of an old office building, cradling a boom box. Today he had a mane of jet black hair, dark glasses, and he wore a jean jacket and denims. That was a new one. Who the hell was he now?

Spencer pondered the black wig and sunglasses for a

good half mile into residential Hamelin before he thought of Roy Orbison, the old fifties rocker from Texas who had helped to make rock and roll. Presley got the credit, and the money. Hadn't the Beatles been Roy Orbison fans? What ever happened to him? Was he still alive? "Only the Lonely" rumbled through the speakers of his private Muzak as he headed for the middle-class section of town.

A few prosperous families had gone to Myrtle Beach for their summer vacation, and they'd asked the sheriff's department to keep an eye on their houses. The night patrol would have done that, but Spencer took a drive up Ashe Lane just to make doubly certain that everything was all right. The "prank" deaths in Hamelin had made him uneasy.

The houses looked undisturbed, and the newspapers had been collected by next-door neighbors on schedule, so that the houses would not look abandoned, an invitation for thieves. Spencer turned his car around in the Prentice driveway and headed back toward the Dandridge place. No matter how long Peggy Muryan lived there, it would still be the Dandridge place to Hamelin.

There were just enough clouds in the sky to make the town look like a postcard. Buffalo Mountain seemed to curl around the valley, shielding Hamelin from the expanse of sky and from any view of the rest of Tennessee. To get out of Wake County, Spencer's father used to say, you had to sneak past the mountains: on the two-lane blacktop that wound around the mountain like a corkscrew; on Cade's Creek, which snaked through the valley and underground before it joined the river in the next county; or on the Appalachian Trail, which threaded its way through the hills and fields linking wilderness from Maine to Georgia. To *stay* out of Wake County was even harder: then you had to get the mountains out of *you*. Most people never managed it. Back in the twenties, Spencer's great-uncles had all gone to work in the car factories up in Dee-troit, and they'd stayed gone for forty years. They were all retired now, and one by one, they had all come back to East Tennessee to take up residence on hardscrabble farms way back up Pigeon Roost. Spencer guessed he could have amounted to more than he had if he'd been willing to go to Knoxville, or even farther afield, but he didn't think a high salary could buy anything that would compensate him for the loss of these mountains.

By the time he swung into the Dandridge circular driveway, he had called Martha to say that he'd be off for a while, and he had switched off his radio. The day was too fair to waste. It was a feeling that he had been getting more and more often lately, a sense of wanting to savor every sunny day, every long talk with his mother, every good time. These won't go on forever, he found himself thinking. But he was only thirty-eight. Why did he feel that life was hemorrhaging away?

He knocked on the door, wishing that he weren't wearing his uniform. It was a day for jeans and T-shirts, but he couldn't spare the time to change, and he couldn't take the whole day off, so he'd have to make do in starched khaki.

After a brief delay—long enough for someone to take a precautionary glance out the window—Peggy Muryan opened the door. Spencer wondered if she had been on her way out, because she was wearing white slacks and a white cotton sweater that looked too dressy to wear while you sat around your house and stared at the wall "composing."

"Hello," she said, glancing past him at his car to see if he had come alone. "Did you catch him yet?"

"Who?"

She looked exasperated. "The person who killed my dog. Have you caught him?"

Spencer shook his head. "We're making inquiries, as they say in the cop business. I just came by to see how you were doing. We need to talk some more about it."

She shrugged. "Okay, I guess. Do you have time to come in?"

"Do you have time to come out?" Spencer grinned. "Look, it's a beautiful summer day, and I thought I'd take a ride out in the country. Want to come along? You might get some inspiration for a new tune."

She hesitated. "Can we stop at a grocery store on the way back? I've been meaning to go, but . . ."

"You aren't afraid, are you?"

"Of course I am!" Her eyes flashed. "And don't try to make me feel guilty about it."

Spencer held the door open for her. "Come out," he said. "We'll go out in the warm sunshine, and you'll feel better. I know a place where you can see the whole valley spread out before you like scenery on a model railroad." In his head, Roy Orbison had switched to "Pretty Woman."

He took the north road out of town, a street that started as a tree-lined avenue between old white houses or houses sided with fieldstone, each with a full porch. At the town limits, the neighborhood dwindled to four-room frame dwellings in need of paint and repair, then to mobile homes with plaster deer on the lawns and whitewashed truck tires encircling flower beds. One mile out, the scene changed to sparse pastures with a few mixed-breed Herefords grazing behind wire fences. Thickets of scrub pine divided one field from the next, like the dark squares on a checkerboard.

As the pastures petered out, and the trees became tall hardwoods, the road began to rise. It coiled around the mountain, so that one side of the highway was a red clay cliff and the other side overlooked a steep slope, thick with trees. Through the leaves of the oaks, one could catch occasional glimpses of the farms and meadows below.

"It's beautiful country up here," Spencer remarked, with a glance out at the view. "Wait till we get around the bend here."

The car finished its climb and emerged on a straight stretch of mountainside. To the left was a place to pull off the road, beside an overlook. There the embankment had no trees near the top, and most of Wake County sparkled below them in shades of green. In the center of the valley, Hamelin was a squat package of red and white blocks tied up with black ribbons of asphalt. Beyond it loomed the dark shape of Buffalo Mountain, with ridges of distant hills fading into the haze at the edge of the sky.

Spencer eased the car off the road and walked to the lookout. He helped Peggy up on the stone wall and pointed out the roof of her house, cupped in the trees below. "You should see this in October," he told her. "Every one of these mountains is a different color then. So you see bands of color. The maples make a red hill, and the oaks turn that ridge golden, and Buffalo—straight in front of you there—goes flaming orange. It doesn't last more'n a week, but it's the most beautiful thing in the world."

"It seems like such a peaceful place," said Peggy, studying the trees on the slope. "I wonder why it never was."

"Hamelin?"

She shook her head. "Appalachia in general. Every song I ever heard is about some feud, or a hanging, or a girl getting murdered by her lover. This place looks like paradise. It should have been enough."

Spencer waved his hand at a yellow jacket that had come too close. "It isn't always paradise," he said. "I'll grant you it is today, though."

Peggy looked at the road stretching off into the trees away from civilization. "Where are we headed?"

"Pigeon Roost, if you can spare the time."

She burst out laughing. "*Pigeon* Roost? What a name! I always thought pigeons lived in downtown Knoxville!"

"It was called after the passenger pigeon. These hills used to be full of them. They looked like doves."

"I don't think I've seen any around."

"No. The last one died around 1914 in the Cincinnati Zoo. Her name was Martha. So Pigeon Roost is just a name for something that doesn't exist anymore."

Peggy looked back out across the valley at the shadows of the clouds on the ribs of Buffalo Mountain. "What's in Pigeon Roost?" she asked softly.

"Just a farm, where my great-grandparents lived."

"And is the tree that grew from a riding crop still in the front yard?"

"That, or one like it. My grandfather's sister lives there now, and she's way past eighty. I like to look in on her every now and again."

She smiled up at him. "Sure. Why not?"

She started back to the car, just as a gray Pontiac rounded the bend and headed up the mountain away from Hamelin. "Let's wait a couple of minutes before we start out," said Spencer. Seeing her look of surprise, he explained, "That car's tags said Sullivan County, and those people drive slower than cement."

He looked back across the collage of greens encircled by the dark forested mountain, made blacker by the shadows of clouds across its flank. "I used to want a house out there in the fields near the river, where I could look up at these mountains," Spencer remarked. "But you know, the older I get, the higher I want to be. Now I think a house on the ridge above this road would be just perfect. You wouldn't have a yard, just a view. I guess that means I'm willing to be a spectator now instead of a doer. You reckon?"

Peggy shrugged. "Maybe you want to get away from people."

"It's in my blood," he admitted. "And even if it weren't, this job could make you feel that way."

She leaned against the hood of the patrol car. "You said we need to talk about my dog—you know. About what happened."

"Well, we do have something to go on. A design was cut into the body of the animal, and my deputy thinks he recognized it. It's an Army insignia. So we wondered if you'd had any dealings with this outfit."

She frowned. "I haven't had any dealings with *any* outfit. I didn't go on tour with Bob Hope, or anything, if that's what you mean."

"Well, there are other possibilities. One of your fans, maybe, who served with them. The group is the Twenty-fifth Infantry Division, nicknamed the Electric Strawberry. Does that sound familiar?"

"No."

"You never knew anybody in that outfit? You never dated any soldiers?" He heard the edge in his voice.

"No." She wouldn't look at him.

He sighed. "Okay. We'll keep asking around. LeDonne thinks it means something."

They got back in the car then and headed up the road toward Pigeon Roost, once populated by grandparents, passenger pigeons, and the ballads of Britain—now a ruin of weathered shacks, kudzu vines, and the last stragglers of the generation before America came to the mountains.

* * *

It was mid-morning when Joe LeDonne arrived at the Wyler farm, and he could tell right away that they already had a visitor. Parked in the driveway next to the shed was a black station wagon with simulated-wood paneling and an "I Brake for Animals" bumper sticker. It belonged to Alex Kessler, the county game warden. That would save some time. LeDonne didn't spare a glance at the white saltbox farmhouse, in need of a lick of paint. He ambled up to the board fence and scanned the pastures for signs of life. He spotted the two men halfway up the hill toward the trees: a stout man in gray work clothes and a taller young man in a dark uniform. They were too far away to hear him shouting. He climbed over the fence and trotted toward the sheep pasture to examine the scene of the crime.

Wayne Wyler wasn't one of the "regulars" with the sheriff's office; LeDonne had never met him. He was past sixty, retired from whatever job he'd had to keep the farm going, and now he worked the land by himself. His sons had gone on to college, which meant that they wouldn't be coming back to live in Wake County. The Southern mountains were a luxury that middle-class America could not afford, so the young people of Appalachia went up and out to a better standard of living in a grayer place. As far as LeDonne knew, there were no feuds between Wyler and his neighbors, and no controversies over politics or religion that would single out this farmer for an act of vandalism. He'd have to ask, though.

The hot sun was already beating down on the meadow, bleeding the color out of the grass itself and making the air congeal into hot, tangible puffs. The dead smell hovered around them. LeDonne batted a green fly away from his eyes and squinted down at the mound of dirty, white wool. Dead sheep didn't look much different from live sheep. Same vacant expression. Only this one didn't mind the flies crawling in and out of its slack mouth. The rusty stain of dried blood was confined to its throat and forelegs. Why was a vine of green leaves wrapped around its neck?

Alex Kessler, who had been game warden in Wake County for twice a coon's age, was kneeling beside the sheep, probing its wounds with deft, gloved hands. He glanced up at LeDonne and nodded. "You need pictures of this?" he asked.

LeDonne shook his head. "Just some opinions. Things you might not have thought to look for." He knelt beside the game warden and began to examine the sheep's body, taking care not to get the blood on himself. He didn't find what he thought he would.

"If I see any stray dogs on my land, I'm going to blow their goddamned heads off," said Wayne Wyler. His bald spot glistened with sweat from the morning sun, and there were already dark patches on his gray work shirt.

LeDonne almost smiled. "Coyotes, I thought you said."

"Coyotes—German shepherds—whatever. If I see any stray dogs . . ."

"You're not looking for a canine here, Wayne," said Alex Kessler, without looking up. "Not for *canis latrans*, either! This was no coyote. See this throat wound here?"

Wyler glanced at the seeping redness and looked quickly away. "What about it?"

"Clean incisions. Predators make tearing wounds. This was done with sharp steel, my friend. You're looking for a sheep killer that walks on two legs."

LeDonne nodded, his suspicions confirmed. "Did you find any carvings on the body. Something like a tattoo?"

Kessler looked puzzled. "They don't brand sheep, LeDonne."

"No. I meant some mutilation done at the time of death. Anything unusual."

The game warden stood up, brushing dried grass from his trouser legs. "Look for yourself, Deputy. There's no marks anywhere except the death wound."

LeDonne fingered the green vine. "Was this on the animal when you found it?"

Wayne Wyler nodded, with a look approaching satisfaction on his pudgy face. "Yeah. It was. And you don't need no expert to tell you what it is, neither. That stuff is fresh poison ivy."

The comic outburst that Wyler was expecting did not happen. LeDonne looked down at his hands in mild surprise. "Okay," he said. "That makes sense."

Pigeon Roost was a good ten miles from the lookout point on the main highway. The road snaked around bends, cutting through meadows and thickets of oaks choked with underbrush, turning the climb into a gentle ascent. They were on a plateau now, a thousand feet higher than Hamelin, but seemingly in lowland, because of the mountain barricades on either side of the valley. Spencer turned down a spur road marked with only a number on a signpost. He slowed to twenty miles an hour.

"Deer," he said, to Peggy's unspoken question. "Even in broad daylight here."

She directed her attention to the wooded hills beyond the tall grass, but all was still.

"Look ahead of us!" he said, touching her arm.

She turned in time to see a flash of red disappear into the trees on the left side of the road. "What was it?"

"Red-winged blackbird. You don't see too many of them. They don't like people, either."

"I haven't seen any of those in my yard," said Peggy.

"You won't see them in Hamelin. We have different

birds in town. A lot of robins, sparrows, blue jays. Suburban birds. Up here you get the wilder ones—bluebirds and orioles. Owls at night. Buzzards, who constitute our rural sanitation department. Even golden eagles."

The landscape was as still as a postcard. She stared out at the sagging wire fences and the weathered barns, their ugliness softened by the rich green of summer grass and the bird's-egg-blue sky. "Have you ever seen an eagle?"

Spencer slowed the car as the lineless blacktop changed to gravel. "Not up close," he told her. "They aren't golden, anyhow. Just big brown birds. My uncle Trace says you can tell them by the way they fly. They're about the same size as turkey vultures, but they fly with their wings right straight out. Turkey vultures fly with their wings in a V shape."

He turned again, this time into a narrow lane whose center line was a grassy hump skirted by tire tracks. "Almost there," he announced. "This was where my dad's kin settled."

"How long ago?" asked Peggy, looking out at the unmown pastures and ramshackle outbuildings.

"Hundred and fifty years, at least. I had great-great-uncles who were draft dodgers in the Civil War."

Peggy grinned at him. "Ahead of their time," she said.

The old home place of the Arrowood clan was a one-story white-frame farmhouse with a wide front porch, all in need of a coat of paint. At each corner of the house stood an ancient oak tree. Their full-leafed branches almost touched above the roof, their size testifying to the age of the farmhouse. A few scraggly irises struggled among the weeds at the front steps, and a child's metal hobbyhorse had been set amid a patch of tiger lilies as a garden ornament. Up the hill, to the right of the house, tomato plants, pole beans, and cabbages grew in the well-tended garden. Aluminum pie plates strung from nearby tree branches twirled soundlessly in the wind; they would keep the birds out of the garden. The brassy orange marigolds planted in rows between the vegetables would keep out the insects, a form of pesticide that went back to pioneer days.

Spencer parked on the dirt driveway that snaked up to the house. "Did I tell you they used to make their own electricity?" he asked.

Peggy shook her head. "Out of what?"

He grinned. "Around 1910, I guess it was, my granddaddy and his brothers learned how to build a homemade power plant. They dammed up the creek and rigged themselves a generator that would run lights on the farm for free. They ee-lectrified the house, the barn, the chicken coop, the outhouse, and the backyard with their homemade power. And the folks in town were still using gas lighting."

Peggy looked up at the graying house that seemed to be sliding back into an underbrush of smothering vines and thick grasses. "Too bad they didn't study carpentry," she said softly.

"Oh, that was seventy years ago," said Spencer. "They were teenagers then. When it came time to get jobs, they left the mountains like most everybody else. When I come up into these hollers, I feel like I'm taking a time machine instead of a car." He shrugged. "Of course, it could be worse. At least no Earth Shoe people have come in here building solar log homes and tripling the land prices." As soon as he said it, he realized that he had offended her, but a movement on the front porch ended the discussion.

"Somebody has seen us," said Peggy, straightening up and patting her hair.

Spencer was already out of the car. "Come on!" he called. "They won't be toting shotguns!"

By the time they reached the porch, Spencer's great-aunt Til (Short for Mathilda? He had never asked) had slipped out the front door and was smiling nervously at her visitors. She wore a faded print apron over a blue cotton housedress, and shapeless black slippers. The furrows in her cheeks made her look all of seventy, but her thinning hair was still a light brown. "We-ell, Lord," she said, addressing the sheriff. "Why'n't you-uns tell us you was a-coming?" There was a musical cadence to her speech, almost a melody. It was a variation, perhaps a descendant, of the Irish lilt.

Spencer gave her a perfunctory hug. "Aunt Til," he said (pronouncing it *ain't*), "like you to meet Miss Peggy Muryan, who just moved to town."

Aunt Til crumpled her apron with blue-veined hands and sighed again. "We could'a had you some dinner fixed if we would'a known." She smiled uncertainly at the blond stranger.

"Didn't want to put you to any trouble," said Spencer. "Just dropped by to say howdy. How's Uncle Trace?"

"About the same, I reckon. You-uns come in." Aunt Til held open the screen door and motioned them into the dimly lit interior.

The faded linoleum in the hallway gave way to a scuffed wood floor in the parlor. An old sofa of indeterminate shape and color was pushed up against a pale green wall, and next to it, in a threadbare morris chair, sat Uncle Trace, as still as a scarecrow.

Peggy feigned interest in the picture over the mantelpiece: a black wolf on a snow-covered ridge against a blue night sky. Below the wolf in the snow, the orange lights of a distant cabin glowed. "It's a Kowalski print," Peggy murmured to no one in particular. "They used it in the dining room set of *All in the Family*."

Spencer knelt down in front of the easy chair and put

his hand over the old man's. "It's Spencer, Uncle Trace!" he said slowly. "How's it going?"

The old man turned his head, and his eyes seemed to focus. "What air ye driving?" he asked in a rasp that was more air than sound.

Spencer smiled. "I got the patrol car out there now. But my personal car is the same old rig, I reckon. You know I'd come tell you if I was to go horse-trading cars." He glanced over at Peggy, who was smiling vaguely. Funny how I slip into the old dialect up here, he thought. It was as if he could speak another language, but only did so when prompted by the time and circumstance on the mountain.

Til came back into the room, then, carrying a tin tray with four jelly glasses. "Iced tea," she said. "With mint from up around the chimney."

Spencer and Peggy sat down on the old couch and sipped their already sweetened tea. "Uncle Trace used to play a pretty mean bluegrass fiddle, didn't you, Trace?" said Spencer with a hollow heartiness.

The old man was tracing the pattern on his jelly glass. He seemed to have forgotten that they were there.

"How's your mother, Spencer?" asked Til, pulling a straight kitchen chair up near the sofa. The cadence of her speech made every statement a lament. The falling inflection of her tone implied that tragic things had befallen Jane Arrowood—perhaps they had, at that—but the question held no more than simple politeness expressed in the keen of a Celt-based dialect.

"She's doing fine, I guess," said Spencer. "The tomato plants could be better, though. Not enough rain."

"A-lord, I know what you mean," said Til with a mournful nod. "And what's worse is that we've had a deer in after ours. He's ruint nigh on every one of 'em."

"Want me to come up and shoot it for you?"

Peggy set down her iced tea glass, a little too hard. She didn't want to hear about shooting things. "Bluegrass fiddle," she said carefully. "Did he play in a group?"

"Nothing formal," said Spencer. "Not like the Carter Family."

"My daddy didn't hold with all that music business," Aunt Til volunteered. "I reckon Trace could'a been real good at it, but he wanted to marry me, and my daddy wouldn't stand for it. My daddy was a preacher."

"The circuit rider," said Spencer, reminding Peggy of the family legends.

"He said stringed instruments were of the devil, and he wouldn't have them on the place.'Course, all my brothers played mandolin and guitar. But they had to sneak around to do it. Trace used to play some with them."

Spencer laughed. "The funny thing about the Reverend was that he believed stringed instruments were evil, but here in the parlor he had an upright piano, just as big as you please. Thought it was a percussion instrument, because you beat on the keys."

Peggy smiled. "An eighty-eight-string demonic instrument."

"Peggy plays guitar," Spencer offered.

Aunt Til smiled politely. Sara Carter and Mother Maybelle were all very well, but when it came to mountain music, women mostly listened. At least in the old days. Or maybe they had been too busy to play in any sense of the word.

"I taught school after that," said Peggy quickly.

Spencer could tell that she didn't want to be trotted out as a famous folksinger in front of his elderly relatives, and truly he hadn't intended to do that. He had been trying to make conversation with these two kindly people who might as well have been from another planet. He seldom saw them, and their lives did not touch at any point. The Arrowoods were not a close family. It seemed to Spencer that when a mountain child reached the age of eight he became a stranger to all his kin. Before that he was the general pet, but thereafter he became the object of distant politeness—an invisible wall that wasn't ever going to go away. He had hoped that Peggy would be able to charm his kinfolk into reminiscences of the old days, but she had been walled out, too. They were in a cultural museum, relegated to the tourist side of the velvet ropes.

Spencer stood up. "I'd better check in with the office," he announced. "It's been a good hour since I signed off. Might be a cat stuck up a tree in Hamelin."

He hurried outside, motioning for Peggy to stay and visit.

Peggy glanced around the room, as if looking for cue cards. The old man was still motionless in his chair, indifferent to her presence. "It's so pretty up in these mountains," she said at last.

Aunt Til nodded. "I like it when the mountain laurel blooms. Or in the spring, for the wild dogwood and the redbud. That whole road out there is lined with purple ever' April from the redbud bushes. And then the forsythia bush there in the side yard comes in yellow, and in mid-April the lilac bush is a flowering glory."

Peggy smiled. "I know about lilacs," she said. "That's how I remember when Lincoln was shot. Walt Whitman has a poem called 'When Lilacs Last by the Dooryard Bloomed.' And I know that lilacs bloom in April, so that's how I remember."

Aunt Til digested this bit of information. "You're not from around here?"

"No. I'm from Norfolk. I went to Carolina. But I have studied folk music for years, so I feel a kind of . . . kinship with the mountain people."

The old woman did not smile at her chauvinism. She said simply, "Spencer went to college. His father was always real restless. The Depression took some people that way. Seems like he was always afraid of not having. Spencer's not so bad as that. Did you know Cal?"

"Spencer's brother? No. I haven't been here long." And he has been dead for twenty years, thought Peggy.

"Oh, he was a one. That Cal could take a crow off the smokehouse with a pistol. And he could sing a blue streak. Spencer just sort of tagged along behind him when they were young'uns." She went to the mantelpiece and brought back a dusty three-by-five picture frame. The fading black-and-white snapshot showed two blond boys, the older boy about twelve years old, sitting with a small white mutt between them. They wore shorts and sneakers, but no shirts. The younger one was rib-thin and was looking at his brother, who grinned confidently into the lens of the camera.

Aunt Til smiled happily at the picture. "I remember when Cal wasn't but a little thing, and his daddy would be a-sitting up in the backyard swapping war stories with Wes and L.J.'s boys. They were in the Red Ball Express with Patton in the Big One. Cal would toddle around after them, picking up beer cans when they wasn't looking, and drinking what was left in them."

"And Spencer?"

"I seem to remember he tried it once—on account of Cal, I reckon. Got sicker'n a mule. Never did bother Cal, though."

"Spencer is a quiet one," Peggy offered. "He's not the way you expect a sheriff to be."

Aunt Til nodded. "In the old days you wanted them big and tough, but nowadays, it's mostly politics. They get a lot of help from the state police and all. But he's doing all right." She grinned. "Don't nobody hunt on our land without our leave, and nobody takes our chickens. It's nice having the sheriff for kin. And I reckon it's nice for him to have a job that don't make him move away. He's the only one of all of 'em that's left. I get Christmas cards from fourteen states."

They heard footsteps on the porch, and the conversation halted. The screen door banged, and suddenly Spencer was in the doorway, looking troubled. "We have to go back now," he said to Peggy. "Something has come up."

Peggy heard the urgency in his voice. "Is it something about my dog?"

"No. It may be nothing at all. Just a high school girl reported missing."

Spencer and Peggy Muryan carried their iced tea glasses back to the dark kitchen and said hasty good-byes at the screen door. They drove downhill to the present in silence.

DEAR PEG,

EXILE. THAT'S ABOUT WHAT THIS AMOUNTS TO, I GUESS. BUT DON'T FEEL GUILTY ON MY ACCOUNT. YOU CAN MAKE IT WITHOUT ME, AND YOU COULDN'T HAVE MADE IT WITH ME—ISN'T THAT WHAT THEY SAID? (AH, BUT YOU DID MAKE IT WITH ME. REMEMBER "ON THE BEACH"? THE FREE FLICK, NOT MYRTLE BEACH. ALTHOUGH, THAT TIME WAS NICE, TOO. BUT THE FIRST TIME IS THE ONE THAT YOU'RE SUPPOSED TO BE NOSTALGIC ABOUT, AND I TRY TO REPLAY IT IN SOFT FOCUS WITH MUSIC, AND TO AIRBRUSH OUT THE ASS-FREEZING COLD IN THE ARBORETUM AND THE SOUND TRACK OF YOU BABBLING ABOUT NUCLEAR WAR AND THE DESTRUCTION OF CIVILIZATION. WELL, YOU SURE PUT A STOP TO THAT, DIDN'T YOU, PEGGY? TWENTY MINUTES ON THE OLD ARMY BLANKET, AND WORLD PEACE IS ACHIEVED. (THERE'S A PUN IN THERE SOMEWHERE.)

I REMEMBER A LOT. EVEN THE BAD STUFF IS GOOD. EXHAUST FUMES MAKE ME THINK OF YOU. (I KNOW YOU WORE "KHADINE," BUT

THERE'S NOT MUCH OF THAT AROUND HERE TO JOG THE OLD GRAY CELLS.) EXHAUST FUMES, THOUGH . . . WE'D BE DRIVING ALL NIGHT TO GET TO SOME TWO-BIT GIG THAT "HIT ATTRACTIONS" GOT US IN ATLANTA, OR CHARLOTTESVILLE, OR TUSCALOOSA, AND I'D SMELL EXHAUST FUMES AS WE CHUGGED DOWN THE OLD INTERSTATE, PULLING THAT RENTED TRAILER FULL OF SOUND EQUIPMENT. I CAN GET A BACKACHE JUST THINKING ABOUT LIFTING AN ALTEC LANSING. AND WE'D BE EATING BOLOGNA SANDWICHES WHILE WE DROVE, BECAUSE WE WERE AFRAID TO STOP AT A DINER. LONG-HAIRED GUYS AND FLOWER-CHILD LADIES DON'T STOP IN REDNECK DINERS. PASS THE MAYONNAISE. AND WE'D PRACTICE FOR THE GIG. I CAN HEAR YOU SINGING "LITTLE MARGARET" WHILE YOU SLAPPED SANDWICHES TOGETHER. AND AS WE DROVE INTO TOWN, I'D BE TRYING TO GET CLEANED UP FOR THE GIG, AFTER DRIVING ALL NIGHT. SHAVING WITH A SAFETY RAZOR AND THE MELTED ICE IN THE COOLER. YOU FLY TO ALL YOUR GIGS THESE DAYS, DON'T YOU? I WONDER IF YOU EVER MISS THE OLD DAYS. (PROBABLY NOT.)

DO YOU EVER LOOK OUT AT A SEA OF PEOPLE WHO PAID EIGHT BUCKS TO SEE YOU AND THINK ABOUT THAT TIME AT U.VA. WHEN THEY BOOKED US INTO A FRAT THAT WANTED A DANCE BAND? POOR PEGGY. THEY THREW RITZ CRACKERS AT YOU AND YOUR FOLK TUNES. YOU CRIED ALL THE WAY BACK TO CHAPEL HILL. THE NEXT DAY I BOUGHT YOU A BUNCH OF MARIGOLDS AND DAHLIAS

FROM THE FLOWER LADIES ON FRANKLIN STREET. . . .

YOU'RE PROBABLY NOT HAVING HALF THAT MUCH FUN NOW, GETTING ROSES IN YOUR DRESSING ROOM FROM PEOPLE THAT CAN AFFORD TO SEND THEM.

I'M NOT HAVING THAT MUCH FUN, EITHER.

YOU SHOULD SEE THE HOOTCH THAT THE AIR FORCE IS PROVIDING FOR ME TO LIVE IN. IT IS A PRIZE. WOODEN HOOTCH, OPEN SIDES, SCREENED IN, NO AIR-CONDITIONING, NO SEPARATE ROOMS, LIVING OUT OF A METAL LOCKER. GODDAMN AIR FORCE, GODDAMN HOOTCH (? HUTCH, AS IN RABBIT—OR DO RABBITS LIVE IN WARRENS?) BUILT FOR DWARFS. (DWARVES, BOZO.)

IS THIS ALL THE AIR FORCE THINKS OF ME, THAT THEY'D DARE PUT ME UP IN AN ABOVE-GROUND HOGAN/LEANTO/HOVEL/TOOLSHED? HUH, IS IT? APPARENTLY.

WELL, CONSIDERING THAT I DON'T DO MUCH, NOTHING SEEMS TO PAY PRETTY WELL.

THE MOSQUITOES HERE ARE ALMOST AS BIG AS A-5 FREEDOM FIGHTERS.

MY "NATIONAL LAMPOONS" HAVEN'T COME FOR A COUPLE OF MONTHS, AND I HAVEN'T HAD ANY NEWS FROM HOME IN MONTHS. NO NEWS AT ALL. ALTHOUGH THE "PACIFIC STARS & STRIPES" COMES CLOSE EVERY SO OFTEN. LATELY, I'VE BEEN LISTENING TO THE ENGLISH NEWSCASTS FROM LIBERTY RADIO, SOUTH VIETNAM, WHICH TRANSMITS FROM THE COMMUNIST-HELD SECTIONS OF SOUTH VIETNAM. I CAN ALSO GET RADIO AUSTRALIA FROM MELBOURNE—THE TOP 20 HIT

TUNES. LOVE IT. ALSO THE BBC WORLD SERVICE. ALL VERY INTERESTING.—SO IF I AM IMPRISONED, I DON'T SUFFER A WHOLE LOT, BEING ON SUCH GOOD TERMS WITH MY JAILER. (YEAH—ME.)

IS THAT HEAVY? OR IS THAT HEAVY?

ACTUALLY, THE ONLY REASON I KEEP WRITING IS SO THAT I CAN KEEP DRINKING. DRINKING. AND GOING TO WORK. AND THE BX. OR DOWNTOWN. (WHEN NATURE-HORMONES DICTATE.) AND BEATING OFF (FURTIVELY) WHEN THERE'S NO TIME TO GO DOWNTOWN. OR GOING TO THE NCO CLUB AND DRINKING THERE.—THAT'S LIFE FOR ME HERE.

ON THE GROUND.

AND SINCE THIS IS THE LAST PAGE I HAVE. AND THE LAST BEER. I'M AFRAID ALL THIS BROUHAHA WILL HAVE TO DO.—I'D WRITE MORE, BUT MY ATTENTION SPAN IS GETTING SHORTER AND SHORTER.

TIME FOR "WORK" ANYWAY . . . UP IN THE AIR, JUNIOR BIRDMAN,

TRAVIS

CHAPTER 8

The only thing that we did wrong,
Was staying in the wilderness too long. . . .
"KEEP YOUR EYES ON THE PRIZE"

A MISSING TEENAGER was a rarity but not a novelty in Hamelin. Usually, though, it was the same kids who went missing for the same reasons. The Hollister boys were third-generation hell-raisers who'd go off on a bender at the drop of a beer can tab. Only the school guidance counselor bothered to report them; everybody else hoped they stayed gone. Crystal Teague would drop out of sight sometimes when things got bad at home, but neither she nor her mother would testify, so there wasn't a lot anybody could do about it. Reva Teague didn't think the law could protect her from her permanently enraged husband, and she was probably right. Spencer never pushed her to press charges. Local law enforcement tends to see the same faces over and over, committing new crimes or suffering new abuses. They did a lot of repeat business in Wake County.

What worried Spencer was that this missing girl was not one of his regulars. He hoped that she'd had a fight with her boyfriend, or an argument with her mother. Those were relatively minor problems that could be solved without lasting effects. If it was drugs, it would be bad news for everybody, especially for Wake County, which so far was off the beaten track for the hard stuff.

Spencer glanced again at the address he'd scribbled down on his clipboard. This was it. The tan mailbox was appliquéd with a color decal of cardinals on a dogwood branch, surrounding the name "Winstead." The straight concrete driveway led to a carport and a one-story white brick ranch house, flanked by boxwoods. The parents were out the front door and waiting nervously on the concrete stoop before Spencer turned off the engine of the patrol car. He was alone now. It hadn't been much out of his way to drop Peggy back at her house before coming over.

He looked at the two people who were waiting for him to get within conversational range. This interview would be conducted in hushed tones, a tacit acknowledgment of the possibility that their daughter might be dead. The parents were about Spencer's age, maybe younger. Spencer always felt mildly surprised that someone his age should be the parent of a near-adult. It reminded him that he was getting old.

The woman held her years better than her husband did. She was a faded study in beige: limp brown hair, dull brown eyes, a muddy tan from garden work, and a scrawny thinness that had never been sexy. She wasn't going to do much of the talking.

The man looked like a football player run to fat. His blue-black hair was streaked with gray, and he wore it long and bushy, in the style of Conway Twitty and fundamentalist television evangelists. His reddened round face radiated unctuous sincerity, probably a cover for a drinking temper. For the occasion of speaking to a police officer, he had added a clip-on tie to his see-through polyester shirt.

Spencer had never met them before.

"Emory Winstead," said the beefy man, holding out a sweaty hand.

"We sure 'preciate you coming out," said his wife, holding the door open for them. "We're just so worried."

They shepherded him into an oatmeal-colored living room and boxed him in between them on the couch. Spencer opened his vinyl legal pad and tried to look official. "I'll need to get some background first," he said, writing "E. Winstead" at the top of a clean page.

Their names were Emory and Debra Winstead, and they were thirty-six and thirty-four, respectively. They had moved to Hamelin eight years ago from Sullivan County. Winstead worked at the granite quarry, driving a dump truck.

Spencer recorded these details in neat printing. He had learned early on not to make indecipherable notes. "Now," he said, looking up. "A few hours ago, you called in and reported your daughter missing. Could we go over the details of that from the beginning, please?"

"I don't know whether to be furious or worried!" Emory Winstead declared. "I think Rosemary knows better than to pull a stunt like this, though. By God, I do."

Spencer's pen was poised above the yellow sheet. He had written nothing except a line of biographical information on the parents. He waited. After a moment's silence, Emory Winstead got the point and tried again. "Our daughter Rosemary is sixteen—going to be a junior this fall. She didn't come home last night."

Spencer looked at his watch. "And you didn't report it until after noon?"

Mrs. Winstead touched his arm. "She told us that she was spending the night with a girlfriend. Jennifer Showalter."

"I'll need her address and phone number," said Spencer, without looking up from his writing.

Emory Winstead took up the tale. "When she wasn't home by lunchtime, the wife called over to the Showalters', and they said they hadn't seen hide nor hair of our girl. First they'd heard of it."

Spencer nodded. He had been expecting something like that. "Does Rosemary have any brothers or sisters?"

Mrs. Winstead pointed to a photograph on the coffee table—a little boy in a cowboy hat on a wooden rocking horse: he recognized the scene as the Kmart Christmas photo package. "Travis is four," she said.

An age difference of a dozen years. There would be no sibling confidences in this family, then. The sheriff went on to the next logical question. "Did your daughter have a boyfriend?" *That you know of,* he wanted to add.

They shook their heads.

"Rosemary was kind of shy," said her mother. "She wasn't what they call a popular girl."

"I'll need to see her room," said Spencer.

Parents sometimes objected to this, afraid of making a temporary situation worse in case the room search turned up marijuana or stolen property. Rosemary's parents had no such reservations. Winstead nodded to his wife, and she led the sheriff down a short hallway to a small, sunny bedroom decked out in shades of pink.

"While I'm in here, could you find me a good, recent picture of Rosemary?" Spencer did not want the Winsteads at his elbow while he searched. He closed the door as she left.

It shouldn't take long to do the room, he thought. Rosemary Winstead was neater than most teenagers, or else she hadn't owned much to create clutter. A pink polyester bedspread and two stuffed bears adorned the single bed. There was a white chest of drawers, a desk-and-bookcase, and a record player on a metal stand.

Spencer wondered if she kept her diary in her underwear drawer.

He looked at the books first: a row of paperbacks and a couple of library books on the shelf attachment above her desk. He thumbed through *Wuthering Heights*, *The Master of Blacktower*, and a well-worn copy of *Spoon River Anthology*, but there were no notes or photographs tucked away among the pages. The titles themselves didn't tell him much about her, except that she seemed bright for a high school kid. The library book was a hardcover edition of *Long Time Passing*. Spencer read the orange words under the title: *Vietnam and the Haunted Generation*. Not the reading matter he'd have expected of a shy teenage girl. He made a mental note to ask her parents about it.

The rest of the room offered no clues to the personality of Rosemary Winstead. There were no drugs, no cigarettes, no dirty books under the mattress or tucked in among her panties. She had kept no notes from friends, no pictures of boyfriends. The entries in her yearbook were bland: "Best of Luck to a Real Sweet Girl." Spencer wondered why this mouse of a girl would suddenly leave home. Maybe her friends could tell him. Her parents wouldn't know. With kids that age, they never did.

"Did you find anything, Sheriff?" Rosemary Winstead's mother asked as if she'd rather not know.

Spencer shook his head. "There are no indications of problems. I didn't find any drugs, or any suicide note—nothing useful. Do you know anything about why she might have run away—if she did?"

"She wouldn't have done that," Mrs. Winstead said. "She wasn't that kind of girl."

"Had either of you quarreled with her in the past few days?"

They both shook their heads. "Rosemary wasn't a

quarreler," her father said. "She was the sneaking kind. Tell you right what you want to hear, and then do as she pleased when your back was turned. She didn't like to make scenes, though. She was sly-stubborn."

Spencer held out the copy of *Long Time Passing*. "I found this library book in her room," he said. "I thought it was unusual reading for a girl. Vietnam. Do you know anything about it?"

"I was in Vietnam," said Winstead. "Reckon she wanted to read up on it, on account of me. Kids like to know family history."

"Did she ever discuss it with you?"

"Wouldn't have told her beans about it," said Rosemary's father proudly. "Not fit talk for a girl. Reckon she wanted to find out on her own. Sly. Like I told you."

"But we never had any trouble with her," said Mrs. Winstead earnestly. "She always kept her room real neat. And her grades were good. She studied."

Emory Winstead stuffed his fists into the pockets of his gray polyester trousers. "What do we do now?" he asked.

"The policy is to wait twenty-four hours," Spencer told them. "She really hasn't been gone very long. She could have sneaked off to a rock concert in Knoxville for all we know. So we'll give her time to turn up. If you haven't heard anything from her by ten o'clock tomorrow, we can file a runaway report with the Juvenile Intake people, and I'll contact the next jurisdictions—the neighboring counties, I mean—to see if they've heard anything."

"If they've found a body, you mean," Winstead growled.

The girl's mother had begun to weep silently. Large pear-shaped tears tottered on her cheeks, but she did not reach out for her husband.

"Do you have that picture I asked you to get?" Spencer asked, speaking gently to her.

She nodded silently and handed him a five-by-seven color print—obviously Rosemary's school portrait. Spencer looked at the photograph, noting the resemblance between the two women. Rosemary, a dreamy waif with light brown hair, would have the same faded look as her mother by the time she was thirty-five. If she was lucky enough to get there, he thought.

"Here's Jennifer's address and phone number, too. Her friend," said Debra Winstead.

"I tell you what I can do now," said Spencer, trying to sound encouraging. "I can take this picture over to Jeff McCullough at the newspaper office and ask him to run it with a little article mentioning that Rosemary is missing. The paper goes to press this evening, so the word will be out by noon tomorrow when the papers are delivered."

"Then the whole town will know!" snapped Emory Winstead.

Spencer's eyes narrowed. "You want her back, don't you?"

Emory Winstead scowled. "Depends," he said, and stepped back into the house, slamming the door behind him.

His wife looked stricken. "I'll walk you to your car," she whispered. She glanced behind her nervously.

"I'll be in touch with you as soon as I know something, ma'am," said Spencer, sounding more reassuring than he felt. "Try not to worry."

He started to get back into the car, but the woman touched his arm. "Wait," she said. "There's one thing I wanted to say. It probably don't mean nothing, though."

"What's that, Mrs. Winstead?"

"About that book Rosemary was reading. That *Long*

Time Passing. It's because of her father being in Vietnam that she was a-reading it."

Spencer nodded. "Yes, ma'am. I believe your husband said that."

"No," she said, hugging herself as if she were cold. Her eyes were wet again. "He said she was reading it on account of him, but she wasn't. Rosemary's real dad was killed in Vietnam, and then I married Emory in '72. I don't reckon it matters."

Spencer sighed. "I don't know, ma'am. It might."

He decided that his next stop ought to be the office of the *Hamelin Record*. The more advance notice he could give Jeff McCullough for tearing up his front page, the easier it would be to ask him for a favor. Spencer turned the patrol car back toward town. He glanced at his watch: there was still time to check in with Martha. Since Hamelin could not afford a dispatcher twenty-four hours a day, they employed one (Martha) for the day shift—the busiest time—and for the rest of the time, they arranged to transfer the calls to the Unicoi County sheriff's department. Martha did this by "dialing forward" to the Unicoi number. In the evening, calls—maybe two a night—were relayed to the second shift from the Unicoi dispatcher. There was no third shift in Wake County: nothing was expected to happen in Hamelin after eleven, and that was usually the case.

She answered his call at once. "Hello, Spencer. Where are you?"

LeDonne liked to use the police ten-code system, but Martha seldom bothered with it. "Everybody already knows what's going on around here anyway," she would say.

"I just finished talking to the parents of the missing girl," he told her. "I'm headed for the newspaper office now. Is anything else going on?"

"Negative," said Martha, irony heavy in her voice. "I'm taking off at four-thirty. Reunion committee meeting at my house. In case you want to stop in."

"Negative yourself," Spencer said into his microphone. "I'm going to keep asking questions about this girl. It could be something serious."

"Oh Lord," said Martha. "I hope not."

"Is LeDonne back yet?"

"Typing up a report on the sheep."

"Ask him to wait for me. This shouldn't take very long."

He signed off. Perfect timing, he thought, pulling the car into the gravel parking lot beside the *Hamelin Record*'s small brick office. Jeff McCullough's old green Ford was still in the parking lot. The newspaper office in Hamelin was just a base of operations for newsgathering and circulation. The actual typesetting and printing of the *Record* took place in Johnson City at a large print shop that put out two dozen community newspapers a week.

Spencer opened his notebook and took out the photograph. Rosemary had been too shy to smile at the photographer, but she had managed to look pleasant and sincere. Mostly, she looked young. It was too soon to tell who she was going to be. He hoped the photograph would reproduce well in the black-and-white pages of the newspaper. It was their best shot at finding her—if that still mattered. If she was dead, he reckoned that the best chance of finding her would be deer hunting season, when an unpaid army of "searchers" scoured the hills in search of eight-point bucks and sometimes came back with a skull instead. Sometimes it was an Indian burial uncovered by erosion; sometimes it was an old person who had wandered away and died of exposure. He made a mental note to ask about Rosemary's dental records, in case it ever came to that.

Jeff McCullough looked up from his typewriter when the sheriff walked in. "Uh-oh," he said, trying to grin. "You know I hate to see you on Wednesdays, Spencer Arrowood. Here I am trying to get to press with a halfway decent paper that's taken more than five minutes' advance planning in layout, and then you walk in with that *High Noon* look on your face, and I just know it means more work."

"I'm afraid it does this time," Spencer agreed. "But you could look at it as free news."

"I would if it wasn't Wednesday," McCullough replied. "What is it this time?"

Spencer set the photograph on the top of the counter. "This is Rosemary Winstead. Her parents reported her missing this afternoon. I've just started doing the investigating, but I thought I'd stop by here first so that we could get this in tomorrow's paper. It doesn't have to be much. Just the picture and caption: 'Have You Seen This Girl?' You know."

The editor nodded. "Sure, I know. 'Anyone having any information about the whereabouts of this missing girl is asked to call the Wake County Sheriff's Department at once.' Front page, right-hand corner, I suppose? Would a two-column headline do you?"

"Whatever," said Spencer. "Have you found out anything about our other case yet? Peggy Muryan's background?"

"Not yet. I've put the word out, though. A friend of mine works for the *Knoxville Journal*. She says she'll see what she can come up with and get back to us. Now what's the story on this girl, Spencer? Is she a runaway, or did she elope with her boyfriend?"

"All I've talked to is the parents."

McCullough laughed. "You don't know beans, then, do you?" He picked up the photograph. "Well, I hope she didn't run off to Hollywood. No potential for it. Looks like the mousy type to me. I'll bump the Ruritan roadside cleanup picture and put—what'shername—Rosemary in the place of honor. Bet she'll be back by tonight, though."

"Want me to call you if she is?"

"Don't bother, Sheriff. I'm headed for Johnson City right now to do the printing. Anything that happens after five minutes from now is next week's news."

Martha was sitting on the floor in her living room surrounded by faded and battered covers of record albums. "I thought these would sort of jar our memory," she explained.

Beside her, Tyndall sat cross-legged on a throw pillow, balancing a clipboard on her knees. Sally Howell lay on her stomach, with her chin propped on her hands. The Class of '66 Reunion Committee Music Meeting was more or less in session. They had arrived at six, wearing jeans and *Hamelin High* sweatshirts, bringing with them the fixings for hamburgers and a two-liter bottle of Coke. Martha was still in her working clothes: a tailored dress and high heels. She had used the time before their arrival to vacuum the rug and to tidy up her small living room. Tyndall and Sally weren't the "popular girls in class" anymore, but Martha couldn't get over the feeling of intimidation. Well, not intimidation, really. Just being overly impressed—she had a crazy urge to tell somebody about their visit: you know, *casually*, "Oh, Tyndall Johnson Garner and Dr. Sally Howell dropped by my place for dinner last night." As if they were royalty. She hoped her feelings didn't show.

"Brian Hyland!" said Sally, examining a yellowed album cover. "I hadn't thought about him in *decades*! Remember 'Sealed with a Kiss'?"

"Yeah," said Tyndall. "You never could keep the alto part straight on that one."

Sally made a face. "Well, I had to invent it, didn't I? Brian Hyland sang alone. Anyway, you only liked that song because it reminded you of David Gordon."

Martha, who knew that such reminiscences would exclude her, and that she might still mind, interrupted. "I figure we have about three hours to fill with music, so we ought to consider playing a lot of different types of songs. You know: some country, some rock, some folk . . ."

"Does it all have to be from '66? I can't keep my years straight," said Tyndall.

Martha considered it. "I think we should extend it to songs of that era," she said at last.

"Right." Sally nodded. "They played some of them for years anyway. Seems like every fraternity party I ever went to was a three-hour rendition of 'Double Shot' by the Swinging Medallions, and 'May I' by . . . by . . . oh God, I'm *old*! Who the hell was it?"

"Maurice Williams and the Zodiacs," said Tyndall solemnly. "I suppose you want them put on the list?" She scribbled the titles under the heading "Beach Music."

"Remember the Shirelles?" said Martha. " 'Soldier Boy' was popular when Leon got drafted, and I remember I used to cry every time I heard it."

" 'Where Have All the Flowers Gone,' " said Sally.

" 'Eve of Destruction,' " said Tyndall, writing furiously.

"I just hope we can find this stuff." Martha sighed. "We only have a couple of weeks, and we should put the songs on cassettes for continuous play."

"I still have all my old records," said Sally. "When we finish the list, I'll check off what I have, and I'll tape them this week in Knoxville."

Tyndall made a face. "Oh, Dr. Howell, you are so-ooo efficient."

"Damned straight." Sally grinned. "They don't give Ph.D.s to airheads—actually, they do, but only to *male* airheads. What about civil rights songs? Remember those?"

Martha blinked. " 'We Shall Overcome'?"

"No. I was thinking of the catchier songs of the movement. 'I Ain't Scared o' Your Jail 'Cause I Want My Freedom,' and 'Keep Your Eyes on the Prize.' Songs like that."

Martha frowned. "I think they'd be out of place at a party. And, besides, we didn't have any black people in our high school back then. Where would you find recordings of them, anyway? Newsreels?"

"Pete Seeger made a record of them. I still have it. It's a memento of my only date with Michael Donnelly. 1964 . . . I think."

Tyndall nodded. "Your Joan of Arc period."

Martha looked puzzled. Nostalgia over civil rights songs? It was a part of the era that she wanted to forget. And anyway, "Michael Donnelly was white."

"Yeah, but he was a Yankee. His folks had just moved to Hamelin because his father was going to be a pediatrician at the hospital in Erwin. We started hanging out together because I was smart, and he needed somebody to talk to. And one day we started talking about race, and I told him I just didn't believe in integration. Straight Confederate party line, direct from the mouth of my grandmother Howell."

"Michael Donnelly looked almost exactly like James Darren, and you talked *politics* to him?" Tyndall giggled. "You're hopeless, Sal."

"He was a very serious boy. Anyway, he didn't try to argue with me. He just asked me to go out with him the next night, and of course I said yes. I guess I thought we'd go to a movie in Johnson City. I remember getting all dressed up: my new paisley shirtwaist, a dab of old English Leather behind each ear." She laughed. "We went to Johnson City, all right. To a civil rights meeting!"

Martha shook her head in wonder. "At the university?"

"No," said Sally, smiling fondly at the memory. "It was in a little black church. Black neighborhood. Pitch-dark outside. And Mike parked the car in an alley. I remember holding his hand—terrified!—as we crept up the steps into the church. There was no one around, and it was all dark. At first, I thought we had come to the wrong place. Then we heard voices singing 'We Shall Overcome.' I was scared to death! First, of having to go into that meeting, and then of just being there. I think it must have been just after that church in Mississippi had been firebombed. I remember looking up at the stained-glass windows, waiting for the crash."

"So what happened?"

"Everybody was very nice. Michael and I were the only two white people there, and the 'We Shall Overcome' was coming from the Pete Seeger record. They were playing it over the church speaker system. We sat down in the second pew, and they said hello to us. I remember they sang some songs and made some speeches, and then we went home. But I was converted. When I got my allowance that week, I went out and bought the record album. Mother wouldn't let me play it while the maid was around."

"Michael Donnelly," said Tyndall. "What ever happened to him?"

"He spent a couple of years in Bolivia with the Peace Corps, and then he went to Penn State for a Ph.D. in economics."

"Is he coming to the reunion, Sally?"

"No," said Sally. "He died of cancer a couple of years ago."

Joe LeDonne worked late if he felt like it, not out of conscientiousness, but just to show his indifference to the clock. Besides, he seldom had anything better to do. He had gone out to Denton's Café at five and had brought back a couple of hamburgers that were slowly leaking grease stains through the white paper bag on his desk. He would eat them when he felt like it. He didn't mind cold food.

Just now he was looking over his notes in the Muryan case and checking them against his newly typed report on the dead sheep on Wyler's farm. The sheriff was going to ask him if they were the work of the same person, and he wanted to be sure of the facts behind his opinion. The sheep had been lying in the field—not hanging—so there were no knots to compare. The wounds were similar, though. He wished that they had kept the dog's body for further comparison, but at the time it had seemed like a nasty but isolated case of vandalism, and there had been no reason to preserve the evidence.

Poison ivy. He was tempted to go out and talk to Roger Gabriel again, but it would have been an indulgence. He really didn't need a second opinion.

LeDonne glanced impatiently at the clock. Six-fifteen. The sheriff should have finished his questioning by now. He decided to go into the inner office and watch the news on Spencer's little black-and-white portable. He picked up the phone to transfer incoming calls to the next county's dispatcher.

"Excuse me, sir?"

LeDonne looked up. The visitor was a teenage boy.

LeDonne's mind automatically classified him: white, male, Caucasian, approximately seventeen years of age. Five-five, slight build, wearing khaki trousers and an olive-drab T-shirt. No distinguishing marks. "Yeah?" he said.

"Um. I just came in for some information," said the kid, sounding nervous.

"What's your name?"

"Pix-Kyle Weaver, sir," he said. With a belated attempt at courtesy to his elders, the boy extended a sweaty hand. LeDonne shook it, grinning ironically at the charade. The sheriff would have made some small talk to put the kid at ease, but then, that was his job. LeDonne just waited.

"Uh—I wondered if you all had a ride-along program."

"A what?"

"Well, I was reading in this magazine about how some places—like San Diego—have a ride-along program where citizens can go out on patrol with the local cops." He blushed when he said "cops," wondering if this was a term of disrespect. LeDonne said nothing. "Anyway, the article said that you just go in and sign up, and they let you ride along with the police. And I wondered if I could do that."

"Call San Diego and ask."

The boy frowned. "I meant here."

LeDonne leaned back in his chair and looked at him through half-closed eyes. "I don't know, kid. You'd have to ask the sheriff, and he's not here right now. Check back tomorrow. He might take you around with him."

Pix-Kyle Weaver shook his head. "I wanted to ride with you."

"With me?" LeDonne sat up.

"Yeah. I thought maybe we could talk. You know, while we were out on patrol."

"Talk about what?"

The boy looked down at the floor. "You know—things," he mumbled.

LeDonne waited. Finally Pix-Kyle Weaver shrugged and said, "I'm kinda interested in Vietnam." There was more silence, so he hurried on. "I'm going to be a senior next year, which means that we're allowed to do one course of our own choosing as an independent study. I got permission to do Vietnam as a project for history in fall term, and I'm trying to line up some information on the subject. The library's got a couple of books on it, but a lot of them are just political. You know: *why* we went there, and what the brass decided to do strategically. And stuff about the French being there first. But that's not what I want to know. I mean, it doesn't tell me what it was *like* over there. What it felt like to be in a war, in combat, you know?"

"Yes," said LeDonne, "I know."

Weaver relaxed a little. "So, do you think we can talk about it?"

LeDonne looked at the kid with his twice-a-week shaved face and his clean khakis and his fake Army T-shirt. He waited for a moment until the cold rage had settled back in the pit of his stomach instead of clotting there in his throat, waiting for him to open his mouth. Finally he stood up, kicking the chair back against the wall. "No," he said quietly, "I don't think we can talk about it. It's not a horror movie, kid. It's somebody's *life*. You want to know what it was like, watch John Wayne in *The Green Berets*. About ten times. You still won't know shit." He ushered the kid to the door, closed it firmly behind him, and locked it. Then he flipped off the lights in the outer room and retreated to Spencer's office.

Pix-Kyle Weaver stared for a moment at the gray wooden door in front of him. "But I already did that," he said softly as he turned away.

Jennifer Showalter's father was the local Methodist minister, but his attitude toward the sheriff's inquiry did not strike Spencer as being much in the way of Christian charity. When Spencer had explained that he wanted to talk to Jennifer, he was grudgingly invited in, and both Showalters had insisted on being present during the interview. At one point, Mrs. Showalter had wanted to call a lawyer in Johnson City, but Spencer assured them that witnesses—or nonwitnesses, as it were—usually did not need legal representation.

They ushered him into their furniture-showroom parlor as if he were a panhandling leper. Spencer noticed that there were no religious items on display. The mantelpiece held brass candlesticks and a collection of family pictures in small brass frames. Above it hung a large gilt-framed mirror, reflecting an immaculate room furnished in pastel blue and white.

They were in their early fifties, he thought. Sitting on the blue brocade sofa with narrowed eyes and forbidding expressions, they looked like the painting *American Gothic*, only instead of a pitchfork between them, they had Jennifer, who seemed amused by the whole thing. She had straight copper hair down to her shoulders and carefully mascaraed green eyes. Her breasts looked much too large for the rest of her small body, and the low-cut sundress did little to counteract the effect. He pictured her naked and moaning, himself cupping her breasts in his hands, sucking her nipples. Too bad he wasn't eighteen anymore. As soon as she opened her mouth, she'd be just a kid to him, and he would cease to notice her . . . attractions. He wondered if all men his age had this schizophrenic view of women: there were women who were people—friends—and there were pieces of meat—centerfolds—the ones you didn't know. He still saw a pretty girl as a delicacy first, for maybe ten seconds, and forever thereafter as a human being. Maybe the psychos and the perverts were the people who couldn't make that transition. He took a last look at Jennifer the Playmate, arching her back a little as she twisted a silky strand of hair. He almost grinned. Good thing her gargoyle parents weren't mind readers.

He told them that he had come about Rosemary Winstead and explained that her parents had believed her to be spending the night with Jennifer. Now they had reported her missing. Reverend Showalter's frown deepened. "We have met the parents," he said carefully. His tone spoke volumes on the distinction of social classes. "I hardly see what that has to do with our Jennifer," he said, patting his daughter's clasped hands.

"It seems she told her parents that she was spending the night here," he told them.

The Showalters looked at each other. *Certainly not,* their expressions said.

Jennifer didn't look frightened, but she didn't look puzzled, either. "Her dad is a real creep," she offered.

"Jennifer!" said both her parents.

She scowled. "Well, he *is*. I can't help it. She was always complaining about him. Anyway, they wouldn't let her do much. She was supposed to stay around and babysit that little brother of hers."

Spencer hoped her parents would shut up before he had to ask them to. "Go on," he said.

"I don't know where she went," said Jennifer with a shrug. "Nowhere interesting, I bet. Rosemary was kind of a stick. She read all the time."

"But you were friends?"

"I wouldn't put it that way," said Mrs. Showalter. "They were classmates, of course."

"Jennifer's friends are the young people in our church," said her father. Apparently their attitude was that if Rosemary had run away to join a motorcycle gang or to become a junkie on the streets of Memphis, no taint of association should attach itself to Jennifer.

Spencer ignored them. "Jennifer? Were you friends with Rosemary?"

She sighed. "Yeah. I guess so. She hung around. I was lab partners with her last year, 'cause she didn't mind doing the write-ups."

He believed her. He didn't understand why plain girls chose to become best friends with someone beautiful, but it was a common pattern. Like a jackal following a lion. Maybe, like jackals, they got the leftovers, he decided.

"And did Rosemary call you yesterday to say she wanted to come over and spend the night?"

Jennifer thought it over. What followed would be an edited version of the truth. "She told me she wanted to get out of the house, and she said that if her parents called, that I was to say she was invited here."

"And you didn't ask what she was really going to do?"

"Get laid, I figured."

"JENNIFER!" Her parents sounded like small dogs, both barking at once. Spencer suspected that the "interview" would continue long after he had gone.

"By whom?" asked Spencer, ignoring them.

"I have no idea," said Jennifer, bored with the subject of someone else. "Probably some older guy. She didn't date anybody at school. I saw her only a couple of times this summer, and she said she was interested in somebody, but she wouldn't talk about it. The way she acted, it was like there was some secret about it. I figured he was, like, you know, married."

Another chorus of yaps from her parents.

"Did she refer to him by any names, even a nickname?"

"I don't remember."

Spencer tried one last gambit to spark her interest. "This could be very important, Jennifer," he said urgently. "Rosemary is *missing*. Something may have happened to her. Is there anything you could tell us that would help us locate her?"

Jennifer thought hard. "Well . . . you could call around to all the motels in Johnson City."

Spencer thanked them politely for their time and said that he might have to come back. When he took his leave of Jennifer at the oak-and-stained-glass front door, he felt nothing of his original spark of desire.

The door to the sheriff's department was locked, but there was a light on in his office. Spencer opened the front door with his key and stepped cautiously inside. "LeDonne!" he called out.

"Yo!" came a voice above the drone of a televised newscast.

LeDonne was sitting in the straight-backed visitor's chair, hunched over the television and finishing the last of his cold hamburgers. "What'd you get?" he said between mouthfuls.

Spencer looked to the coffeepot, but it was empty, rinsed out by Martha before she left. The ceiling fan was turning at slow speed, but it couldn't come up with any cool air. He sat down behind his desk and put his feet up. "I don't know." He sighed. "The parents say she was a pure little homebody who studied all the time, and her so-called friend thinks she went into heat and headed for Johnson City."

LeDonne made a perfunctory smile. "Ain't it ever the way?"

"Have there been any calls?"

"No. Why?"

"I don't know. I was halfway thinking she might have turned up by now. Her and the boyfriend. With a story about a flat tire, maybe."

"Well, she hasn't. Now what?"

Spencer rubbed the back of his neck. He was suddenly tired. "I'll notify Juvenile Intake in the morning. Call the neighboring jurisdictions. The *Record* comes out tomorrow, and McCullough is running her picture on the front page. Maybe that will help. Right now I'm going to call the assistant principal at the high school. I have his home number around here somewhere."

"Front of Martha's phone book," said LeDonne.

"Thanks. He should be able to tell me something about the girl. Schoolteachers see more than parents. Or maybe they're just more willing to believe it."

This time, though, it didn't help. Assistant Principal Samuel J. Rogers, reached at his home and interrupted over dinner, was finally able to recall Rosemary Winstead after some prompting from the sheriff, but he was able to tell them nothing useful. She had not been truant, or loud, or a troublemaker. She had not been an honor student, a cheerleader, or a school politician. She had made no lasting impression. Assistant Principal Rogers could offer nothing except his opinion that Rosemary was not the type to have gotten into trouble. Except, of course, in the euphemistic sense of the word. After fifteen years as an assistant principal, Mr. Rogers would have believed *that* of any adolescent female.

"That's about all we can do tonight," said Spencer, placing the telephone receiver back in its cradle. "How did your investigation go this morning?"

LeDonne handed over his report. "The animal was killed in the same way as Miss Muryan's dog," he said. "Except that it was not hung from a tree."

"So you think it's the same person?"

"I do."

"What about the mutilations we found on the German shepherd?"

LeDonne hesitated. "Well . . . you can't carve tattoos on a sheep. There's all that damn wool in the way. But I think our boy did manage to leave a message, anyhow."

"A note?"

"No. But there was a vine of poison ivy draped over the body." He gave a grunt of satisfaction at the look of bewilderment on the sheriff's face. "This could be a coincidence, I know. But after the first carving, I thought we ought to consider it."

"Consider what?"

"Poison Ivy. It was the nickname of another outfit in 'Nam. Fourth Infantry. It had an ivy design on its shoulder patch, and its official title was the Ivy Division."

Spencer put his head in his hands. "So what do you make of that?"

"I don't know," said LeDonne. "Symbols for two outfits. Maybe it's two people, working together. I thought I'd check with the Vietnam Vets Association in Knoxville. See if they have any members in this area."

Spencer nodded. "What outfit was Roger Gabriel with?"

"Hundred and First Airborne out of Fort Bragg, North Carolina," said LeDonne. He turned to go.

"LeDonne?" said the sheriff quietly. "What outfit were you with?"

The deputy grinned. "I thought you'd never ask."

* * *

" 'Poison Ivy'!" cried Sally Howell, waving her spoonful of ice cream. "Now *that* was a stupid song!"

Tyndall jumped up from the table and sang the line about calamine lotion, using her glass of Coke for a microphone. It was past nine o'clock now, and they had adjourned to the kitchen for dessert. Sally had wanted to go out and buy the ingredients for S'mores (graham crackers, marshmallows, and Hershey bars), but in the end they settled for low-calorie strawberry ice milk and Diet Coke.

"I think 'Poison Ivy' is a little early for this reunion, isn't it?" asked Martha with a worried frown. "I seem to remember singing that in junior high school."

"I heard my daughter singing it a couple of months ago," said Tyndall. "And I started feeling sorry for kids today."

"Yeah." Sally snickered. "They don't have real parents. Just *us*."

Tyndall sat down again. "No," she said. "I guess it's really stupid if you say it out loud, but it just seems to me that a lot of kids' childhood nowadays is hand-me-downs from our childhood. I mean, we were the generation that Disneyland was built for. And we were the first kids to have 'Rudolph the Red-Nosed Reindeer.' And McDonald's. And so many of the songs you hear today on the radio are remakes of our music. 'The Locomotion.' 'Great Balls of Fire.' "

Sally looked at her solemnly. "Tyndall Johnson *Garner*, that is without a doubt the stupidest thing you have ever said. And if I wanted to I could completely refute that thesis of yours with a ton of historical examples, because *I* have a Ph.D." She struck a pose, head thrown back, nose in the air, and then spoiled it by laughing. "To give you a brief example: 'The Night Before Christmas' was not written for us. Neither were nursery rhymes. Or

Winnie the Pooh, or *Alice in Wonderland*, or *The Jungle Book*. Culture *is* hand-me-downs. That's all it is. Twit."

Tyndall rolled her eyes in mock exasperation. "And what are my little cherubs going to have to pass on to my grandchildren, huh? I ask you. Strawberry Shortcake, the imbecilic Care Bears, and those godforsaken Smurfs!"

Sally grinned at Martha. "This from a woman who used to plan every Saturday morning around a couple of rodents named Pixie and Dixie."

Martha, who felt blitzed by a camaraderie she did not share, said nervously, "I used to like *Bullwinkle*."

"Oh. *Bullwinkle*," said Sally. "Now *that* was a *religion*. Not for children at all. Very classy stuff."

"Speaking of religion, Sal, remember how you used to watch *The Man from U.N.C.L.E.* every week and moon over David McCallum?"

"Yeah. No regrets. I still like wiry blonds. Do you think we could get some posters from back then? *Man from U.N.C.L.E.? The Avengers?* And maybe some political ones. I have a Robert Kennedy poster taped to the side of my refrigerator."

Tyndall made a face. "Hypocrite. You were for Eugene McCarthy. I remember when you got bused out to Indiana to campaign for the Democratic primary. They wouldn't let you wear jeans or sloppy clothes—didn't want you to offend the voters. *Clean for Gene,* you all called it."

"Maybe a JFK poster, too," Sally mused.

"He was dead before '66," said Martha.

Sally looked at her. "Well, of course he was, Martha! But that was such a big deal to the members of our generation. I remember, we were in fifth period, about to have a Spanish test, and Mr. Turley came on the intercom and said, 'Boys and girls, your president has been shot.' "

Tyndall nodded. "And you said, 'Who would want to shoot Bill Walsh?' "

"Bill—oh! The student body president," said Martha, finally remembering.

"Well, it just seemed incredible to me that anybody could shoot *Kennedy*. I mean, we *loved* him, and he had those two little children . . ."

"And all those girlfriends," said Martha.

"Yeah," said Sally. "So much for Camelot. We were so innocent back then!"

"We were. But we digress," said Tyndall, glancing at her watch. "I can't leave Mother with Mrs. Mitchell for too much longer. I don't want to make her mad, or I'll never get out of the house again. Have we dredged up three hours' worth of songs yet?"

"We may not need the whole three hours," said Martha. "Weren't there a couple of guys in the class who had local bands?"

Tyndall nodded. "Yeah, but I bet they haven't picked up a guitar in years. I could ask around, though."

"There's another possibility," said Martha. "Spencer Arrowood is supposed to be inviting Peggy Muryan to come to the reunion. As his date! And I figured we could ask her to sing."

Tyndall and Sally looked at each other. "Not for long," said Tyndall. "I mean, we wouldn't have any backup band for her or anything."

Martha smiled brightly. "Maybe we could play her old record album, and she could lip sync!" As soon as she said it, she could tell from their expressions that she had said something uncool—gauche—not *with it*. After all these years, they were still an alien culture. After all these years, it still hurt.

* * *

LeDonne had finally gone home, and Spencer was about to call it a night. Tomorrow's investigation promised a long and tedious day, and he was beginning to get hungry. On impulse, though, he picked up the phone and dialed Peggy Muryan's number. After four rings, the receiver was picked up, and her voice—guarded and solemn—said, "Who is it?"

"Spencer," he said.

He heard her sigh of relief. "Hello. Did you find your missing girl?"

"Not yet. There's rumors of a boyfriend, though, so she could be shacked up anywhere between here and Bristol."

She laughed. "I hope *that's* not illegal."

"Well, not at your age. It is at hers. Anyway, I'll start trying to trace her in the morning. Meanwhile, there's something I've been meaning to ask you. . . ."

"What's that?" She sounded serious again, anticipating a discussion of the vandalism, he figured.

"Well, I wondered if you had any plans for August ninth?"

She was too experienced to commit herself at that stage. "Go on," she said coolly.

"That's the night of my high school reunion here in Hamelin, and some of the people on the committee were wondering if you'd like to attend. But that's not why I'm asking you."

"Oh? Why are you asking me?"

"Because I need a date. Showing up alone to a twenty-year reunion would absolutely wreck my image. I tried to get Barbara Mandrell, but she was busy."

She was laughing now. "I'll bet! Well, I can't make any promises right now, but you get a definite maybe. Will that do?"

"I guess it will have to," he said amiably. "So unless

you're going to invite me over, preferably for dinner, I'll say good-night."

There was a pause at the other end of the line, as if she were making up her mind, but finally she said, "Good night, Spencer. Maybe another time."

He heard the hum of the dial tone, and then he was alone again.

CHAPTER 9

Which of us has known his brother? Which of us has looked into his father's heart? . . . Which of us is not forever a stranger and alone?
THOMAS WOLFE

JOE LEDONNE CAME out of the café balancing a paper plate on top of his can of Pepsi: his breakfast doughnut. It was not yet eight o'clock, but his shades were firmly in place. The bright, cloudless morning heralded the beginning of a scorcher.

As he walked toward the office at the back of the courthouse, he looked around for Vernon Woolwine. It was kind of a habit, seeing who Vernon was today—like reading your fortune cookie in the Chinese restaurant in Johnson City. The benches in the little park across from the courthouse were empty, and the sidewalks were deserted. It was too early for Vernon. Maybe the airless heat of last night had left him as fatigued as everyone else, and had made him sleep late in the morning. Maybe he wouldn't be anybody at all today. LeDonne knew that Vernon was crazy, but he was always courteous to him when their paths crossed. There were worse things than crazy: most things, in fact.

He had spent the hot predawn hours thinking about the dead sheep. The missing girl was Spencer's case, at least for now, and maybe it would turn out not to be a case at all. But the gutted dog and the butchered ewe were his business. He wished he knew what they meant.

He squinted up at the morning sun. Hamelin's brick-front stores and concrete sidewalks seemed faded by the light. The signs could do with a new coat of paint, and the drugstore awning was tattered. Neglect. His hand went to the holster straddling his right thigh. The first thing he would do today would be to clean his gun, the Colt .45 automatic that made him the object of good-natured ribbing from other lawmen. They called him Hotshot, pretending not to realize that he carried it because he was familiar with it. It was an Army weapon. Not that being Army issue was always a good recommendation. He'd had an M-14 in basic training, and it had been a satisfactory weapon, but the M-16 he'd used later in combat was less to his liking. He had found the pistol grip awkward, and the blunt sight had impaired his accuracy in firing. The .45 was a good weapon, though. It showed you meant business. The sheriff carried a .38 Smith & Wesson with a four-inch barrel.

When LeDonne was a kid in Ohio, he had a .22 rifle, a tenth-birthday present from an uncle who had been in Korea. That summer he had spent long afternoons by himself shooting tin cans and beer bottles off a stump in the woods near his house. Later, he'd discovered rats at the city dump, and they had become unwilling participants in his war games, playing the parts of Krauts or Japs in his imaginary battles. Eight summers later in Indochina, the game had been reversed: the dinks in the luminous jungles of Vietnam had been transformed by his weary terror into junkyard rats, all teeth and glistening eyes, to be blasted into ribbons of gore by his M-16, with its lousy horizontal drift and its squat black stock—an eighteenth-birthday present from Uncle Sam.

He wished he could spend the day target practicing, instead of making polite phone calls to bureaucrats trying to run down the Poison Ivy thing. He took a swig of Pepsi from the can; it was hot already. Holding the doughnut between his teeth, he pried open the screen door to the sheriff's office, catching the door against his hip and easing his way through it.

Martha saw him in the doorway, and ran over to help. "Ugh," she said, eyeing the shiny glazed doughnut with distaste. "I don't know how you can keep that thing down. You might as well just eat right out of the sugar bowl."

He spat the pastry back onto the paper plate. "Want a bite, Martha? Make it a suicide pact?"

"No, thank you. I ate enough last night to last me all week. Hamburgers. Ice cream. I had no idea that nostalgia could be so fattening."

He took off the sunglasses and sat down in the straight chair beside her desk, positioning her small floor fan so that it blew in his direction. "Another meeting of the reunion committee?"

She nodded. "Tyndall and Sally came over to my house last night. They were big shots in high school."

He took another sip of Pepsi. "And what about now?"

"I don't know. One of them is a professor, and the other one is married. I guess they both have me beat. Always did, always will."

"Only if you believe it," said LeDonne. "You're okay, Martha. Believe me, compared to what there is in this world, you're okay."

"It's funny how people from high school can make you feel so small and useless all of a sudden. Just like your parents can. One minute, you're a happy, functioning human being, and the next minute you're a gawky, socially ignorant adolescent again! It's like voodoo. Do you ever feel like that?"

"No," said LeDonne. He hadn't been home to Ohio in years. He had lost touch with the family, and he couldn't even remember the names of most of the people from his high school. He was somebody else now. He had gone home for a few days when he came back from Vietnam, but he'd known almost immediately that it was a mistake. He felt alien in his parents' house, or like someone remembering a past life. He felt angry at his father, his friends. He didn't know why. Perhaps because they hadn't been where he had been. The war had changed him past accommodation. It had drowned him and thrown his body back on a familiar shore, leaving him as silent and uncommunicative as a corpse, bloated with memories, unable to say what he was. He had spent most of his days there in silence, staring empty-eyed at the fields beyond his parents' house, or lying wide-eyed in the dark waiting for thunder. Finally he had packed a canvas bag with clothes and hitched a ride to the bus station. He had never gone back. He was somebody else now, and that somebody did not belong in Gallipolis, Ohio.

"I just feel eighteen again," said Martha, "and it is not the thrill you might suppose."

"It's the reunion," said LeDonne. "An overdose of 1966."

"Yes." Martha sighed. "The reunion. I thought it was just going to be like planning a big party, but it isn't. It's like exhuming a corpse. It's coming together, though." She looked at him carefully, trying to gauge his mood. "After I get over all these agonizing preparations, it should be a great party," she said. "Whether you went to school here or not. In fact, maybe better if you didn't. No ghosts to contend with."

LeDonne nodded. He knew about ghosts.

"Like poor Spencer. I know he is dreading this, but he is *not* going to weasel out of going. So, if he tries to trump up some emergency for that evening—like an impromptu license check—or if he tries to juggle shifts around so he'll be working then, don't you let him get away with it. We're counting on him to present that plaque to the school."

"Why shouldn't he want to go?"

Martha sighed in exasperation. "Because of Jenny, of course. His ex-wife. Funny, though, I never think of her that way. Never think of them as a couple. He's afraid she's going to show up, and he doesn't want to have to deal with it."

"Will she?"

"Will she what?"

"Show up."

"I wish I knew. We haven't heard from her yet. I think Tyndall might know where she is. She said that if we don't hear from her in the next few days, she'll try to track her down. When I find out for sure, I don't know whether to tell Spencer or not."

"Tell the truth."

"I just think he'd be sorry if he didn't go. There's going to be so many people there that we haven't seen for years. And we're going to play sixties music. It should be a really nice party."

"I'll take your word for it," LeDonne mumbled.

Martha took a deep breath. "Well, you don't have to. Take my word for it, I mean. You could come along. I happen to be in need of an escort."

He didn't say anything, and Martha, who was hearing all the possible refusals in her head, was trying to think of ways to change his mind. She wondered how anybody who looked so unlike a movie star could manage to be so sexy. Maybe it was because he never smiled—or if he did, you could tell that he didn't really feel it. His features were clean and straight, and there was just one streak of gray in his dark hair, which made his eyes seem that much more blue. They were a cold blue that made her think of Watauga Lake, man-made by the TVA back in the forties. Its deep, opaque blue water covered a treacherous lake bed of drowned houses and bridges, and the tangled undergrowth of still-standing trees. When somebody drowned in Watauga Lake, they always sent scuba divers, and boatloads of volunteer crews dragged the bottom and searched the forested shoreline that was inaccessible by road, but it was never any use. Watauga Lake never did give up its dead.

"Okay," said LeDonne, shrugging.

"What?"

"If it fits in the work schedule, I'll go to this reunion thing with you. Sure. Why the hell not?"

Martha felt the blush spread across her cheeks. She nodded quickly, afraid of saying too much. "Well, fine, then. Okay." She looked up to see that LeDonne had taken the .45 out of its holster, and he was staring at it with a bemused smile.

"You ever see *The Deer Hunter*?" he asked quietly. "First time I saw it, back in the seventies, I went home and played Russian roulette with my dad's revolver. Tried it three times. Never did it since."

She froze, her hand at her throat, for maybe two heartbeats, and then the phone on her desk began to ring. The sound seemed to come from far away. Without looking away, she reached for the receiver.

"If anybody wants me, I'll be in Spencer's office, cleaning my pistol," said LeDonne. As she picked up the phone, he gave a little wave and ambled away.

"H-h-hello?" Martha wiped her wet cheeks with the

back of her hand and tried to listen to the voice on the other end of the phone.

Tyndall knew that she looked like hell before nine o'clock, but after last night's get-together, and her mother's restless night, she was too tired to put on makeup. It was only a trip to the grocery store. Besides, why should she care how she looked? A suntan would have made up for the absence of makeup, but all the talk about skin cancer had made her uneasy about tanning, which was just as well: her mother's condition did not allow for hours of inactivity, anyhow. Sometimes the old woman would just sit for hours staring at the television, or even at the wall; but without warning, she could suddenly begin to wander about the house or outside, and she had been destructive at times, as well. Twice she smashed the mirror in her bedroom dressing table. Tyndall wondered if it had been deliberate. Perhaps some last shred of a functioning intelligence had looked into the mirror and had seen the ruin of herself: the fat, unexercised body, dressed in the cheapest, most washable polyester; the short-cropped haircut of a prisoner, her hair allowed to grow out iron-gray and unpermed, after all her years of careful grooming; and the expression—the tentative smile of one who is lost, is confused by technical details, doesn't speak the language, got on the wrong bus, forgot her lines. A smile that asked for patience and a little kindness to straighten the matter out. But when the matter is a brain full of tangled neurons, nothing will straighten it out; it will only get worse, and the smiler will die lost. Perhaps she had understood some of that in a flash of coherence as the mirror showed her what she had become, and she had picked up the hairbrush and smashed the mirror to kill the messenger that brought the dreadful revelation. Tyndall wondered if any part of her mother was still inside her, alert and aware of what was happening. She hoped not.

The old woman was asleep now, after a long, restless night of crying out and trying to walk about the house. Perhaps she resented Tyndall's going out for the evening. Tyndall had decided to risk a quick trip to the store before her mother woke up. She hated to leave her alone, but sitters for deranged old women were hard to come by.

Tyndall decided that she would run in to the grocery store, grab the jar of coffee, a can of applesauce for her mother, and Tampax, and then dash out again before any of her mother's old friends could corner her in the aisle to ask how *dear Evelyn* was getting along. Dear Evelyn had forgotten them all months ago in the haze of her illness, and they had returned the sentiment. None of them came to see her or offered to help Tyndall. It was as if Evelyn Johnson were dead. Tyndall supposed that she was. The nursing home decision would have to come soon; Steve was right about that. She had reached the point that no matter what she did, she felt guilty because she wasn't doing two other things instead. And Steve was beginning to complain about being left to manage the children alone. When she thought that her mother might ruin her marriage, she felt a cold shiver of fear and then shame at her terror that her mother might not die in time.

This made her doubly careful not to leave her mother alone or to let her harm herself, and to see that the doctor came by to check on her regularly. Tyndall washed the bedsheets twice a day and sat with her mother making cheerful conversation as if it were understood. She managed to convince everyone but herself that she was a tireless nurse and a loving daughter, but Tyndall knew that as she put each spoonful of soft, bland food into her mother's slack mouth, her own heart was beating an accompanying litany: *Please die. Please die. Please die.*

"Don't put me in a home," her mother had pleaded when she was still able to talk through her growing clouds of confusion. "You know what they do to old people in homes. They beat them. Starve them. Don't put me away." Sometimes Tyndall had heard her alone in her room, weeping.

Don't put me away. Tyndall had promised, but she didn't know how long she could keep her word. In fifteen years, she too would be old, and the disease that had taken her mother might be lying in wait within her brain, ready to claim her, too.

She reached for the cheapest can of applesauce, and then put it back, choosing a more expensive name brand. Only the best for Mother. *Please die.*

"Tyndall Johnson? Is that you?"

When she turned around, Tyndall was careful to have her friendliest smile in place. She studied the face in front of her. A heavyset, dark-haired woman in a salmon-colored polyester pantsuit. The woman was smiling back. "I declare, Tyndall, I didn't know you was in town again."

"Just visiting," said Tyndall, still trying to place her. "It's been a while, hasn't it?"

"Lord yes. Seems like I work so hard these days, I don't hardly get to see nobody. I've been meaning to answer your letter, though."

"Letter?"

"About the reunion."

The printed notice that they had sent to all the members of the class. Tyndall studied the face again. Somewhere under the lines and the extra poundage was a fleeting resemblance to Dolores Whitchard. She risked it. "Dolores?"

"Yep." The woman leaned against her shopping cart, mashing a spongy loaf of white bread with her forearm.

Tyndall remembered being in classes with her, but try as she might, she couldn't summon up anything special to remark on. Had Dolores written poetry? Sung in the glee club? Made the Beta Club? The pages of *The Papyrus* remained closed in her mind. "Well, how *are* you?" she said with all the warmth she could muster for a stranger.

"Tolerable," said Dolores with a sigh. "Still married to Bobby Ray. Got four kids."

"Well," said Tyndall, trying to sound hearty. "That must keep you busy."

"I work, too. Clerk over in Johnson City at Kmart. Bobby Ray got laid off at the plant last winter, but we're making do." She reached past Tyndall for cans of green peas and Green Giant Mexican Corn. "Bobby Ray and the kids keep the house real good while I'm gone. It's just like turnabout. He takes the kids to the doctors and the ball games, and I bring home the paycheck."

"He doesn't mind?" asked Tyndall. Of course, Steve had taken over the chores while she came to stay with her mother, but he never missed an opportunity to voice his dissatisfaction with this temporary inconvenience.

Dolores Whitchard smiled. "He's not the greatest cook in the world," she said, "but between canned food and frozen dinners, we get by. And my mom helps out a lot."

"You're very lucky," said Tyndall faintly. "I have to go now." She lugged her armful of cans and boxes to the checkout counter. On the rack facing the front aisle, the new copies of the *Hamelin Record* had just been put on display. As she waited for the dogfood-laden cart in front of her to pass through the line, Tyndall picked up the newspaper and glanced at its headlines. A girl was missing. Tyndall wondered what the story behind that was. A murder victim or just a rebellious teenager? Martha would know, since she worked at the sheriff's office. Tyndall sighed. Martha had such an interesting life.

Spencer came in a little after nine, wearing his "dress-up clothes"—navy blue blazer and khaki trousers—and carrying a copy of the *Hamelin Record*. "There," he said, showing the front page to Martha. "That ought to get some results."

Martha looked at the solemn young face staring out at her from beneath black typescript: HAVE YOU SEEN THIS GIRL? She looked familiar—or had Martha gone to school with her cousin?—or did all teenage girls look alike? Martha read quickly through the article that McCullough had thrown together in Johnson City. It said little more than who her parents were, how old she was, and when she had been reported missing.

"It's always young girls, isn't it?" She sighed. "I wonder why."

"Easy targets."

"No. I meant I wonder why men don't see them as people. Maybe we should teach our girls to be less passive and sweet. I never heard of a bitchy woman getting kidnapped by a pervert, did you?"

LeDonne looked up from his magazine. "No, Martha. In that case her friends usually do her in."

"Anyway," said Spencer, "we don't know that anything has happened to her. She may be taking in the sights at Dollywood with the boyfriend."

Martha was not convinced. "Well, Spencer," she said, shaking her head. "I hope it helps. Those look like your interview clothes to me. Who are you going to talk to next?"

"I don't know. I've seen her folks, her so-called friend, and the assistant vice principal of the high school, and that's all I know to do. They weren't much help. Now I'll have to wait and see if someone comes to me."

He did not have long to wait.

A little past ten, when the mailman had finished delivering to addresses within the town and was headed out to his rural route, the telephone rang in the sheriff's office.

Martha, who was typing up a warning letter about cattle straying onto the road in Dark Hollow, snatched up the phone and cradled it between her shoulder and her ear. "Sheriff's Office," she said, tapping out the final letters of "Sincerely" with one finger.

"Yes," said an anxious voice on the other end of the phone. "Could I speak to Spencer, please? I mean—the sheriff?"

"It's for you, Spencer," called Martha, holding her hand over the mouthpiece. "Peggy Muryan."

Spencer waved to show that he had heard and picked up the extension in his office. "Good morning—"

"No, it isn't," she said. He could hear her taking deep breaths, the way people do when they are trying very hard to stay in control.

"Peggy? What's wrong?"

Another long pause. "Can you just come over here—right now?"

"Well . . . I'm on duty."

"Will you please come over here right now *as the sheriff*, goddammit!"

"I'll be there in five minutes," he said, but she had already hung up. He thought of calling her back, but in a town the size of Hamelin, you could go there just as easily. He hoped it wasn't a dead animal in her yard again. Or worse.

Joe LeDonne looked up from his paperwork as Spencer put down the phone. "Want me to go along?"

"I don't think so," said Spencer. "I don't know what this is about yet."

LeDonne nodded. "I'll be here. Another half hour, at least. If you don't need me by then, I'll start patrol."

He eased the patrol car out of the parking lot and turned left, toward the big shaded houses on Elm Street. If he flipped on the siren, he could be at her house in two minutes. Maybe less. But he'd also be answering questions about it from nosy townspeople until the middle of next Tuesday, and for all he knew her emergency could just be an obscene phone call or some other minor matter. He decided to forgo the theatrics and just get there in reasonable time. She had sounded upset on the telephone—maybe frightened. It might be a good time to ask her more about her past. She was keeping something back; he was sure of it. People who are victims of vandalism or harassment usually know why they have been singled out. Often they know who's doing it. He wasn't sure if this rule applied to famous people or not.

The lawns were beginning to turn brown from the July sun, and the flowers were past their peak. Spencer shook his head at the sight of a lawn sprinkler going full blast in one parched front yard. Didn't those people know that watering a lawn in the morning just boils the grass in the noonday sun? A lifetime of helping his mother with her gardening chores had taught him things like that, but unlike his mother, he didn't particularly care.

He spun a few pebbles of gravel taking the first curve of Peggy Muryan's driveway a little too fast. The white-columned house looked as peaceful as ever in its grove of oaks. The porch light was still on in mid-morning, though. By the time he had cut the motor, Peggy had slipped out the front door and was on the front porch waiting for him. She looked pale and tired—the way a woman her age looks when she hasn't bothered to put on makeup. She wore jeans and a man-sized T-shirt that looked slept in, and her feet were bare. He glanced at the yard and the outside of the house for any signs of vandalism or forced entry, but everything seemed normal.

"Are you all right?" he asked, ushering her inside.

She hesitated for a moment. "Something else has happened."

They went into the parlor, and she motioned for him to sit down on the flowered sofa. He noticed that there was a pile of advertising circulars and unopened letters beside a yellowing houseplant on the coffee table. The *Hamelin Record* lay faceup near the pile of mail.

"I thought you didn't subscribe to this," he said, indicating the newspaper.

She shrugged. "They called me up and asked if I wanted a subscription. I couldn't figure out how to say no without being insulting about it. It seemed easier to send them the ten bucks. It takes about two minutes to read it, but it's great to peel vegetables on." She stared at the newspaper, but she wasn't smiling.

Spencer waited for her to continue.

She sighed and tapped the front page with her fore finger. "Spencer, is this girl still missing?"

"As far as I know. Why?"

"Well, I think I know something about her disappearance."

Spencer frowned. "Did you know her?"

"No. But this came in the mail today." She reached under the pile of advertising circulars and brought out a color postcard, a picture of pink mountain laurel in bloom on the Blue Ridge Parkway. It was addressed to "Peggy Muryan, Elm Street, Hamelin, Tennessee." Block capitals, printed in ballpoint. He handled it carefully by the edges—just in case.

The message, also printed in block capitals, read:

I TOOK HER BY HER GOLDEN HAIR,
I THROWED HER ROUND AND ROUND—

He looked up impatiently. "This is addressed to you."

"Yes."

"Well, what does this have to do with a missing high school kid?"

She got up and walked to the cabinet beside the fireplace, where several hundred record albums were stacked against the wall. She flipped through the first few covers and selected a dark cover, Vanguard label, illustrated with a black-and-white photograph. She looked at it for a minute and then set it down on the table beside the newspaper.

"*That's* what this has to do with the missing girl."

The title on the album read *Peggy Muryan: Mountain Ballads*. He had never seen it before; it must have preceded her classic, *Carolina Blue*. But it wasn't the music that interested him. It was the jacket photo. Spencer looked at the solemn face of the young girl staring out at him from a twenty-year-old record cover: long, light hair, an oval face with dreaming eyes, and delicate features. Just like the face on the front page of the *Hamelin Record*.

He looked again at the words scrawled on the back of the mountain laurel postcard. "I took her by her golden hair, I throwed her round and round."

"What's the next line?" he said hoarsely.

CHAPTER 10

I drew my saber through her, which was a
bloody knife,
I threw her into the river, which was a dreadful
sight.
My race is run beneath the sun, and Hell is
waiting for me,
For I have murdered that dear little girl whose
name was Rose Connally.

"DOWN BY THE WILLOW GARDEN"

PEGGY MURYAN LOOKED at the face on the front of the album cover, a young face with shining eyes. It might as well have been someone else. "It was a long time ago," she murmured, "but I thought you might know this one. It's a local variant of 'The Wexford Girl,' an English broadside."

"What is the next line, Peggy?" He wanted to shake her, to make her look at him.

"It dates from around 1700, but people have always changed the words to fit whatever local crime is current. 'The Oxford Girl.' 'The Cruel Miller.' There's always a new dead girl to sing about. Always a dead girl."

Spencer reached for her hand, but she edged away. "Isn't it funny how in the American versions, they never say why he kills her," she mused. "She's pregnant, of course." Peggy had a faraway look, as if she had forgotten that he was there. "So many songs about that. 'Omie Wise.' 'Poor Ellen Smith' . . . So many murdered girls. All pregnant, all trusting."

She was badly frightened, Spencer decided. And if this was a mild form of shock, he wouldn't get anywhere by bullying her. "I don't recall that song," he said gently. "Could you tell me the words?"

She nodded absently, closed her eyes, and began to sing. Her fist beat soundlessly against the cushion of the couch, keeping time to the rhythm of the song.

I met a little girl in Knoxville, a town that you all know,
And every Sunday evening, into her home I'd go.
I took her for an evening walk about a mile from town.
I picked a stick up off the ground and knocked that fair girl down.

She fell upon her bended knee. "Have mercy," did she cry,
"Oh, Willie, dear, don't kill me here; I'm not prepared to die."
She never spoke another word; I even beat her more,
Until the ground around us shook, and with her blood did flow.

In his impatience, he started to interrupt her, but Peggy held up one finger to indicate that the crucial lines were coming, so he settled back and tried to keep his mind on the words to the song. A cluster of images of past crime scenes, and Rosemary's timid face, kept distracting him from the simple ballad. Peggy sang it with a mountain accent that was not present when she spoke: flattened vowels and compressed syllables. He wondered where she had learned it.

I took her by her golden hair, I throwed her 'round and 'round;
I throwed her into the river that flows by Knoxville town.
"Go there, go there, you Knoxville girl, this dark and stormy night.
Go there, go there, little Knoxville girl, you'll never be my wife."

I started back to Knoxville, got there about midnight;
My mother she was worried, and woke up in a fright.
"Oh son, oh son, what have you done to bloody your clothes so?"
I told my anxious mother I was bleeding from the nose.

I called for me a candle to light my way to bed.
I called for me a handkerchief to bind my aching head.
I rolled and tumbled the whole night through. There's trouble ahead for me.
The flames of hell around my bed before my eyes did see.

They took me down to Knoxville, they locked me in a cell;
All my friends tried to get me out, but none could go my bail.
I'm worrying my life away in this old dirty jail,
Because I murdered the Knoxville girl, the girl I loved so well.

The song died away into silence, and neither of them spoke. Spencer was thinking about jurisdictions, and search parties, and the absurdity of listing a folk song as his source of information. He looked again at the album cover. The Peggy Muryan of two decades ago stared back at him with big, solemn eyes. Her long, straw-colored hair was fashionably straight and cascaded over one shoulder of an embroidered peasant dress. The back cover listed the songs, all credited as Traditional: "Little Margaret," "John Riley," "Farther Along," "Fennario," "The Knoxville Girl," "Poor Ellen Smith," "Down by the Willow Garden," "Whiskey in the Jar," "True Thomas," and "The House Carpenter." The producer and the musicians were listed on the back, but he saw only one name that seemed familiar: Backup vocalist—Travis Perdue.

"I'd like to take this record album with me," he said. "It strengthens the theory that the threats involve you."

"Fine."

"And I'll also need to take the postcard with me. The other one, too. Do you still have it?"

She nodded. "Somewhere."

"Try to find it for me, please. I'm going out to the car to get an evidence bag to put them in. It may be too late to test for fingerprints, but we'll have to try. And after that, I'll go back to the office and call."

She narrowed her eyes. "Who are you going to call?" she asked thoughtfully.

He sighed. "The Knox County sheriff's department." *I throwed her into the river that flows by Knoxville town . . .*

"Call from here." She had put her feet up on the couch now, and she hugged her knees against her chin, as if for protection. He hesitated. "Please," she said. "I want to know."

"All right. But you can't tell anyone, no matter what. It's police business."

Peggy nodded. "Get an autopsy. Find out if she was pregnant."

"She may not be dead," said Spencer, but he had been composing this request to the coroner in his mind.

He went out to the car and got the clear plastic evidence bags for the postcards. He wished he had thought to treat the first postcard as evidence when Peggy had first received it, but he had thought it was just a piece of hate mail. Not serious enough to pursue. When it turned out to be more than that, the evidence was compromised, both by careless handling and by time. What postal official would remember seeing such a postcard now? What store clerk would remember selling one?

When he came back, Peggy was still on the couch in the position he had left her, but two postcards were lying facedown on the coffee table. He inserted them carefully into the small bags.

"Make the call," she said, pointing to the phone in the hall.

He pulled his card list of phone numbers out of his wallet and went to the telephone table. Maybe it was just a joke. Maybe the postcard was just a coincidence, unrelated to the girl's disappearance. He thought of the white German shepherd hanging stiff and bloodied from a wire at the edge of the woods. *Please,* he thought, as he began to dial, *don't let her be tore up*.

He identified himself as the sheriff of Wake County and asked to speak to the information officer. "We've got a situation here," he began, lapsing into police jargon. He told the Knox County deputy about the threats and the mutilated animals.

"And now we have a missing girl," he said. "White female, fifteen years of age, approximately one hundred and ten pounds. We have reason to believe that she may have been . . ."

I took her by her golden hair; I throwed her 'round and 'round,
I throwed her into the river that flows by Knoxville town. . . .

The words sang in his head in a discordant jangle. "We have reason to believe that she may have been placed in a river in your area."

Silence at the other end of the line.

The sheriff cleared his throat. "This is just a long shot, but if you can assist us in this, we'd appreciate it if you'd—"

The Knox County officer cut him off. "Sheriff, I think you'd better get down here right away. Bring whatever information you've got."

"Are you saying—"

"Somebody just phoned in a report of a body in the French Broad River."

He was headed for Johnson City. From there he could pick up I-81 and I-40, a straight shot into Knoxville, just over an hour away. There was a new four-lane out of Unicoi County that might have been faster, but it was out of his way. He preferred the dozen miles of country road that bypassed urban traffic and city clutter. The old road was lined with rolling pastures and shaded trees. Ironweed, like clumps of blue daisies, grew by the side of the road, and an occasional groundhog watched the cars speed past.

With the mountains falling behind him in the distance, he drummed his fingers on the steering wheel, wishing he had an AM-FM radio in the car so he could tune in to WJCW in Johnson City, the country station. A dose of country blues might distract him from what was to come. The criminal investigation unit had just been dispatched to the crime scene, they told him. If he hurried, he could meet them there, maybe identify the body. He had set off right away, pausing long enough to call Martha at the office to tell her where he was going. Later he would question Peggy Muryan—or somebody else would. If it was Rosemary Winstead floating in the French Broad River, then it wasn't his case anymore. Except for notifying her parents. He had not informed them of the Knox County find; he would have to assume that it was a false alarm until proved otherwise. There was no point in distressing them with an unsubstantiated report. But he had their daughter's picture tucked into the notebook beside him, and in a few hours he would know for sure. He would spend the long drive back figuring out how to tell them.

The highway stretched before him, hot and boring, an obstacle between him and the urgent business in Knoxville. At night, twenty years ago, that road had been a stream of headlights. He was crammed in the backseat, between Buddy Jessup and Gary Barker. Cal was driving, coming back from seeing *The Great Escape* in Johnson City. They were arguing about whether or not Gary could jump a barbed-wire fence on his motorcycle, the way Steve McQueen had done in the movie.

Suddenly Cal yelled, "Pruitt!" and gunned the motor.

Behind them two pools of headlights danced in the darkness. Delos Pruitt, in his father's beat-up Fairlane, was trying to catch them. Delos Pruitt was always trying to catch them. He was the last chosen for any team, the clumsiest lab partner, and the most fawning of lackeys: 120 pounds, slick black hair that looked painted on, and a perpetually pleading expression. Delos wanted to be "one of the guys," not realizing that the most intoxicating thing about being one of the guys was the ability to inflict cruelty and humiliation on lesser beings, Delos Pruitt in particular.

That night he had wanted to catch up with them to tag along to the Stetson Grill, a beer joint out on the highway where the "cool guys" went to drink beer, and where they could buy some for their underage cronies, no questions asked. Delos didn't want the beer, just the company, but he wasn't going to get it.

When the wavering headlights of Delos's daddy's Fairlane flashed in the rearview mirror, Cal had jammed his foot to the floor, and the car roared and leaped forward into the darkness. They spun around blind curves, teetering along the mountain roads, with Pruitt's little Fairlane dogging them at a steadier pace, never quite out of sight. Finally, after one switchback turn—with all of them yelling for him to slow down—Cal threw a switch and the road went away. The faint band of headlights in front of them vanished, and the darkness closed around them. But Cal didn't slow down. He drove the road he remembered. He might have killed them all. Far behind them, the lights of Delos Pruitt's Fairlane seemed to stop, and then they rounded another bend, and the darkness was complete.

Cal let them scream for another mile or so until he was sure he'd lost Pruitt for good, and then he flipped the lights back on and headed for the Stetson Grill. The next day Delos Pruitt tried to pretend that nothing had happened, but Spencer saw a puzzled look in his eyes, like he really couldn't figure out how they had vanished. Pruitt was too cautious and law-abiding to think of the obvious. It was a miracle Cal hadn't driven them over the side of a mountain: himself, Spencer Gary, Buddy, and . . . who was sitting up there in the front seat beside Cal? He let his mind construct the scene again: the tattered interior of Cal's sedan beneath the light in the movie theater parking lot. Whose face had it been on the front seat passenger side? He pulled at the steering wheel as his patrol car lurched for gravel. It was Jenny.

If she stayed cooped up in the house any longer, she was going to go crazy. There was still a lot of work to be done on the Dandridge place, and Peggy had looked forward to a happy summer once she had the songwriting underway, sanding floors and stripping paint off the woodwork. Instead, the house had taken on the gloomy aspect of a prison, and the work undone spoke of squalor, rather than decorating potential. She looked at the clock. There wouldn't be any messages from Spencer for hours yet, and it was a fine cloudless day. The trees looked like bouquets against the sky. It was too pretty to stay inside. Maybe it was time to go out into the backyard. She hadn't been out there since she'd found Blondell; if she didn't go soon, she'd never go. She hurried out the kitchen door before she could change her mind.

The back porch steps needed a coat of paint, she decided. And the shrubbery could use a trimming. She ought to make a list. Maybe she should put up floodlights in the backyard as a security precaution. A sudden movement near the privet hedge caught her eye, and she froze, feeling her muscles constrict with fear.

It was a white rabbit.

She watched the fat long-haired bunny with drooping ears as it tried to wiggle through the hedge, and then she heard the cry of "Mel-lee" from the adjoining lawn. Jessie Traynham appeared above the hedge. She was wearing a white sundress and a necklace of polished stones. Her dark eyes flashed in search of her pet.

"He's in there!" called Peggy, hurrying to the boundary. "I just saw him."

"She hardly ever leaves the yard," said Mrs. Traynham,

frowning. "You hadn't seen her before, had you? I call her the vegetarian kitty."

Peggy stared. "You have a pet rabbit?"

Her neighbor sighed. "I suppose I do. A couple of years ago, the Dandridges rented your house to a family with young children, and they kept caged rabbits. That one escaped the day they moved, and they never could catch her, so here she stayed."

"It's odd that she's still around," said Peggy. The rabbit poked its head out of the hedge to reach for a dandelion.

"Oh, my dear!" Mrs. Traynham sighed. "Domestic rabbits don't have the sense that God promised animal crackers. The concept of hiding and starting a new life in the wild is not built into the bunny brain. This one just bounces around the yard eating grass—and flowers when I'm not looking! She had just enough sense to figure out that someone sneaking into her presence with a gunnysack should probably be avoided. If you become really insistent about stalking her, she'll go under the shed until you recover from your compulsion to disturb her."

"She should be easy to catch in the winter when there's nothing for her to eat."

"That was my reasoning," Jessie Traynham agreed. "I thought I'd wait until the grass was gone, and then she'd be too weak and hungry to escape, but before winter arrived, I found myself thinking, Why?"

"Why?"

"Yes. Why bother to catch her? There weren't any vicious dogs around to attack her, and she is as large as any of the neighborhood cats. They think she is eccentric, but they are polite. If I put her back in a cage, I'd have to find a home for her, or take care of her myself. That would mean feeding her twice a day, unfreezing her water dish in winter, changing her straw . . . I decided that it would be a lot easier to pretend she's a cat and to give her the run of the place. Believe me, a vegetarian kitty is a lot less trouble than a caged rabbit."

Peggy was smiling now, and the tense look in her face was gone.

Jessie Traynham was watching her closely. "I wonder if you'd like to come over and have some iced tea," she said. "It's made with mint grown right here in my yard."

"I guess I could," said Peggy, glancing back at the dark shape of her own house, shaded by the sprawling oaks. "Thank you. It would be good to talk."

Jessie Traynham settled her in a redwood lounge chair, talking all the while of Melisande, the wayward bunny, and about her roses. On the concrete patio, wreathed in pink rose bushes, were an assortment of lawn chairs and a glass-topped table shaded by a yellow canvas umbrella. After a few minutes, the white rabbit appeared and lurched toward a water dish in the shade.

"I'll just go in now and get the pitcher," said Jessie. She disappeared through the curtained French windows, and Peggy looked out at the well-kept lawn, wondering if her neighbor was motivated by a love of beauty, an obsession with order, or sheer boredom. The result was pleasant, though. Manicured flower beds of pansies and thrift encircled the lawn, and a huge white-flowered magnolia occupied pride of place in the center of the yard.

After a few minutes, Mrs. Traynham returned, carrying a cut-glass pitcher and matching glasses on a silver tray. "I could have brought out slices of pound cake," she said, attaching a sprig of mint to Peggy's glass. "But you are not a cake eater, from the look of you."

Peggy took a sip of her drink. "I haven't been eating at all," she murmured.

Jessie Traynham shook her head. "Not good," she

said. "If you can manage it, my dear, I think you will find that anger is more productive than fear."

"It's not the dog," said Peggy.

"No." Jessie Traynham set down her glass and leaned back in her chair. "I believe that you and I have something in common."

Peggy shrugged. "We're neighbors."

"That is not what I meant. I am given to understand that your dog was butchered in a fashion associated with Vietnam, was it not?"

"Yes. So?"

"It would seem that we are both victims of a war. My husband was a scientist at Oak Ridge. In August 1945 I left him. And he held no bitterness against me for it. I wonder if in your case it might be different."

Peggy rubbed her fingers against the cold side of the glass. "Do you believe in ghosts?"

Jessie Traynham's voice was harsh. "No, I do not," she replied. "And neither do you. Now let us dispense with theatrics and face this matter squarely so that it can be dealt with. Who is it that has such good reason to hate you?"

"I don't know that he has much reason to hate me," said Peggy slowly. "And, anyway, it shouldn't matter, because he has been dead for twenty years."

The older woman pointed to the oak tree at the edge of the woods in Peggy's yard. Its bark was still rusty with bloodstains. "Are you sure?"

"I was. I used to have an MIA bracelet with his name on it. He was in Vietnam, but he didn't make it back."

Matter-of-factly, Jessie Traynham refilled the glasses and drew her chair closer to Peggy's. "You will need to talk about this, in order to decide how you are going to tell the sheriff."

"What makes you think I haven't?"

"You can't eat. You start at noises. You haven't faced it yet."

"Okay," said Peggy with a sigh. "But I don't think it has anything to do with what's happening here. When I was in college, I used to sing with a guy I was sort of engaged to. He was from East Tennessee. Travis Perdue. We played coffeehouses and folk concerts around Chapel Hill. In our junior year we went to the Union Grove Fiddlers Convention, and somebody from a record company heard us. He offered me a recording contract, but only as a solo act."

"I see. And you took it."

"Of course."

"With your generation it is *of course*," said Mrs. Traynham grimly. "Perhaps that is wise."

"Well . . . I went on with my career, and he went back to Carolina. But I think he quit. Or flunked out. I don't remember. Anyway, he ended up in Vietnam. He used to write me letters. I wrote him back every so often. He was pretty hurt when we broke up. Then I got a letter from one of his buddies telling me he was missing. I never heard from him again."

"Perhaps until now."

"Oh, I don't know. It was a long time ago. He wouldn't even know where to find me."

"Celebrities are not hard to keep track of, if one is interested."

"Well . . . maybe. But I don't see why he'd want to harm me after all this time."

"Don't you, my dear? Let me see if I can explain it to you. You are partners, singing the same songs at the same places. Perhaps the act was even his idea." Peggy nodded. "You are discovered by a talent scout, and you abandon him both professionally and personally. I take it that the engagement was terminated?"

"It was never official."

"You go on to fame and fortune with a singing career that he can only watch from a distance. And where is your young man? In a jungle? In fear of his life? Dirty, sick, tired, afraid . . . I think you would make an excellent focus for his hatred."

"It isn't him," said Peggy. "You don't understand about being a celebrity. People think they know you. Whoever is harassing me will turn out to be someone I never heard of. Probably someone who is mentally unbalanced."

"Perhaps you are right. In any case, I see no harm in telling the sheriff about the young man you sang with. He may be able to advise you."

Peggy smiled bitterly. "Most of the mistakes in my life have come from taking a man's advice. What I should do is buy a gun."

Jessie Traynham sighed. "How we have changed since the days when Melanie sat on the steps of Tara waiting for Ashley to return from the war!"

Peggy met her gaze with a stony stare. "If I remember correctly, Melanie had a gun and used it."

"But not on Ashley."

"It isn't Travis, Mrs. Traynham. He's dead. You saw what they did to my dog. And now there's a young girl missing."

"From Hamelin? Who?"

"I don't know. I wasn't supposed to say anything. But she looked like I did when Travis knew me."

The silence stretched beyond them to the sun-dappled garden and the woods beyond the hedge. Melisande sat motionless in the short grass staring at shadows. Finally the old woman said, "Very well. If you want a weapon, you shall have it. My father had a pair of pistols, and I have kept them in very good condition, as I do my silver.

They are .45 caliber and rather cumbersome, but shooting them at close range requires no skill. Shall I lend you one?"

Peggy stood up and followed her into the house. "Yes, please."

It didn't take the full hour and a half to reach his destination, because he wasn't going all the way to Knoxville. He'd radioed the sheriff's department on the last stretch of I-40, and they had given him directions to the crime scene: a bridge site on a two-lane blacktop road a few miles south of I-40. At Exit 407, Spencer left the four-lane expressway to Knoxville and picked up the state road he had been told to follow. He had driven for several minutes through oak and beech woods before he realized that his internal Muzak was on again. It was playing an old Pat Boone tune, "Moody River," a song about a girl who drowned herself. Odd that Pat Boone should have recorded it; Spencer remembered him as almost mindlessly cheerful. The song had been a big favorite with the girls in his class—death for a lost love appealed to their morbid teenage romanticism. Maybe it was the backdrop of the war that had made them melodramatic. But none of them ever did kill themselves, except Robert Laurie, and that wasn't exactly for love. He had gotten his girlfriend pregnant, and he couldn't face telling his Baptist-strict parents. Abortions were illegal back then, and illegitimate babies were not casual occurrences. That had changed. "Moody River." The guy is standing beside the oak tree, staring into the river where the girl's body is floating. That was why the song was running through his mind. Spencer saw the concrete bridge up ahead, and in the level space to one side, he saw two white unmarked cars—Knox County detectives—and the crime van. There were going to be a lot of guys standing among the trees looking at the girl in the river, and they were all going to be as cheerful as Pat Boone. Crime scenes were like that.

He introduced himself to the Knox County deputy standing guard, and made his way along the riverbank to the investigation team. As he approached he could hear their laughter.

"This is the worst case of suicide I ever saw!" one of them said.

"You reckon she's French? Some tourist sees the sign 'French Broad River' and he follows the directions!" More laughter.

They were distancing death. Spencer understood it and said nothing. He introduced himself to the state investigator in charge, a big-boned man with Cherokee features and a forbidding expression. He was an ex-trooper named Winnow Ross.

"Yeah, I heard you were coming," Ross said, narrowing his eyes. "Dispatcher said you knew who the floater was. Is this some psychic shit or what?"

"Let's see if I'm right first. I brought a picture. Who found her?"

"Tourists. They stopped to take pictures of the bluffs." He pointed to the steep cliffs on the northwest side of the river. "One of 'em looked over on this side of the bridge and saw the body in the shallows. Freaked, of course."

They walked around photographers and measurers to the blanket-covered stretcher, set a little apart from the bustle of the crime scene. Ross opened the body bag, exposing the waxy face of a young girl, frozen in death. Her long, light hair was streaked with mud, and her mouth was open, like an inelegant sleeper. Spencer could see the red line on her neck, just above the edge of the covering.

"I don't think you want to see the rest, Mr. Arrowood," said the detective.

Spencer closed his eyes. "Was she ripped open?"

"Oh, yeah. Just like you'd butcher a deer." Ross looked at him intently. "How do you know so much about it?"

Spencer eased the photograph out of the pocket of his shirt and handed it to the detective. "I'll need to sit in on the investigation," he said. "It's her."

"Okay," said the investigator. "You can give the particulars to Boyd."

"There's something else I need to know about the body," said Spencer. "Is there any evidence of mutilation?"

Ross scowled. "We *will* need to talk, won't we?" He pulled the sheeting back to reveal the girl's bare shoulder, with the neatly razored incision open and bloodless.

They ended up at Peroulas, the restaurant on Market Square that was within walking distance of the City-County Building. They had time to kill before the coroner finished the autopsy, and, as Ross pointed out, it was as good a place as any to have a meeting. Besides, he had missed lunch.

The meeting consisted of Spencer, State Investigators Winnow Ross and Zee Boyd, and Fred Hall, a detective with the Knox County Sheriff's Department. With plates of fried chicken and cole slaw on the table, the problem of the murdered girl became a philosophical exercise, rather than a tangible horror. Because it did not threaten their own mortality, they could discuss it in solemn terms.

"The way I see it," said Spencer, "you all are going to end up in Wake County sooner or later, and I think it had better be sooner. This girl is from Hamelin, and I have reason to believe that the killer is someone familiar with that area." He brought out the postcards. "Y'all go ahead and eat, because this explanation is going to take a while."

He told them about Hamelin's new celebrity resident and the threats she had received. He showed them the photographs of the dog and the sheep, and he described the carving on the dog, relating LeDonne's theory about a Vietnam connection. Finally he showed them the album cover and explained the tie-in with the songs.

"We'll want to see that wire from the dog incident," said Ross, between mouthfuls of chicken.

"Was wire found on the victim?"

"No, but we may be able to do some matching with the nature of the wounds. Depends on water damage to the body. Not that there should be much. He heaved her into the shallows, damned near missed the river."

"You think the body was dumped off the bridge, then?" asked Spencer.

"That's what I'd do," said Boyd.

"The coroner can tell us if she was dead when she went in," said Hall.

"She was," said Boyd. "That riverbank was not the death site. She was killed somewhere else. The killer's car is probably a mess."

"Good," said Hall. "Then all we need is a suspect."

"I think you'll find him over my way," said Spencer.

"So you think that this individual was killed because she resembled this show business personality?" asked Ross, stabbing his fork in the air for emphasis.

"I think that possibility should be thoroughly checked out," said Spencer carefully.

"So maybe this singer woman knows who is doing it," Boyd suggested.

"She says not."

The two state investigators exchanged looks that said:

We're professionals. He's a politician. "We'll ask her again," said Ross.

"I've got my deputy checking out Vietnam veterans' organizations."

"We can check the ones in this area, too," said Fred Hall.

"Background check on this folksinger?"

"It's under way," said Spencer. He looked up just then and saw a familiar face staring at him from a nearby table. He didn't look away in time to pretend he hadn't recognized the tanned face with lean well-chiseled features that spoke of Nautilus machines and racquetball courts.

Chuck Winters, also something of a politician, whispered something to his tablemates and ambled over to Spencer with an almost-believable grin. "Hello, buddy!" he said. "What are you doing in the big city?"

"Police business," said Spencer, feeling the other officers' impatience at this interruption.

He had known Chuck Winters all his life, but he would never have thought of him as a friend. From the earliest days of elementary school, Chuck seemed to be practicing for his career as lawyer and civic gadabout, friend to those in power. There had always been a rushed quality to his charm that had made him seem important. Every phone conversation began with "I can't talk long," and every encounter with him was a breathless interval on his way to somewhere else. Chuck's parents may have established this routine, enrolling him in a succession of tennis lessons, swimming lessons, Scout activities, and piano lessons. Spencer always thought of Chuck Winters as a grainy photograph on a school election poster; he was always running for something.

"I can't talk long," Chuck went on, straddling a chair at the empty table next to Spencer. "I hear we're having a high school reunion soon. Just wanted to say that if there's anything I can do, you let me know."

"You can present the class plaque," said Spencer. "You're good at making speeches."

He had hoped that Chuck would agree to this without further inquiry, but he had been born with a lawyer's wariness. "What plaque is that, old buddy?"

"It's a list of the guys who were killed in Vietnam."

The attorney's smile faded. "I can't see my way clear to do that," he said, shaking his head. "The war didn't affect me very much at the time. I guess I was just so busy with classes at Duke, and we had a lot of fraternity work for charity. I had friends who were on both sides." He looked at Spencer and seemed to downshift from his public speaking mode. "Sometimes I get the crazy feeling I missed something. Anyway, I think you ought to get a vet to present it. Lord knows they deserve some respect now. But if you want to get up a scholarship fund for the children of KIAs, put me down for a grand."

"Why don't you handle that, Chuck? It sounds like something a lawyer ought to be in charge of."

Chuck's attention had wandered. He looked back at his own table, where plates were being stacked and napkins folded. "Well, gotta run," he said hurriedly to Spencer. "Sorry to interrupt your meeting. Just wanted to touch base with you."

When he was gone, Spencer said, "Sorry about the asshole."

"No problem," said Boyd. "Too bad he isn't a suspect."

Ross drained his coffee cup. "Okay," he said. "I think we're about done here anyway, Sheriff. Leave the postcards with us. We'll see what the lab can do with them. I guess that's all we need from you right now. You need to be getting back. I take it that the parents of the victim have not been notified."

"No," said Spencer. "I wanted to do it in person."

"Naturally. Well, you get on with it. We'll do what has to be done in Knoxville, and you can expect us in Hamelin sometime tomorrow."

"Looking forward to it," said Spencer.

Zee Boyd scowled. "I'm not."

DEAR PEGGY-O,

YOU WRITE ME ABOUT HOW TIRED YOU ARE, AND WHAT A DRAG IT IS BEING A PERFORMER, AND HOW ALL THESE NAMES ON RECORD COVERS ARE JUST SHALLOW, ORDINARY PEOPLE INSTEAD OF THE MYTHIC FIGURES WE THOUGHT THEY WERE. MAYBE YOU'RE A MYTHIC FIGURE, YOURSELF, PRETTY PEGGY-O. ANYWAY, I THINK YOU'RE JUST BULLSHITTING ME BECAUSE YOU FEEL GUILTY ABOUT MY LESS THAN DELUXE ACCOMMODATIONS.

MAYBE I'D LIKE TO HEAR ABOUT THE FANCY DINNERS YOU GO TO, AND THE STATELY MANSIONS YOU VISIT, WHERE YOU NO DOUBT DINE ON HUMMINGBIRD TONGUES AND PEASANT UNDER GRASS.—OOPS! SORREE. PHEASANT UNDER GLASS, I AIMED TO SAY. PEASANT UNDER GRASS IS WHAT WE HAVE.—MAYBE I'D LIKE TO HEAR ABOUT THE HIGH LIFE. I'M NOT SURE. IT WOULD MAKE A CHANGE FROM THE ATROCITY STORIES I HEAR THROUGH THE GRAPEVINE.

WELL, NOW I HAVE AN ATROCITY STORY OF

MY VERY OWN. SHALL I SHARE IT? MAYBE YOU CAN WRITE A SONG ABOUT IT. AND YOU CAN RECIPROCATE WITH THE INSIDE DOPE ON SHOW BIZ.

WE WERE TOOLING AROUND OUTSIDE THE COMPOUND IN A LIBERATED JEEP (WE WERE ARMED, OF COURSE; YOU NEVER COMPLETELY PLAY HOOKEY FROM THE WAR) JUST THE FOUR OF US, PLAYING TOURIST IN INDOCHINA. ME, MCKINNEY, SORENSON, AND WHAT'S-HIS-FACE, TAKING SNAPSHOTS OF THE GREEN MOUNTAINS, AND THE EXOTIC LANDSCAPES, AND THE PEOPLE WITH FUNNY HATS WALKING WATER BUFFALO. ANYWAY, WE SEE THIS LITTLE GIRL. TWELVE . . . MAYBE THIRTEEN. WHO KNOWS HOW OLD THEY ARE? THEY'RE SO LITTLE TO BEGIN WITH. SHE WAS DRESSED IN HER LITTLE PAJAMA COSTUME, LONG BLACK HAIR, SHY BROWN FACE THAT MAKES YOU THINK OF FAWNS.—AN UNFORTUNATE COMPARISON I AM SOON TO LEARN.

SHE'S SELLING RICE WINE.

AND OF COURSE MCKINNEY HAS TO HAVE SOME, BECAUSE HE WILL DRINK ANYTHING THAT DOESN'T COME OUT OF SOMEBODY ELSE'S—WELL, WE MUSTN'T BE CRUDE, MUST WE?—WE MUSTN'T CHEAPEN THE MOMENT, AS IT TURNED OUT TO BE MCKINNEY'S LAST. . . .

IT WAS BOOBY-TRAPPED.

SORENSON AND I WERE OFF WITH THE DAMN CAMERA, ME POSING WITH MY RIFLE ON A CONVENIENT BOULDER, MOUNTAINS IN BACKGROUND, BUGS GROOVING ON MY FEET . . . VERY SERGEANT YORK, WHEN ALL OF A SUDDEN WE HEAR A ROAR BEHIND US,

AND THERE IS A PILE I DON'T WANT TO LOOK AT WHERE MCKINNEY AND (WHAT WAS THE BASTARD'S NAME?) USED TO BE.

AND TINKERBELL IS RUNNING LIKE HELL.

AND I'M SITTING THERE POSING LIKE A GEEK, HOLDING MY RIFLE. SO IT WAS ME THAT HAD TO SHOOT HER. NEVER HAD TO DO THAT TO A PERSON BEFORE. JUST DEER BACK HOME. HUNTING WITH DAD TO PROVE THAT OLD TRAVIS HAS BALLS. ONLY I DON'T WANT TO DO IT THIS TIME. OLD DADDY ISN'T THERE TO BE IMPRESSED, AND HE MIGHT TAKE A DIM VIEW OF BLASTING LITTLE GIRLS ANYHOW. SO I'M THINKING MAYBE I'LL JUST WING HER, JUST TO STOP HER, YOU KNOW?—AND I RAISE MY RIFLE, WITH NO INTENT TO KILL IN MY HEART, BUT JUST HAVING TO USE THIS MECHANISM I HAVE HANDY TO STOP A FUGITIVE. AND AT THE LAST SECOND WHEN I SQUEEZED THAT TRIGGER, SOMETHING IN MY BRAIN SAID, "WHY THE HELL JUST STOP HER? DO YOU THINK IT WILL CHANGE ANYTHING? DO YOU THINK SHE CAN GET A LAWYER?" SO I FIXED THE SIGHT ON THE BASE OF HER NECK—MAYBE A LITTLE HIGHER—SO THAT THE BULLET WOULD GET HER IN THE HEAD.

IT SEEMS LIKE I TOOK TWENTY MINUTES LINING UP THAT SHOT, WHILE SHE'S RUNNING AWAY, KICKING UP SLOW-MOTION DUST WITH HER LITTLE SANDALS. IT SEEMS LIKE I HAD ALL AFTERNOON TO CONTEMPLATE THE PHYSICAL AND MORAL FACTORS INVOLVED IN MY INTENDED ACTION. BUT IT HAD TO HAVE BEEN SECONDS. JUST A COUPLE OF SECONDS.

IT WAS LIKE A SAM PECKINPAH MOVIE—

WHERE THINGS DIE IN SLO-OOW MOTION. PULLING THE TRIGGER WAS LIKE A BALLET EXERCISE, AND IT TOOK FOREVER FOR THE LITTLE GIRL TO BREAK STRIDE, AND TO THROW OUT HER ARMS AS IF TO CATCH HERSELF, AND FLOAT GENTLY TO THE GROUND. AND THEN THE SLOW MOTION STOPPED, AND SORENSON AND I RAN TO HER IN REAL TIME, BUT SHE WAS ALREADY DEAD.

NOT AN ATROCITY, YOU SAY? MERELY AN UNPLEASANT BUT NECESSARY ACT OF WAR? PERHAPS. BUT I HAD SHOT HER, AND THAT LEFT SORENSON STILL ACHING FOR HIS OWN REVENGE ON BEHALF OF MCKINNEY AND . . . MCCARTHY! THAT'S WHO HE WAS. OH YEAH. MCKINNEY IS DEAD, AND MCCARTHY DON'T KNOW IT. MCCARTHY IS DEAD AND MCKINNEY DON'T KNOW IT. THE BOTH OF 'EM DEAD AND THEY'RE COVERED IN RED, AND NEITHER ONE KNOWS THAT THE OTHER IS DEAD.

SO SORENSON TOOK HIS K-BAR AND GUTTED HER LIKE A DEER, AND WE HUNG HER ON A TREE BRANCH AS A MESSAGE TO CHARLIE.

HAVE YOU MET JOHN WAYNE YET, PEGGY? TELL HIM I REALLY LOVED HIM IN SANDS OF IWO JIMA.

TRAVIS

CHAPTER 11

I cheer a dead man's sweetheart,
Never ask me whose.

A. E. HOUSMAN

THE DRIVE BACK to Hamelin seemed twice as long because it consisted of one endless rehearsal of the unpleasant task ahead: telling the Winsteads that their daughter was dead. Being the bearer of bad tidings wasn't the worst aspect of the job of sheriff—car wrecks claimed that dubious honor—but it was a ceremony of anguish, and Spencer had never managed to establish a routine. No matter what the circumstances, he never escaped a taint of self-imposed guilt, as if his bringing the news was the only thing that made it so.

It was nearly seven o'clock, but daylight saving time made it an endless summer afternoon, without a hint of the coming dark. Spencer thought that darkness would have been a more appropriate accompaniment to his solemn duty.

Most of the people on the Winsteads' street were still enjoying the day. Children were shooting baskets at driveway backboards while their parents grilled hamburgers or watered lawns. Only the Winstead house looked shut and empty, its curtains drawn against the shining day.

As Spencer stopped the patrol car in their driveway, he felt them watching him. From behind drawn curtains they would try to read the message on his face, even before he reached their door. The spoken news was only a formality, the adding of detail to the truth already made known. As he got out of the car, his face was solemn. They deserved that warning, that time for preparation. He would not lie to them by smiling at thoughts of other things.

As soon as he reached the concrete stoop, Debra Winstead opened the door, smoothing her checked shirt over faded jeans. "Come in," she whispered, with a pleading look. He often wondered what that beseeching expression meant. *Lie to us? Don't say it, and it will not have happened?* What good does it do to beg the messenger?

Emory Winstead leaned against the mantelpiece, looking as if he wanted to fight. *(Okay! Okay! I take it back. She isn't dead!)* He motioned for Spencer to sit on the couch, but the sheriff shook his head. This had to be said standing. He waited while Debra crept over to join her husband.

"I'm sorry," said Spencer. "We found her."

Emory Winstead squinted at the sheriff as if he were questioning a suspect. "Found her where? Where is she now?"

"Would you like to sit down, sir?" said Spencer quietly.

"I want some answers."

"Her body was found today in the French Broad River. The case has been declared a homicide, and the state investigators have been called in. Your daughter's body is now in the Knox County morgue. You will not be called on to make an identification. I did that. If you would like to make arrangements with a local mortuary, her body can be returned to Hamelin for burial after the coroner has released it." He doubted that they took it all in, but he wanted to get it all said.

The girl's mother began to cry silent tears, but Emory Winstead's reaction was combative, as usual. "Who did it, Sheriff?"

Spencer looked away. "We don't know yet. The investigation has just begun."

"I'll kill him myself. I'll shoot him like a dog!"

"There are better ways to deal with your grief," said Spencer. Or your guilt, he finished silently.

Eight o'clock, but still light. There was one more thing that Spencer wanted to do before he called it quits for the day, but first he wanted to hunt up LeDonne. A call to the office got him the other county's dispatcher, so he figured that his best chance of finding the deputy was to try him at home.

LeDonne lived two pastures past the town limits, in a small white frame house that he rented. The lawn was mowed almost often enough, and the hedge bordering the road was trimmed back so that it did not impair motorists' view on the curve; other than that, LeDonne was an indifferent tenant. The faded linoleum and discolored paint were decades old, and the furnishings were second-hand and sparse. LeDonne didn't seem to care. He had few visitors—none by invitation.

The sheriff pulled into the dirt road that led to the adjoining farm and parked in the space beside LeDonne's Volkswagen. As soon as he slammed the car door, he heard the barking of LeDonne's Samoyed husky. LeDonne walked out to meet him.

"Evening, Sheriff," he said. "I take it we're headed into overtime?"

"That's right. The body in Knox County was our missing teenager. The state boys will be here in the morning." He followed LeDonne to the backyard, where two lawn chairs were set out under a mountain ash whose red berries brightened the otherwise plain expanse of lawn.

"You want a Pepsi?" asked LeDonne.

"No. We need to hurry. I want us to go and talk to Peggy Muryan again tonight, but I figured we needed to exchange information first. How'd it go today?"

"Not much to tell," said LeDonne, sitting down in the other chair. The white husky lay down beside the chair, just out of reach. "Alderman Tyler stopped by. He's still got that bee in his bonnet about the war on drugs. Wants us to get the state's helicopter and cruise the county looking for marijuana crops."

"Not a bad idea," said Spencer. "It's about harvest-time. Just because Tyler is a jerk doesn't mean he's always wrong."

"No. But I assume the present situation will take priority. Do you want me in on the investigation?"

"Sit in on it tomorrow and see how it goes," said Spencer. "The death seems to tie in to the threats on Peggy Muryan, so there is a possibility of a Vietnam connection. What did you get from the veterans' groups?"

"Nothing definite. They're going to go through their files and get back to us. What did you get in Knoxville?"

"I think it's our animal killer, Joe. The victim was nude, with some insignia carved on her right shoulder. I couldn't make it out, though. All this seems to be a vendetta against the folksinger, somehow related to Vietnam." He told LeDonne about "The Knoxville Girl," and about the resemblance between Rosemary Winstead and the face on the old album cover. "The dog belonged to Peggy Muryan, and the girl looked like her," said Spencer. "I don't see where the sheep fits into this, though."

"Maybe he needed one more warm-up round before he killed a human being," said LeDonne.

"Yeah, maybe. Anyhow, I think it's time we broke the news to Miss Muryan and pressed for some answers."

LeDonne shrugged. "If he's a real psycho, she's probably never heard of him."

"She's the only lead we've got."

"Okay. Before we go, let me go inside and call Martha."

"Call Martha? Why?"

LeDonne looked away. "Oh, I said I might drop by for dinner."

The sheriff tried not to look surprised. "You were going to have dinner with Martha?"

"Unless something came up."

LeDonne's indifference was hardly flattering to his would-be hostess, but Spencer considered the possibility that he could be faking it. Spencer almost smiled, picturing Martha's excitement over this breakthrough. Why spoil it? LeDonne was off duty, after all, and the case technically belonged to the TBI, anyhow. "Listen," he said carefully, "I believe I can question one ninety-eight-pound folksinger without an officer for backup. And if I do need you for anything, I know Martha's phone number by heart. So why don't you take her up on that offer of a free meal?"

"Whatever you say."

"No, you go on. This questioning isn't official, anyhow. The state boys will do it all over again tomorrow. I just thought I'd let her know what's going on." Besides, he thought, Martha would kill me if I blew her chance. As Spencer walked back to the car, he felt a half-serious urge to turn and say: *Bless you, my children.* He wished them luck.

* * *

He closed the car door, but before he could go up the steps to the circular porch, a voice from the shadows said, "May I help you?" and he turned to see Peggy Muryan, guitar in hand, watching him from beneath the oaks in the side yard. If she hadn't been wearing white slacks and a white sweater, he wouldn't have seen her at all.

"I was just about to go in," she told him. "It's nearly dark, and I could feel myself waiting for something. Maybe I should get another dog. For protection."

Spencer hesitated. "Maybe you should."

Something in the tone of his voice made her frown. "It's bad, isn't it?"

"Do you want to go in now?"

She shook her head. "Have a seat," she said, pointing to a wrought-iron bench under the largest oak. She eased onto the seat beside him, cradling the guitar against her. As he talked, she strummed it softly, never looking at the frets as her fingers set the chords.

"I don't want to upset you . . ." he began. "And if you want us to post a guard, we will. But I think your best bet is to be straight with me on this investigation."

"You found her." She bent her head, listening to the ripple of the strings. "The Knoxville Girl."

"Yes. Just like the song says. And there was a mark on her similar to the one that was carved on your dog." He waited, but she continued to play. "The Tennessee Bureau of Investigation will be here tomorrow. They know of your connection to the case, and they will want to talk to you. If you don't cooperate, we'll do background checks on you until we know everything there is to know about you, including what kind of toothpaste you use. If you tell me now, we can start doing something about this just that much sooner. Maybe before somebody else gets hurt."

Almost imperceptibly, the song changed. After a

moment's reflection, Spencer thought he recognized an old Bob Wills tune called "Faded Love."

"I will tell you," said Peggy. "And it isn't going to do you a damn bit of good."

"Who's doing this?"

"I told you once that when I was in college I used to sing with a guy named Travis Perdue."

Spencer nodded. He remembered the name from the back of the record album he had taken to Knoxville. "You sang those songs with him? 'Little Margaret'? 'The Knoxville Girl'?"

"Yes. And when I went national, they used him for backup vocals on that first album, and then they dropped him completely." Her fingers paused, arched over the steel strings. "I guess I dropped him, too. We had called ourselves engaged, back at Carolina. Before there were other possibilities."

"So he has a grudge against you?"

"He didn't get over it, no," said Peggy. "But considering that he has been dead for twenty years, I don't see that it matters."

"Dead?"

"Yeah. He was killed in Vietnam. Well, missing in action. It's the same thing. He used to write me, and one day the letters just stopped coming, and later I heard that he had been shot down. I never heard from him again. But he used to type his letters to me, using all capital letters. He said it was faster, and he didn't like to have to worry about grammar."

"All caps . . . like the postcards. Were they in his handwriting?"

"I couldn't tell. His trademark was that portable typewriter. I haven't seen his handwriting in a long, long time. He's been dead a long time."

"Apparently not. Do you remember his Social Security number?"

"Of course not! After *twenty years*?"

"His birthday, then?"

"Sometime in October. The third, I think. 1948. Why?"

"If we have his full name and date of birth, we can trace him through the Defense Department. Where was he from?"

She shrugged. "Erwin. I think. His parents moved, though, while we were in college. I forget where."

"Is that why you're here?"

Peggy considered it. "I guess it is, in a way. He took me home with him one time, and we drove through Hamelin while he was showing me the sights. We passed this house, and I said, 'Someday when we get rich and famous, let's buy this place!' I guess I never got it out of my system."

"Maybe he didn't, either."

She shook her head. "He's dead."

"Yeah, maybe. The name and date of birth should be enough to go on," he told her. "Is there anything else? Have you received any other threats? Phone calls? Any signs of a trespasser?"

"No."

"Is there someone who can come and stay with you? Parents?"

"My dad is still alive, but I'd never call him. He feels about me the way he feels about UNC's basketball team—tremendously proud and concerned with their achievements, but he'd never let one of them into his home, and he wouldn't want to spend time actually talking to them. He feels the same way about me. I'm somebody to root for that he doesn't much like as a person."

"I can get you a guard."

She smiled. "I have a standing invitation to visit my neighbor, Mrs. Traynham. I might just do that."

"Good. As I said, the investigators will be over here to see you tomorrow. I'll tell you about this, though, and we'll call Washington first thing in the morning. I'll check on you tomorrow. And, of course, the reunion is day after tomorrow. Are we on for that?"

"Sure. What could be safer than a room full of people?"

"Are you sure you're all right?" He stood up to leave.

Peggy nodded. "I'll call you if I need to."

"Good. Now that we know what we're looking for, things will be easier. You'll be glad you told me everything."

As he walked away, she continued to strum the guitar, as if she had forgotten his existence. Before the intricacies of the chord progression absorbed her attention, it occurred to her that she had not told him everything. She had failed to mention that she had a gun.

Nobody worked at the *Hamelin Record* after five, but if you knew the workings of Wake County, you would always have a pretty good idea where to find Jeff McCullough. This was Wednesday night, which meant either the Board of Education meeting or the County Board of Supervisors, depending on which Wednesday it was. In either case, it meant the courthouse, and since it was nearly nine o'clock, the meeting should be within minutes of breaking up.

Spencer parked the car in the gravel lot behind the building and slipped in through the side entrance, hoping to catch McCullough in the hall. It wasn't that he didn't trust Peggy Muryan, but experience had taught him that everyone edits the truth, and the more respectable a person is, the more likely he is to gloss over unpleasant facts because he has an image to preserve. He wanted to know what McCullough had come up with on the folksinger's glamorous past.

Spencer stood in the doorway listening to L. J. Harrelson trying to wind up the meeting. The sheriff suspected that L. J. was a secret fan of a ten o'clock TV show, and that he wanted to make sure he got home in time for it. Certainly his civic patience dwindled rapidly after nine-twenty.

As the final formalities were taking place, people began to file out of the meeting room, trying to beat the parking lot traffic jam. Spencer waylaid McCullough on his way to the men's room.

"Jesus, can't it wait?" McCullough complained. "I've been holding my breath for the last twenty minutes!"

"I'll be out here," said Spencer, and settled back against the wall, nodding a greeting to the local politicians as they strolled down the hall.

The reporter returned just in time to extricate Spencer from a one-sided discussion of the local speed limits. Theodore Nelson, no doubt the recipient of a speeding ticket, was insisting that residential speed limits in Wake County be raised to forty-five miles per hour. The sheriff was nodding, trying to look interested; he had found that this approach worked better than explaining the facts to a fanatic who mainly wanted to hear himself talk.

"Sorry, Mr. Nelson," said McCullough with a toothy smile. "I have to confer with the sheriff. Police business." He steered Spencer Arrowood down the back stairs before Nelson could voice an objection. "That was a close call, wasn't it?" he remarked to the sheriff. "You could have been standing in that hallway all night."

"Yeah, thanks. You got a minute?"

"You mean an hour? Sure. You gonna read me my rights?"

"No. I might give you some coffee, though. Come on over to the office."

"I was going to come and see you tomorrow, anyhow," said McCullough, as they crossed the gravel parking lot. "The funeral home called about an obituary for Rosemary Winstead."

"They don't waste much time, do they?"

"They can't afford to. Neither can I. I have to run some kind of story on it next week. What can you tell me? Is it tied in to this business about Peggy Muryan?"

Spencer reached for the keys to the office. "Off the record?" he said. "I think it is."

Jeff McCullough walked over to the collection of coffee mugs on Martha's worktable and inspected them, trying to pick the cleanest one. "Off the record?" He groaned. "I'm a *reporter*, Sheriff. I'm not asking you all this stuff out of a disinterested quest for knowledge!"

Spencer was scooping coffee out of the can. "This is a murder case," he said.

"I'm printing whatever Knoxville prints," said McCullough. "Now what about local stuff?"

Spencer shrugged. "Interview her friends. Talk about what a sweet kid she was."

"You have no leads?"

"Nothing I want to read about in the *Record*," said Spencer. "Later on, maybe. What did you find out about Peggy Muryan?"

"Nothing earthshaking. Are you going to rinse that pot out? Maybe you ought to scrub it."

Spencer glared at him. "I know how to make coffee," he said. "Now tell me what you found out."

"Well, I talked to the guy at the National Public Radio station. You know, the one who does the offbeat music show. Bill Adamson. He said that Peggy Muryan was a really good singer, and that she'd been moderately successful. Bill says talent doesn't have much to do with it."

Spencer blinked. "Not with heavy metal, maybe, but Peggy sang alone."

"Yeah. What he meant was that talent by itself won't put you in the top ranks. Some of it is luck, and the material you do, what the pubic happens to want at the time, and how skillfully you are promoted. Joan Baez had a beautiful voice, but she was also the ethnic Madonna that the idealistic left wanted for a patron saint in the sixties. Peggy Muryan was white bread—less appeal. She did okay. Bill's not sure she has comeback potential. He says he sees a lot of people like her, most of 'em wanting to do a guest shot on his show. They can't wean themselves from the spotlight, so they become gypsy troubadours. They play county fairs and folk cafés, and they do benefits for the Central America crowd, and they hustle albums under their own label. It's a marginal living, but it's show biz. If they went to law school, they'd have to admit they were finished."

Spencer nodded. Peggy had told him much the same thing over dinner at the Parson's Table. He set a steaming mug of coffee in front of the reporter. "Okay," he said. "She isn't rich. Is she influential? Are there any groups that might have cause to hate her?"

"Bill says that insanity is practically a requirement in music fandom, and if you don't believe it, he'll let you kneel on his Graceland prayer rug . . . but he said he doesn't associate Peggy Muryan with any specific cause. She wasn't all that political. He figures that could have hurt her career back in the sixties, when being political was the way to go. He said she could *use* some craziness. It would help her comeback."

The sheriff and McCullough looked at each other. Could she be staging this just to get some free publicity?

"I don't think so," said the reporter, responding to the unspoken question. "She hasn't called any press conferences, and she hasn't tried to draw attention to herself. I can't see her killing a young girl just for publicity, either. If we were talking Satanist heavy metal, I'd consider it, but this stuff won't attract the folkies. It has undertones of Manson, and you know what *he* did to the commune culture."

"How about Peggy Muryan's personal life? Is there any gossip about her in the business?"

McCullough took another gulp of coffee and made a face. "Bill says the music business is like a small town. The word on Peggy Muryan is that she's committed to her music, and that's all. She's not out to be a big sister to newcomers in the business, and she doesn't do many benefits unless there's something in it for herself. She's not the party type, he said."

"Did he mention any singing partners she's had?"

"No. Why?"

"Never mind," said Spencer. "It isn't much of a lead."

"You don't have much to choose from," McCullough pointed out. "Anything I can help with?"

Spencer thought about it. The TBI would take over in the morning, and their resources were better than his and McCullough's put together, but he decided to offer the reporter something to work on, as a reward for his efforts so far.

"In college she used to sing with a guy from East Tennessee. His name was Travis Perdue. She thinks he was killed in Vietnam. Wouldn't hurt to find out."

McCullough nodded slowly. The mention of Vietnam was not lost on him. "I'll check around," he said. "Where in East Tennessee was he from?"

"Try Erwin."

The reporter let out a low whistle. "Close enough."

"Yeah. If he made it back."

"There's more to this than you're telling me, isn't there, Sheriff?"

Spencer sighed. "Maybe so. But remember that I warned you: you could go to a lot of trouble tracking down a dead man."

Joe LeDonne sat in the darkness, as still as the timbers of the porch itself. Only his hand, resting on the wooden railing, was illuminated in the moonlight.

"I used to know how to read palms," said Martha softly, holding out her own hand.

After a moment's consideration, LeDonne turned his palm upward, as expressionless as if he had not heard. Martha let it rest gently against her fingers, tilting it a bit to catch the light. She felt her muscles tighten against the urge to embrace him.

He had arrived at twenty past eight, saying only that Spencer was back from Knoxville, and that the girl was dead. Martha changed the subject; she didn't want police work to intrude on her time with him. She set the table with her grandmother's linen tablecloth, and she'd fried a chicken and made biscuits, remembering that this was LeDonne's favorite meal. She had made bright, rehearsed conversation during dinner, and he had said little in reply, but occasionally he smiled. The restlessness wasn't there, for once. She hoped that it was a start.

She looked at the filament of lines in his right hand. Martha had forgotten most of what little she had known about palm reading—which line was the head and which was the heart? Did it matter? Both stopped far short of the heel of his hand. One thing she did remember, though: the meaning of those little criss-crosses all over his palm, as if he had been grasping at razor blades. "You worry too much," she told him.

Joe shook his head. His hand in hers felt cool and tense, but he did not pull it away. She slid her forefinger across his palm. "I wish I could touch you," she said.

"Want me to spread my legs?" The razor was in his voice now.

She swallowed her breath. "I didn't mean . . . Maybe I did. If I did make love to you, it would feel like touching you, for that long, anyway. I keep fighting against this feeling that you're not really here. I mean, you talk and you listen, but it's like . . ."

". . . somebody in a sentry box. And the real me is in the compound, behind an eight-foot wall." He sounded amused.

"It's true, isn't it?"

"Maybe. But there's no way in. And even if there were, you don't want in. I'm not worth it. There's things you couldn't ever understand, Martha."

"I've been trying. I . . . I read some books. About Vietnam and all."

He shook his head. "I can't sleep. I can't hold a job. You're looking for security and, lady, I am anything but that."

"You seem so alone. And I care about you so much it hurts." She hugged him gently, pressing her face against his shoulder, because that hadn't been something she could say looking at him. She felt his muscles tighten as she pressed her cheek against him, and then his hands touched her lightly in the small of her back, a perfunctory response, almost an afterthought.

Joe pressed his nose against her hair, letting her scent remind him that he was holding a woman, not one of the nugs . . . not the kid who got it in the gut in his first firefight . . . his face had been wet, too, against the shoulder of Private LeDonne.

"I can fuck you, if you want, Martha," he said at last, over the noise in his head.

She looked up at him and nodded, with that same pleading look of something that wants you to put a stop to its misery.

DEAR PEGGY,

I KEEP WANTING TO TALK TO YOU ABOUT THE PAST—OUR PAST, TO BE SPECIFIC—AND I HAVE GIVEN SOME THOUGHT AS TO WHY THIS IS. THE PAST WAS NOT PERFECT (KIND OF PRESUMPTUOUS TO HAVE A VERB TENSE CALLED PAST PERFECT, DON'T YOU THINK?), BUT IT SURE AS HELL BEATS THE PRESENT TENSE, WHICH I MUST SAY IS VERY APTLY NAMED.

AND THE FUTURE IS NOT SOMETHING I DWELL ON, FOR I HAVE READ THE FORTUNE COOKIE, POPPET, AND IT HAS CRUMBLED. I HAVE FACED THE VERY REAL POSSIBILITY THAT I AM NOT IMMORTAL. THAT GOING DOWN IN BLACK SMOKE IS NOT JUST A COLORFUL EVENT IN OTHER PEOPLE'S LIVES. I REGRET TO STATE THAT I AM NOT COMING BACK, AND WHILE THIS THOUGHT MAY DISTRESS YOU, IT PISSES THE HELL OUT OF ME. I WANT TO COME BACK SEASONED AND WISE FROM MY MILITARY SERVICE, A NEW JAMES JONES, CREATING A BODY OF LITERATURE OUT OF THE PAIN OF MY WAR EXPERIENCE. I

WAS THE IMPORTANT ELEMENT; THE WAR WAS ONLY A BACKDROP TO MY TALENT. UNFORTUNATELY, I OUTGREW THIS EGOISM, AND BECAUSE I NO LONGER BELIEVE IT, IT HAS CEASED TO BE TRUE, AND I AM GOING TO DIE.

YOU CAN ADD ME TO YOUR LIST OF SAD SONGS. TRUE THOMAS, MAYBE, WHO FOLLOWED THE QUEEN TO FAIR ELFLAND AND WAS NO MORE SEEN ON EARTH. ONLY THIS THOMAS DIDN'T GET INVITED TO DISNEYLAND; THE QUEEN TOOK OFF WITHOUT HIM. I ENDED UP IN THE WRONG SONG. ME AND SORENSON, WHO SIT AROUND AND JAM WITH MY GUITAR ABOUT "OLLY-OLLY-OXEN FREE" AND BROTHERLY LOVE . . . ALL OF A SUDDEN WE FIND THAT WE ARE IN A DIFFERENT KIND OF SONG, AND WE ARE THE BAD GUYS.

POOR ELLEN SMITH . . . HOW WAS SHE FOUND? SHOT THROUGH THE HEART, LYING COLD ON THE GROUND.

WHEN YOU AND I SANG THAT, PEG, IT WAS JUST A SONG. SORENSON AND I SANG IT AND WE CRIED. THEN WE GOT STINKING DRUNK. I CAN STILL SEE THAT LITTLE BODY CRUMPLED ON THE GRASS, WITH HER LITTLE GIRL FACE. SORENSON STAYS DRUNK, AND LORD KNOWS I TRY, BUT I CAN'T SEEM TO GET THERE. WHY BOTHER WITH REMORSE? THIS WAR IS GOING TO GET ME, TOO.

IF I DON'T DIE, PLEASE MANAGE TO LOSE THIS LETTER SO THAT I WILL NOT BE REMINDED OF WHAT A MELODRAMATIC LITTLE

SNOT I WAS AT TWENTY-TWO. IF I EVER SEE YOU AGAIN, THAT IS.

IF EVER I RETURN, PRETTY PEGGY-O . . .

I DON'T THINK I WILL, PEG. JUST LATELY I'VE BEEN TRYING TO CONCENTRATE ON FUTURE EVENTS—SAYING TO MYSELF, I WILL GET OUT OF HERE EVENTUALLY—BUT IT ALL SEEMS IRRELEVANT AND UTTERLY UNREAL. WHO IS GOING TO MAKE IT TO THE NCAA FINAL FOUR NEXT YEAR? WILL YOU AND I EVER PICK UP WHERE WE LEFT OFF? WHAT WILL I DO FOR MY BIRTHDAY? WILL I LEARN TO SKI?—AND I FEEL DETACHED FROM IT, FROM ALL OF IT. IT'S LIKE READING SOMEBODY ELSE'S HOMETOWN PAPER: FACTS WITH NO EMOTIONAL CONTENT. AND I THINK THAT MEANS I'M MOVING AWAY FROM HERE. GETTING READY FOR CHECK-OUT TIME.

MAYBE WHEN YOU ARE OLD, YOU WILL UNDERSTAND WHAT IT IS TO GET ACQUAINTED WITH DEATH, ON A SLOW AND CASUAL BASIS, BEFORE DEVELOPING A RELATIONSHIP. MAYBE IT'S BETTER TO GO QUICK WHILE YOU STILL CARE ABOUT THINGS. THE PEOPLE OVER HERE SAY THAT GHOSTS ARE PEOPLE WHO WENT TOO QUICK, BEFORE THEY GOT USED TO THE IDEA. I THINK I'M JUST WANDERING OFF, LIKE SOMEONE LEAVING A BIG SUNDAY AFTERNOON GARDEN PARTY. I'LL JUST KEEP WALKING, AND I'LL NEVER BE MISSED.

IT'S OKAY IF YOU FORGET ME, PEG. SOMETIMES I EVEN FORGET MYSELF. MIDNIGHT . . .

LAST CIGARETTE . . . LAST SHOT IN THE FIFTH.
SIGN-OFF TIME FROM:

TRAVIS PERDUE AND JACK DANIELS

CHAPTER 12

If ever I return, Pretty Peggy-O,
If ever I return, Pretty Peggy-O,
If ever I return, all your cities I will burn,
Destroying all the ladies in the area-o.

"FENNARIO"

TOMORROW WAS THE reunion.

It was an early morning, even for Martha. But, then, she hadn't been able to sleep. She got to the office by seven-fifteen, which was full sun by that time of an August morning anyhow. She wore her khaki skirt and a scoop-necked olive tee. Very military, she thought, catching a glimpse of herself in the bathroom mirror as she filled the coffeepot. It showed where her thoughts were. She sat at her desk, waiting for coffee noises from the percolator, and tried to think of something to do besides rearrange her pencils. She watered the plants and ran a wet paper towel across the filing cabinets. It was twenty to eight before she remembered to switch off the night call forwarding from the neighboring county. Just as well. She had her own thoughts to keep her company; most of them centered on Joe LeDonne and the potential ruin he could make of her life.

They hadn't talked much the night before. Not that Joe LeDonne ever talked much, anyway. But he had been more gentle than she had expected, and he didn't seem to forget that she was there. So often it seemed to Martha that during sex men became so involved with the female body at their disposal that they forgot that there was a person *inside* it, so to speak. Martha had expected Joe to be one of those, but he wasn't. Still, he hadn't been much on spoken endearments or late-night chatting. A little after one, he'd whispered, "I ought to go now," and she'd offered him coffee, but he said that tomorrow was going to be a long day, and so he'd left.

Martha had tried to sleep, without much success. Her mind kept replaying the evening, as if there were some clue to their fate that would be revealed to her if only she examined each word and gesture closely enough.

Martha poured coffee into her green chipped mug and took a tentative sip, savoring the bitterness. You'd think she would have learned her lesson about men with Leon Jarvis. Or with any of the other jokers she'd been dealt in the years that followed. It didn't take a palm reader to tell that Joe LeDonne was trouble. Falling for a Lost-Cause Man was a young woman's luxury, and Martha knew that she no longer qualified as a young woman. She avoided mirrors in strong sunlight: the lines were already there. When you are closing in on forty, relationships should be short-term investments, calculated to produce quick dividends in upscale home ownership, a midsize American car of one's own, and freedom from the neurasthenia of self-support in genteel poverty. Such an emotional investment usually meant an older man—widowed or newly divorced—who needed an agreeable companion, someone willing to trade sex for upkeep. Martha knew that she had another decade before her search for such an arrangement became urgent, but the sooner she took care of it, the better. Pickings were limited in a town the size of Hamelin. And the brittle women who drank too much and let the desperation leak out of their pores like cheap perfume—they usually ended up as regulars at the Mockingbird Inn. It wasn't something Martha wanted to think about. She didn't plan to join them.

Joe LeDonne was not the answer to any of her troubles—except that he made them seem small by comparison. Imagine growing old worrying about the *two* of you to support. Wondering if he'd get sick with that Agent Orange thing, or if he'd have a mental breakdown and have to have long-term care. She shook her head, smiling at her own folly. Talk about confidence! Planning your health coverage after a one-night stand!

She wished LeDonne would hurry up and get to work. She thought that she could tell with one long look whether or not there was any future between them. Until then, there wasn't much point in worrying about it. Besides, she had enough on her mind as it was. Tomorrow was Friday—the first night of the reunion—and Martha expected to be pestered with phone calls all day. People would be getting into town and using her for a message center. Plus there was all the stuff she had to see about: the food, the flowers, name tags to buy. Damn this murder business! She couldn't very well ask for the day off with Spencer up to his holster in state cops. Martha began to make a list of Things to Do.

It was like the senior prom all over again. Or was it? After twenty years Martha had a hard time remembering what she had done on the day of the prom. She remembered the white net ballerina-length dress that her mother had insisted on buying. Was there anything she could have looked worse in? Her shapeless stick-legs seemed to plummet for miles beneath the snowball skirt, and her bony neck and shoulders stuck out above it, making her look like a fat white goose. The memory of the night was colored with her hatred for that dress, and whenever she thought of it she always wondered the same thing: did her mother make her look ugly on purpose?

Martha's mother had an upholstered figure that added ten years to her age. Perhaps she begrudged her daughter a shapely body, just as she resented every mouthful of food that Martha could eat without fear of calories. Martha could never rid herself of the feeling that her mother had wanted to sabotage her adolescence in small, hurtful ways—like the ugly prom dress. Martha remembered that Tyndall had looked elegant that night in a floor-length gown of emerald silk. She had seemed to be on the dance floor every minute, gliding about the room on the arm of one football player after another: Cinderella playing the field. In Martha's memory of that night, Tyndall was always looking upward into some boyish face and laughing with pleasure. To this day Martha wasn't sure whether she envied Tyndall Johnson her effortless beauty or the mother's love that made it possible.

What *had* the prom been like? It had smelled like English Leather and White Shoulders cologne—and smuggled beer. The popular people had all crowded together, laughing and talking as usual, accustomed to social events. They danced with each other, as if no one else were there. The rest of the class stood awkwardly about the crepe-papered room, feeling the bass notes in waves from the speaker system, wondering what they should be doing, and whether this was *fun*. They knew that going to the prom was the high point of their senior year, but they weren't sure what was required of them, and so they hung back. Not that the girls had any choice in the matter, Martha reflected. Back then, girls were supposed to stand around in clumps waiting for some teenage martyr to ask them to dance. It didn't seem to happen very often. So you stood and chattered to your friends, and you pretended not to be mortified that no one wanted you. Martha remembered drinking endless cups of sugary strawberry punch and talking to Joyce Overton about which one of the men from U.N.C.L.E. was the cutest: David McCallum or Robert Vaughn. But both she and Joyce would have traded a roomful of U.N.C.L.E. agents and assorted movie stars for just one gawky high school boy on prom night.

Was it that way for the guys, too? Did they dread rejection as they hung in corners on the opposite side of the room, pretending indifference to the whole affair? Martha thought of asking Spencer when he got in, but then she remembered that Spencer hadn't gone to the prom. No one knew why he hadn't shown up. They didn't find out until later that Cal had been killed. Martha couldn't remember being too concerned about Spencer's absence, though. She hadn't known him very well back then. Besides, her own misery that evening had overshadowed everything else.

Tomorrow's party was going to be different. If it had taught them nothing else, twenty years of living past high school had taught them self-preservation. Most of the class of '66 would bring their own dates to the reunion dance, just as she was bringing Joe LeDonne. No one was going to risk putting his ego on the line; they would come prepared with dates, flattering clothes, and a well-rehearsed, carefully edited biography. They would all be kind to each other. High school was enough torture for one lifetime.

Martha had eight things on her To Do list by the time Joe LeDonne arrived. She pretended to be so absorbed in her task that she did not hear him come in. Let him save face, she thought, if he doesn't want to deal with me right now. She began to draw little stars in the margin beside some of the items on the list.

LeDonne looked at her for a minute. "Morning," he drawled, scooting a chair next to her desk.

She looked up and managed a smile. "Hi, Joe."

"Brought you something." He laid a waxed-paper-wrapped honey bun on the edge of her desk. It glistened with melted sugar, sticking to the wrapping like a fly in a spiderweb.

Martha eyed the noxious pastry. "You first!" she said.

"I've already had mine," said Joe, rocking the chair back and forth. "Thanks all the same."

Martha set down her pen and looked at him. "How are you?" she said carefully.

He shrugged. "I slept okay. That's more than I can say most of the time. What about you?"

"Distracted," she said, tapping the list. "This reunion."

He nodded. "Yeah. Plus the state cops. Doubt if we'll get much of a breather for a while. But, if we don't have to work next Tuesday night . . . are you busy?"

"No," said Martha. Instantly she wondered if she should have been more hesitant. Playing high school hard-to-get was still second nature.

"Okay. I'm supposed to go to Knoxville, and I thought maybe you should go along." He wasn't looking at her now. His voice was husky with some kind of emotion, she couldn't tell what.

Martha waited.

"There's a support group there for vets. And people who have to deal with 'em. Thought you might like to meet some folks. Other women, you know. Hear how it is."

Martha nodded slowly. "Yeah. Yeah, I want to go," she whispered.

"Good," said LeDonne. "I think . . . I think it won't be easy."

"I know," said Martha.

He walked away then, as if the conversation had not taken place at all. Martha could hear him in Spencer's office, whistling as he ran the copy machine. Slowly she reached for the honey bun and unwrapped it from the sticky paper. Wincing a little, she took a tentative bite.

Sally Howell eased her white Mercury Lynx into the gravel parking lot beside the sheriff's office; she didn't want to stir up too much road dust—no time to wash the car before the reunion. "Maybe I should have borrowed Tom Howard's BMW." She grinned to herself, thinking how amused her office mate would be at the request. After all, weren't reunions supposed to be about impressing people? She struggled with the cardboard sunshade, positioning it against the front windshield to ward off the already blazing morning sun. That ought to keep the car reasonably cool until she got back—not that this visit was going to take long. After twenty years, she still couldn't think of anything much to say to Martha. She didn't dislike Martha; that wasn't it. There just didn't seem to be any point at which their lives touched.

She scooped up the tapes and her straw handbag and carefully locked the door as she got out. Living in Knoxville had taught her that. Just as it had taught her to walk quickly and purposefully to wherever you were going and to carry a sharpened "church key" on the end of her key chain, positioned for ready access in case anyone approached her. She was wearing dressy flat shoes—because high heels are hard to run in—and a blue sundress—not too short, not too revealing. Knoxville was a long way from Hamelin—not in miles but in light-years. Her fingers played with her key chain weapon, and she remembered the talks she and Tyndall used to have about "how to say no to a boy." They had concentrated on psychology in those days. Now people tended to focus on handguns. Now there was a rape counseling center on campus, and half the women Sally knew had taken classes on self-defense. Where had all the crazy people come from?

Across the street on the park bench, she saw a black-caped Ninja eating a doughnut. Where the *hell* had all the crazy people come from? Now it seemed that not even sleepy old Hamelin was immune. All the radio news broadcasts had carried stories about the murder of the Winstead girl. I wonder what she was like, thought Sally, and she realized that, like everyone else who heard the news, she was really thinking, *I wonder why she had it coming to her.* Blame the victim, so you're sure it can't happen to you. That's why her students called the German people stupid every time she taught about the rise of Hitler in twentieth-century history. *It can't happen to us,* they were saying. Sally glanced again at the Ninja watching her from the shady bench. She quickened her step. She wasn't the victim type.

By the time she reached the door of the sheriff's office, the news of the murder case had been pushed to the back of her mind by a more personal source of anxiety: tomorrow night's reunion. She tapped on the glass and waved to Martha, who smiled and motioned for her to come in.

"I'm not interrupting, am I?" asked Sally in hushed tones.

"No," said Martha. "I just answer the phone, you know. We're never very busy."

"Well, I thought now, because of . . . you know."

"The murder?" Martha shrugged, trying for the nonchalance of a television cop. "It's not our case anymore. The Tennessee Bureau of Investigation has it." She nodded toward the closed door to the sheriff's office.

"In there?" whispered Sally.

"Yep."

"Do you know any more about the case, Martha? All I've heard is what's on the radio." Sally looked around the sheriff's office with ill-concealed curiosity. The place smelled of coffee and furniture polish. Martha must have come in early, she thought.

Martha had no news about the Winstead case. Not even the sheriff knew the autopsy results yet. But she hated to lose face in the eyes of Sally Howell. "I can't talk about the case yet," she said, looking away. "Maybe later."

Sally frowned. Her fingers traced the smooth edge of her key chain church key. "Do you think we ought to warn the people at the reunion?" she asked.

"No!" said Martha, a little too quickly. She paused a moment to justify her reaction. "We have two dead animals and a teenager whose body was found near Knoxville. That doesn't exactly make Hamelin the murder capital of the South. I don't think we ought to get people all worked up over nothing."

Sally nodded. "I guess," she said. She reached into her straw handbag and pulled out a stack of tapes. "I finished doing the music, Martha. Do you think this will be enough?"

Martha picked up one plastic cassette case, holding it a bit away from her so that she could read the fine print. "It's an hour long. So that's four hours all together, right? I think that's plenty. Especially if Peggy Muryan is still coming." She glanced at the sheriff's closed door. "I haven't had a chance to ask Spencer yet."

Sally sat down in the visitor's chair and propped her elbows on Martha's desk. "So who else is coming?"

Martha pulled out her red "Reunion" folder and consulted the list. "Ray Elgin . . . Chuck Winters . . ."

"A doctor and a lawyer. That figures. They want to come back to prove how well they did."

Martha shrugged. "Slater Phillips. He makes minimum wage at the Texaco station. So much for your theory, huh?"

Sally thought about it. "Slater Phillips . . . I remember locking myself in the bathroom and crying once because Slater Phillips said I was an egghead. He was co-captain of the football team at the time. Remember that letter sweater of his? Julie Matthews wore it all the time, and it came to her knees. I guess she must have looked like a bag lady, but we were so awed by the status symbol that we didn't notice."

Martha frowned. "What's your point?"

"Back in high school, Slater Phillips was royalty. He impressed the hell out of us, with his trophy and his car, and his Joe Cool attitude. So that's why he's coming to the reunion. It doesn't matter that he's nobody now. We're still his fans—or some of us are. In fact, we're probably the only people in the world who *would* be impressed by Slater Phillips these days. So of course he's coming back. It's a chance to relive his glory days." Sally sighed. "It's kind of sad, isn't it?"

"Just be glad you didn't peak at seventeen," said Martha. She thought Sally still looked like a kid, with her pixie haircut and her large brown eyes. Maybe staying single meant that you never had to grow up.

"Are we all set for tomorrow night, then?" asked Sally.

"I think so. I heard that the John Sevier Motel is all booked up through Sunday, so people have already started arriving. Some have been here all week, too. I saw Ray Elgin and his family in church last Sunday."

"And, of course, some people don't have far to come," said Sally.

"Not many of us stayed in town," said Martha. "But there's folks in Johnson City and Knoxville that could commute, I guess. Are you driving in?"

"No, I'm staying over tonight, so I'll be around if there's anything to be done."

"Thanks," said Martha. "Are you staying with Tyndall?"

Sally shook her head. "No. I'm at the John Sevier. I couldn't take it at Tyndall's house! You know about Mrs. Johnson, don't you?"

"Yes." Martha remembered the haggard look on Tyndall's face at their first reunion meeting. "How is she?"

"She's coming down with a cold. Tyndall had the doctor out there yesterday."

"Oh. Well, I hope she gets to feeling better soon."

"No," said Sally with a little shiver. "Don't wish that."

"What you need in this town is a fast-food joint," said TBI detective Winnow Ross, scowling at the pack of Nabs beside his coffee cup. He looked tired. He and Boyd had driven to Wake County that morning, a drive that had begun at 6:00 A.M. His gray suit still looked pressed and his appearance was businesslike, but there was a sag of weariness about his face, as if gravity were proving too strong to be overcome by will. He stifled a yawn. The yawn was echoed by Deputy Godwin, who had been called in early to attend the meeting. He'd be on evening shift as usual, but they wanted him to know about the investigation. Godwin, a red-faced ex–football player who liked night work, didn't look too interested.

Spencer, seated at the head of the conference table, put

down his own mug of coffee. "We could adjourn to the café," he said. "They serve breakfasts."

Ross frowned. "That place up the street? I saw the damnedest thing when I drove past there this morning."

Spencer and LeDonne looked at each other. "Elvis?" Spencer asked, trying to keep from grinning.

"What? No. It was some fool in a Ninja costume. Big enough to be *two* Ninjas. You mean you got Elvis, too?"

"No," said the sheriff. "It's the same guy. He likes to dress up."

Zee Boyd's eyes narrowed. "Uh-huh. Have you checked him out?"

"He's harmless," said Godwin. "Been around for years."

The expressions on the faces of the state investigators suggested that the matter would not end there, but first they would see what better suspects the local boys had to offer.

"The thing is," said the sheriff, "old Vernon isn't a vet. And we're pretty sure that it's a vet we're looking for. I told you about the carving on the dog."

On cue, Joe LeDonne pushed a folder across the table. "Here's a list of local vets. Myself included. We've talked to 'em. Also my notes on calls made to veterans' organizations in the area."

Ross glanced through the folder. "Are there any Vietnamese people living near here?"

"Not that we know of," said Spencer. "We can check on that."

"Okay. Thanks. Anything else?"

The sheriff picked up another sheet of paper. "Photocopy of a list of people interviewed. Acquaintances of the victim. I think, though, that you ought to start by talking to Peggy Muryan. She's been receiving threats that seem related to the case."

Boyd nodded. "Yeah. You gave us the postcards." Dressed in a nondescript blue blazer and a red tie, the burly detective looked like a wrestler-turned-car-salesman. "Was there any connection between her and the victim?"

"Only the resemblance," said Spencer.

Godwin stifled a yawn with his fist and reached for his coffee mug. Spencer glared at him and went on, "She thinks she knows who's sending them. There's just one problem."

"Yeah?"

"Guy never came back from Vietnam."

Boyd gave him a sour look. "Is that right?"

"That's what she says. I expect the Army will tell you differently."

Winnow Ross flipped open his notebook with an air of weary resignation. "Name of suspect?"

After Ross and Boyd had received all the local information they thought they'd need, they relaxed a little and stopped complaining about the coffee. They were ready to discuss their end of the case with the sheriff.

"We have the autopsy report," said Boyd, taking a manila folder out of his briefcase. "Thought you might want to take a look at it."

Spencer examined the report. "Not pregnant," he said to Joe LeDonne. "Death occurred before victim was placed in river . . . mutilation occurred postmortem."

LeDonne scowled. "You said there was something carved on her shoulder. Is that identified?"

Spencer ran his finger down the page of the report. "Here it is. Right shoulder . . . two vertical parallel incisions."

"We've got photos of that," said Ross. "Nice close-ups."

LeDonne drew two lines on his yellow legal pad and stared at them thoughtfully.

"That mean anything to you?" snapped Ross.

The deputy looked up and shrugged. "Captain's bars?"

The state investigators remained impassive. Long silences were among their stock-in-trade. LeDonne stared back.

Spencer cleared his throat. "Well," he said, "I guess it's too early to come to any real conclusions. I did have one question about the Winstead girl. When can we have her back? Her parents will want to know."

"We're through," said Boyd. "You can tell the funeral home to arrange it with Knox County whenever they're ready."

Spencer handed the autopsy report back to Winnow Ross. "Did you get anything else out of all this?"

Ross frowned. "Not much. I guess we'll try to trace this folksinger's dead boyfriend. Talk to the parents. The usual. We'll check back here before we leave, see if anyone has come forward with information." He stood up and stretched, straightening his red-striped tie.

"Would you like me to come with you to Peggy Muryan's house?" asked Spencer.

The two agents looked at each other. "Just draw us a map," said Boyd.

They carried their coffee mugs over to the sink, gathered up their papers, and left.

Godwin yawned again. "Well, I sure hope they get to the bottom of this," he said cheerfully. "You mind if I take off home, Sheriff?"

"Go ahead," said Spencer. Even if it had been their case, he wouldn't expect much help from Godwin. He was good in everyday stuff, but he wasn't going anywhere.

Joe LeDonne made no move to get up from the table. He was making squiggles on his yellow legal pad, seemingly lost in thought. Spencer would have given anything to say, "How'd it go last night?" but something about

LeDonne made that impossible. He waited. Finally LeDonne looked up, scowling at the necessity of talking. "I didn't say anything to those hotshots," he said, jerking his thumb toward the door through which the agents had just left. "But I think they're wrong."

"Wrong about what?"

"About the killer being a vet."

Spencer sat down again. LeDonne looked dead serious, but in the light of what they already knew, what he was saying made no sense. "You don't think there's a Vietnam connection?" Spencer said carefully.

"I didn't say that," LeDonne told him. "I said I wasn't sure that the perp was a vet. He or she sure as hell knows about the war, though."

"Why don't you think it's a vet?"

LeDonne sighed at the necessity for more words. "Some of it is gut feeling that I can't express too well. It has to do with the hokiness of the whole operation. It's not something you'd do on a spur of the moment. It's not like a flashback thing fueled by rage."

"But it is Vietnam-style killing, isn't it?"

"Almost. But like with the dog: usually with a killing like that, guys would leave the ace of spades as a calling card because it bugged the hell out of the VC. One of their little superstitions. I thought it was funny that it wasn't done."

"Maybe the killer didn't have a deck of cards on him."

"Okay, but then there's this mutilation business. Remember I thought the dog-killer was a vet because of the lightning bolt carved in its hide? But even then it bothered me that there was no playing card. But, okay, I figured we had a guy from the Twenty-fifth Infantry freaking out, and that made a certain amount of sense."

"Except that we didn't find anybody to fit that description? Well, maybe Ross and Boyd can—"

"No, I'm willing to believe in suspects that haven't turned up yet. It was the inconsistency that stuck in my craw. Remember the dead sheep?"

"Yeah. No carvings. It may be an unrelated incident."

"I figured that, until we got the autopsy report on Rosemary Winstead. Remember it said that she had incisions cut in her shoulder? That got me to thinking about Wayne Wyler's dead sheep again. Somebody had put a vine of poison ivy around its neck."

"Yeah. I remember your saying so in your report."

"Poison Ivy is the Fourth Infantry Division, because it's called the Ivy Division, because of its patch insignia. And then they find this Winstead girl's body, and she's got parallel lines cut in her."

"Whose insignia is that?"

"Nobody's. But it got me thinking. The Eleventh Infantry got nicknamed the Butcher Brigade after My Lai. It would fit. Two vertical cuts: the number eleven."

"Why didn't you tell the investigators this?"

" 'Cause they were acting superior as hell, and they'd give me a hard time about it anyway. My point is that the killer is outfit-hopping. I can see a vet carving *one* insignia on bodies, but unless we're looking for General Westmoreland, this is too damn many units!"

"Or maybe it's a coincidence. But since the sheep was draped with poison ivy, we could check to see if anybody has been treated for poison ivy recently."

LeDonne held out his hands, daubed with the chalky pink of calamine lotion. "You just buy it over the counter in Johnson City, Spencer," he said patiently.

Zee Boyd looked out the window on the passenger side, admiring the well-kept flower beds and the sprawling lawns of Ashe Lane. "What do you reckon houses cost around here?" he mused aloud.

"Your sanity!" snorted Ross, keeping his eyes on the road. Ross liked his apartment in Knoxville, with its chrome-and-glass tables, red vinyl couch, and the beige shag rug that looked okay with a twice-a-year vacuuming. He was ten minutes away from the take-out pizza place, and he had no lawn to mow. Boyd's yearnings for the trappings of suburbia left him unmoved. Boyd and his wife lived in a run-down white frame house, but they wanted to buy an old place and fix it up. They spent their Saturdays prowling around the antiques warehouse near the Knoxville zoo, looking for cheap oak furniture that they could restore. Ross didn't see why. He wouldn't want to own anything that couldn't be cleaned with Windex.

"Big white house with columns," said Boyd. "That shouldn't be hard to find. I wonder if she got it for less than a hundred K?"

"Wonder if she can heat it for less than that," said Ross. A hundred K, indeed! Boyd's use of computer jargon irritated him, but he didn't want to start in on it now. He looked at the house numbers on the mailbox. "Coming up!" he announced.

"Jesus!" whispered Boyd, looking at the white-columned house, wreathed in the dark green of oak leaves.

Winnow Ross was unimpressed. "You couldn't afford to put gas in the lawn mower, Zee," he said.

"Wonder why the sheriff wanted to bring us here himself?" Boyd remarked as they pulled into the gravel drive.

"I don't like to think," said Ross. "Just keep an open mind, will you, Zee? Remember, drug money finances a raft of mansions. And lots of show business people are tight with organized crime, so don't kiss her hand if she offers you a mint julep, okay?"

Boyd nodded, staring up at the carved leaves on the top of the white columns. "Corinthians," he muttered.

"Which comes before Revelations, let's hope!" said Ross, snickering at his pun.

Boyd was inspecting the beveled glass on the porch light while Ross thundered against the oak door with his beefy knuckles. "If she gets a B&E, I'm taking your prints first, Zee," Ross told him. "Now knock it off!"

The sheer curtain in the living room window flicked aside for a second, and then they heard the sound of the door being unlocked. Ross reached for his shield. When Peggy Muryan opened the door, she glanced at them and then looked past them to see if there was someone else with them. An instant later, she met Ross's eyes and said with a child's polite precision, "Yes, may I help you?"

She knew we were coming, thought Ross, who had trained himself to notice such things. Her hair was carefully brushed back to reveal small gold earrings, and she wore fresh lipstick and blush on her cheeks. In one practiced glance he took in the white jeans and Indian-patterned cotton sweater: it was meant to look casual, but it wasn't an outfit for knocking around the house in. This was somebody who had to worry about stray reporters dropping by, and who was careful of her image. She worked at not looking her age. A jogging type, he thought, with an inward sneer.

"TBI, ma'am," he said politely, letting the badge flash in the sunlight. "Like to talk to you, if we may."

She took the badge from him and inspected it carefully, which both annoyed Ross as a waste of time and impressed him with her wariness. Some serial killer—was it Bundy?—actually bought a fake badge and flashed it at women to get them to let him in. This one was smarter than they were, anyway. At her unspoken invitation, he and Boyd followed her into the house.

The summer hangout for the youth of Hamelin County was the local swimming pool, built with county recreation funds, down a gravel road that dead-ended at the foot of Torch Mountain. Two dollars got you in for all day, with the services of a lifeguard and the chance to lunch on candy bars and soft drinks at fifty cents apiece. Every year the council worried over whether the rising costs of insuring public facilities would force them to close the pool, but so far they'd managed to keep up the premiums. As long as nobody drowned, they'd be all right.

Nobody in Jennifer Showalter's crowd was likely to drown. As far as they were concerned, the mouthwash-blue water of the pool was merely set decoration around which to hold court on their rainbow of beach towels. Jennifer's long red hair, which shriveled into rattails when wet, was a burning bush in the midday sun, offset by the glow of her tan and her white bathing suit. The two-piece suit, of a simple cut and exclusive of decoration, had looked all right to her mother while it was hanging on the rack in Alexander's. At least there were no sequins, fake leopard skin, or other gimmicks to cheapen its look into teenage haute couture. On Jennifer, however, this bit of spandex, with its straps slipped artfully off the shoulder, evoked images of strobe-lit stripjoints or porno movies with titles like *The Sultan's Nymphet*. She sat curled up on her beach towel, her chin resting on one knee, as she painted her toenails bright scarlet. She was surrounded by four of her girlfriends who had attracted their own following of boyfriends, would-be boyfriends, and casual acquaintances. Dawn Jessup, a short dark-haired girl in a green one-piece, lay on her stomach next to a boom box the size of a loaf of bread. Beside her sat Crystal Teague, in a ruffled suit to cover her bulging hips. She was reading a tattered paperback. Amy Barker and Debbie Pruitt were lying facedown on their towels trying to even out their tans. A couple of the more popular boys sat next to Jennifer's towel, dangling their legs in the water. Near Crystal's blanket sat Pix-Kyle Weaver and his cousin Kevin, skinny adolescents somewhat lacking in social skills; they were tolerated by the popular kids. Usually, though, Kevin made a jerk of himself and was ignored by the group, and Pix-Kyle didn't seem to care whether they talked to him or not. Today, though, everybody wanted to talk about the local sensation: the murder of Rosemary Winstead. The bigger the audience, the better. You never knew who might have a new scrap of information to enlarge the myth.

Dawn's radio lapsed into silence. "Shut up, every-body!" she hissed. "News time!"

Ordinarily when the local rock station interrupted its pounding blare for four minutes of news, the sunbathers chattered through it, or went to the concession stand for another can of soda. But this time they sat at attention, all eyes on the radio. The murder of Rosemary Winstead was the top story of the hour.

"Gee. Poor Rosemary," said Dawn Jessup, adjusting her sunglasses.

"I already knew about it," said Jennifer. "Arrowood came by my house wanting to know if I'd seen her."

"Had you?" asked Crystal Teague, abandoning her copy of *Sweet Valley High*.

Jennifer shrugged. "She called me up. Said she wanted to stay out late." Carefully, she set the brush back into the bottle of nail polish. She pushed her sunglasses back to the top of her head and gazed at the group of guys sitting at the edge of the pool.

Jason Jordan, junior class president, looked disgusted. "You make it sound like it was her fault, Jennifer!"

She flashed a feline smile. "My father says it usually is. He says that if you don't hang out in bars, you don't get raped on pool tables."

Crystal Teague looked worried. "But Rosemary was a nice kid. She was kind of fannish, but she wasn't a tramp."

Pix-Kyle Weaver grinned. "Unlike *some* people!"

Jennifer gave him a cold stare. "You were pretty tight with her, weren't you, P.K.?"

He shrugged. "She could carry on a sensible conversation. And she didn't make her toes look bloody!" With that parting shot, he plunged into the pool, splashing the sunbathers with his spray.

Amy Barker looked after him and shuddered. "What a creep!"

Beside her, Debbie Pruitt raised her head long enough to say, "Rosemary didn't think so!"

"Yeah, she should have stuck with him," said Jason sadly. "What happened to her was really gross!"

"Maybe there's a killer stalking Hamelin, like in one of those teenage slasher movies!" said Kevin Sanford. His chief preoccupations in life were horror movies, Dungeons & Dragons, and a video game called *Time Pilot*.

Crystal Teague shook her head. "It's not funny, y'all!" she wailed.

"Did Rosemary say anything to your cousin about who she was seeing?" asked Amy, ignoring the outburst.

Kevin shook his head. "He don't know nothin' 'bout it. We're going to the funeral, though! Reckon they'll have the casket open and you can see anything? Maybe she'll have her neck stitched up!"

"Shut up this minute, Kevin," said Jennifer Showalter briskly. "It's a truly tragic event, and we must all go to the funeral to pay our respects."

The others nodded in agreement.

"What are you going to wear, Jennifer?" asked Dawn.

Spencer was eating a sandwich at his desk, while Martha used her lunch hour and a bit more to run errands in preparation for tomorrow night's reunion. He was supposed to be working on his presentation speech, but every time he tried to compose a speech dedicating the plaque to the Vietnam war dead, his mind strayed to the case. The Vietnam vet foremost in his mind was Travis Perdue. Was he back, and if so, who was he? And if that turned out to be a dead end, where were the postcards coming from?

It wasn't his job, he thought, taking a bite of tuna fish and stale bread. Three-men departments weren't supposed to worry about real crimes. They were supposed to check for expired county tax stickers and keep the good old boys from taking each other apart on Friday night. Mostly they were just supposed to be around so that people would think twice about vandalism or ignoring the speed limit through the one-horse town. The TBI had the facilities and the manpower to handle big cases. They had labs to analyze the evidence and a staff that could ask questions day after day without neglecting other business. When the TBI solved the murder case, after dozens of hours of routine police work in half a dozen counties, they would let him know what they found out. But they didn't expect any input from him.

Spencer picked up the phone and dialed the newspaper office. Jeff McCullough, he knew, was in the same boat that he was in. His publishers would be expecting him to write up the local aspects of the story after the *Knoxville Journal* broke the case. He sat there with the phone cradled against his shoulder, listening to the ringing and hoping that McCullough wanted answers as bad as he did.

"Record," said McCullough in his tinny mountain twang.

"This is Spencer Arrowood. Did you get anything on that tip I gave you?"

The newspaperman laughed. "You talk like there's still an operator putting calls through, Sheriff! Yes, as a matter of fact, I've got something for you. A classmate of mine got a job with a real paper in Washington, and I got her to check on Travis Perdue. She just called me back."

Spencer scratched through "We the class of '66 dedicate this plaque," and wrote "Travis Perdue" at the top of the yellow sheet. "I'm ready," he told McCullough. "What have you got?"

McCullough sighed. "I wish we had a fax machine."

"A what?"

"It's a cross between a photocopier and a teletype. You can send a copy of a document across country in about a minute. Carla's office has one, of course, but we're a shoestring weekly. We're lucky to have a Xerox machine. You ought to ask the county to buy one for the sheriff's office."

"I doubt we'd have much call to use one," said Spencer. "Just go ahead and read it out to me over the phone."

"Okay. On March 17, 1968, Sgt. Travis Perdue (USAF) was part of a crew that left Ubon Air Force

Base, Thailand, on an armed reconnaissance mission over North Vietnam. Apparently, he was an interpreter. Not fluent, though; Air Force–trained."

"Go on."

"Do you want to know how he happened to be doing interpreting from the airplane instead of monitoring radio broadcasts from a hut in the hills?"

"Not right now. What happened to Perdue?"

"According to the reports, the plane crew sighted . . . I can't read my notes here. . . . Anyway, they saw something that they wanted to take a closer look at, approximately one mile south of Dien Bien Phu Airport. They radioed that they were going down to examine the area. And that was it. Attempts to make radio contact with the plane were met with silence. And because it was enemy territory, an organized search was not conducted."

"He died in a plane crash," said Spencer, drawing the outline of a cross beneath his notes.

"Maybe not," said McCullough. "In 1975, Travis Perdue's mother was asked by the Air Force to view photographs of unidentified American prisoners of war. She swore that one of them was her son. A couple of his uncles and cousins also testified that the man in the photo was Travis. But later the Air Force told them that the man in the photo was positively identified as somebody else, and, citing privacy reasons, they have refused to provide the family with any information about the photo. So we don't know where, when, or how it was taken. And we don't know how the Air Force came into possession of it."

"Well, then, wherever he is, he's not here," said Spencer.

"Unless he escaped, or got quietly freed and we don't know about it. Remember, the family saw the picture in '75. It might have been taken years earlier."

"Where does the family live?"

"His mother used to live in Erwin, but there's no telephone listing for her," said McCullough. "I already checked."

"Do you have any pictures of him?"

"I'm going to Erwin this afternoon. We can get a high school yearbook picture, at least."

The sheriff sighed. "Okay, thanks. I'll give this information to the TBI when I see them."

"Don't bother," said McCullough cheerfully. "Somebody at their headquarters probably had it before I did. *They've* got a fax machine!"

Martha had ordered the plaque from the engraving place in the mall in Johnson City. There weren't any businesses in Wake County who did that sort of thing, so she went for the best price she could get elsewhere. It was going to take her a little longer than her lunch hour to pick it up, but Spencer said he'd be in the office anyway, so she went to pick it up. She wanted to make sure that it was ready and that there weren't any mistakes. She wouldn't want anybody's name to be misspelled on the plaque. Dying in a stupid war in a place nobody could find on a map was bad enough without that final insult. The clerk at Things Remembered unwrapped the finished plaque for Martha to look at.

It was a shield-shaped wooden plaque, about twelve inches high, with a bronze plate attached that said: THE HAMELIN HIGH SCHOOL CLASS OF 1966 DEDICATES THIS PLAQUE TO THE MEMORY OF THEIR CLASSMATES WHO BRAVELY FOUGHT AND NOBLY DIED IN THE WAR IN VIETNAM.

The names of the three boys who died were printed in block capitals beneath the inscription. Cal Arrowood's name was first. It was fitting that Spencer should give that presentation speech, whether he wanted to or not. Martha ran her fingers across the other two names: Michael Gibbs, a tall, quiet guy who liked garage electronics more than school, and Steve Heyward, a bandy-legged farmboy who had a crush on Martha once. His constant clowning had irritated her, and she had been cruel to him. When he died, she felt guilty about the fact that she had so disliked him. Years later, the guilt remained; so did her dislike of him.

She thanked the sales clerk and paid for the purchase with a check from the reunion account. It was only twelve-twenty-five. Perhaps there was still time to look at dresses at Penney's before she went back. They always had size fives on the rack at sales time; it was one of the few triumphs of Martha's life, the ability to buy good clothes at bargain prices because she was thinner than average.

She was making her way around the coin-filled reflecting pool when she heard someone calling her name. Martha wasn't surprised; half the older women in Wake County prowled the Johnson City malls on weekdays. She turned and saw Georgia Barker in her pale blue polyester pantsuit, carrying a stuffed tiger. Looped around her wrist was a white plastic bag, counterbalanced with her purse on the other arm.

"Are you going back to the parking lot?" she asked a little breathlessly. "I sure could use a hand."

"So it seems," said Martha, eyeing the tiger. She knew Georgia Barker from church. Martha tucked the tiger under her arm and headed for the downstairs escalator. It was getting late anyway, she told herself. She ought to get back. Her white linen dress would be good enough for tomorrow night.

"The tiger is for Ashley Nicole, in case you're wondering. Her birthday is Sunday," said Georgia.

Martha nodded. Ashley was Georgia's granddaughter. "How are Kathy and Carlyle doing?" she asked, her thoughts elsewhere.

"Just fine. They're coming over for the weekend. You've got the reunion coming up, don't you?"

"Tomorrow night," said Martha, blinking in the bright sunlight of the mall parking lot. Georgia Barker led the way toward her car.

"I read about the reunion in the paper. Article said you all were giving a plaque for the boys that went to Vietnam."

"That's right. I was just picking it up." They had reached the car by now. As Georgia fumbled with the keys to the trunk, Martha steadied the tiger under one arm and drew the plaque out of its plastic bag.

Georgia Barker unwrapped it and peered through her glasses at the inscription. "You left some out," she said quietly.

"Who?" asked Martha.

"Ernie Weaver. And my son Gary." She pushed the plaque back at Martha, her eyes stern.

"No," said Martha. "This plaque isn't people who *served* in Vietnam. It's people who *died* in Vietnam. Ernie committed suicide a couple of years ago in Dark Hollow, and Gary's still around, isn't he?"

Georgia Barker took a deep breath. "Gary hasn't held a job for more than ten months in all the years he's been back. He drinks too much—says it's his nerves. And Ernie Weaver wasn't the same person when he came home from that place, neither. The old Ernie would never have done such an awful thing to himself. You want a plaque listing people who died in Vietnam. You better put them down, 'cause, believe me, they did." She climbed into her car and slammed the door. Martha stood in the glare of the parking lot, staring up at the flag by the front entrance. She wondered if the girl in the engraving shop could change the plaque while she waited. *"In Memory of Those Who Served in Vietnam . . ."*—that's what they would put.

CHAPTER 13

This living hand, now warm and capable
Of earnest grasping, would, if it were cold
And in the icy silence of the tomb,
So haunt thy days and chill thy dreaming nights
That thou would wish thine own heart dry of
blood
So in my veins red life might stream again,
And thou be conscience-calmed—see here it
is—
I hold it towards you.

KEATS

THE SCENT OF roses mingled in the twilight with the smell of new-mown grass. Jane Arrowood sat on the steps of her front porch, watching the sky above the elm tree bleed the last of its color into the clouds and fade to black. From the eaves of the house, a bat dropped into flight and slid away toward the green heart of the woods beyond the fence. The crickets chirped in the stillness, perhaps as loud as the lawn mower had been but less intrusive. Jane was glad that Spencer had finished mowing. She liked the evening quiet.

He was inside taking a shower now. After that he would drink exactly three-quarters of a cold beer, and by then the stuffed pork chops with Vidalia onions ought to be ready to come out of the oven. The mashed potatoes were already done. Jane still had plenty of time to slice the tomatoes and to brew fresh iced tea before dinnertime. She could afford a few more minutes of quiet darkness on the porch.

Jane Arrowood had lived alone since her husband died—nearly eleven years now. Most of the time she didn't mind being by herself, but it was nice to have Spencer come over twice a week or so. It gave her the illusion of family closeness. That's just what it was, she thought. An illusion. They were still friendly, and concerned about each other in an offhand way, but she and Spencer had lost the thread of each other's thoughts some years back. Lately he had fallen into the habit of answering her small talk with Pronouncements, just as his father had done. "My back is sore," Jane would say, hoping for a little sympathy. "Take an aspirin," Spencer would reply. Or she'd say, "I wonder what I ought to do about that old pier mirror of your grandmother's? It's really too big for the parlor." "Sell it," Spencer would say.

He could solve every problem in creation with one impatient sentence. Why should he settle for being Wake County sheriff? she thought bitterly. Surely, since he had all the answers, he could rule the world.

She sighed. It was only men who thought that everything was cut-and-dried, black or white. The older Jane got, the more she seemed to see the ambiguity in everything. She wanted to know *why* things were and *how* they happened. Men wanted to fix everything, but she would settle for understanding things. She liked to savor the subtleties, perhaps because she had never had either the power or the inclination to do much fixing in the world. She had married Hank Arrowood after a year of Woman's College, and she'd never had any job or responsibility greater than being secretary of the Sunday school class. Hank had seen to the taxes and the finances and maintenance of home and automobiles. By the time

Hank died, Spencer was a veteran and a college graduate, so he had taken up where his father left off, mowing the lawn and balancing the checkbook. She wondered, sometimes, if her menfolk had thought her stupid. Perhaps so; they were not likely to see that there could be other forms of wisdom besides their own.

Jane was not concerned with the world of carburetors and certificates of deposit. It had always been her business to anticipate people's needs, and to *ensure domestic tranquility* (the Preamble to the Constitution, memorized long ago in Miss Yopp's civics class, because young girls back then were expected to make good grades in school, and then to let their minds fall fallow forever after. No one seemed to see any irony in that). In the smallest scale, Jane Arrowood, homemaker, was a philosopher and a diplomat.

Now that she was old enough to have some perspective on the whole business, she saw life as a field of tangled kudzu vines, with endless runners going in all directions beneath the surface. In her mind she wanted to unearth the kudzu and examine the roots, to find the hidden connections between people and events. She didn't want to affect anything at all, the way men did; it would satisfy her simply to know.

Take the case of the murdered girl (which Spencer would not discuss. "We'll get the guy" was his one-sentence solution). When they found out who had done it, Jane would want to know why he did it, and what indications of trouble there had been in his past, and whether there was a history of violence among his kinfolk. She'd want to know whether the murdered girl resembled the killer's mother, or if he had seen a horror movie the night before the killing. Spencer wouldn't much care. Motives were the district attorney's job, he would tell her.

Spencer didn't want to talk about the reunion, either,

but that, too, interested her. She knew his high school friends so much better than she had known anyone since in Spencer's life. She wondered how his playmates had turned out, and whether they would still see one another as friends. She didn't suppose that Jenny was coming, or that she and Spencer would talk if she did. They would each be full of pride and ego and the self-absorption of the young. They were not yet old enough to treasure acquaintances not for their own virtues, but just because they were people who remembered one's youth. It would be a few years yet before they would feel the urge to band together as a generation against the young aliens who had become the world's doctors and lawyers and congressmen, while one's own thoughts had been elsewhere.

Jane did not mind being old, except for her concerns about her health and the disquieting specter of dependence upon family strangers. If her generation could all be twenty-five again together, then it would be a fine thing, but she herself would not want to go alone into the enemy camp, to have to like *their* music, *their* clothes, *their* politics.

Perhaps Spencer's uneasiness about the reunion stemmed in part from his realization that he, too, was being displaced by another tribe of young people. The high school did not belong to his group anymore; they were there on sufferance for a brief reunion. They weren't eighteen anymore. Spencer still looked young enough—blonds don't gray as dramatically as other people—but he was holding the newspaper at arm's length now, and the veins in his hands were beginning to surface. Jane knew the signs and the self-mourning that began with them.

She tried to picture her other son, Cal, approaching middle age, but the image would not come. Cal had been a rather loutish young man, and she could find in her imagination no seeds of maturity in that boy to project into the flower of manhood had he lived. Spencer knew that she still grieved for Cal, but he did not understand the nature of it. He saw it, as he saw everything, in terms of himself, as a reproach to him. But in fact it had nothing to do with him, and not much to do with the young soldier who had died. She was not mourning the brash youth whose future had been lackluster at best, but the irrevocable loss of the little blond boy, her firstborn. That Cal had been gone long before he fell in a firefight in Southeast Asia, but his death had canceled any chance that for even one moment she could reach her trusting baby son again. Her husband might have mourned the future Cal who had never lived, but she missed the toddler who would never die. The fact that Spencer was worth two of him was neither here nor there.

"Mother? You out here?" He was standing at the screen door, calling out into the darkness.

"Yes, hon," she said, struggling a little to get up. "I'm just about to take the pork chops out of the oven."

He held the door open for her. "Doesn't look like it's ever going to cool off," he said.

She looked past his faintly lined face to the pictures of children on the mantelpiece. "Oh, yes," she said. "It will."

He followed her into the kitchen, and set the table while she bustled around getting things into serving dishes. She had put out his favorite red-and-white-checked tablecloth and the old dishes with the farm scene etched in blue across the plates. Sometimes Jane wished that she could take all those old things to the Women's Club rummage sale and get some rose-tinted glass plates and new stainless steel flatware for herself. She'd like to repaint the kitchen, too, and put in green appliances, and put in air-conditioning so she wouldn't have to have the tube of flypaper dangling from the ceiling fan. Spencer wouldn't like any changes, of course. This was the home of his childhood, and while he wouldn't want to live here anymore, the fact that the house existed unchanged made him feel safe in the world, because here it was still 1959, just the way he remembered it. She was used to providing this museum of comfort for the last surviving man of her family; it was part of her job as a diplomat.

Spencer was preoccupied tonight. He wasn't making polite conversation as he usually did, and of course she noticed. Had the situation been reversed, he would have sensed no difference.

"Are you ready for tomorrow night?" she asked.

He set the basket of biscuits in the center of the table and carefully unfolded the red covering cloth before he answered. "Not really. I was in conference with the TBI for most of today, so I haven't given social activities much thought. I'm escorting the local celebrity to the mixer tomorrow night, though."

"Peggy Muryan. I read about her in the paper." Jane wondered what there was in that. Polite indifference was the way to play it for now.

"I don't reckon it'll be too wild a party," he said, smiling.

"I imagine not," Jane replied. "One of your classmates is a grandmother now."

The smile faded from Spencer's face, and Jane felt a guilty twinge of satisfaction that she had scored a direct hit. Let him see what it feels like to be dismissed as old, she thought. True, Patsy Joyner had married at sixteen, and her daughter at nineteen, but that didn't change the fact that there *was* a grandmother in his precious class of '66.

"I just wish I didn't have to dedicate that damned plaque!" said Spencer.

But you are the authority figure in town, Jane thought. It would never have occurred to people to ask Mike Gibb's widow (though she remarried) to present that plaque. Or poor Gary Barker, who knew what it was like over there in Vietnam. No, they wanted a showpiece classmate, to make it all respectable. She was sure that Spencer's reluctance had to do with Cal's name on the plaque. Yet another trophy for Big Brother. And perhaps he saw it as a reproach that his own bravery had not been tested in the crucible of his generation.

"I'm sure they meant it as an honor, Spencer," she said gently. "Have another pork chop?"

LeDonne's little Volkswagen scooted up the ruts of the dirt road toward Roger Gabriel's place. It was nearly dark, and the flicker of fireflies in the long grass beside the road made LeDonne think of the flash of sniper fire at night. He looked away, steadying his gaze to the path ahead. Something about this road always made him think back. Maybe Roger haunted it already, he thought, without even being dead. Or no deader than the rest of them were. It was getting hard to tell who was dead and who wasn't, he told himself. Thanks to Travis Perdue, who by all accounts had been dead a good long while but who was apparently taking more of an interest in the world than LeDonne himself had felt for a long time.

He thought he'd better see how Roger was doing. Just before five, the two state cops had come back to the office to say that they had finished their fieldwork. They'd talked to Peggy Muryan, and she'd repeated what she'd already told the sheriff. Then they'd talked to the dead girl's parents and to some of her friends. They'd also checked out Roger Gabriel.

"I think you got a hot one out there, Deputy," Ross had told him.

And Boyd told him how they'd been so spooked by the atmosphere of the place that they had drawn their guns as they approached the door. LeDonne figured they were lucky not to be dead, but apparently Gabriel had been in one of his more charitable moods. He had come out to the porch and answered their questions in a tone bordering on civility. They couldn't think of anything worth charging him with, so they'd left.

They weren't coming back. From now on the case would be pursued via lab work and phone calls, an amorphous departmental thing: crime-solving by committee. Wake County was left to Sheriff Arrowood and his deputies. They would have to reassure the relatives that everything possible was being done to solve the case, and they would have to deal with those whose lives had been disrupted by the investigation.

LeDonne didn't have any theories about the identity of the killer. He wasn't paid to have theories. Besides, assuming that one person was guilty would automatically exonerate a dozen other people, and LeDonne no longer had such benevolent illusions. Nothing that anyone did surprised him anymore. He was willing to venture an opinion that the killer was not a vet, based on a few pieces of information he'd come by the hard way, but he didn't really care one way or the other, and he didn't want any credit for the information. It was all the same to him.

He did want to check on Roger, though. If he was guilty of the murder of the Winstead girl, the state cops might have rattled him into doing something incriminating, and if he wasn't guilty, the officers might have shaken him into doing something unfortunate. Like putting a pistol in his mouth and squeezing the trigger. LeDonne thought Roger Gabriel might be in the market for an excuse to do just that. He knew that if Roger intended to die, a visit from him could do little more than postpone it, but if that suicide happened tonight, it would be on LeDonne's conscience that he didn't take the ride out here, so here he was. It was hard enough for LeDonne to sleep as it was; another nightmare would make it impossible.

The shack was a dark shape in the clearing, melting into the trees behind it. There were no lights in either of the windows. LeDonne blinked to accustom his eyes to the grayness. There was one flash of light from the porch. LeDonne stiffened, waiting for the sound of the gunshot, but a second later, when the glow persisted, he recognized the circle of light as a lit cigarette. Squinting into the darkness, he thought he could make out Roger Gabriel's dim form seated on a wooden bench beside the front door. He flashed his headlights once before shutting them off, and climbed out of the car. The fact that he had not brought his gun was not an oversight.

He advanced toward the porch in silence, glancing about for the dark form of Chao, the black Lab. Finally a muffled thump from the porch told him where the dog was. LeDonne ambled up the steps, and by now he found that his eyes had adjusted and that he could see the man on the bench.

"Evening," he said softly. "Mind if I set awhile?"

The pause before Roger Gabriel's reply was just a few seconds too long to be courteous. "What happened to your friends?"

LeDonne let half a minute go by. "They didn't make it past Tet," he said, deliberately misunderstanding the other's question.

Gabriel understood. With a grunt of satisfaction he patted the bench. "Couple of fascist bastards," he remarked. "Reminded me of officers."

LeDonne eased himself onto the bench, holding his hand out for Chao. "Well, as far as they're concerned, you're Charlie," he said, stroking the dog's dusty coat. Roger made no reply to this observation, so LeDonne ventured another gambit. "You okay?"

The cigarette glowed again. "Compared to what?"

"I thought the state boys might have given you a rough time," LeDonne said carefully. "Which I figured was pretty pointless, because I don't think the killer we're looking for is a vet."

"Is that a fact?" Roger Gabriel didn't sound too interested.

"Of course, I can see why they'd be uptight about the whole thing. That kid they pulled out of the river was messed up pretty bad. You remember those pictures of the dog I showed you?"

"I've seen worse."

"Not in Tennessee," said LeDonne.

"So what's the word?"

"The prime suspect as far as they're concerned is a grunt who's been MIA for twenty years."

Roger stubbed out his cigarette under the heel of his boot. "Yeah. They mentioned that. I think they were hoping that I'd turn out to be him."

"And did you?"

"Not to their satisfaction, no." Roger Gabriel sounded amused. "I didn't like to rule it out entirely, though, for fear of disappointing them too much. They mouthed off at me a lot, talking macho. They didn't say I was under arrest, though. And they didn't say not to leave town."

"They couldn't stop you," LeDonne remarked, suspecting that a question had been posed. "You going somewhere?"

Roger Gabriel nodded. "Somewhere." After a pause he added, "And I'm taking the dog."

LeDonne did not need to inquire further. Taking the dog meant that he was going somewhere, anyway.

Somewhere other than a hundred yards into the trees with a fifth of bourbon and his pistol. Sooner or later the vets usually did move on. They never actually went home, and they never figured out how to make someplace else home, so they kept moving. LeDonne felt the urge to go, but he was trying to outstubborn himself. He reasoned that what he was looking for was not a place, and that the urge to search for it was futile. Sometimes it helped to argue that, when every nerve in his gut said "Run for it!"

"That support group still meets in Knoxville," he said softly.

"I know," said Roger. "I'll keep it in mind. And if the state cops take a notion to look me up, I haven't seen you."

LeDonne stared out at the incoming fireflies. "Chao," he said.

The old woman coughed again. A tentative sound, as if she couldn't quite remember why you were supposed to cough, but some part of her brain still sparked the impulse.

Tyndall gripped the arm of her chair, feeling her own throat tighten in response to the sound. It was nearly eleven, and she had been sitting at the kitchen table staring at the telephone for a couple of hours. The doctor had been by yesterday, and he hadn't seemed very concerned about her mother's cold. He hadn't offered to check back, either. After all, it was dead summer, hardly the weather to fear pneumonia. Should she run up another doctor bill—a house call yet!—for something as minor as a head cold? Or was it a more serious illness?

Tyndall was too tired to make any decisions. Why did she have to make all the decisions, anyway? Her mother had drifted through a pleasant little life making no more command decisions than the average sheep. It seemed to

Tyndall that Evelyn Johnson had been carried over the threshold and over every other possible obstacle in her life by her domineering husband. Tyndall alternated between pity and envy of the circumstances of her mother's life.

Steve was not like that at all.

He met every discussion with a shrug: "Whatever you want to do." She thought of calling Steve, of telling him about her mother's labored breathing—but what would be the point? She could do whatever she wanted to do without the formality of consulting him. He would offer no insights to inform her decision. He did not share in the care of her mother; he would not share the burden of any decision to cease caring.

Sally, then? But Dr. Sally Howell thrived in the rarefied atmosphere of academia. She was an idealist, fonder of causes than of individuals. Tyndall could have her conversation with Sally without lifting the telephone. "Call the doctor, Tyndall. Better safe than sorry. They might find a cure next week. Then how would you feel?" *Cheated out of a week, Sally.* After a lifetime of friendship, Sally was a second self. She could hear the arguments without need of a telephone. She could play both parts. Why bother?

Her mother's physician? Of course he would come round at midnight if she asked him to, but was her mother's congestion a serious condition or was it not? Either way, he might think Tyndall was a fool. Why should we make every effort to preserve life within this human husk? he might wonder. Tyndall wondered, too. Was the whole world really leaving the decision in her hands?

The cough came again, echoing through the stillness of the house, while Tyndall turned the pages of the

Hamelin telephone directory trying to think of someone that she could call.

"Hello?" Peggy Muryan's voice was cautious, just above a whisper. She had picked up the telephone after one ring.

"It's Spencer," he said. "I just got back from my mother's place. Thought I'd check on you. Are you all right?"

"Yes." A touch of impatience slid into her voice. The circle of light from the bedside lamp threw menacing shadows on the white walls of her bedroom and made the roses on the curtains and bedspread look like bloodstains. Peggy was curled up on the four-poster bed, two pillows propped behind her, reading *The Foxfire Book*.

"I was going to sit in on your interview with the state police," he told her, "but they wanted to do it their way. Everything all right?"

She sighed. "It wasn't a pleasant experience. Cops are so—I don't know how to put it—you know. Or maybe you don't, since you sort of are one."

"Tell me."

"Well, they have sort of a condescending attitude. Very self-righteous. If they stop you for running a stop sign, they act as if they are fully entitled to sit in judgment of you-a-sinner because their lives are models of holy rectitude. And I always think: what a lot of crap, because I do read, you know, and it's common knowledge that cops have a very tidy rate of alcoholism, personality disorders, episodes of violence . . . so who the hell are they to act so high and mighty?"

"Did they read you your rights, Peggy?" Spencer tried to sound amused.

She pushed a straggling shock of hair away from her ear. "No. It was just the way they acted. Like they could smell shit, you know? No matter what answer I gave to one of their supposedly polite questions, they accepted it with a little smirk or a gesture that meant *This is a load of manure.* God, I see why people give false confessions. After twenty minutes with those guys, I was ready to admit to anything."

"The attitude is an occupational hazard," he said. "We don't deal with innocent people very often; with nice people, almost never. It's easy to start feeling holier-than-thou. But they are good at their jobs. You should feel reassured that they are after the creep."

"He deserves them."

"You don't sound much in need of police protection, ma'am."

She eased open the drawer to the bedside table. The gun lay on top of a neatly folded stack of pillowcases. "This house is like a fortress. The doors are locked. The phone is beside my bed. I'll be fine. Those two goons this afternoon almost have me convinced that the Winstead girl's death is just a coincidence." She paused for a moment. "It doesn't sound like the sort of thing Travis would do."

"We're running a check on Travis Perdue. Should know something by Monday."

"Fine. I hope the next cop I see is in an unofficial capacity."

He laughed. "You're an unreconstructed hippie, ma'am."

"Damn right. Speaking of which . . . what am I supposed to wear to this séance tomorrow night?"

"Uhh—it's not a costume ball, as far as I know. Love beads and madras are optional."

"I know that. I didn't want to have to go looking like Barbara Mandrell. You don't want glitz, I hope?" She looked at the open door of her closet. How formal did country high school reunions get? Would the white cocktail dress be too much?

Spencer sighed. "I take whatever I can get."

"Good. I'll see you tomorrow."

Spencer thought she might ask him whether she'd be called upon to sing, or whether she was likely to be pestered for autographs, but apparently that did not concern her. He wasn't sure how the class of '66 would react to Peggy Muryan: it could be anything from wild adulation to total indifference, but since mountain people are a reserved bunch, he'd bet on the latter. He hoped she wouldn't expect too much. At least it would take her mind off the case, he thought.

THE WOODS WERE lovely—dark and deep. The promises he had to keep belonged to another time, perhaps, but he felt obliged to honor them nonetheless. Not tonight, though. Tonight he would keep his own rituals, and leave Her to stink in her fear, waiting for him to come. He pictured her staring out the window, looking for shadows in the grass, listening for sounds from the black woods. Good. Let her see what it felt like to be On the Line. Waiting. Looking for omens of your own impending death. War was no fun if you had to play it alone.

He wouldn't come tonight, though. Tonight he was going to shirk his duty in that respect . . . take it easy . . . be absent from his mission. Back in 'Nam they used to call that Ghosting. *So tonight he was being a ghost.*

He wiped his forehead with a dirty forearm. Darkness had not taken away the heat. It was a steaming jungle, and his utilities were sweat-soaked before he had even begun. No wonder the Red Haze flights could see people in the dark; he could feel the rays emanating from his own body heat. He pictured the waves enveloping him like a red aura, transforming him into an avenging demon.

He wondered if she had heard about the Knoxville Girl, about how she'd looked when they pulled her out of the river and washed the mud off so that they could see his handiwork. He was only guessing, of course. He wasn't there when they took her out of the river. But he watched her go in; falling fast and hard from the side of the bridge, like a sack of rocks. Let Pretty Peggy-O dream about that.

The whine of a mosquito near his ear made him jump in the darkness, but he did not slap at it. Silence was necessary. Not now, perhaps; not here in the fields with no one any closer than the faint glow of house lights; but sometime silence would mean survival, and so he practiced it whenever he could. Maybe if he worked silently and well, he wouldn't have to stop after Peggy-O. Maybe he could kill a few more fair and tender ladies. After twenty years of silence, the world ought to be charged interest for the loneliness and suffering of Travis Perdue. He would see that the payments were made in blood.

CHAPTER 14

Where is little Maggie?
Over yonder, there she stands:
With a rifle on her shoulder,
And a six-gun in her hand . . .

"LITTLE MAGGIE"

FRIDAY . . . AUGUST 8.

At the newspaper office Jeff McCullough saw the notation on his desk calendar that Saturday was the forty-first anniversary of the bombing of Nagasaki and wished he had done an editorial on it. The old-timers from World War II, a large percentage of his subscribers, would probably have liked that. He could do it for next Thursday's edition, but it wouldn't be the same. Anyway, for that issue he had planned an editorial eulogy for Rosemary Winstead, and most of the rest of the paper would be devoted to the reunion. McCullough had been asked to stop by, take a few pictures, and talk to the folks from out-of-town. The issue ought to sell well. While he was there, he could talk to Spencer Arrowood about the murder case, and maybe set up an interview with Peggy Muryan, just in case they ever *did* find Travis Perdue. They probably wouldn't give it much play in the local weekly (his publisher liked *good* news), but he could freelance it, with some help from his buddies at bigger papers. He needed the money.

* * *

The reunion committee paid a visit to the American Legion Hut, getting ready for the mixer that evening. Tomorrow night there would be a party at the old high school, and they would have to decorate the gym for that one, but all that was required for the Friday party was a quick tour of inspection to make sure that there were enough tables, to see that the flowers had been delivered, and to double-check the buffet menu.

At the John Sevier Motel, a Mount Vernon replica on the road to Johnson City, the No Vacancy sign had been on all day, and most of the doors to the rooms stayed open, as newly arrived classmates from far-off places visited with old friends before the party itself. The level in the ice machine was low by three o'clock, as people gathered in one room or another to catch up on twenty years of living. Nearly every motel room contained a copy of the 1966 *Papyrus*, so that the returning graduates could refresh their memories before the big event. They studied the faces smiling out from black-and-white ovals and wondered if they had changed all that much, and whether they ought to drop the word "assistant" from their job title when they talked about what they were doing now. Most of them had come back because there were a few old friends they wanted to see, and they were prepared to be polite to everybody else.

If Spencer Arrowood hoped for a crime wave to get him out of going to the reunion, he was disappointed. Maybe it was too hot for crime. He took the patrol car on a cursory tour of the main roads, and he drove past Peggy Muryan's house to make sure that she was all right. He caught a glimpse of her on the side porch, cradling her guitar, so he decided not to interrupt her work. There was no news, anyway. Even with a lot of personnel working on a case, inquiries take time. He thought of driving past the motel to see who had come to town, but decided against it. He would see them all tonight.

Peggy Muryan was one of the few people in Hamelin who did not spend that Friday thinking about the twenty-year reunion of the class of '66. The fact that she would be attending the party tonight was only a small detail in the back of her mind; the rest of her consciousness was focused on the song she had been writing for the past few weeks, "Song for Travis."

She had awakened early, troubled more by the breathless heat in her upstairs room than by the menace of a human predator. She slipped on shorts and a pink T-shirt, swept her bangs back with a terrycloth headband, and went downstairs to make coffee. She took the gun with her; the heft of warm metal felt good in her hand. She would keep it hidden—under a cushion or behind a potted plant—but it would always be in whatever room she was in. She liked to feel that she was in control.

The dog's dishes were put away in the pantry now. For the first few mornings she had gone automatically to the cabinet to scoop dry dog food out of the bag; only then would she remember that Blondell was gone. By now, though, the habit had worn off, and she seldom thought of the white shepherd. She sat at the glass-topped kitchen table sipping black coffee and wondering what, if anything, this incident would do to her career plans. There was always the sympathy factor, of course. The story was sensational enough to make the wire services and the tabloids, and people might feel outraged on her behalf. She had thought of talking to a publicist, to capitalize on the tragedy, but something made her feel that it might not be wise to do so. She didn't want people to see her as a victim; the American public tends to shy away from losers, despite its reputation as a champion of the underdog. The other possibility that worried her was the natural tendency to think that people mostly got what they deserved. No matter how sympathetically the articles portrayed her as a harassed celebrity, a lot of people would say to themselves: I wonder what the real story is. I bet she had it coming.

Peggy Muryan had been wondering that herself since the messages began. She had used her youth as an excuse for her treatment of Travis Perdue. Yes, she had dumped him for a chance at the big time. Yes, she had come to think of him as an emotional nuisance when his letters came from Vietnam; she wrote him patronizing replies, fueled by guilt. But what did all that matter now? Surely it had ended when he died in the war.

She got her guitar from the living room and carried it to the sun porch so that she could work among the plants and enjoy the beauty of the day, if only from behind the panes of glass. She slid the gun behind the wicker container of the corn plant. She didn't think such a precaution was necessary: she kept the doors locked. But Peggy Muryan had never liked leaving anything to chance. She supposed that she might have got the TBI officers to give her a guard if she had become weepy and clinging during their interview with her. The sheriff would have camped out in her living room if she'd asked him to, but Peggy liked her independence and her image as a competent woman. To give in to fear would be an admission of weakness, and she suspected that Tennessee's Good Ole Boys had enough hang-ups about liberated women without her living down to their expectations of hysterical, defenseless females. Screw them, she thought, I can take care of myself. I always have.

She positioned her fingers on the neck of the guitar—second, third, and fourth strings. A-minor. A haunting chord that began many a sad song, from "House of the Rising Sun" to "In the Pines." She liked songs in minor key; they seemed to linger in the memory after the notes had died away. But this song needed some strength to it—maybe a blend of major and minor. She strummed A-minor, D, and G7: a nice progression. Somewhere in there was a song. Odd that she wanted to write a song for Travis. She had begun it in May, after she was settled in the house. Then the first postcard came. Had she summoned Travis up from some jungle grave? She smiled ruefully at her own thoughts: Don't tell that story outside California, she thought. But since the incidents began, she had abandoned the song to go back to other things. What did she want to say, anyway?

She looked at the notes about "The Redwood Woman," from her early efforts at composing the song. A West Coast image. No, that wasn't Travis. He had belonged in these mountains. She thought of him as the embodiment of Appalachia, in all its positive and traditional aspects. What were those symbols, then? She picked up a pencil and scribbled "quilts" and "vistas."

She would write a line and then try to fit it to the chord progression—from minor to major. The story of my life, she thought. Half an hour later, she played the notes more deliberately and with a definite rhythm. The paper in front of her held a verse boxed in amidst scribbled notations:

You are a memory of a mountain sky,
Of kettled fires and hands upon a plow;

It is the feel of quilts, a nighthawk's cry,
And clay-cut roads that lead me to you now.

When she tried to extend the metaphor for another verse, she tried to picture Travis Perdue. It was then that she realized that the mental image she had been writing about was Spencer Arrowood, not Travis.

What did she really remember about Travis, anyway?

She had been somebody else then: a shy little blonde, who had gone along with her boyfriend's dream of bringing mountain music to the masses. The idea was his, the songs had been his, the first contacts with booking agents had been his—but ultimately the talent had been hers. She was the one whom the national promoters wanted. She had the voice and the image that promised a shot at fame. What else could she have done? Married him anyway, and dragged him along—a folk Gladys Knight with one hillbilly Pip? Surely he would not have wanted that. It had been better her way: a clean break without pretense.

What had he been like?

He was funny, with a sense of irony that was usually directed at himself. He drank too much sometimes, and he didn't talk much about his feelings, except to make a joke of them. He had wanted her to wear short-cropped hair like the actress Sandy Duncan—the one who later played Peter Pan. Travis was maybe the only man in America who saw Duncan as a sex symbol: he would go to Disney movies just to look at Sandy Duncan. When Peggy tried to picture him, she got snapshots from old photo albums. All the real memories had been replaced by celluloid: Travis with his guitar, ginger-haired and grinning from the stage of the coffeehouse; Travis, stocky and sunburned in cutoff jeans in front of the Kitty

Hawk Memorial on their beach trip in '65; Travis with unnaturally short hair and solemn expression in his Air Force picture for the folks back home. He had been a *situation* to her for so many years that she had almost forgotten him as a person.

The attic, she thought. Somewhere in all the boxes of junk in the attic were letters from Travis stuffed in among old playbills from their music gigs in college, along with the photos and other flotsam from the life of that other Peggy Muryan, the one who wasn't famous. She set down the guitar and hurried up the stairs. She was opening the door to the attic before she remembered the gun. Let it stay where it was, she thought. There's nothing in the attic but ghosts.

Spencer Arrowood looked at his watch: twenty past five. He could close up the office if he liked; Godwin was already on duty, and there hadn't been any serious calls all day. LeDonne and Martha had left half an hour ago, but he wanted to get his notes on the Winstead case organized and, then, if there was time, look over his speech about the goddamned plaque he had to present.

When the telephone rang he was sure it was Peggy. "Sheriff's office," he said in a softer voice than normal. He had been hoping she'd ask him to drop around early for a drink.

He heard a woman crying.

"Peggy?" he said, louder than he meant to. "What's happened?"

The sobbing ended in a gasp, followed by silence. Finally a quavering voice said, "Spencer?"

It wasn't Peggy.

"Who is this?" asked the sheriff.

More choking sounds, as if the speaker were forcing herself to speak calmly. "This is Tyndall Johnson Garner.

Can you . . . I don't know . . . can you come over here, please?"

"Where are you, Tyndall?" He found himself picturing the Dandridge place, searching for some connection to the case that was foremost in his mind.

"I'm at home. At my mother's house. I need you to come over. I think I killed her!" The sobbing began again.

It took a minute for Spencer to assimilate this. The Johnson place. Dark Hollow. He knew about Evelyn Johnson's condition; Martha had mentioned it in one of her interminable monologues on the fates of their former classmates. He answered her calmly, "What happened, Tyndall? Do you need an ambulance?"

"It's too late for that! Just come over!"

The line went dead. Spencer thought of calling her back, but he decided that it would be simpler to go over there. He dialed the rescue squad instead and asked them to meet him at the Johnson place. As an afterthought he called Peggy Muryan.

"I'm going to be late," he told her. "Something came up at the office."

He heard her gasp. "Have they caught him?" she demanded.

"No. Nothing to do with that. It's a senior citizen. Medical emergency. I'll be there a little after eight, I guess. I expect I'll have to go to the hospital, and then I'll go home and change. I'll be there by eight-fifteen, though, or else I'll call you back." He waited, but she said nothing. "Are you okay?"

"I guess so," said Peggy. "I went up to the attic this afternoon to look for my letters from Travis. I thought I might find a picture of him that you could use. But the stuff wasn't there. I looked in all the boxes, and it wasn't there."

"Don't worry. The TBI can get photos from Washington. Anyway, I need to get going. We'll talk about this when I see you."

Peggy Muryan set down the phone. It was nearly six o'clock. Where had the day gone? It was still full sun outside, but the day was over, and "Song for Travis" was still unfinished. She could allow herself only a few more weeks of the luxury of a country idyll. After Labor Day, she would go to Nashville and talk to some people in the business. She had to have some material to show them by then. She had written to a few of her old contacts in California, asking if they could offer suggestions, but so far none of them had responded. She hadn't even checked the mail today. Peggy sighed impatiently: six months in a Southern town, and she was turning into a hermit. She opened the front door and stuck her hand into the wall-mounted mailbox.

Tucked into a circular from the local hardware store was one white envelope addressed to her in block capitals. She stared for a moment at the familiar lettering and then out at the rolling lawn, shadowed by its canopy of oaks. All was quiet; the street beyond was empty. She glanced over at Jessie Traynham's house and saw that her car was gone. She went back inside and locked the door before she opened the letter.

It was not postmarked at all. Someone had come to her porch and put it in the box today, after the mail had been delivered. Her throat tightened at the thought of his being so close, yet unobserved. She opened the envelope carefully, wondering if she need bother about fingerprints. Since she had already handled it, she supposed it was too late to take precautions. She wondered if they could get Travis's fingerprints off his old letters. If she managed to locate them, that is. Had she overlooked them in the attic, or were they still at her father's house?

The envelope contained a postcard, as she knew it would. He must have resorted to this subterfuge in case the local post office was monitoring her mail. This way he made sure that she—not the police—would receive the message. The postcard showed the rocks and gray-green water of the French Broad River surrounded by even greener mountains. On a rack of postcards in a gift shop such a picture would be taken for a peaceful country scene, but Peggy knew the menace implied in that view of the river. *Remember what they found in that river,* it said. Rosemary. Peggy swallowed the bile in her throat and burned over the card. The message was printed in the same block capitals used on the other cards:

IF EVER I RETURN, PRETTY PEGGY-O

She wanted to tear it to bits, but beneath her anger, common sense told her that the police would need the postcard for evidence. They would want to know the next line, and of course she could supply it. It had been one of the best numbers performed by Carolina's Folksinging Duo, Peggy & Travis. She reached for the telephone on the hall table, but she set the receiver down without dialing. There was no point in calling the sheriff; he was out on his medical emergency. Well, he would see this new bit of evidence soon enough. In the gilt-frame hall mirror she saw her own face—a pale oval of taut lines and shadows. She looked old and tired, she thought. And in two hours she was supposed to play the glamorous celebrity for the locals. Peggy pushed a lank strand of hair away from her face. She would have to start getting ready fairly soon. Just as well—it might take her mind off this new development. Maybe she would ask Spencer to stay the night after the reunion. He had probably been expecting it anyhow. She was glad of a safe chance to get out of the house for an evening. She just hoped they wouldn't play "Fennario" or "The Bonnie Streets of Fyvie-O," or whatever they cared to call it, at the reunion tonight. The rhythmic, martial-sounding tune drummed in her head. The last verse:

If ever I return, Pretty Peggy-O,
If ever I return, Pretty Peggy-O,
If ever I return, all your cities I will burn,
Destroying all the ladies in the area-o.

Any other time Spencer might have enjoyed the drive to the Johnson house. It was located several miles out of town on a paved but winding back road that followed Laurel Creek along the base of the ridge. Modest frame houses with big trees and well-kept lawns sat far back from the road. Farther along, the road curled back into the valley, past miles of open pastures and a few cultivated fields, but the Johnsons had lived on the residential part of the road, just half a mile past Shiloh Methodist Church. Regardless of the urgency of the summons, the sheriff didn't see any reason for flipping on the siren: there wasn't anybody else on the road.

The Johnson house was at least fifty years old, but it had been taken care of. It was a small two-story with a wide front porch, nestled among clumps of rhododendron bushes. He remembered it from high school: the Beta Club had met there once to plan its spring picnic. He would have known this was the right house, anyway, though, because the rescue squad ambulance was parked in the driveway, its red light still flashing in the deep shade under the elms.

He eased the patrol car into the driveway and parked a little to the right of the ambulance, in case they needed to get out in a hurry. With a brief wave at Clarence Aliff, who was waiting in the driver's seat with the motor running, the sheriff hurried toward the open front door.

Tyndall was sitting in her daddy's old morris chair in the living room, staring at nothing. The prettiest girl in high school looked much the worse for wear. From down the hall, Spencer could hear the sounds of the squad members, presumably in Mrs. Johnson's room. He'd talk to them later; they wouldn't want him underfoot just now.

"How are you?" he asked Tyndall, pulling a straight chair up beside her.

Her face was blotched and tear-stained, but she was quiet. "I can talk," she said. "Mother's dead, Spencer."

He nodded. "I'm sorry to hear it. Can you tell me what happened?"

She took a couple of deep breaths and twisted the shreds of a tissue between her fingers. "Well . . . she had this cold that started a couple of days ago, and I had the doctor out, but he didn't seem to think it was too serious." Her voice trailed off.

"You're doing fine," said Spencer, patting her shoulder.

"And last night I thought she sounded worse, and I thought about calling him back, but I didn't." Tears seeped out of her eyes, and her voice caught, but she swallowed and went on. "She kept coughing all night, and the later it got, the more I wished I'd called, but then I kept saying that I didn't want to disturb the doctor if it was a false alarm. But, Spencer, part of me was thinking, *it's better this way*. I mean, if she just *goes*, without a big to-do, I can sell the house and go home without having to worry about affording a nursing home, and without having to stay here with Steve resenting every minute I'm away from the family. I mean, I'd be out of it, just like magic, you see?"

He nodded.

"So, I think I didn't *want* to see how sick she was! Spencer, *I think I let her die*."

"Have you had any sleep, Tyndall? Have you eaten anything today?"

She stared at him. "Haven't you been listening?"

"Yes. I think you need some coffee, but I could be wrong. I'll slip in and ask Millie Fortnum if she thinks a sedative would do more good."

"But, Spencer, I—"

He cupped her hands in his and looked her in the eye. "Tyndall, did you *do* anything to your mother? Hold a pillow over her face, or anything?"

She shook her head, eyes wide in horror.

"You didn't. Well, that's good. Then I wish you'd stop talking about murder and all. The doctor said he didn't think it was serious, and you believed him. Now maybe he was wrong, and maybe you were wrong to set such store by his opinion, but that's neither here nor there." He spoke slowly and carefully, making sure that she didn't look away. "What happened here is that an incurably ill old woman died peacefully in her own home in her own bed, without a lot of tubes and wires. And her daughter, who loved her, is in shock over the suddenness of it, and she's half-crazy with fatigue and grief, so she said a lot of things that just aren't so. Isn't that right?"

She closed her eyes and nodded.

"Now I'm going to go down the hall for a minute and speak to Millie and John. And I want you to be thinking about what you want to do. I think you ought to pull yourself together before you call your family, and for that I recommend coffee. If you don't want to be alone—and I hope you don't, frankly—why, I can get somebody to come sit with you, or I can take you down to the class reunion, because, Tyndall, I tell you what's the truth, half the people that'll be there came to see you."

She was smiling a little. Spencer straightened up. "Now you think it over while I speak to the rescue squad." He could tell that she was coming out of it. His folksy speech usually did work on people in shock. He called it his "Andy Griffith rap," and he was very good at it. It made people look up to him as sheriff, and it often eased a bad situation.

As he walked down the hall, Spencer idly wondered whether she *had* played any part in the old woman's death. He would prefer not to have to find out. He would explain the circumstances to the doctor; he doubted that there would be an autopsy.

She had been able to kill about forty-five minutes getting ready for the party: a shower, several try-ons of outfits, and careful attention to hair and makeup had diverted her attention from her fear. It was like getting ready for a performance—make sure you'll look good for the audience, dress to match their expectations. She still wasn't sure what image she was supposed to project. The quilted two-piece outfit with the square neckline said "folksinger," but people might think that she was showing off. The white cocktail dress might make her overdressed for a small-town party. She delayed that decision by leaving both outfits on the bed and slipping on her white kimono with the embroidered silk flowers. It was only seven o'clock: too early to get completely dressed, anyway. All of her life was a performance, really, Peggy thought; the trick was to appear unaffected. She went downstairs for a drink.

Bourbon and Coke. She had learned to drink them in college, when she and Travis were still playing frat parties at Southern schools. Bourbon didn't taste as bitter to her as Scotch, and it was the one drink that all the fraternities had on hand; she mixed it with Coke to limit her consumption of alcohol, and to cut the taste. She could make a bourbon and Coke last for two hours. Only one drink tonight: alcohol and singing do not mix.

She carried the drink into the living room and was surprised to find that the room was nearly dark. The trees kept out the light, but outside she saw that the twilight had deepened. Summer was fading fast. She drew the curtains against the grayness.

She had perhaps half an hour to herself before she needed to finish getting ready. She glanced toward the sun porch, where she had left her guitar. Should she work on the song some more? She closed her eyes and blocked out the stream of thoughts, trying to gauge her feelings. She could feel no rush of energy from within that would signal a creative mood; what she felt instead was a charged atmosphere like that of an impending storm. Something was not right. She heard a muffled, unfamiliar sound that tightened her muscles and stifled the breath in her throat.

Someone was in the house.

It's Spencer, she told herself. *This can't be happening to me.* And I'll give him hell for scaring me like this.

She forced herself to get up from the couch and to call out, "Who is it?" The question hung in the air of the high-ceilinged room, followed by silence. She listened for more footsteps, but there were none. Peggy ran to the telephone in the hall.

"I already cut the line."

* * *

Spencer glanced at his watch: twenty minutes to eight. All things considered, the situation at the Johnson house had been resolved with efficiency and dispatch. The rescue squad had taken the body to the funeral home for the doctor's inspection, and he had been able to persuade Tyndall to come to the reunion: "You don't have to do the Twist, Tyndall, but that's where your friends are tonight, and you sure as hell don't want to be alone."

Her husband and children would be getting in to Hamelin sometime tomorrow. In the end, Tyndall agreed to go to the reunion because it was the fastest way to find Sally, and because she couldn't stand being inside her mother's dreary little house any longer.

They had not spoken for nearly ten minutes.

Spencer kept his eyes on the road as if it were alien territory instead of part of his regular patrol. The sky was fading to a smoky haze, making the trees stand out in sharp relief against the distant hills. He glanced at Tyndall and found her watching him, a glint of amusement in her expression.

"Are you going to wear *that* to the party?" she asked.

He looked down at his sweat-stained khaki uniform. "Well," he said, "if you'll tell them I'm on my way, and to hold up that plaque ceremony till I get there, I may have time to go home and change before I pick up my date."

"I think that's a real good idea, Spencer." She hesitated. "Just who *is* your date?"

"Peggy Muryan. You know, she was a folksinger back then."

"Yes, of course. I still have *Carolina Blue*. So—is it serious between you two?"

Spencer coughed. "I expect it's too early to tell. Why?"

"Well . . . I just wondered if Jenny was going to be there tonight."

"I don't know," said Spencer.

"I'd like to see her again. We were all sorry to hear about the divorce. I know I'm being nosy, Spencer, so just put it down to the raving of a hysterical woman. Do you think there's any chance you and Jenny could patch things up?"

He shook his head. "No, Tyndall. There is no chance at all." *Because one summer night years ago, I beat the hell out of her,* he finished silently.

They were living in Atlanta at the time. He had been trying to escape from the mountains and become a big success, but he had hated every minute of it. Atlanta was a dingy one-bedroom apartment in a high-rise with Mo-Town noises coming through the walls and a view of concrete and steel that made him want to jump every time he looked at it. He wanted to go home; Jenny thought Atlanta was a sophisticated place, and she wanted to settle there: never mind that it took both their paychecks to get from one month to the next.

That hot night they had been quarreling about something—probably about the fact that he wasn't interested in barhopping in the Underground every night. Atlanta tired him physically and spiritually, and he just wanted to sit on the plastic couch in their tiny living room and stare at the television. He wanted to watch *The Waltons*.

The air conditioner was broken, and the food had been overcooked and tasteless—and Jenny was sick of their shabby little apartment and sick of his indifference, so the quarrel began. *"I'm sick of living with you!" she had screamed at him. "I wish I had married Cal! He was a better lover than you are! I should have kept the baby, and let my daddy make him marry me!"*

She had calmed down real fast when she saw the look

in his eyes, but it was too late to stop talking about it then. He shook her until she told him about seeing Cal, home on his last leave before Vietnam, and how a combination of a schoolgirl crush and his manipulation of her patriotic guilt toward the departing soldier had fueled their week-long affair. Spencer wondered why Cal had never boasted of it; he usually did. Jenny said that she had started dating Spencer just to hear news of Cal, and she had thought that when Cal got out of the Army, they would get back together.

When Spencer heard how she'd gone to South Carolina and had an abortion that Christmas before graduation, and that the baby was Cal's, he felt that he had just heard his brother pronounced dead all over again, and he'd started to hit her with his fists until the sticky feeling of blood made him stop.

He had taken her to the hospital that night, and they had tried to pretend it hadn't happened, but before the month was out, he had given notice at his job and was getting ready to go back to East Tennessee. It was understood that Jenny would not go with him.

Sometimes he wished that night had never happened, but too much time had passed for him to miss her. All that was left was a fear of getting too close. He didn't want to ever care that much again.

"Tell them I'll be back," he said to Tyndall, stopping the car in the parking lot of the American Legion Hut. The sign said: WELCOME, HAMELIN HIGH CLASS OF '66.

Tyndall touched his arm. "And if Jenny's there?"

He shook his head. "She won't be back."

Peggy swallowed her scream and turned in the direction of the voice. He was sitting in the darkness on the staircase, about halfway up. She could just make out a dark form beside the banister. She could see his hands in the dim light, but his face was dark. Was he wearing a mask? Camouflage?

Peggy clutched the kimono tighter around her. Steady on, she thought, taking a deep breath. Life is all an act. What does *this* audience want from you? She looked up at the dark form on the stairway and gave him a bright smile. "Travis! Thank God you're back!" She had to keep talking, establish the tenor of the conversation before he became menacing. "I'm working on an idea for a comeback career, and I think this time we could make it as a team!"

He laughed. It was more of a grunt, really, a sound of disbelief.

She kept her voice steady. "It has been so-o-o long. Half my life since I've seen you! I've grown up a lot since then, Trav. I used to think that being successful was everything, but now I realize that other things are more important."

"I think revenge is important." From the darkness of the stairs, she saw something flash in his hand. He had a knife.

She wondered if he *had* cut the telephone lines, but since he was armed, it would be too dangerous to find out. What time was it, anyway? Spencer would be here soon, or he'd try to call, and the dead phone line would be her distress signal. She would have to keep him talking until then. That shouldn't be difficult, she told herself. She had always been able to wrap Travis Perdue around her little finger.

"Can I get you a drink?" she asked.

Silence.

"We have a lot of catching up to do, don't we? Where have you *been* all this time? Couldn't you find me? I wrote to your mother once, after you were listed as missing, but she never answered."

"Don't you feel any guilt at all, Peggy-O?"

She swallowed. "People change, Travis. You should know that. The old Travis wouldn't have been into this. No way."

He stood up and went down one step.

"I think we should talk," said Peggy. "Do you want to come in here? I want you to hear a song I've been working on. It's called 'Song for Travis.' It is. Honest. I can show you the notes."

He motioned her into the living room with the blade of the knife. "Go slow!" he said.

She reached for the light switch beside the doorway, but he touched her arm with the blade. She could see that the knife was very long—like a bayonet or a small machete. Peggy didn't know much about things like that. It looked like the sort of thing they might have used in an Asian war, though. She looked from the blade to the person holding it. He was dressed in camouflage, and he wore a ski mask. She turned away quickly. *Get out of the range of his weapon.*

"I want you to hear this song," she said, still sounding cheerful. *Did men think women were that stupid? Did he think that she was unaware of the danger? Or do mad dogs know nothing except their own pain?* "I want to get my guitar, though. Maybe we can do some numbers together." She walked slowly toward the sun porch, keeping up a flow of chatter about the house and what she wanted to do with it.

Once, back in '68, when she had been visiting friends in the Haight, a drugged-out guy had waylaid her in an alley and tried to rape her. It was dark then, too, and there were street noises and party sounds to drown out her screams. She had realized that at once, before she even tried to resist. So she'd acted drunk and hugged the guy, whispering, "Why don't we do it at my place?" It had surprised the hell out of him, but animals aren't capable of much reasoning, so he'd groped her some more, and she'd whispered, "My car's out front here. Can you drive a Jag?" He'd followed her out of the alley then, too brain-fogged to work it all out, mumbling something about how he'd always wanted to do it in a Jag. Once out of the alley, she began to run, screaming, into the first lighted shop she came to. She never saw the guy again, but for years she'd wake up in a cold sweat, back in that alley.

She picked up the guitar and handed it to him. "Isn't this a beauty?" she said, keeping her voice steady. "Remember that first guitar I had? The one we bought at Sam's Pawn Shop in Durham? Take this in the living room for me, while I get the music."

He looked around the tiny sun porch. There was no telephone, no other door, no way of escape. Just a lot of plants and some wicker furniture. Sheets of yellow lined paper and pages of sheet music were scattered across the floor. Peggy was still smiling at him like a child about to show off a new trick. With a shrug he took the guitar and headed back toward the sofa.

She waited until he was ten feet away from her, then she knelt as if to pick up the papers. "I know it's here somewhere!" she called out. "You know how disorganized I always was . . ." She reached behind the corn plant and felt her hand close around smooth, cold metal. She had remembered where she had left the gun. She exhaled a long sigh: she wouldn't have to play geisha anymore.

Peggy Muryan stood up with the borrowed .45 in her hand and walked to the living room doorway. The fool in the ski mask was sitting on the couch tweaking the guitar strings with his knife. "Now," said Peggy, leveling the gun at his head. "Just who the hell are you?"

* * *

Spencer Arrowood flipped through the pages of the phone book for Peggy's number. His hair was still wet from a quick, cold shower, and he hadn't begun to fool with his necktie yet, but he thought he ought to give her a call, just to say that he was on his way. It was a little after eight now. If he hurried, they would be there by eight-thirty.

He punched in the seven digits, but instead of a ring, he heard a click and then silence. He decided that he had been in too much of a hurry. More slowly this time, he hit each of the numbers, and waited. The result was the same. He had punched in 0 to report the problem to the operator, when the implications of the dead telephone hit him. Why wasn't Peggy Muryan's phone working?

He ran out to his car. No time to change clothes now; he had grabbed his pistol and holster without even taking time to strap it on. He thought of radioing Godwin for backup, but decided against it. If LeDonne had been on duty, he would have called him, but Godwin wasn't worth the time it would have cost to summon him.

He went up Ashe Lane at sixty, part of his mind thinking of all the times they'd hot-rodded this street as kids. Now he just wanted to get to where he was going. He even wished Ross and Boyd had stayed in town another day. He didn't care who got the credit for this, as long as they were in time.

In Peggy Muryan's living room the lights blazed. She sat on the piano bench, still holding the gun on the intruder. "Throw the knife toward the sun porch door," said Peggy in pleasant conversational tones. "And if you try anything stupid, I will shoot you in the stomach and watch you bleed to death."

After a moment's hesitation, he lifted the weapon and tossed it toward the open doorway.

"Much better. Now take that stupid ski mask off. I knew you weren't Travis Perdue the minute I saw you. You're too little, and you don't sound like him at all. I want to know who the hell you are, before I have you arrested."

"I didn't mean nothing," said the voice defensively. He eased the black covering off his head and tossed it on the floor beside him.

Peggy stared. She had never seen him before in her life. The armed assailant who had broken into her house was a kid. He looked about fifteen—almost girlish, with wide-green eyes and longish hair. His camouflage outfit seemed oddly out of place on such a child.

"*You* sent the postcards?"

He licked his lips, his eyes moving from her to the gun and back.

"Who are you? Why were you doing this?"

He shrugged. "It was a game, kind of. Are you going to call my parents?" When Peggy did not reply, he continued, "Okay. My name is Pix-Kyle Weaver, and Vietnam is, like, my hobby. I watch war movies, and sometimes I go out and pretend I'm on patrol in the jungle." He glanced at the knife lying in the shadows of the porch.

"Don't even think about it."

Pix-Kyle wiped sweat away with his forearm. "Aren't you gonna call somebody?"

Peggy steadied the gun; her eyes narrowed. "You cut the phone line, didn't you? Now, what's your connection to Travis Perdue?"

He lifted the sleeve of his shirt and showed her the bracelet. "See? Travis Perdue's MIA bracelet! I got it and a box of his letters at the Women's Club rummage sale. I used to play like I was him. I'd put lampblack on my face and crawl around the fields pretending they was mined. I burned a car once. Before I went on to other things." His eyes flicked then, watching her face.

"Were you high?"

"You mean stoned? Sure. I smoked. That was authentic. They smoked a lot over there. You ever see *Apocalypse Now*?"

"That was a movie."

He shrugged. "Anyhow, combat's a high in itself. I heard that from real G.I.'s. They were right, too. You go crawling through the woods, feeling a rush of fear and the power of being able to blow away whatever you want, and you get a hard-on that won't quit. Fear does that." He looked down at the bulge in his jeans and grinned. "See?"

"I see." It was a game, but Peggy wasn't interested in playing. The music of the sixties was now a collection of golden oldies, and the youth movement was seen by the children of today as a series of postures: long hair, bell-bottoms, peace signs, and love beads. *Her past.* What was missing was the substance. And Vietnam was a variation of Dungeons & Dragons: let's pretend we're soldiers and go out on patrol.

Her lips tightened. "You killed that girl who looked like me. You killed my dog."

"Yeah. Killing is the biggest high of all. Sex is good, but killing is better. You can *remember* killing clearer. Sex and *then* killing is awesome." When she did not reply, he shrugged and went on. "I started playing Travis, and I could tell from the letters that you had been shit-awful to him, so I figured he'd want me to pay you back. That's why I sent you the postcard and killed your dog. That was just like a combat mission, ripping your doggie's throat out. All that blood. Being scared of getting caught. I got off on it. You were a nice target, but basically, it was fun." He had brightened up during the explanation of his actions. Since this adult was not yelling at him or showing any sign of disapproval, he found that talking about his game was pleasurable.

Peggy Muryan had never felt older. "And why did you kill Rosemary?"

Pix-Kyle Weaver rubbed his chin. "That's a little mixed up," he admitted. "My folks had your record album, so I knew she looked like you, and I thought that was a pretty neat coincidence. Made me feel more like Travis. I started hanging around with her, when her parents weren't home, because it was more fun to play Travis if I could have a *Peggy* as my girlfriend." He frowned. "I wouldn't let her tell anybody about us, because it was part of my Travis secret. I even rented the video of *On the Beach* and took it over there, but she wouldn't let me do it to her. Not then." He shrugged. "Big deal. So I went out on patrol instead. I got stoned and took my knife to an old mattress out in a field. I pretended it was Rosemary. First Rosemary, then you, then Rosemary again, till it got all mixed up in my head." He smiled and stretched, savoring the memory.

Peggy felt her throat tighten at his casual reference to *On the Beach* and her own first sexual experience. It hadn't been like that. There had been some real emotions there, concern for the world, and fear for the bleak future. She looked at the sullen teenager, a product of that bleak future, and shivered. "Why did you kill her?"

He scowled. "Because she was getting all whiny! I told her about killing the dog and she didn't like that, but she didn't tell on me, so I thought I could trust her. Then I took her with me on patrol one night." He looked up at

Peggy to see if she understood what he meant. Reassured, he went on. "I even let her watch me kill a sheep. Just to show her what combat was like. And she really freaked. Said I needed professional help and shit. They were just *animals*." He looked disgusted. "Anyway, I decided that if I wasted her, it would be okay, because the cops would all be looking for old guys as suspects. Vietnam vets. They'd figure that old Travis was back." He laughed. "It was easier than the dog. I really got off on it."

Peggy nodded. "And you were going to kill me?"

He smiled and nodded toward his erection. "I'm going to rape you first. For a long time."

He killed the lights before he turned into the driveway of the Dandridge place. He left the car at the beginning of the loop, near the road, and walked quickly to the house, holding the pistol at his side. All was quiet. It was nearly full dark by now, and an early moon had just risen above the trees. The columns of the house looked like bones in the twilight; she had not turned on the porch light.

As he edged closer to the house, he could see lights shining from behind the drawn curtains in the living room, but the windows were too high up for him to see. He wondered if there was a way in. If it turned out that Peggy was all right, and that the telephone problem had been in the wiring, he would apologize for scaring her by breaking in, but he wouldn't really be sorry: he wasn't going to take any chances. If he was too late to save her, he would call the TBI and give the case back to them, but right now every second counted. There was a chance that he'd be in time.

He crept around the side of the house looking for a way in, and when he reached the back of the house, he found it. It looked as if it had already been used. Behind a clump of rhododendron bushes, the window to the kitchen pantry stood wide open, and a concrete block had been placed on the ground beneath it. In her zeal to keep all the doors locked, Peggy had overlooked one small, out-of-the-way window. Spencer wished that he had gone over the house himself. He stepped up on the concrete block, laying the pistol down on the windowsill, and eased himself through the opening.

The pantry was dark and smelled of dust and onions. Spencer retrieved the gun and put his hand out to steady himself on one of the shelves that ran floor to ceiling against each wall. It was a small room: no more than six feet across and twelve long. If it were like the one at Aunt Til's place, there would be a string dangling from the light socket in mid-room. He would risk turning it on so that he wouldn't trip over anything on his way to the door. With his left hand he struck out and felt his fingers brush against the cord. He pulled it, illuminating the tiny room with a dim glow. The door was the kind that pushed open and shut; he hoped it didn't squeak. Catching his breath, he crept toward the door and leaned against it. It gave with only a slight scraping of wood against tile, and an instant later he was in the dark kitchen, listening.

Peggy heard the sound, faint as it was, but she did not react. It was past eight o'clock now: the sun porch windows were dark, and she knew who the new intruder must be: Sheriff Spencer Arrowood, come to save her. Only she didn't need saving. She gave no sign of having heard; nor did the boy in camouflage. He was hunched up on the couch, mumbling about calling his daddy to come and get him. The adrenaline of his night raid was wearing off now, and he looked tearful. And young.

Peggy could imagine him on the witness stand, neatly dressed in a blue suit, looking like a schoolboy caught throwing eggs. He would be much aggrieved that the court was making such a big *deal* of this. He just wouldn't get it. The idea that a woman's life might be worth his own would strike him as completely bizarre. He would never understand the enormity of his crime. It had been fun. "I didn't mean nothing," he had told Peggy, and that would be his litany, with a defense based on too many war comics and too many movies about Vietnam. He would get a slap on the wrist, but Rosemary would still be dead. As dead as Travis. As dead as the sixties. Where *have* all the flowers gone?

She heard quiet footsteps coming down the hall from the kitchen. There wasn't much time. "Well, kid," she said softly to the sullen boy, "I wish we had time to go on talking, but . . ."

She raised the gun.

He looked at her with a stare of complete disbelief that said dozens of things. Grown-ups are supposed to let you off, it said. Women don't shoot guys, it said. Women are supposed to beg for mercy. Women always forgive you. Hippies love everybody. Kids are allowed to make mistakes. Your parents will always get you out of whatever mess you're in. Death is something that happens to other people.

She pulled the trigger.

The stare dissolved into a grimace of pain as his body slammed back against the couch. Her face was impassive. She fired three more times without hesitation before the sheriff reached her side.

Peggy looked up. Spencer Arrowood's face was pale as death. He looked at the gun in her hand, and his gaze traveled to the still form lying in a red stain on the couch. There was no sign of a weapon near the body. He looked back at the woman with the gun, seeing triumph on her face, mixed with defiance.

"He killed that girl," she told him. "He confessed to me. He killed my dog. He sent the postcards, and he broke in here with the intention of killing me." Her voice shook with anger. She did not glance at the boy on the couch.

Spencer stared at her. "But you didn't have to kill him. You could have waited for help. He was a kid!"

"He was a vicious bastard, and a killer, and he broke into my house. Do you think a Tennessee jury will convict me of anything for shooting him? Me—a poor helpless *woman*?"

"But it wasn't self-defense," he whispered. "You murdered him."

Her smile was bitter. "Prove it, *Sheriff*."

CHAPTER 15

And gentlemen in England, now a-bed,
Shall think themselves accurs'd they were not
here,
And hold their manhood cheap while any
speaks
That fought with us upon St. Crispin's Day.

HENRY V

THE AMERICAN LEGION Hut was in a time warp. Candlelight eased the lines from no-longer-youthful faces, and the blare of beach music drowned out the voices comparing children's ages and job descriptions. It didn't look like a high school reunion, Martha thought, because it seemed impossible that all these people were the same age. Most of the women were still young—still recognizable, anyway. They had shed the long straight hair of the sixties (except for Joyce Overton, who didn't know any better), but most of them were still trim and attractive. She hadn't seen a gray hair on any of them.

The men were a different story. Either they had not tried so hard to impress their old classmates, or else there was less that they could do to disguise the aging process. Some of the athletes looked ten years younger than they were, but there were others she wouldn't have known in a million years. They had beer guts and receding hairlines that made them look fifty. Early on,

Martha had scrapped "You look wonderful!" in favor of "How nice to see you again." She had mixed feelings about having brought LeDonne: true, he was one of the better-looking men at the party, but on the other hand, he was not especially friendly. He tended to stare at people he didn't know as if he were tempted to read them their rights.

And where was Spencer? She looked at her watch. It was nearly time for the presentations. They would do the gag gifts first: an award for the classmate with the most children, most times married, still single, and so on, but the grand finale was the plaque that Spencer was presenting on behalf of the class. Martha had staked out a table near the entrance so that she could see who came in, but so far there was no sign of the sheriff.

"Did he say anything to you?" she whispered to LeDonne, who was staring meditatively into a beer.

"No. He wasn't thrilled about doing that speech, Martha, but he wouldn't just stand you up."

"He's supposed to be bringing Peggy Muryan. If they don't come, I'll have to start replaying the music."

LeDonne looked out at the clump of people talking and laughing in small, closed groups. "Nobody's listening anyhow, Martha."

On the dance floor, Sally Howell was engaged in earnest conversation with Delos Pruitt. Pruitt, who had been gnomelike and hopelessly square in high school, had filled out well in the years that followed. Now, sporting contact lenses and a deep tan, he looked better than some of the football players. Certainly better than Slater Phillips, whose linebacker muscle had turned to gut-fat. According to his reunion biography, Delos Pruitt was now with a computer corporation in the Research Triangle outside Raleigh. He looked confident, pleased with the impression he was making. Sally, with her pixie face, dressed in a white sundress and sandals, could have passed for twenty-five.

Suddenly, there was a relative silence in the room, and people turned to stare in her direction. Martha looked around to see if the sheriff was making his entrance and saw that the late Elvis Presley had decided to attend the reunion. He stood in the doorway, squinting into the candlelight, with a tentative smile. He was wearing a white fringed jumpsuit, his favorite dead-black wig, and cowboy boots. Tucked under his arm was the boom box.

Martha took a deep breath and stood up. "Hello, Vern—er—Elvis," she said, solemnly shaking his hand. "We're so glad you could make it to our party. Would you like to do a few numbers for the crowd?"

"Thank ye, ma'am," he said, in a well-practiced breathy drawl.

"Is that your music?" asked Martha, pointing to the tape player. "Come on, then."

As she led Vernon Woolwine past the balloons and streamers to the stage, it occurred to Martha that if he had tried to crash the prom twenty years ago, the class of '66 would have jeered at him and ordered him to leave. By now most of them had outgrown the urge to humiliate the different ones. If the decades had given them nothing else, it had taught them tolerance. The revelers clapped and cheered as the imitation Elvis mounted the steps to the stage.

"Way to go, man!" somebody yelled.

Martha leaned into the microphone. "Listen, everybody! I have a real treat for you tonight! Our special reunion guest is the King himself! I know that will bring back some memories! He'll be entertaining you with some of his greatest hits! And we'll do the regular program later."

They gathered around the stage, still applauding, while

Vernon Woolwine switched on his tape player and began to lip-sync "Don't Be Cruel."

Martha edged her way through the crowd and took up her post at the table by the door. LeDonne was smiling. "That was good of you," he said, raising his plastic cup in a toast.

She smiled back. "Hey, who would you rather have as the evening's entertainment, Peggy Muryan or Elvis?"

"No contest."

They settled back in their seats and watched the man in the white jumpsuit shake, rattle, and roll.

"Excuse me, Martha?"

She turned at the sound of a familiar voice. The Homecoming Queen had arrived. Martha's first thought was the inevitable comparison between Tyndall *now* and Tyndall *then*. The golden girl in the green silk dress had not come back to the reunion: she had sent her mother. This tired, middle-aged woman with dark circles under her eyes and bloodless lips bore a slight resemblance to the yearbook photo of Tyndall Johnson, but there seemed to be more than twenty years' distance between them. She stood there in a plain brown dress, clutching her purse as if she were lost. She didn't seem to notice the crowd.

"What happened to you?" Martha whispered.

Tyndall shook her head. "I have a message from Spencer. He said to tell you he's going to be late—something came up. I don't know when he'll be here."

LeDonne leaned over, frowning. "Does he need me?"

"He didn't say so. Just that he'll be late." She looked around the room. "And I have to find Sally. . . ."

Martha pointed to the laughing dark-haired girl dancing with Delos Pruitt. "Right over there," she said.

Tyndall watched the couple for a moment and then

turned back to Martha. "Can we go someplace and talk?" she asked. A tear trickled down the side of her face.

Martha stood up and hugged her. "You bet, hon," she said, giving LeDonne a look that said *I have to do this.* He nodded. "We'll go just as soon as I go tell Chuck Winters that he's dedicating that plaque."

It was after eleven, and Spencer had run out of things to do. The doctor had been summoned to the Dandridge place to examine the Weaver boy, and the body had been taken to the funeral home. He had called the Tennessee Bureau of Investigation and told them that the perpetrator had been shot while trying to attack Miss Muryan. It was an open-and-shut case of self-defense, he said; the assailant was inside the house when he had been shot. No, he didn't recommend further inquiry: it was an open-and-shut case.

At least he had saved the taxpayers the cost of a pointless trial.

When the routine had been taken care of to that extent, he had driven out to Dark Hollow to tell the Weavers that their son was dead.

He never made it to the reunion.

The drive along the dark winding road to the Weaver farm was too quiet. There was nothing to hear but his own breathing, and nothing to look at except the pool of light in front of the car. Vietnam had cost him another prom, he thought sardonically. He had lost another date with a woman he was better off without. Now here he was in his dress shirt and blazer, reliving that summer night in '66 when he had watched two adults face the death of their son.

Good-bye again, Cal, he thought.

He didn't want to go home. His duties were done for the night, but he knew that it would be a long time before he slept. Even with the radio turned up full blast, he could still hear the Weavers' voices in his head. *Not my little boy . . .*

He supposed that there would still be parties going on at the Sevier Motel, but there wasn't really anybody that he wanted to see. He wasn't in the mood for reminiscing and catching up on old times.

The Dark Hollow Road came out on the south side of Hamelin, near the curve where LeDonne lived. Spencer supposed that the deputy would still be out partying with Martha, but he decided to drive by, just in case. If they were there—and decent, he amended to himself—he'd stop in for just a minute. He needed to apologize to Martha for not showing up at the reunion. He supposed he would get all the details from her sooner or later.

He slowed down at the privet hedge that edged LeDonne's yard and pulled into the gravel driveway. The Volkswagen was parked under the tree, and there were lights on in the house. Spencer got out of the car, taking care to slam the door loudly; it wasn't a good idea to sneak up on Joe LeDonne. He waited a moment before setting off across the gravel toward the front door.

"I'm around here, Spencer," said a voice from the darkness.

"Joe?"

"Back porch. Want some coffee?"

"Yeah. About a quart of it." The back door was open, and the light from the kitchen made it bright enough for him to see LeDonne, back in his jeans, sitting in a lawn chair with the husky at his feet. The sheriff opened the other lawn chair and sat down across from him. "Martha here?"

"No. She wanted to visit with her girl friends, so we agreed that I'd be a third wheel, and I came on home. Let me get your coffee." He ambled into the house, calling back over his shoulder, "Where were you, sport?"

Spencer waited until he came back with two steaming

mugs, and then, between sips, he told him what had happened that night. LeDonne listened in silence. He listened better than anybody Spencer had ever met. Finally, after another dose of coffee, he found himself talking about Peggy, and then Jenny, and how tonight had been a rerun of the senior prom in so many ways. His voice rose and fell in the darkness.

"Did they get that damned plaque dedicated?" he asked finally.

"You bet. Some lawyer from Knoxville did the honors. Said he didn't go to Vietnam himself, you understand, but he wished he had. Talked about how he hated to have missed the *quintessential experience of our generation*." He laughed. "They'd have fragged his ass in twenty minutes."

Spencer nodded. "Chuck Winters."

"That's him."

He sighed. "Joe—I did *not* want to dedicate that plaque tonight, but I couldn't tell anybody why." The silence from the deputy was the only response that could have let him go on. "You know my brother, Cal, was killed over there. My parents never got over it, I guess. He was the football hero, and the oldest, and all that. They used to make me feel guilty that I didn't grieve enough when he died—and I *was* sorry. He was my brother. But I don't think my parents really knew him."

"No?"

"No. The last letter he sent before he died was addressed to me, and I destroyed it. My folks never let me forget that. 'Your only brother,' they said, 'and you tore up the last letter he ever wrote without even letting us read it.' But, Joe, I had to. I couldn't let them read that stuff he told me about killing civilians for the hell of it, and how combat was like pulling a three-day drunk. In that letter—he sent me an ear."

After a moment's pause, a cigarette glowed in the darkness, and LeDonne said, "How old was he?"

"Nineteen. I can still see that thing, shriveled up like a dried apricot in the wrapping. God knows how he sent it out of there. But I took it out and burned it, and the letter, too! I couldn't let them see it. My mother—"

"It was a tough place to be nineteen, Spencer. We found out a lot of things about ourselves that we'd be better off not knowing. But your brother died out there. I'd let it go at that."

"They never knew what he was really like."

"Neither do you, Spencer." LeDonne stood up and stubbed the cigarette out with his boot. "Are you off duty tomorrow?"

"Yes. Why?"

"I think I'll get Godwin to take my shift. He owes me, and with the Winstead case behind us, we can afford to take comp time." He yawned and stretched. "How long do you reckon it would take us to get to Washington?"

"*Washington?* You mean driving? All night. Ten hours, at least."

"I've never seen the Wall, have you?"

"The Vietnam Memorial? No."

"A guy in my group explained it to me. It starts off real low to the ground, level with the path. That's for the early years, when we first got involved over there, sending in advisers. There's just one or two names there. Then the ground slopes down, so that the path descends, and the wall is made taller. That's our progression into the war. Finally—in the mid-sixties—the wall towers way over your head—like we were in over our head in the war—and there are thousands of names before you. Gradually, as we started pulling out in the early seventies, the path slopes up again, and the wall tapers off.

They say people leave notes on the Wall. I know there's some people there I haven't said good-bye to."

"Cal's name is there, isn't it?"

"We could find it." LeDonne poured the rest of his coffee into the grass. "You want some more?"

Spencer shook his head. "We have a long way to go."

"Whenever Sharyn McCrumb suits up her amateur detective Elizabeth MacPherson, it's pretty certain that a trip is in the offing and that something deadly funny will happen."
—*The New York Times Book Review*

Sharyn McCrumb's
ELIZABETH MacPHERSON NOVELS

SICK OF SHADOWS
LOVELY IN HER BONES
HIGHLAND LADDIE GONE
PAYING THE PIPER
THE WINDSOR KNOT
MISSING SUSAN
MacPHERSON'S LAMENT
IF I'D KILLED HIM WHEN I MET HIM . . .

"Sharyn McCrumb has few equals and no superiors among today's novelists."
—*San Diego Union-Tribune*

Murder on the Internet